Winter of the Snowfox

Age of the Unifier, Volume 1

by Nik Heikkilä

Winter of the Snowfox

ISBN 978-0-578-04346-3

www.ageoftheunifier.com

Acknowledgements

Writing this novel has been a long journey, and not one I've made alone. There have been many who've helped me out along the way and who I owe a debt of gratitude, and while this list is by no means exhaustive, I'd like to recognize a few names without whom this book might never have been completed: My very first readers, Anne and Liz, whose appetites for new chapters helped keep me going on the frustrating days when the words just didn't want to cooperate; Robin, for her editorial insight and persistence in making me see the sense in her comments even when I didn't at first want to; Angie, for helping me tell one end of a horse from the other; Amy, for organizing the writers' group that has given me such valuable feedback on my work over the past year; Donovan, for his friendship and being an excellent sounding board for my ideas (even when they were bad ones); Aimée, for the effort and skill she marshaled for the illustrations, and her patience in dealing with this graphic arts illiterate during the process; my brother, Eric, for all his work pushing me along in the final stages of this project; and most of all my parents, John and Carol, without whose incredible support and encouragement I'd have never been able to start writing this book, let alone finish it.

"A great deal has been written of the Unifier, and of the epochal war that arose along with the prophesied savior. Far less scrutiny is usually given by my fellow historians to the Northern conflict which preceded these events. This, I believe, is a terrible oversight, for much was set in motion during that struggle which would ultimately shape the nature of what was to follow."

-Elena Kethrace, from *The Dark Before Unity's Dawn: A History of the Necromancer War*

Prologue
Flames and Tears

Rania awakened from a deep sleep as her mother pushed open the door to her room. Rubbing the sleep from her eyes, she looked out her window. It was still night, but in the absence of sunlight the window frame flickered with a ruddy glow, as if the entire city were lit with torches. Sounds drifted up to her room from below as well, thin and indistinct from the distance. Screams.

Frightened, the eight year old looked wide-eyed back to her mother.

"Rania, dear," Emereen Amoran said gently to her daughter, "I need you to get out of bed and get dressed."

"What's happening, mother?" Rania asked in a quavering voice, "Is everything okay?" She knew it wasn't, but mother and father would make things right. They were the Lord and Lady of the city. That's what they did.

"No, dear. There are bad men in the city, burning the buildings and hurting the people." Emereen was going through Rania's wardrobe, pulling out clothes. She laid a bundle of them on the bed. They were some of Rania's play clothes, the comfortable ones she didn't have to worry about ruining when she was playing outside with the other children of the household.

Obediently, Rania crawled out of bed and began getting dressed. "Where's daddy?"

"He's with the guards, dear. They're keeping the bad men out of Felmorinen." That was the name of the castle Rania lived in, as well as the small city surrounding it. It was old, so old that nobody remembered when it had been built. People sometimes said that it was cursed, that bad things had happened here long ago, but Rania had never really paid them much attention; it had always seemed a wonderful place to live.

As Rania finished pulling on her tunic and was about to put on the scratchy wool cloak her mother had picked for her, Emereen pressed a small knapsack into her hands. "Put this on, Rania." She said, "I need you to take this with you."

"What is it, mother?" It was a little heavy, but not so bad once she had the straps over her shoulders. "And where am I going?"

"It's a book, dear, a secret book. Only your father and I know about it, and now you. It's the biggest secret ever, so you can't tell anybody about it. Can you do that for me?" Emereen was on her knees, looking Rania in the eyes. She looked sad and a little bit frightened, with tears glistening at the corners of her eyes.

"Yes, momma. I promise I won't tell anyone." Rania put the cloak on over the sack. "Where are we going?" she asked again.

Emereen brushed a stray lock of red hair out of her daughter's eyes. "Captain Drevaan and some of his men are going to take you out of the city, Rania, in case any of the bad men get into the castle. I can't come with you. I have to stay here."

Rania felt her eyes getting wet. "No, mother," she sniffled, "I don't want to leave you here."

"I don't want that either, Rania, but sometimes we have to do things we don't want to because they're so important." Emereen hugged her daughter close. "This is very important, honey. You have to be brave. Do it for me, please?"

Rania bit her lip and nodded.

"That's my girl." Rania's mother stood and took her daughter by the hand, giving it a little squeeze. "I'm so proud of you, Rania."

Captain Drevaan, who led Felmorinen's household guard, was waiting in the hall with five of his men. They were all dressed in plain clothes like commonfolk from the city below, but they were all wearing their swords and the armor under their clothes jingled when they moved. Drevaan smiled gently at Rania as her mother led her into the hall, and then addressed Marquess Amoran, his liege. "We're ready?"

Emereen nodded decisively. "Yes. Remember, get out of the city quickly but take no unnecessary risks. More depends on your success than you could possibly know."

The captain saluted, fist to heart. "It shall be as you order, my Lady."

Emereen bent down to her child, absently straightening the collar on Rania's cloak. "Go, Rania. Remember I love you. I love you very much." A single tear dripped down the noblewoman's cheek.

"I love you, too, Mother." Rania said, trying to sound less frightened than she was. The guards surrounded her and they started down the hallway.

Emereen stood and watched until they disappeared around the corner. "Goodbye, my darling daughter," she whispered.

They took the back ways down through Felmorinen, the narrow passages usually used by the servants. It was long past the time that the last of the servants finished their duties for the night, and the narrow halls and stairways were dark and frightening to young Rania. As they descended lower and lower, ever closer to the ground floor of the ancient keep, the sounds of fighting drifted up to them, distant but still scary. Rania tried not to tremble as she walked, tried not to make a sound. She had promised mother she would be brave, but it was so hard.

As they drew near the kitchens and the delivery door by which foodstuffs were brought into Felmorinen, they heard the heavy footsteps of running men headed their way. Drevaan flattened himself against the wall, holding out an arm to press Rania likewise to the stone. The sounds moved thankfully past them without anyone coming into the darkened passage they occupied, but they continued to wait. Rania could hear her heartbeat pounding in her ears, and she counted thirty beats after the running men passed before the Captain moved again. Drevaan motioned to the rest to stay where they were as he crept down the hall to furtively look around the corner before he signaled them forward.

When they emerged into the kitchens, they found two soldiers wearing strange livery of white and gold. Their uniforms were spattered with crimson, and they stood amidst the corpses of several of the household staff who had apparently tried escaping by this same route. They turned in surprise toward the men entering the room.

Drevaan's men acted without hesitation. The terrified Rania was pushed back behind them as they charged forward, drawing swords to fall upon the invaders.

Their foes surprised and outnumbered, it was over quickly. One of the guardsmen stared in consternation at the still forms of the two men while Rania sobbed with fright. "Those're the colors of the old kingdom. Is it true, then, what they're saying? Are these ghosts?" Fear quavered in his voice.

"Don't be daft," Drevaan answered gruffly, wiping his sword blade on one of the white uniforms before resheathing it. "Ghosts don't bleed." He walked over to Rania and gently took her by the chin, turning her face upward to look into her eyes. His other hand wiped the tears from her cheek. "Come, child. There's no time for tears now."

Rania gulped and nodded. She didn't dare open her mouth to reply, afraid that she'd start crying again.

Drevaan picked the girl up, carrying her out of the fortress.

The courtyard was a scene of bygone chaos and destruction. Bodies littered the ground, friend and foe alike tangled where they had fallen. There looked to be more friends among the slain than foes. Above the inner wall of the castle, flames could be seen crackling up to the sky. Aside from the flames, there was no sign of movement. It appeared the struggle had moved on into Felmorinen itself.

"Try not to look at them, my Lady." Drevaan murmured. He started cautiously toward the inner wall.

Rania tried to do as he said. She was afraid to look at the corpses, afraid she would find her father among the detritus of the battle. Mind recoiling from her surroundings, she stared straight ahead as Drevaan carried her to a small sally port set into the wall.

On the other side of the wall they found a dying city. Flames danced in many of the buildings, and several had already collapsed in on themselves. Corpses lay scattered in the streets, but here they were all townsfolk, cut down as they tried to flee. None of the bodies wore the white and gold they had seen inside. Whereas the inside of the wall had been the remnants of a battle, these streets had witnessed a massacre.

Anger contorted the face of one of the guards who escorted Rania. "How could this happen? Where was the city garrison? Why didn't we put up a fight until they were on top of us?"

Drevaan shook his head. "Somehow, I don't know how, they got into the city without the alarm being sounded. The first warning we had was when the fires started, and the city barracks were the first buildings to go up in flames. They probably barricaded our men inside and let the fire do their work for them." He surveyed the carnage grimly. "Let's pick up the pace a bit. We've got a ways to go, but these streets seem empty. Stay sharp, though, there's no doubt stragglers out here somewhere."

They trotted down the streets as fast as their attempts at stealth would allow. Rania's fear bordered on unreasoning panic. The city seemed a nightmare of mauled bodies, flames, and heat. Small clusters of white-clad invaders roamed the streets, and several times they had to fight off attackers. She lost track of how many times they had to turn and fight, how many times she cowered in the street while Drevaan and his guardsmen fought like cornered mountaincats to keep her from harm. The occasional struggles took their toll on her protectors, though. By the time they were nearing the outer wall that ringed the city, two of her guards had fallen, and two more bled from wounds taken before they felled their assailants.

Still they continued on, the gate in the looming stone wall ahead beckoning them on. Beyond that wall lay safety, Rania remembered her mother saying. They ran, and soon were passing under the wall, the great stone of the arch swallowing them. As they emerged from the other side, Rania wanted to breathe a sigh of relief. Then she looked around, and screamed.

With a roar, the men who had been lying in wait to either side of the gateway charged them, encircling the smaller party.

Drevaan hastily set Rania back down on her feet and drew his sword, turning his back to her to face the attackers.

Steel clashed on steel, and Rania had nowhere to run. Her protectors were outnumbered six to four, and bloodied where the attackers were unwounded. Men fell screaming around her, and not all of them enemies. In the initial rush, three of the men in white and gold went down. So did two of the Felmorinen Guardsmen.

4

Rania had her opening. She began backing away, not daring to look away from Drevaan. The last guard aside from the Captain himself was run through even as Drevaan landed a mighty overhand blow on the soldier in front of him, nearly taking the man's arm off at the shoulder. The two remaining assailants circled the last of Rania's protectors, ignoring the young girl for the time being.

Rania's foot caught against something soft and she sprawled backwards over one of the fallen attackers. She tried to catch her fall, struggling not to cry out at the warm stickiness that her one hand found. The other came to rest on something hard and contoured. Rania pulled, and found herself holding the dagger that had hung at the soldier's belt. She struggled back to her feet, clutching the weapon awkwardly.

Drevaan was still locked in his dance of death with the two men. Rania clenched her teeth and summoned up her last ounce of courage to begin creeping back towards the struggle.

With a bellowing roar, Drevaan lunged at the soldier before him, knocking aside the man's sword to thrust his own through the soldier's abdomen. At the same time, the other attacker swung low, cutting deep into one of Drevaan's legs. The captain foundered, falling forward and losing his grip on the weapon still stuck through the man he had just killed. He hit the ground with a grunt, struggling to rise again as the soldier moved in for the killing blow.

Rania saw her opportunity and jumped forward, stabbing down with the dagger toward the back of the bad man's leg. She felt a tearing sensation through the blade and warm blood welled forth as the soldier howled. Somehow, she managed to pull the dagger free before the man fell to one knee.

"Run, child!" Drevaan yelled, his voice urgent and laced with pain. "Run and don't look back!"

Rania did as she was told and ran for all she was worth, off along the outer edge of the wall. Man-shaped shadows lined the walls, and she had to remind herself that they were just the stone guardians, statues of soldiers set into embrasures lining the entire outer wall of Felmorinen, relics left over from the past ages of the city. Her breath came ragged in her throat as she ran and ran, fear giving her strength to go on long after her legs would normally have given out. Well away from the gate, she turned and fled away from the city toward the surrounding mountains.

At long last she could run no more and collapsed, her legs trembling from exertion. She crawled over to huddle against a nearby large rock jutting out of the ground, finally daring to look back at the city she had called home for eight years. The flames were dying down, but her eyes were drawn upward, to the great stone spire of Felmorinen itself. Smoke belched from the ancient keep, rising toward a sky that was just starting to turn grey with the first rays of the sun. With that sight, it all came crashing home. Everyone she knew, everyone she cared about was surely dead, taken from her in the flames and blood of the night.

Rania cradled the dagger she still carried to her chest, and cried until she thought no more tears could come.

1
Eyes

Someone was watching Talaren. It was a peculiar thought; standing as the young lord was in the midst of the Grand Melee at the annual Harvest Tournament of Val Zherrane, a roaring throng ringing the tourney field, of course he was being watched. But this feeling was different, a persistent tingling at the nape of his neck that whispered to him that he specifically was under intense scrutiny from some unknown watcher.

Tal pushed the feeling aside, though, to focus on the task at hand. He had a competition to win. All about him armored men with blunted weapons hewed at one another to win the honor of the title of Champion of Arms for this year's tourney. Tal had taken that honor last year, and he had every intention of doing so again today.

A bulky fellow in chain mail with sword raised overhead rushed at Tal, who casually brushed the crude attack aside and struck back with a series of rapid blows that left his attacker groaning on the ground. Tal had already put the man out of his mind as he turned to face another three attackers, howling like madmen as they came at him. He danced deftly around their attacks, tangling the three men up with each other as they all sought to strike him a disqualifying blow. The foremost of the three pushed forward aggressively, trying to break through the young nobleman's guard. Tal ducked under a high swing and swept the man's legs out from under him. Before the fellow had even struck the ground, Tal had launched himself forward, blade rising swiftly crosswise to dash aside another attack and strike his astonished attacker all in one flowing motion. The third foe gave a startled cry as Tal stepped smoothly forward, inside the arc of his quarry's swinging blade, his free hand reaching out to catch his opponent's swordarm by the wrist even as he drove his knee up into the man's abdomen. He pivoted, still grasping the captive arm, and heaved his gasping opponent over his shoulder to the ground. Snatching up the man's dropped sword in his left hand, Tal turned and strode into the nearest boiling cluster of combatants.

The young heir to the Duchy of Val Solus moved through the fighting with a skill and grace that bordered on the inhuman. Mind, body and weapons in accord, as he had been taught, Tal moved through the fray bringing down the best of Valeran's warriors with either hand. For nine years he had practiced in the fighting arts of the Armslords, the inheritors of the legacy of the most fearsome and infamous warriors history had ever known, the Shevestra'ken. His tutelage under Armslord Malry Zhierren had been punishing but effective, pushing him beyond all normal endurance to surpass limits he'd never dreamed he could reach in the first place. The training had become part of Talaren, rooted itself in his reflexes and instincts such that it came without effort now. He fought without fear, without doubt, and without hesitation, as was the way of an Armslord. Against that, few foes could hope to contend.

Tal swept an incoming attack aside with one sword while striking a disqualifying blow to his attacker's mailed chest with the other. A swift kick to the side executed right atop his swordplay staggered another man bearing a mace, its head padded for the competition, and Tal surged in with both blades swinging before his opponent could regain his balance. The maceman just managed to block the first blade, but the second caught him low in the chest, knocking the wind from his lungs and removing him from the fray. Tal glanced quickly about, blades held in readiness to meet another attack, and found that while there were still contenders on the field, all those immediately around him were downed.

The feeling of probing eyes came over him again, overpowering, as palpable as if the watcher had reached out and touched him. Tal cast his gaze across the stands in his brief moment of respite, seeking the source of the odd sensation. Like iron to a lodestone, his eyes were drawn to a young woman sitting amongst the crowd not fifty paces distant. She was strikingly attractive, with shoulder-length red hair framing a face that somehow managed to be both delicate and bold at the same time. There was an enormous sense of presence about her, as though she were somehow more real than her surroundings. All those around her were cheering and yelling with wild abandon, but she sat almost motionless, quietly watching. Watching Talaren. Why did he feel as if he should recognize her, when he couldn't place her anywhere in his memory? Their eyes met, and the defending Champion of Arms felt an electric thrill shoot up his spine. He thought he saw the hint of a smile cross that breathtaking face.

Suddenly, a heavy impact crashed into Tal's left shoulder. By instinct he rolled forward with the force of the blow, but from the way his shoulder protested he knew that he'd already been eliminated from the contest. He silently berated himself for his moment of inattention even as the man with the padded axe who'd just struck him leapt past Tal in search of another foe. *Had this been real, I'd be minus an arm and bleeding to death.* That thought stung far more than the fact of having just lost his title from the previous tourney.

Tal watched on from the place where he'd been struck down as the few remaining competitors converged on one another towards the center of the field, swinging and slashing at each other until after a few minutes only one remained standing. The victor, a man Tal didn't recognize, held his blunted sword aloft to the cheers of the crowd as a herald in the black and red livery of the Royal House of Zherrane declared him this year's Champion of Arms. *Good for him,* Tal thought. *He's likely either a mercenary or hedge knight,*

8

and winning this recognition might earn him a high place in service to one of the Houses. It was more benefit than the young Lord would have taken from a win today.

Footmen were rushing onto the field from the sidelines to help the defeated to their feet, or carrying off those whose injuries precluded moving on their own to be tended by Jhessaillian-trained healers. Tal waved off one of the men as he got back to his feet. There were others who would need the help far more. He cast his gaze back to where the mysterious woman who had so distracted him had been sitting, but she was nowhere to be seen.

With a regretful sigh, Tal made his way to the edge of the field, which was hemmed in by rank upon rank of spectators. They stepped back to open a narrow passage for him to walk through, those closest to him offering words of support and wishing him better luck in the Melee next year.

After clearing the crowd Tal was free to wend his way to his tall black-and -silver striped tent. A small pennant with the silver running fox on a black field that was House Solus's crest fluttered atop the tent in a gentle breeze. Tal pushed through the door flap and went inside.

Malry was already within, waiting for his pupil, a stern scowl on his face and in his voice. "What happened out there, Talaren?" Beside his student the silvery-haired Armslord seemed a small man, but his slender frame was all muscle and sinew, and anyone assuming his age made him a less formidable warrior would be setting themselves up for a rude surprise. Tal knew from years of training with Malry that the older man was stronger, tougher, and far swifter with a blade than most men half his age. He held himself with an easy grace that the young Lord hoped he would one day be able to duplicate. "One moment your performance was nearly flawless, the next it seemed as though your focus completely vanished. I've not expected you to have difficulties like that since your first year working with me."

"I'm sorry, master," Tal replied contritely, his face flushing with embarrassment, "I let myself be distracted. There was someone in the stands, a woman..." He shook his head, struggling to find the proper words to explain himself. "There was something about her..."

"You're telling me you were too busy looking at women to defend yourself?" Malry's tone was incredulous. "That's ridiculous. I know for fact that you've better discipline than that."

"You're right, or you should be," Tal agreed with a frown. How could he describe the odd feeling that had overtaken him? "This was different, though. I could feel her watching me, before I even saw her. And when I spotted her, I had the strangest feeling that I knew her, even though I'm certain I've never laid eyes on her before today." He shrugged apologetically. "Still, I shouldn't have let my concentration slip. It was a foolish mistake."

"So long as you realize that," the Armslord said gruffly, "I suppose I can let it pass without further reprimand this time." He gave his student a searching look. "It sounds to me as though you read something within the Sephira about this woman. I couldn't tell you what it may have been, but I can tell you that when the Sephira speaks to you, you ignore it at your own peril."

The Sephira was the animating force of reality, an all-pervasive energy field in which the entirety of existence was suspended. The Shevestra'ken had learned how to somehow merge with it, channeling its raw power through their bodies to attain the unnatural strength, speed, and stamina for which they had been renowned and feared. Though the secret to that ability had disappeared along with its practitioners, the Armslords of the present learned through meditation and discipline to read the ebb and flow of combat through the Sephira. Some few, Malry included, claimed it could even occasionally grant other, deeper intuitions.

"So it could have been a warning, then?" Tal began the work of removing his armor, a complicated affair based on the traditional design favored by Armslords and the Shevestra'ken before them. At first glance it resembled a light suit of plate and mail armor, but with segmented plates to allow the wearer the greatest possible range of movement. The gaps between the segments were protected with an extra layer of mail, the whole assembly held together by a network of straps and buckles that also served to distribute the armor's weight evenly. It afforded an excellent balance between protection and mobility, at the price of being irksomely involved to put on and take off.

Malry set to helping his pupil with the armor. "Did it seem like a warning? Did you feel threatened, endangered, uneasy?"

"No," Tal answered with a shake of his head, "nothing like that. It was just like I said, a sense of familiarity that I know rationally shouldn't actually have been there." He grunted softly as the Armslord worked at a buckle on the dented pauldron where he'd taken the axe blow.

"I'd suspect it to be something else, then," Malry said as the strap came free. "Perhaps you were sensing a potential friend or ally in this woman. Or maybe there was something between your spirits in a previous life. I really couldn't say. It's on you to interpret those things you may sense in the Sephira. That's why you felt it and not I."

"Are you filling my son's head with Battleborn mysticism again, old friend?" Duke Daron Solus asked as he pushed through the door-flap into the tent. Talaren's father was a broad, solidly built man only barely taller than his son. The golden hair Tal had inherited was on Daron beginning to fade to silver, but his face was yet unlined by the years. His black doublet and mantle were of the finest cut, the Solus fox insignia embroidered boldly across the chest. The Duke leveled a paternal gaze at his son. "It's clever tactics and sound leadership that win battles, not archaic philosophies and exaggerated legends."

Tal had heard this argument any number of times over the past several years, and knew from his past attempts that it was useless trying to change his father's opinion. Though Daron appreciated the value of the Armslords' martial skills and training, he considered the esoterica of Shevestra'ken lore to be little more than a curiosity of history, questionable in its accuracy and lacking practical application. So Tal simply bowed his head acquiescingly toward his father.

Malry, on the other hand, wasn't so easily deterred. "With the utmost respect, Your Grace, Talaren is but a few short steps away from becoming the first noble-born son of Valeran to attain the title of Armslord in at least a dozen generations. It would seem appropriate for him to have some knowledge of those from whom we inherited our ways."

"You've certainly seen to that over the past several years," the Duke commented wryly. "Tal knows almost as much trivia about the Bloody-Handed Maiden's followers as you do." That was a reference to Shevestra herself, who some claimed had been a demon and others a minor deity, and who the Shevestra'ken had claimed as their founder and patron in naming themselves after her. "What I overheard sounded far more specific than general lore, though. What were you discussing?"

"Talaren sensed something unusual in the Sephira about a young woman among the onlookers," Malry answered, "which is what distracted him in the middle of the competition. I was simply trying to help him interpret whatever it may have been."

The final strap on the outer layer of Tal's armor came loose and he shrugged off the plates with a relieved sigh, then promptly set to stripping off the mail shirt underneath. It made for a convenient way to cover his embarrassment at the Armslord's disclosure.

"One hardly needs a convoluted Sephiral explanation for taking notice of a woman at the tourney," Daron chuckled, making Tal's ears burn all the redder, "though to have kept you from noticing an armored man coming up behind you, she must have been quite something to look at."

"It was a foolish lapse on my part," Tal muttered as Malry took the mail from him to hang on a nearby wooden armor rack. "It won't happen again." He flexed his left arm to test its range of motion after the blow it'd absorbed.

Thankfully, Daron didn't press his son about the mysterious young woman. "How's your shoulder, Tal?" he asked instead. "That looked like quite the brutal hard hit you took."

Tal shrugged. "It isn't that bad. A bit stiff, but otherwise it seems fine."

"I'll send for a healer," Daron said decisively.

"I suppose," Tal agreed halfheartedly, "though I'm sure there are others who need their attention more than I do."

"Don't be ridiculous," Daron scoffed. "None of the other contestants are in dire need, and if any were, they'd have been taken care of by now. A whole team of Jhessaillian-taught healers will hardly be so overtaxed they can't spare one man for a few minutes to heal you." Healing was one of the few, and the most popularly studied, of the Sephiral disciplines that the Jhessaillian Order taught to those outside its own ranks. A healer who had studied under them could mend in mere moments wounds that might otherwise cost a man his life.

Malry lifted the back of Tal's tunic to examine the injured shoulder. "You've got quite the bruise back here," he noted dryly, applying gentle pressure with his fingertips. "But nothing appears to be broken."

Daron took note of Talaren's slight wince during the Armslord's examination. "That decides it. You've got the competition for King's Champion tomorrow, Tal. You don't want to have a stiff shoulder slowing you down." He ducked out of the tent.

Within a few minutes Daron returned with a slight, sandy-haired woman in tow with a healer's scrip at her side. She coolly ordered Tal to strip to the waist, and he complied without protest. She gently ran her hands over the injury. Tal's skin seemed to prickle as she read his Sephiral pattern to determine the severity of the wound.

"This is fairly minor. I'll have it taken care of in no time," she said matter-of-factly as she reached into her scrip and pulled out a small tin. She opened the tin and dabbed her fingertips into a faintly greenish ointment inside, which she then tenderly rubbed into Talaren's shoulder. A cool tingling spread through the area, washing away all hint of stiffness and ache. "There," she said crisply when she finished, refastening the lid and putting the tin back, "good as new."

Tal rolled and stretched the shoulder to check for any lingering aches. It felt, just as the healer had said, good as new. "My thanks, dear lady," he said, rummaging in his pocket to produce a pair of silver coins which he pressed into her palm.

"Oh, it was no trouble," the young woman said as a smile dimpled her face. She really was quite pretty. "My husband will be cheering for you tomorrow, and he'd never forgive me if I let you go into the Joust injured."

"Well then, I'll just have to try not to let him down," Tal replied with a smile.

The healer dropped a graceful curtsy. "Thank you, milord, I'll tell him you said so. I'm sure he'll be very happy to know I tended to you myself. But if you'll excuse me, there are others who yet require my attention."

"Of course," Tal said graciously, "I wouldn't want to keep you too long."

The healer bowed her head and let herself out of the tent. Tal turned to a chest in the corner and pulled out a clean tunic, black with understated silver trim and House Solus's running fox emblem embroidered on the left breast, also in silver.

As Tal pulled the clean tunic on, Daron cleared his throat. "Tazmin asked me to tell you that he'd wait for you at The King's Lancer, Tal." Tazmin was Tal's cousin and best friend, the son of Baron Remarr Joseth, whose House was among the closest of allies to House Solus.

Tal chuckled. "He probably wanted to get a head start on me in the drinking." The Harvest Tournament was among the biggest of events in Valeran, equaled in merrymaking only by the Festival of Liberation which commemorated the fall of Empress Anakara the Undying and the founding of Valeran by Korven Zherrane. The streets and taverns tonight would fill with celebrating folk, and Tazmin had never been one to miss an opportunity to celebrate.

"We'll let you get on to Tazmin and the festivities," Daron said, "just be careful not to celebrate yourself into a hangover in the morning."

"Of course not, father," Tal replied, "I'm the sensible one, you'll recall." Not that Tazmin lacked sense so much as restraint.

"And yet it seems you let your cousin talk you into trouble more often than not," Daron chuckled. "But no matter, so long as you can ride and lance straight in the morning. Enjoy yourself, Tal."

Malry met Tal's gaze and gave a curt nod before following Daron out of the tent.

Tal gave himself a cursory inspection in a small hand mirror, taking a moment to regather his shoulder-length hair into the silver ring he used to keep it pulled back in a neat tail. He rubbed his strong, lightly stubbled chin for a moment, and decided he could put off shaving again until morning. Setting the mirror aside, he gave his tall boots a quick brushing to remove the dust of the Grand Melee before departing from the tent himself and making his way from the tourney field, where workmen were already erecting the lists for tomorrow's joust, and into the city proper of Val Zherrane.

The capital city of Valeran had been built a scant three centuries past by Korven Zherrane himself, following his defeat of the Undying Empress, making Val Zherrane the youngest of Valeran's great cities. Situated on the northern coast, the city was laid out like an enormous semicircle, with the Royal Palace on its promontory overlooking the sea at the center. Straight, broad avenues ran like spokes of a giant wheel out from that center, with smaller connecting streets between. With sturdy stone construction for most of the city's buildings, streets kept meticulously clean, and a healthy trade passing through the harbor, Val Zherrane was the crowning glory of what had once been the largest and mightiest of nations, prior to the Bhellan Revolution twenty years past in which Bhellus to the East and later Amberyl to the South had broken away.

The King's Lancer was familiar to Tal, one of the larger taverns located in the richest part of the city near the Palace. As he walked there the streets were already beginning to fill with people, musicians and the folk dancing to their music, hawkers selling ale and mead from booths erected just for the festivities surrounding the yearly tourney. Many on the streets called out to Tal as he passed, and he waved back or exchanged a few polite words with those who did. When he arrived at the tavern, the sun was just beginning to slip below the horizon.

"Tal, you glory hound!" Tazmin declared over his mug as Talaren walked into the common room. "Finally you manage to find your way here! I was starting to wonder if you'd gotten lost!" Tal's cousin was a few inches shorter than the heir to Val Solus, with close cropped reddish-blond hair and a ready smile. Aside from the mug in his hand, a full one sat on the table before him, which he slid over to Tal. The common room was filled with men and women in their finest festive dress, drinking cool ale or enjoying a pipe or dancing to the tune being played by three musicians on a small platform at the end of the room.

"Not lost," Tal said as he sat down and took a sip of the dark, bitter ale, "just not quite so eager as you to start getting drunk."

"I'm just trying to get a start in on the drinks you owe me," Tazmin grinned, "for the money I lost on you today."

"Tazmin, you didn't..."

"Of course I did," Tazmin cut Tal off merrily. "Just a small wager, mind you. The Grand Melee is unpredictable enough that the odds were quite agreeable. You're so heavily favored tomorrow that a bet would hardly be worth my time."

Tal grunted noncommittally as he reached into his belt pouch to produce his carved wooden pipe and a pouch of pungent dried herbs, the finest smoking blend from the fields of Val Solus. He began thumbing the bowl full as Tazmin followed his example, pulling out and filling his own pipe. Tal puffed his pipe alight with the aid of a long splinter that lay beside the candle on the table and then offered the small flame to Tazmin.

"I must admit, though," Tazmin said as he exhaled a long streamer of smoke, "I'm still rather perplexed as to how you let that fellow smack you across the back. How did you manage to miss him clanking up behind you?"

"I was busy looking at a girl," Tal sighed.

"Is that so?" Tazmin chortled. "It's about time. Talaren Solus, the great swordsman and Armslord-to-be, who can never be bothered to find time for

14

the swarms of ladies that sigh over him, finally notices a woman. This is a banner day." He took another long sip of ale and chuckled again.

"Just because I don't play at courting every pretty pair of eyes that cross my path, unlike some people I know, is no reason to laugh," Tal said with a grin and a twinkle in his eye before puffing deeply on his pipe. "I'm just selective."

Tazmin laughed heartily. "And I'm just trying to have my fun before my father marries me off. With my luck, I'll end up with some rich, powerful, and above all ugly and old harridan." Tal's cousin shuddered, but the smile never left his face. "So who's the lucky girl, Tal? No, wait, let me guess - is it Korine of House Eldarion? She's quite the eyeful. Or maybe Joseen of Dorath - not only is she beautiful and her House strong, I know she's had an eye for you for quite some time. Well, Tal, who is it?"

Making a disgusted sound at the back of his throat, Tal rolled his eyes. "Tazmin, you know how I feel about the so-called 'ladies' of the Royal Court. They're taught from childhood to smile, bat their eyelashes, and find themselves a husband who'll advance the standing of their Houses. And never to say anything controversial, never to have a thought that's too original lest they raise eyebrows, never to do anything that breaks the mold of a 'lady' that they've been crammed into. It's all terribly sad, and dreadfully boring to have a conversation with, let alone anything further. I'll pass on that, thanks."

Tazmin's grin grew through Tal's brief tirade. "So she must be a commoner, then. The plot thickens." He waved over a buxom, dark-eyed serving girl. "Would you mind getting the former Champion of Arms and I each another ale?"

The girl assented with a smoky gaze and inviting smile for Tal. He smiled back and nodded in acknowledgement.

"You see, there you go again," Tazmin grumbled, watching as the serving girl swayed back to fetch their drinks, "the less you give them the more they want it. I wish I knew how you do it." He drained the rest of his mug with a sigh. "So tell me about this mystery woman of yours, Tal. What's she look like?"

"Red hair to the base of her neck," Tal said, picturing the mysterious woman in his mind, "with a flawless face and eyes that bore right through you. What I really noticed, though, is that there's an intensity about her that I can't quite put my finger on. I've never seen anything quite like it, but I could feel it from across the field like she was jabbing a finger into my chest."

Their new mugs arrived, and Tazmin began drinking his while Tal finished off his first one. "That narrows the field a bit, but she still doesn't sound like anyone I know of. You'll have to point her out to me, I suppose. Or you could make her your Queen of Roses when you win tomorrow."

"If I win tomorrow," Tal corrected absentmindedly.

"Oh, would you stop that, Tal?" Tazmin sighed in exasperation. "You're the best in Valeran, and everybody knows it except you, apparently. There's not a knight in Val Zherrane tonight who isn't praying to every god he can think of that he not have to lance against you tomorrow."

"Not true, Lord Joseth," a too-familiar voice called insolently. "I, for one, don't fear to face Talaren in the lists. He did well enough in the melee today against ruffians and mercenaries, but some nameless commoner still defeated him. I look forward to showing him tomorrow how a true nobleman fights." The speaker, Lord Joren Jerak, was of an age with Tal, an inch or two shorter, and broad of shoulder. A fine fuzz of blond hair covered his head, and his pouty lips were now twisted in a mocking smirk. In Tal's experience, Joren was a fair swordsman, an exceptional lancer, and a superb braggart. He swaggered up to Tal and Tazmin's table flanked by a pair of lesser lordlings who Tal recognized only by the insignias on their coats, all well in their cups judging by their gait.

"I stand corrected," Tazmin announced merrily to Tal. "I should have said instead that there isn't a man with an ounce of sense who wants to lance against you."

Joren glowered at Tal's cousin. "Were I you, Tazmin, I'd not go picking fights with three men when you've but one at your back."

"I'm not the one picking a fight. And were you me, Jay-Jay, you'd be a great deal more popular with the ladies," Tazmin laughed. "You'd also realize that the man at my back is worth the lot of you twice over."

Tal groaned as one of Joren's companions reached for the sword at his side. Tazmin just *would* have to goad them. He stood and caught the younger lord by the wrist before he'd bared more than an inch of steel.

"Nobody's questioning your prowess, Joren," Tal said, drawing the other nobleman's gaze, "or that of your friends. You'll have ample opportunity to demonstrate it tomorrow, no need to cause a disturbance now. Let's drink instead to your success at the joust. I'll buy."

Joren sneered. "No Jerak needs a Solus to buy him his drinks. You can drink to me tomorrow night instead, after I knock you in the dirt at the lists." He shouldered rudely past Tal, his friends in tow, and stormed out of the common room.

Tazmin sighed and shook his head. "There are times I just don't understand you, Tal. Joren comes on blowing smoke out his arse like that and instead of kicking it back to Val Jerak for him, you stroke his already bloated ego?"

"Better than letting you needle him into starting a fight and spoiling our welcome here," Tal grumbled back.

Tazmin opened his mouth to reply, then shifted his gaze past Tal and smirked instead, murmuring, "I'd say that welcome looks plenty unspoiled."

"Excuse me, milord," the serving girl with the inviting smile said as she laid a hand lightly on Tal's shoulder. "I wanted to thank you for seeing that lot off," she nodded toward the door Joren had so precipitously exited through. "They'd been hassling me and the other girls something fierce."

Tal shrugged modestly. "I didn't really-" he cut himself off abruptly when Tazmin kicked him in the shin under the table.

"If it wouldn't be too forward of me," the girl went on, "would you care for a dance? Alsibeth's covering for me a few minutes."

Tal smiled and bowed his head to her. "It would be a pleasure." Offering her his hand, he let her lead him out to the cleared space of floor where folk were merrily dancing. He flashed a quick grin over his shoulder at Tazmin, who tipped his drink in reply before taking another long sip.

Once on the floor, Tal had no shortage of requests for the next dance. Tazmin came out himself after a short while, trailing another serving girl who giggled at whatever it was the heir to Val Joseth was whispering in her ear. So the night passed in dancing, drinking, and merriment. That was what festivals were all about, after all.

He felt her eyes on him again as soon as he had taken his place at the sidelines of the field to await his first match. Searching the crowd, Talaren's own eyes came to rest upon her almost immediately, just as he remembered her from the day before. The peculiar intensity that he had almost convinced himself was a trick of his mind was still there, and her gaze remained fixed on him just as intently as before. This time he was certain she smiled when she saw him looking back at her. And then slowly, deliberately, she bowed her head toward him in acknowledgement. Curiosity filled Tal anew. Who was this woman? Why was she watching him, seemingly to the exclusion of all else? And why did he feel so powerfully drawn to her? He had to have answers. But not now. Now, he had the most important event of the tournament to focus on. He promised himself, though, that he wouldn't lose track of her this time, that he would find her and get his answers once the Joust was over.

The competition was expected to last most of the day, as virtually every knight and young noble with any amount of martial training had come to contend for the title of King's Champion. Tal's first bout, the seventh match of the morning, was against Lord Jonos, the son of Baronet Orman Ygris. Jonos was a few years younger than Tal, this his first time in the Harvest Tournament. Tal unseated him on the first pass.

Two bouts later Tal watched Joren face Boral, youngest son of the Earl of Val Goren. Joren won on the third pass, but from the way he wavered in the saddle, Tal suspected the heir to Val Jerak was feeling the aftermath of the previous night's drinking.

The second matchup an hour later proved a bit more of a challenge for Tal. Facing him at the other end of the lists was Sir Roddik of Gahane, who had been King's Champion at the Harvest Tourney twice in the past. He and Talaren each shattered five lances against the other's shield to the pleased roaring of the crowd before Roddik was finally thrown from the saddle on the sixth charge.

Roddik was followed by Famrir of Val Oryx, and then Dellim of Harost and Sevwin of Val Lorran who tenaciously kept his saddle for eight passes and nearly knocked Tal from his twice. Joren made it to his fourth match before being unhorsed by Sir Galnar Larch. Apparently he'd not have the opportunity to make good on his promise to knock Tal into the dirt.

The entire time, Tal remained aware of the eyes watching him. So long as the feeling persisted, he found he didn't even have to look to be certain the mysterious girl was still there.

At last, well into the afternoon, the championship match was announced, pitting Tal against Sir Wyman Mavis, a seasoned warrior who had earned his knighthood in service to House Arvin during the Bhellan Revolution. Tal had never before faced Sir Mavis, but had watched his matches both this year and the last, when Mavis had taken the honor of King's Champion. The man was formidable, his form little short of perfection and his aim as close as Tal had ever seen to unerring.

A young squire held Talaren's grey warhorse, Stormwind, while Tal climbed into the courser's saddle. He took up a lance from a rack at the side of the field, and took his place opposite his opponent. The crowd grew silent in anticipation as the two men saluted one another, and then Tal pulled down the visor on his fox-headed helmet and kicked Stormwind into a charge, his lance coming down as he and Mavis hurtled toward each other. The impact when lanceheads met shields was enormous. Both lances exploded into clouds of splinters, but both men kept their saddles. After replacing the shattered lances, the second pass was almost identical, as were the third, forth, fifth, and so on.

By the ninth pass, both men were visibly less than steady in the saddle and it was beginning to look as though the winner would be decided by endurance more than anything else. On the tenth, Sir Mavis's aim was particularly good and Tal barely managed to stay on Stormwind, having to drop his unbroken lance to haul himself back upright in the saddle. The cheering and yelling of the onlookers grew more frenzied with every pass. The eleventh time Tal and Mavis clashed, it seemed for a few moments as though both men were going to lose their saddles, but they managed to steady themselves and turn their horses about again. Tal's ears were ringing from the repeated impacts, and his shield arm felt numb from all the blows taken. Holding the tip of his lance steady seemed a supreme act of will.

18

Taking a deep breath to steel himself, he comforted himself in that Sir Mavis looked to be having similar difficulties. Again both riders set heels to the flanks of their steeds to thunder down the lists at each other. As the last few feet between them flashed away, the tip of Mavis's lance wavered by just a few inches. It was enough. His lance glanced off of Tal's shield, even as Talaren's own lance struck home. As though lifted by a great invisible hand, Mavis flew from his saddle to crash to the earth sprawled on his back.

As the dust began to settle on the knight's prone armored form, the crowd leapt to their feet and roared. Tal raised his visor and held his lance up in victory as cheering rolled across the field. Four men ran out from the sidelines to pick up the insensate Sir Mavis and carried him off to where a healer was already waiting in case he needed any attention. Tal brought Stormwind around and cantered up to the King's Pavilion, where a liveried herald stood waiting for the cheers to die down enough to announce the King's Champion. Tal sat his saddle patiently.

Within a few moments the crowd's din died down and the herald boomed, "Winning the title of King's Champion this year is Lord Talaren Solus, heir to the high seat of House Solus!" Again cheers drowned everything out.

Tal lowered the tip of his lance toward the herald, who placed a crown of roses around the head of the weapon. Tradition held that the King's Champion presented the crown to a woman from among the audience to mark her the Queen of Roses. Whomever was chosen joined the Champion at the King's table for the Royal Feast following the tournament.

Tal turned Stormwind about and rode down along one side of the stands. Women in the crowd yelled to him, beckoned to him, even threw hats or shawls at him trying to draw his eye. His gaze went inexorably to one woman only, though.

Unlike those around her, she made not a move and spoke not a word. She simply sat calmly, watching as Tal rode closer and closer. When the tip of the lance swung over to hold the crown before her, crystal green eyes sparkled amusement at him before she took the wreath of roses. Tal had wondered what color they were, after having felt their touch all day. She raised an eyebrow at him as she placed the crown atop her head.

The red-haired young woman stood gracefully and stepped forward, accepting Tal's outstretched hand to help her up into the saddle behind him. In the instant they touched, Tal was struck by a sudden burst of sensation, like a lifetime's worth of half-remembered recollections flooding through him for a heartbeat and then vanishing.

Also surprising, though a mere curiosity by comparison, the young woman wore grey breeches instead of skirts and carried a sword at her hip balanced on the other side by a long fighting knife. From the way she moved, she was clearly used to wearing them. The weapons didn't hinder her in the slightest as she smoothly pulled herself up by Tal's hand onto Stormwind's back. As she settled down, she wrapped her arms familiarly around Tal's waist to hold on and leaned forward to speak softly over his shoulder.

"I hope milord doesn't mistake me for a wide-eyed admirer, easily impressed and added to a handsome young nobleman's conquests." Her voice was clear and almost musical, her tone playful.

"Not at all," Tal replied back over his shoulder, "I consider you more a riddle waiting to be solved." He could barely see her out of the corner of his eye.

She laughed lightly. "I'll warn you then, Lord Solus, this riddle will take more than a single night to yield up her secrets."

"The best kind then," Tal smiled back. "I'm afraid you have the advantage of me. You know my name, but I haven't yours. What are you called, my Lady?"

"Rania," came the reply, "And don't call me 'Lady.' I claim no such titles."

In spite of himself, Tal had to grin. Though barely past the introductions, he already knew he was going to enjoy the company of this impertinent young woman. "Very well, then. Rania. Shall we join His Majesty for the feast?"

"Yes," she murmured, "I believe we shall."

2
A Feast of Questions

The Harvest Tournament's Royal Feast was held beneath an enormous tent erected a short distance from the competition field. Tal brought Stormwind up alongside the Royal Pavilion and dismounted, handing the reins off to a waiting groom. He turned to offer Rania a hand down from the warhorse, but she simply sprang down from the saddle and flashed a grin at him.

"I'm not so delicate as the women I imagine you're used to," she said, eyes dancing.

"I see not," Tal replied wryly. There was something about those green eyes that tugged at him, something roiling beneath the cheerful and amused surface that he couldn't put his finger on. The sense of her presence that had been so strong from a distance was nearly overwhelming with her standing beside him.

An elderly gentleman was stepping down from the set of stairs at the side of the King's platform. He wore the black and red livery of House Zherrane and had a kind, grandfatherly face below thinning silver hair. Tal had known Gyles, the King's Seneschal, since he had been but a young boy.

"Talaren! You put forth a most impressive effort today. Allow me to offer my congratulations."

"Thank you, Gyles," Tal replied with a small bow.

"Yes," Rania agreed, "from what I've seen you handle both sword and lance extremely well. You've quite a distinctive, and effective, fighting style."

"Lord Solus has long studied the arts of the Armslords, my lady," Gyles volunteered.

With a thoughtful nod, Rania murmured. "Yes, I thought that was what I was seeing. Have you completed the training?"

"Not yet," Tal answered, "but soon, my master says."

The young woman eyed him thoughtfully. "He must be a very thorough man, this master of yours. With the skill you appear to possess, I'd think he would have declared you ready by now."

"That's a fairly accurate description of Armslord Zhierren," Tal agreed. "I've been fortunate to have his instruction."

"You seem to have chosen a most fascinating Queen of Roses, Talaren," Gyles observed, studying Rania curiously. "Beautiful, unconventional, and unusually observant. Who is this lovely lady who causes the unmarried noblewomen of the Court to gnash their teeth in jealousy?"

"Gyles, this is Rania," Tal introduced her. "Rania, this kind gentleman is Gyles Devrin, the King's Seneschal and head of the Royal staff."

"A pleasure, my lady," Gyles murmured with a bow. "I'm to inform you that His Majesty's party will be along shortly and then we may all process to the Feast."

"Thank you, Seneschal Gyles," Rania said, and then flashed an impish grin at Tal before adding, "but what's this about jealously gnashing teeth?"

"Oh, you didn't know?" The Seneschal seemed surprised. "With his position and honors, Talaren here is regularly and relentlessly pursued by the unmarried noblewomen at Court. I'm sure a great many young Ladies are disheartened at his choosing you over them."

"Really?" Rania asked, casting a sly glance at Tal, "How fortunate for me."

"Indeed," said Gyles with another smile. "But if you'll pardon me, I must rejoin His Majesty." The Seneschal turned and mounted the stairs again.

"So, Talaren," Rania asked with a smirk, "why *did* you choose me over all the Ladies of the Royal Court?"

Tal shrugged casually. "None of them are quite as striking as you." He fixed her with a searching gaze. "And because I wanted to know whose eyes those were I've felt on me the last couple days."

Rania gave him a peculiar look. "You could feel me watching you," she mused. "Interesting." A wicked grin crossed her face and with a devilish glint in her eye she asked, "Did you enjoy it?"

Tal let himself smile faintly. "Let's just say it wasn't unpleasant."

Just then the Royal Party began to descend the steps at the side of the pavilion. First came Gyles and Uried, the High Commander of the Valerite Guard, in an ornately crafted breastplate polished to a high shine with Valeran's crossed swords emblem raised and lacquered a slick black and crimson on the chest. Following them were the Lords of the Royal Council with their Ladies, Tal's father among them. Daron walked unescorted; Duchess Nareene Solus, Tal's mother, had died of a winter fever in her son's youth, and the Duke had shown little interest in remarrying since. Duke Solus nodded to his son as he passed by. Last of all came King Garant Zherrane. The King was an elderly man, face creased and wrinkled from the long years. The simple golden circlet that was the crown of Valeran rested on snowy white locks, but face and hair were the only places Garant Zherrane showed his age. His shoulders were unstooped beneath his heavy robes of state, and his clear blue eyes spoke of a sharp, incisive intellect that age had only honed to a keener edge.

As King's Champion and Queen of Roses, Tal and Rania were given a place of honor directly behind the King, the tradition being that the Champion protected his monarch for the procession to the feast. It was a ceremonial role only; In all of Valeran's history the Champion had never been called on to execute it, for no King had ever come under attack at the Harvest Tournament.

Tal offered Rania his arm as they fell in at the end of the procession, and she took it without comment. He was still very much puzzled by her. He'd fulfilled his promise to himself to speak to her, if only for a short time thus far, but had learned little more about her than her name. In fact, it seemed she had learned more of him than he of her. Tal couldn't help but feel that Rania was playing with him. And Gods help him, he was enjoying the game, even if he didn't yet grasp the rules.

It was but a short distance to the massive canvas roof of the tent. Already a thick swarm of nobles, courtiers, and commonfolk of station milled about beneath it, and more were still trickling in as the Royal Party arrived. A line of eight heralds sounded a fanfare on long, straight horns at a signal from the Seneschal. The murmuring crowd fell silent as they all turned to face the raised dais on which the Royal Party would sit.

The nobles of the Royal Council filed in and stood before their seats, their proximity to the King's seat determined by the influence of their Houses and their standing within the Council. Talaren's father stood at the seat just to the left of His Majesty's. One seat down from him Archduke Zharkus Jerak, with his immaculately trimmed blond hair and beard and heavy square jaw, scowled as he took his place. Usually it was he who would be seated at the King's left, with Daron to the monarch's right, but with the right hand seat given to the King's Champion the members of the Council were all shuffled down one rank in the seating scheme. Zharkus's having to relinquish his position beside the King, even for one day, would be a sore reminder to him that although his House's position and wealth were reckoned among the greatest in all of Valeran, its influence had been on the wane since the Bhellan Revolution. His mood would only be worsened by the fact that a Solus would be seated to either side of the King, for there was a rivalry between the two Houses that had grown alongside House Solus's expanding influence over the past couple decades.

When the Council were all in place, the heralds blew another fanfare, and the assembled crowd bowed as the King entered with Tal and Rania following close behind. As King Garant took his place at the great padded central chair, Tal came to stand at the King's right hand with Rania beside him.

The King lifted a gem-encrusted silver goblet from the table before his seat and held it aloft. "Rise, my friends and subjects," he declaimed in clear tones. As the gathered aristocracy straightened themselves, he went on. "Another growing season has passed us by, and our storehouses are filled and ready for the long, cold winter to come. Sit and feast with me, friends, and let us celebrate the bounty the land has given us this year."

A cry of approval went up from the onlookers and as the Royal Party took their seats, the rest of those in the tent began to seat themselves at the myriad of other tables set out for the Feast. Already a small army of servants was streaming into the tent bearing to the tables covered platters from which emanated mouth-watering smells.

While the food was being laid out before them, the King turned to Tal. "My congratulations on your victory today, Talaren. All of Valeran stands in awe of your skills."

"Thank you, Majesty," Tal replied with a bow of his head. "Although I hardly deserve such praise."

"Nonsense!" Garant scoffed. "I seem to recall you saying much the same last year when you won the competition for Champion at Arms. Take a little pride, at least, in your accomplishments. You certainly deserve that much." He smiled soothingly and glanced past Tal to Rania. "And who is your lovely Queen of Roses?"

"Majesty, this is Rania," Tal replied.

He thought he detected a brief trace of something, perhaps recognition, on the King's face, but in the blink of an eye it had become mere curiosity as Garant nodded his head to Rania. "If I may ask, Lady Rania, from which House do you hail? I feel there's something familiar about you, though I regret to say I can't seem to place it."

"I claim no House, Your Majesty," she replied politely, "I am but a humble traveler."

Garant nodded. "Of course. I apologize. Perhaps you minded me of someone I once knew." The King grimaced. "Would you listen to me, nattering on like an old fool about half-forgotten memories? I should permit you the time instead to become acquainted with Talaren. He's quite the charming young man, really, once you get past the fact that he denies anything you say to him that's at all complimentary." Garant smiled indulgently at Tal before turning his eyes back to the young woman. "Be welcome, Rania."

"Thank you, Your Majesty," Rania responded. As the King turned to converse with Duke Solus, she focused her green-eyed gaze back on Tal. "So tell me, Talaren, how long have you trained in the Armslord's ways to so command the awe of Valeran?"

"Nine years," he replied, "and please, call me Tal."

"Alright then," she smiled warmly, "Tal."

"Rania, why *were* you watching me so closely?"

"Maybe I was just admiring a handsome young Lord," Rania replied with a mischievous twinkle in her eye. Then her tone became much more serious. "Actually, I recognized your fighting style. I have something of a fascination with the ways of the Armslords and Battleborn, you see. I've learned a great deal of lore about them, but it's not often that one encounters someone who actually practices their arts."

Tal nodded thoughtfully. "I suppose this interest would arise from your own training," he guessed. In response to the questioning look Rania gave him, he grinned and explained, "You wear your weapons with obvious familiarity. Between that and the way you carry yourself, I'd expect that you might have done rather well in the Grand Melee yourself, had you competed."

Rania gave an approving nod. "Very astute," she conceded.

Tal's grin grew wider. "Every struggle is won or lost in the mind before ever the first blade is drawn," he replied sagely.

"Shevestra'ken philosophy," Rania murmured, her recognition of the ancient adage startling Tal. "It sounds to me like you've learned more than just how to swing a sword in those nine years." She directed a considering look at him that fairly near made his bones melt. Those eyes were weapons in their own right. In a low voice she asked, "So are you expecting a struggle with me then, Tal?"

He kept his gaze locked with hers by sheer force of will. "Certainly a challenge, at the least," he said, and lifted his goblet of wine from the table to hold it out to Rania in a toast. "To interesting company."

Rania plucked up her own goblet and lightly touched it to Tal's with a crystalline ring. They both drank.

Valeran's Harvest Feast was known throughout the North for its grandiosity, and this year was no exception. The trays laid upon the tables by House Zherrane's servants bore delectable foodstuffs of every imaginable description: roasted game hen, fish in a delicate white sauce, stuffed leeks, and a myriad of other dishes, many of which Tal didn't even know the name for. Entertainment was in no short supply, either. A large patch of cleared ground lay between the King's table and those of all the other guests, where there would be dancing later. While the guests ate, though, the space was host to a stream of acrobats, jugglers, minstrels, and fools who plied their trades to the laughter and polite applause of the onlookers.

Tal ate but lightly and paid little mind to the entertainers. His attention was very much focused on the enigmatic Rania, who demonstrated throughout their dinner conversation that her claim of knowledge of Armslord and Shevestra'ken traditions had been no idle boast. It was strangely exhilarating for Tal, being able to engage this alluring young woman on topics that he was accustomed to only being able to discuss in any sort of depth with Malry. From blade techniques to meditation to codes of conduct to history, Rania seemed comfortable and conversant with it all. At times, Tal couldn't help but wonder if she was trying to impress him with the range of her knowledge, or to test the depth of his own. On the topic of the

Four Great Frailties of the Spirit, a cornerstone of Shevestra'ken philosophy, they entered a stimulating debate as to why malice was included with fear, doubt, and hesitation. Tal argued that it was to be shunned because excessive hatred for a foe could incite one to dishonorable and ignoble actions, whereas Rania held the belief that malice was a path to disrespect for an enemy and the potentially fatal mistake of underestimating them. Despite their disagreement, Tal found himself smiling through the whole thing, and noted with some satisfaction that Rania was as well.

As the rhetorical duel wound down still unresolved, Rania gave a satisfied nod. "When I commented earlier that this Armslord Zhierren who trained you was thorough, I didn't have the half of it. He's taught you as much as an initiate to the Shevetra'ken might be expected to know." She paused, lips pursed, staring into Tal's eyes as if she were trying to see through them to the back of his skull. "You can sense the Sephira at times, can't you?"

Tal hesitated for just a heartbeat before answering. "Yes. Sometimes, I think I can."

"That might explain why you thought you could feel me watching you. Although I still don't understand..." Rania frowned and shook her head as though to dislodge a troubling thought.

Tal couldn't take it anymore. The overpowering curiosity that had led him to make Rania his Queen of Roses grew with every word she spoke, and he was well and truly ensnared by it now. "Rania, just who or what are you, exactly?"

She shrugged. "Nobody of consequence, really."

"The more I talk with you, the harder it becomes to believe that."

Rania graced him with a radiant smile. "Maybe I'm being intentionally evasive to keep your interest. Is it working?"

Tal's throat suddenly felt very dry. He had to swallow carefully before answering, "Very much so."

"Good," she said, sounding pleased as could be. Her eyes strayed to where the entertainers had cleared out from some time ago and the Valerite aristocracy were now dancing to the lilting music of five musicians. "I assume that the King's Champion is expected to dance with his Queen of Roses?" she asked, looking back at Tal.

He nodded. "That's the tradition."

"Well, I suppose you'd better start teaching me how, then," Rania said, standing.

Tal looked at her incredulously. "You don't know how to dance?"

"I never really had the opportunity or inclination to learn," she replied, "but I think now seems like a good time to remedy that." She held a hand out to him.

Tal stood and took the offered hand, and led Rania out to the dance space.

One thing he had to give her credit for, she learned quickly. He had only to show Rania the steps to each dance once or twice before she picked them up, and she possessed a lithe grace that complemented dancing very nicely. Before long she didn't even require to be shown the steps, only for Tal to lead her.

At one point Talaren spotted Tazmin in the crowd, dancing with the elaborately coiffed Lady Lauriana of House Raheen. Tazmin caught Tal's look, and his eyes went from Tal to study the beautiful, sword-bearing redhead in his friend's arms. Tazmin's gaze flickered back to Tal, and he grinned widely with an approving wink before disappearing into the mass of dancers again.

For a time, the questions in Tal's mind were silent. He drifted along with the music, his movements and Rania's blending together, and he was able to push aside his curiosity to simply enjoy the pleasure of dancing with a comely young woman. From the bemused smile on her face and the distant, almost wistful look in her eyes, Rania seemed to be feeling much the same.

Hours blurred around them dreamlike as the night grew deeper. Still couples danced, and wine flowed freely beneath the tent of the Harvest Feast. On this, the night of the final day of the Tournament and accompanying festivities, many of the celebrants would not be seeking their beds until the sun rose again.

At length, in the lull between the end of one song and the beginning of the next, Rania pulled herself close against Tal to whisper in his ear. "I feel like taking a walk, and I very much think you want to come with me." There was no question in her voice, only absolute certainty that sent a shock of anticipation up Tal's spine.

Tal pulled back from her to study her face. She looked far more bold than delicate now, a smile playing about her lips that was both inviting and challenging, a challenge echoed in her fathomless green eyes as she looked back at him, daring him to accept the invitation.

Tal nodded in agreement, his curiosity rising anew. Taking Rania's arm, he led her away from the dancers, out of the tent and into the night.

The sky was clear, the air crisp and cool with the coming of autumn. Pale blue ribbons of Sephiral Aurora stretched across the sky, twisting and writhing placidly, heedless of the vicissitudes of the wind. They were bright and strong tonight, an auspicious significator of possibility and change according to old lore. Beyond the gently pulsing curtains of light glittered a myriad of stars, adding their gentle illumination to the brighter provided by the Sephira.

Rania chose their path once they were clear of the tent, leading Tal silently around and past the Tourney field, away from the village of tents clustered about it, and up a gently climbing hill beyond. She stopped partway down the southern slope of the hill, facing away from Val Zherrane and the Festival and, looking out across the countryside ahead, sat down. Tal seated himself beside her.

They sat in silence for a long while, taking in the rolls and folds of the land and the breathtaking spectacle of the ever-changing lights in the sky. Tal would occasionally spare a glance at Rania; her eyes were far away, looking off at some distant point that he could not perceive. He wondered what had prompted her to bring him here.

Finally she spoke, quietly, her voice little more than a whisper. "I've got just one more question for you, Tal." She looked at him then, her eyes dark pools, deep and unreadable. "Why did you do it? The training you've had couldn't have been easy. It's said that the disciplines of the Shevestra'ken and the Armslords are the hardest to learn, and only those with the greatest willpower, discipline, and determination can hope to succeed. Where do you find your determination?"

"That's a complicated question," Tal replied, "and requires a complicated answer."

"I know," she said simply, "I expected no less of a proper answer, and after the rest of the night I expected no less of you than such a response. That's why I brought us out here, where we won't be disturbed."

Tal nodded. Now it was his turn to gaze distantly at the horizon. "In my bedchambers back in Val Solus," he began, "hangs a tapestry. I had it put in my quarters shortly after I began training with Armslord Malry. It's a battle scene, an artist's version of the Battle of the Gilden Hills. The battle that my father is famous for winning, and for which his title was elevated to Duke."

"And deservedly so," Rania said, "I've heard of it. He lured a vastly superior force of invading Bhellans into a series of ambushes and skirmishes in the hills that slowed their advance and whittled away their strength until he received reinforcements and was able to put his enemy to rout with a concerted attack. After that battle, the Bhellans never managed to push as deep into Valeran again. It was the turning point of the Bhellan Revolution, a victory to be proud of."

"It wasn't out of pride that I had the tapestry hung in my rooms," Tal said, "but to be a reminder. My father thought it was pride at first, too. He demanded I take it down until I told him my real reason. I wanted that image of my father leading the charge against the Bhellan ranks where I would see it every morning, to remind me that one day I'll have to equal or even surpass his deeds."

"Why would that be?" Rania questioned. "To make a name for yourself, write it into song and history?"

"No," Tal said softly, shifting his weight uncomfortably.

"So why then," she pressed, "if not for fame and glory? The advancement of your House?"

"That's part of it," Tal admitted, "but only as a means, not an end. What would you say if I told you we've not yet faced the worst consequences of the Bhellan Revolution?"

"I suppose I'd have to wonder in that case why no armies have marched to fight in it for two decades," came the reply, delivered with a grin. Her eyes spoke of interest, though, sharp and attentive.

"The fighting stopped, true," Tal agreed, "but not before both of King Garant's sons had died in it. By then the Queen was past childbearing age, and so Garant has no obvious heir. Granted, most all the Noble Houses of Valeran have some Zherrane blood somewhere in their lineage, but none strongly enough to grant a clear claim to the throne. What many have in abundance, though, is ambition."

"You're talking about a war of succession," Rania guessed.

"That would only be the beginning of it," Tal predicted darkly. "When the King dies and leaves an empty throne, the Greater Houses will surely enough struggle with one another to claim it. In the resulting loss of order, any number of the Lesser Houses may try to carve themselves out a greater portion of the realm. Before long Bhellus and Amberyl would likely enter the struggle, either in alliance with a Greater House or simply seeking to annex as much land as they can. What remains of Valeran could crumble away, and the North would be reduced to what it was in the old days before Korven Zherrane or Anakara the Undying and her Skeletal Legions: a patchwork of territories claimed by petty warlords and tyrants, constantly at one another's throats, where no man, woman, or child could be assured of their safety from day to day."

Tal took a calming breath and stared Rania in the eye. "That's what sustained me through my training. The war I just described is little short of certain, Rania, and I'm going to have to fight in it, to lead Val Solus's forces in it. I don't know how much I'll be able to do, or if I'll be able to change anything about it at all, but I'm going to have to try keeping it from spiraling too far out of control before we lose everything."

Rania looked long and hard at him. Finally she murmured, "Your goals do honor to your master and to the lineage of Armslords and Shevestra'ken who came before him." She nodded. "And to yourself, to be sure. Though I apologize for making you talk about something that obviously troubles you."

Tal shrugged. "I could have refused to answer if I'd really wanted." They were silent for several long moments before he asked, "So will you finally answer any of my questions now that I've answered yours?"

"Soon. You've certainly earned some answers. But there's just one more thing I want of you first," Rania replied. "Fight me."

Tal blinked in surprise. "What?"

"I want to fight you," Rania said, getting to her feet and pulling him up after her, "I want to see how good you really are. Besides, you might learn a little bit about me from it."

"But neither of our blades are blunted," Tal protested.

"We've both practiced with sharpened blades before, I'm sure," Rania tossed back over her shoulder, completely undeterred, "I promise not to hurt you."

"That wasn't what I was concerned about," Tal muttered. Rania didn't notice, or pretended not to.

She led Tal to the bottom of the hill, took several strides away from him, then turned and drew her sword. It was a well-crafted weapon, with a broad, middling length blade well suited to swift slashing attacks and a narrow hand guard. In workmanship, it appeared at least the equal of Tal's own Sephirally-forged weapon. Rania stood with her right side advanced, holding the blade slanting up at an angle with its tip level with her eyes, which were fixed on Tal. "Well?"

Talaren sighed. Argument, it appeared, would be to no avail. He unsheathed his own blade and advanced carefully, leveling a halfhearted swing at Rania. She turned the attack aside with only a slight movement of her blade, standing otherwise completely still.

"Tal, when I watched you yesterday you would never have shamed yourself with such a pitiful attack. Do try, please. You wouldn't want me to think you're not taking me seriously, would you?" Her smile was encouraging, but her tone chiding. "I told you I'm not delicate."

"Alright," Tal agreed grudgingly, and pushed in toward her with a series of rapid slashes. Rania's blade flickered to meet the attacks, responding with a flurry of swift strikes of her own.

Tal parried furiously and danced back from Rania as recognition hit him, and with it realization. "I understand now," he said. "You know so much about the Armslords because you've studied under one yourself."

"I've had some instruction," Rania allowed as she closed with Tal. Blades flashed and rang against one another as they exchanged attacks, Talaren finally pushing Rania back a step.

"How long did you study?" Tal pressed his advantage, stepping forward to keep on the offensive.

"Seven years," Rania answered, startling Tal with a ferocious counteroffensive that pushed him back several steps, barely able to keep her blade away from him.

"You're extraordinarily accomplished for only seven years' training," Tal said, breaking away to circle cautiously around Rania, "I daresay you're better than I was after that much time." He threw himself back at her.

"I'm a quick study." Rania ducked under a high kick and came back up with blade swinging.

They clashed back and forth, struggling constantly for the upper hand. Tal was amazed at how evenly matched with him Rania appeared to be. Their attacks grew more and more elaborate, striking at each other with blades, hands, and feet, yet through all their exchanges neither managed to connect with the other.

After long minutes of fighting, Rania stepped back, nodding approvingly. "You *are* good, Tal," she said. "Extremely good. But there are still some things I think I could show you."

As she spoke, tendrils of misty blue light seemed to seep up from the ground, twisting and winding their way up Rania's legs as Tal's jaw dropped in disbelief. The light seemed to coalesce around Rania, suffusing her with a glowing azure aura. A fearful awe filled Tal unbidden as Rania surged toward him with blinding speed. She seemed suddenly no longer a creature of flesh and blood but an unstoppable force of nature, violence and strife made manifest. Battleborn.

Rania effortlessly swept Talaren's startled attack aside as she flowed forward with a preternatural grace, not a single movement wasted. Even as Tal recovered from his attack, she caught his swordarm by the wrist with her free hand and spun past his side, doubling the arm up painfully behind his back and forcing him to drop his blade. Before the weapon even hit the ground, Rania was sweeping his legs out from under him and Tal came to lie beside his weapon, looking up at the point of Rania's sword poised inches from his throat. As his gaze moved up past the blade to her face, what he beheld there was enough to freeze the breath in his lungs.

Rania's features were contorted into a mask of rage, her lips twisted up in a voiceless snarl. Blue fire flickered in her usually green eyes, the flames cold and hard and cruel. Death danced in those eyes. The tip of her blade began to quiver, as though she were fighting some terrible urge to plunge it through his neck and finish him. Then abruptly she withdrew the sword and sheathed it, the flames vanishing from her gaze even as the glow about her faded away.

"I... I'm sorry, Tal," Rania said, dropping her eyes in shame. "The battle rage nearly took over. I should've reined it in better. Please believe me, I didn't mean you any harm."

Tal sat up, half surprised to find his body still whole. He stared up at the young woman standing above him, still struggling in his mind to accept the impossibility he had just seen. "You're not just an Armslord," he said, his voice barely louder than a whisper, "you're one of the Shevestra'ken."

3
Possibility and Change

Regaining her composure, Rania held a hand out to Tal and helped him back to his feet. "Yes, I'm Shevestra'ka. Protégée to Muzash Finallin, who before me was the last of us."

"So he still lives, then." Muzash had been white-haired and venerable when last he had been seen, and that had been close to a century ago. Shevestra'ken were said to have unnaturally long lifespans if not slain in battle, but even for them such longevity was difficult to credit. The common wisdom had long been that with the disappearance of Muzash, the Shevestra'ken had finally completely vanished from the world.

Rania looked down, her lips tightening as she shook her head sadly. "No longer. He died three years ago, shortly after finishing my training and claiming me for Shevestra. I gave him to the flames myself, in the old way. It was his last request of me."

"I'm sorry," Tal said gently, "I didn't mean to bring up painful memories."

"It's alright," Rania replied, "I finished mourning a long time ago." The strain in her voice and the haunted look in her eyes said otherwise, but Tal decided it best to let the subject drop.

"You didn't reveal yourself to me on a whim," he said instead. "The conversations we've had tonight, bringing me out here to fight you where we'd not be observed - there was purpose behind this. What was it?" Tal suspected the answer, but years at Court had taught him never to give away everything he knew, or thought he knew.

Rania nodded. "Yes, of course there was. It'd take a fool not to see that at this point, and I know already that you're no fool." She fixed him with a deadly serious gaze. "I could complete the training your current Master began, Tal. I can grant you Shevestra's Embrace. I could make you Shevestra'ka, if you desire it."

Tal's heart seemed to skip a beat. It was the answer his own reasoning had brought him to, but suspecting it and actually hearing it were completely different things. Such an opportunity was the fantasy of nearly every young boy ever to play at swordsmanship and imagine himself a hero. But Tal was no longer a boy, and this was no idle daydream. Could he truly give himself into service to the Bloody-Handed Maiden? The rewards were great, to be sure, but it was whispered that so was the price, that in reaching beyond human limits Battleborn risked becoming something other than human.

Some of the legends told of the struggle Shevestra'ken fought internally to keep the violent energies they absorbed in check, and of a few of those who had lost that struggle. Tyrek Varr, who in his madness had laid waste to his own home city before taking his own life. Or Kieran Salamar, said to have blazed a trail of wanton destruction across three nations before finally being hunted down and slain by his own brethren to protect those still in his path. Such tales were one of the biggest reasons folk questioned to this day whether the Shevestra'ken had been a blessing or a curse. Tal had difficulty believing the scale of destruction that legend attributed to those men, but Rania had only moments ago shown him the truth at least of the difficulty presented in controlling the battle rage.

After a long moment of quiet consideration, Tal broke his silence. "I'm not sure I can accept," he said. "I've told you what lies ahead for me, and while becoming Shevestra'ka would no doubt help me fight the succession, it may hinder my goals in the long run. The Battleborn are even more feared than they are respected, and I'm not sure the commonfolk would be very eager to follow one. At the least I would need some time to think it over. This is so sudden, and not a decision I can make lightly."

"No, it's not," Rania agreed. "You don't have to rush to a decision. I can wait. Think it through and choose when you're certain."

Tal smiled hesitantly at her. "Thank you," he said.

Rania nodded gravely. "I'll find you in a few days to see if you've come to a decision. But for now I think I should seek my bed."

"Rania?" Tal asked as she began to walk back toward the city.

The Shevestra'ka turned back around and gave him a questioning look.

"While I'm deciding, can I see you again? I still hardly know you."

She seemed to ponder for a moment. "I think I'd like that," she said finally. "I have a room at the King's Bounty, in the Eastern district. You can find me there. Good night, Tal."

"Good night, Rania," Tal murmured as the darkness swallowed her.

Rania made her way leisurely through the streets of Val Zherrane. Folk were still about, drinking and carousing their way through the night. Rania held on to the Sephira only lightly, taking in just enough for it to bring her its gift of awareness. So small a trickle was far from enough to cloak her in the telltale aura; she didn't want to make a spectacle of herself. There was an unmistakable ebullience to the currents of the Sephira tonight, an intoxicating joy carried on its waves. It tended to do that, taking on the mood of the moment, and at a celebration like the Harvest Festival it soared and sang in tune with the spirits of the people around her.

Rania smiled to herself as she walked down the streets. She hadn't been in such a good humor in what seemed forever. On the whole, it had been a surprising, eventful, and pleasant day. The young Lord Solus had proven to be, aside from a skilled warrior, engaging, courteous, and quite handsome.

She very nearly had to laugh at herself for such a thought, so uncharacteristic for her. Of course, she'd had very little social contact for the past fifteen years, a fact of which she was painfully aware. Her only company had been Muzash, and he had been more like an adoptive Grandfather to her than anything else. With so little prior practice, she had been worried she might embarrass herself with her attempts at wit this evening, but Tal had seemed to enjoy them.

There was a sincerity about the King's Champion that had taken Rania entirely unawares. From someone as deeply embroiled in the Royal Court as he surely must be, she would have expected considerably more guile. Tal had instead seemed remarkably forthcoming with her. Part of her wished she had been able to return the favor in kind, but there were things about her past she wasn't ready to share with anyone yet, regardless of how ruggedly handsome a face that anyone might have or how tempted she might be to lose herself in the depths of his slate-blue eyes. It was for his own safety, she told herself; some of those things were dangerous, and that she'd nearly lost control of herself when she seized the Sephira at the end of their sparring duel was proof of just how dangerous. She'd been terrified when she felt it slipping from her grip, but thank Shevestra she'd managed to regain her hold on herself before doing anything she couldn't take back.

Arriving at the front of the King's Bounty, whose sign bore a faded picture of a stately man with hand held up in benediction, Rania pushed open the door and stepped into the common room. A great many patrons were still at the tables, merrily drinking or smoking pipes. A honey-haired woman danced atop one of the tables, skirts pulled up above her knees, as she sang a bawdy song about a self-important tax collector and his young wife's many infidelities. Several of the drinkers lustily bawled the words out along with her.

Rania picked her way around the edge of the room and mounted the stairs to the rooms above. Two floors up and at the end of the hallway, she let herself into the room she was renting. Singing voices drifted up faintly from below.

The singing brought to her mind the dancing earlier. That had been perhaps the most delicious part of the evening, a taste of a life she had never lived, but might have had things been different. Had Felmorinen never fallen, she might have danced with Lord Talaren Solus many a time before tonight.

"As well to wish night was day," Rania murmured. She looked at her reflection in the mirror atop the room's dresser and shook her head at herself. "Just look at you, Rania. Only a few days in the city and already you're pining after some pretty Lord." The circlet of roses Tal had presented her with still rested atop her brow. Gently she lifted it off, careful not to crush any of the flowers, and placed it on the dresser.

Rania's hand began to tremble as she set the wreath down. She sucked in a deep breath through her teeth, mentally bracing herself. These episodes had become all too familiar to her, occurring with disturbing frequency. Mind-numbing anguish rippled through her, seeming to tear its way from the depths of her soul to rampage through her uncontrolled. Her muscles tensed, her entire body shaking with the strain. Tears seeped from the corners of her eyes. Her vision seemed to blur, overlaid with images of blood and death, of men's faces distorted with their dying cries.

After a moment, the agonizing torrent subsided. Rania's trembling ceased. One side of the rose crown lay crushed in her hand. She bled from where several thorns had pierced her palm, an uncomfortable reminder. There was so much blood on her hands. Entirely too much blood. She had spilled rivers of it over the past couple years, absorbed the energies of countless deaths. With each foe slain her Sephiral abilities had grown stronger, but so had the sense of anguish and loss that she also absorbed with every life taken. It was part of the price Shevestra'ken paid for their powers, but Rania hadn't realized the spiral of madness she had been falling into until she was deeply caught in it. When the vision had come to her at the height of one of these Sephiral backlashes, she hadn't dared hope it was true rather than just another manifestation of her self-inflicted condition. And yet she had followed it, if only because she knew she needed time away from strife and bloodshed to try containing and controlling the forces within her before they tore her mind apart.

Now, it appeared there may have been some truth to the vision after all. Meeting Tal, a warrior already trained as an Armslord and disciplined enough to withstand the Maiden's Embrace, had been entirely too fortuitous for her to believe it mere coincidence. By giving a part of her strength to him, she would be able simultaneously to perpetuate the Shevestra'ken and rid herself of the excess energies that threatened her sanity. Assuming, of course, that Talaren chose to accept her offer, yet despite his own uncertainty Rania felt confident that he would, eventually. She couldn't have said where such assurance came from, but there it was anyway.

Rania grimaced at herself in the mirror as she plucked the thorns from her palm, casually wiping off the blood on the hem of her shirt before pulling it up and off. She studied her reflection again, wondering at some of the compliments Tal had given her. She wasn't accustomed to being around mirrors, wasn't used to looking at herself. More striking than any of the Ladies at Court, he had said. Surely he had to be exaggerating. Her face was pleasant enough, she supposed, with smooth skin and high cheekbones that some might find attractive, but certainly no more so than some of the carefully powdered and painted faces she had seen at the Feast. The same with her straight fiery hair - while it certainly didn't detract from her appearance, it simply hung to the tops of her shoulders in stark contrast to the elaborate styles most noblewomen wore theirs in. Of course, she didn't look as soft as any of them, either. The training and life of a Shevestra'ka had left her slender, with hard and well-toned muscles. Her arms and torso were crisscrossed with thin white scars, the legacy of how hard she had pushed herself in training. They seemed symbolic to her, scars left behind from a life lived too quickly, and the worst of them couldn't be seen in any mirror.

With a sigh, Rania stripped off her boots and breeches. Clad only in her smallclothes she climbed into bed, forsaking the covers. Winter's chill had yet to begin to settle in, and it was a warm night. She blew out the candle that lit her room, and closed her eyes.

Relax, she told herself, *it's going to be alright. The Maiden has brought you to someone who can help you. Things will get better from here.* Amazingly enough, she was almost even able to believe it.

Talaren sat wreathed in the night on the hillside where Rania had left him, staring at the sky. He watched the lazily shifting Sephiral Glow, pondering its serene and majestic beauty. He wondered what it must feel like to have that energy, the raw stuff of all potential life and existence, coursing through one's body. He wondered if he had the courage to find out.

A night of possibility and change, truly, he thought. Rania's offer had certainly opened a new realm of possibility to him, and one that would entail enormous change to his life. Tal found he had two paths before him, and no way to tell which was most right. Were he to accept Rania's offer, become an Adept of Shevestra, the abilities he'd gain command of would surely be of tremendous help in the struggle for the North that loomed in the future. But swearing the Shevestra'ken oaths would also mean renouncing his claim to the high seat of House Solus and with it his right to lead the armies of Val Solus, a role his father had spared no effort to prepare him for. Could he really turn his back on that? There seemed no way, short of knowing the future, to tell which path would better accomplish his goals. Somehow he would have to settle on one and hope he chose correctly.

If you do not find your own way, fate will find one for you. The saying, from one of the old books in the Duke's Library at Val Solus, seemed appropriate to Tal. The unwritten implication was that it was preferable to choose one's own way. And so he sat, lost in thought, trying to decide which way felt more like his own.

An hour passed, and then two. Dawn wasn't far off. Presently, a sound intruded itself on Tal's consciousness, at first a barely perceptible suggestion of sound that over time resolved itself into the rhythmic muted thump of hooves on turf.

Tal shook himself from his musings as soon as he recognized the sound. In the palely illuminated night, he had little difficulty spotting its source. To the southwest, a dark horse plodded toward the base of the hill Talaren sat upon, a cloaked rider hunched forward in the saddle. The rider didn't appear to have noticed Tal despite his sitting out in the open, but the horse's path would take him close past the watching nobleman.

Tal waited silently until the horse was perhaps twenty yards away, and then he stood and raised his voice. "Hello? Who's there?"

The horse stopped as Tal spoke and the rider stirred, cowled head rising to peer at him with frightened, glassy eyes. His face was pale, disheveled hair plastered to his brow with sweat. The tattered black clothing he wore had certainly seen better days. "Who are you?" he gasped between labored breaths, his voice pained and wary. "Have they sent you for me?" His gaze darted about skittishly.

"Easy, friend," Tal soothed, holding his hands out in front of him to show that they were empty. "I am Talaren Solus of Val Solus. You don't have to be afraid. You're safe here."

"No." The man shook his head insistently. "No place safe." He doubled over with a pained groan. "They come from the shadows," he whispered.

"You're hurt," Tal said as he ran forward to support the man before he fell from the saddle. "I'll take you to a healer."

"Chapterhouse," the man gasped, clutching at Tal's sleeve. His feverish gaze held Tal's. "Take me to the Order. Matter of prophecy."

The words struck Tal like a blow to the stomach. He glanced at the man's collars, and surely enough, embroidered on each one in white thread stood the sigil of an open book, crossed diagonally by a sword. Tal hadn't recognized the uniform at first, torn and rumpled as it was, but this man was a Guardian of the Jhessaillian Order.

A Guardian claiming to be acting under the auspices of the Jhessailian Prophecy was a serious matter indeed. Nations were known to rise and fall when such words were uttered. Cities could burn, ruling Houses toppled, almost anything could happen. The Order claimed for itself absolute authority where its agents said the Prophecy was involved, and to deny it such could easily lose a nation the support of the Jhessaillians, along with the prosperity brought by Jhessaillian-trained healers and craftsmen. Few kingdoms survived the Order's displeasure for long.

Tal had to wonder for a moment if helping this Guardian was really wise, but didn't see that he had much choice. His affiliation aside, this was a man in apparently desperate need, and Tal could not in good conscience deny him aid. He just hoped he wouldn't later have reason to regret it.

"Hold on," he said, "I'm coming up to hold you in the saddle. I'll take you to the Chapterhouse." He climbed gingerly up atop the horse's back behind the Guardian. With one hand he took the reins, while the other he wrapped gently around the other man to hold him upright. The Guardian's shirt was crusty with dried blood.

Tal kicked the horse forward, riding toward the city with as much speed as he dared, not wanting to jostle the injured man about too much. He could feel the Guardian still breathing, but he could also feel the unnatural warmth coming from the man's skin. Whatever had happened to him, his condition was dire.

The streets were mostly empty as Tal guided the horse through the city. Here and there were the occasional groups of people still celebrating the festival, and they looked on curiously as Talaren and the wounded Guardian rode past before returning to their own devices.

The Jhessaillian Chapterhouse was in the northern part of the city, not far removed from the Royal Palace, a small walled complex of buildings rarely frequented by any not of or studying under the Order. Tal brought the horse up beside the gate and climbed down from the saddle, gently lifting the Guardian down after him before walking up to the closed doors. Supporting the man's weight with one arm, Tal reached out and pulled a chain that dangled down beside the door. On the other side of the wall, a bell sounded.

A moment later, a small panel in the door slid open and a pair of eyes peered out. The eyes widened as they took in Talaren and his burden, and the panel snapped back shut. Tal heard a bolt being slid back on the other side, and the door opened.

"I found him outside the city. He asked me to bring him here," Tal explained to the black-clad Guardian who emerged.

The Guardian nodded as he took his injured comrade from Tal's arms. "Wait here," he said brusquely, "I'll be back."

After the man disappeared back into the Chapterhouse, closing the door behind him, Tal heard raised voices from the other side calling for a healer. The commotion died down quickly, and he waited for several minutes in the silence.

At length the door opened again, and the same Guardian emerged once more. He was just a shade shorter than Tal, with short dark hair and a penetrating gaze.

"You're Lord Solus, the King's Champion, are you not?"

"I am," Tal confirmed.

"You've done a great service for the Order today, Lord Solus," the Guardian said sincerely. "We will remember your help."

"Is he going to be alright?" Tal asked. This talk of service and remembrance was all well and good, but it failed to address the wellbeing of a seriously injured man.

"It's too early to say for sure," the Guardian replied, "but he's in the best hands possible now. We'll let you know if anything changes. Again, milord, thank you." He bowed, and retreated back behind the gate, leading the horse within and leaving Talaren none the wiser as to the nature of the events he had just been part of. He didn't know what else he could have expected, considering the Order's well-known penchant for secrecy.

Trying to put it from his mind, Tal turned with a yawn to walk back to the Royal Palace. He had rooms there, and sleep sounded a good idea right now. It had been a long, eventful, and quite tiring day.

4
Warnings of the Storm

Tal slept in late the next morning. Having been awake nearly to sunrise it was still hardly a full night's sleep, but he couldn't justify to himself sleeping past midday. He dressed unhurriedly, opting for a pair of loose fitting charcoal colored breeches and an unadorned burgundy tunic rather than his House colors. On his way out of the Royal Palace, Tal detoured briefly to stop by the kitchens and break his fast with a bowl of honeyed porridge. He then continued on, making his way leisurely through the city to the tourney field to oversee and assist with the taking down of his tent pavilion and to see that his things inside were taken back to his rooms in the Palace. With that task, his only real obligation for the day, finished and most of the afternoon yet ahead of him, he decided to go find Rania's inn and perhaps engage the mysterious Shevestra'ka in further conversation.

As Tal roamed the eastern district of Val Zherrane seeking the King's Bounty, his mind wandered with his feet. It was a toss-up as to whether his thoughts lingered more on Rania's offer or on his strange encounter with the wounded Jhessaillian. He was no closer to making a decision on the one, and for the other he knew his chances were between zero and nil of figuring out what the Order was about. Still, both topics were very much thought-provoking.

Far less obvious without his house colors on, fewer people on the street recognized Talaren but some still hailed him as he passed. As was his habit whenever able, he would stop to exchange a few friendly words with those who did, and in the course of doing so got pointed in the right direction to find the inn he sought. In short order he found himself gazing up at the faded monarch on the sign outside the tall, sturdily constructed wood and plaster building.

Stepping through the front door, Tal found himself in a warmly comfortable common room, with a well-swept timber floor and brightly polished tables scattered about. The fireplace set into the wall had several logs piled neatly in it, waiting for the chill of night before being lit. Another wall boasted a shelf containing a modest collection of books, their spines worn from much use.

Rania looked up from where she sat at one of the tables, reading a copy of *The Fall of the Undying*, a pot of tea resting on the table before her and a happily drowsing tabby cat curled up on her lap. She smiled warmly at him as she set the book aside. "Hello, Tal. You're looking rather preoccupied today. What's on your mind?" She gestured for him to take a seat at the table with her.

Tal pulled out the indicated chair and settled down opposite Rania. "My interesting day didn't end when you left last night."

Rania raised an eyebrow at him. "Would you care for some tea?"

"Yes, please."

The matronly innkeep, her steel-grey hair in a neat bun, brought an extra cup to the table at Rania's gesture. As the innkeep returned to her place behind the counter, Rania poured the tea. "So what happened after my departure? Were you perhaps assaulted by a horde of jealous noblewomen?"

Tal chuckled. "No, nothing like that." He recounted to her his encounter with the Guardian in a low voice so as not to be overheard by the innkeep or any of the few other patrons in the common room. He made the account as thorough as memory would permit him, from spotting the rider to the strange things the man had said and the brief, uninformative conversation he'd had with the other Jhessaillian at the Chapterhouse.

Rania listened with great interest, her eyes sharp on Tal. When his tale wound down, she spoke in an equally soft tone. "A matter of prophecy, eh? I doubt you'll find out what you stumbled across last night, then. As closed-mouthed as the Order usually is, they're doubly so when it comes to that subject."

Tal nodded in agreement. "I'd been thinking much the same thing." In addition to sitting atop the greatest collection of ancient knowledge recovered from the time before the Great Purge, when the Sephiral Arts had flourished beyond anything now imaginable, the Jhessaillian Order were also charged with the protection and implementation of the prophecy supposedly given by their founder, Jhessail. It predicted the rise of a savior, the Unifier, to lead mankind against the darkness that had destroyed the Ancients. Little was known about the details of the predictions outside of the Order, and they seemed to prefer it that way.

"I wonder what he meant by 'they come from the shadows?' Who is this they?" Rania frowned. "Could the Jhessaillians' prophesied enemy finally be arising?"

Tal shuddered at the thought. "I certainly hope not," he said fervently, "I don't think the world is ready to face something like that."

"But has it been getting more prepared, or less?" Rania asked, staring into his eyes. "Think about it, Tal. The Bhellan Revolution splintered the north, and you explained to me yesterday how further war and chaos are almost certainly coming again, and soon. It's hardly any better anywhere else. For as long as history can remember, the Shevestra'ken have been in decline. With Muzash gone, I'm the last. Even the Jhessaillians seem to be waning from what they once were. No matter where you look, everything seems to be falling apart. It feels like something is horribly wrong with the world, Tal. I don't know what it is, but it seems to me that we need saving while there's still something left to save." Her hand agitatedly stroked the sword hilt at her side.

Tal moodily swirled the tea around in his cup. He couldn't deny most of what Rania said; he too had often felt that things were not wholly right himself, that somewhere the world had gone horribly awry. What had become of the stories of great cities, nations, and civilizations rising from the ashes of the Great Purge and later from the Harrowing and Second Fall, carried forward by the deeds of fabled heroes? Now it seemed as though the most anyone could hope for was to slow the crumbling of what the past had wrought.

Tal shook his head to clear it of such thoughts. He couldn't accept the hopelessness and impotence they led to. "Maybe the world *has* gone astray, Rania, but that's no reason to give up on it or to think that we can't do anything. We're part of it, and we can't just wait and hope that some savior will come and fix everything. We owe it to ourselves, to everybody, to do everything we can to protect and preserve whatever or whoever we can. That's how ruin is warded off. To do otherwise would be to lose the fight before it's even started."

Rania chuckled at Tal, the hint of a smile showing at the corners of her lips. "Spoken like a true Adept," she murmured approvingly. Again he thought he saw something else in the green depths of her gaze, something he still couldn't quite identify.

"Not an Adept, Rania," he replied quietly, "just me."

"Whether or not you ever choose to accept what I've offered you, Tal, I think that in your heart, you're already one of us." Rania nodded. "It becomes you."

"Thank you," Tal said, "Let's just have no more talk of prophecy being fulfilled and darkness coming for us all. The Order are perfectly capable of worrying about that for us."

"That sounded close to an order, Tal," Rania teased, "Maybe you do have some of the inclinations of a nobleman after all." She pressed her right hand to her heart in imitation of a salute, grinning mockingly. "Yes, milord. Whatever milord says. Even if milord brought up bloodied Guardians babbling about the Jhessaillian Prophecy first."

Tal laughed in spite of himself. "You're impossible," he said between laughs. "I just brought it up as a curiosity. If whatever the Guardian was talking about is really *that* important, I'm sure even the Order would break their silence and inform the Royal Council." As secretive as they were, Tal couldn't imagine them failing to warn the nations about anything truly serious, if for no other reason than to rally support.

"Maybe," Rania said doubtfully, "I suppose time will tell."

Sometimes, Tal hated being right. After spending the rest of the afternoon in idle conversation with Rania, he returned to the Royal Palace shortly after dusk. As soon as he walked into the entry hall he noticed that there was a great deal more activity than he would have expected for the time of day. Servants hurried about, running on this errand or that under the directions of the aged Seneschal. Several knots of courtiers and lesser noblefolk stood about, chattering anxiously among themselves, their voices merging together into a low, worried buzz. Even the guards seemed unusually alert and on their toes, eyes darting to take in everything around them.

Gyles noticed Talaren as the young nobleman was approaching him, and spoke up before Tal had the opportunity to greet him. "Lord Solus, there you are! We've been trying to find you. I dispatched a small army of runners to look for you."

Tal's brow wrinkled with concern. "Why, Gyles? What's going on?"

"A Guardian." As the words left Gyles's mouth, Tal felt a chill pass through him, running down his spine and prickling his skin. "He arrived about an hour ago and demanded to speak to the Council tonight. Demanded!" The Seneschal's bushy eyebrows quivered in outrage at the breach of protocol. "He also asked to speak privately with you." Gyles noted the sickly expression on Tal's face and asked, "Do you know anything about this, milord?"

"Not a great deal, but maybe a little. I think I met him last night."

"Do you know what he's here about then, and in such an unseemly rush?"

"A 'matter of prophecy,' he told me last night," Tal said, carefully pitching his voice not to carry, "though little else he said made sense. He seemed quite delirious at the time. Where is he now?"

"In the sitting room adjacent to the Council Chambers."

Tal nodded. "I'd best go talk to him, then. Thank you, Gyles."

He set out on his own for the room Gyles had mentioned. With as much time as he had spent at the Royal Palace, Tal was nearly as familiar with it as he was with his own home in Solus Keep. Into the western wing of the Palace he went, noting on the way the air of anticipation that hung thick about everyone he passed in the halls. Word could spread quickly at Court, especially word of the unusual.

When Tal arrived, the Guardian was sprawled lazily in an overstuffed chair. Even without the solid black uniform with Jhessaillian insignias at the collars, Tal would have recognized him. The color had come back into his face and his mane of dark hair was now carefully brushed instead of sweat-slicked, but he was without a doubt the rider from the previous night. His eyes flickered up to Tal as the young nobleman let himself into the sitting room, and a rakish grin appeared on his face.

"It's hard to be certain, not being quite so feverish and half-dead as I was last night, but I believe we've met, yes?"

Tal nodded. "Yes, briefly."

"Then that would make you Lord Talaren Solus, the King's Champion, or so I've been told." The Guardian bowed with a flourish from his seat. "I am Guardian Kyril Damarrian of the Eye of Jhessail, and I appear to owe you a debt of gratitude for my continuing to draw breath."

"You're welcome," Tal said with a much plainer bow. "I'm just glad to see you survived. I wasn't sure you would, the shape you were in last night."

"Due largely to the talents of my fellow Brothers and your assistance in seeing me safely to them. I wanted to thank you for that personally. And I'm curious what I said to you last night, if anything. My recollection of our encounter is quite hazy, for obvious reasons."

"You asked me to take you to the Chapterhouse, that it was a matter of prophecy," Tal said. Kyril raised his eyebrows at that but said nothing, so Tal went on, "Then you said no place is safe and that they come from the shadows." He watched the Guardian carefully for a reaction.

"Did I?" Kyril chuckled. "Well, indeed they do."

"I don't suppose you're going to tell me who or what *they* are?"

"You'll be attending the Council meeting?" The Guardian asked.

"Yes," Tal replied, "though with my father there I'll have little to do besides observe and possibly advise."

"Plenty of time for you to hear the horrors along with the others, then," Kyril said airily.

"Oh, that's very reassuring," Tal grumbled.

The Jhessaillian smiled mirthlessly and in a dry voice responded, "That's funny, it wasn't meant to be."

Perhaps a different line of questioning was in order, Tal thought. "Can you tell me at least how you came to be so badly injured when you stumbled across me?"

"I don't see why not," Kyril answered after a moment's consideration. "I took a crossbow bolt to the shoulder, from behind. Though my Sephiral talents allowed me to evade my assailant, healing is unfortunately not my area of expertise. I'd been riding with my injury for nearly two weeks. What little Sephiral Healing I can perform was sufficient to knit it over with tender flesh, but the blasted thing kept breaking open again. I lost a lot of blood, and the wound had begun to putrefy." He shrugged. "I kept pressing on and against all odds, I made it here and ran into you."

"I assume this attack and what you've come to tell us are linked?"

"You assume correctly," Kyril admitted. "Someone wants what I know kept secret."

"It's revolting, the things people will do to keep a secret," Tal sighed.

"There is very little more dangerous than information in the wrong hands, Lord Solus," the Guardian said gravely. "We of the Eye, with our duties of observation and intelligence gathering, understand that danger especially well. In this case, we happen to be dealing with a particularly hazardous piece of knowledge."

Tal simply nodded his understanding of what the Guardian meant. Having moved among the political machinery of Court for several years now, he could appreciate the need to keep secrets sometimes. Still, killing a man for what he knew seemed like taking matters too far.

A light knock at the door preceded the entrance of Gyles. The seneschal bowed to Talaren and Kyril in turn before politely announcing, "Lord Solus, Guardian Damarrian, the Royal Council has assembled and awaits your pleasure."

The Guardian sprang to his feet and beckoned Tal to the door. "After you," he grinned. "You're about to have your curiosity satisfied."

The Council Hall was a sizable room, if not so large as its grand name implied. The wood paneled walls were polished to a dark sheen, and the room was dominated by an enormous table hewn from a single piece of wood. Padded leather chairs with little in the way of decoration lined the table and were currently occupied by the various members of the Council, no few of whom were accompanied by an assistant or heir.

The Councilmen were assembled and waiting at their respective seats when Tal and Kyril entered. King Garant sat at the head of the table in his robes and crown, with Talaren's father to the right and Archduke Zharkus Jerak to the left. Zharkus was accompanied by Joren, who glowered sullenly at Tal as he entered the hall. Also seated at the table were Duke Vernus Aldarrius in the black and green of his House, and Barons Arvin, Ghared, and Orman. Tazmin flashed his friend a quick grin from his seat beside Tal's Uncle, Baron Remarr Joseth, a jolly man with wild red hair and a bristling beard. There were also the two appointed positions, occupied by High Commander Uried who spoke for the Valerite military, and Count Hezig Lorran whom the King had appointed Minister of State and who oversaw Valeran's various domestic affairs. Hezig's appointment to the position had boosted the prestige of his House greatly.

Tal bowed respectfully to the Council before taking the empty seat next to his father, while Kyril stood at his ease at the end of the table opposite the King, awaiting permission to speak.

Garant scanned his eyes across the faces of the men assembled in the room and nodded to himself upon confirming that all were present. He cleared his throat before speaking. "Thank you all for coming here on such short notice. As you may already be aware, we have convened tonight at the request of our guest, Guardian Kyril Damarrian of the Jhessaillian Order. Guardian Damarrian has informed me that he has a matter of the greatest urgency to discuss with us. Guardian?"

"Thank you, Your Majesty," Kyril responded with a flourishing bow. "As a servant of the Eye of Jhessail, I was recently dispatched to the North to gather information relevant to an ongoing investigation we have been conducting. For what I discovered, a Jhessaillian Chapterhouse has been destroyed, several of my brothers slaughtered, and I myself barely escaped with my life. Which is fortunate for you all, for I have come here tonight to warn you of the return of an old darkness to the Northern kingdoms. Once more, we stand under threat from the legacy of Anakara the Undying."

Uneasy murmurs passed through the Councilmen. Most every man, woman, and child in the North remembered the Undying Empress. A mere five centuries wasn't nearly long enough to wipe away the memory of such terror and suffering. Anakara Amoran had been the Guardian who had rediscovered the location of ancient Felmorinen along with a host of dark secrets within, Sephiral knowledge from the time of the Second Fall that enabled one to twist, corrupt, and enslave the energies of the dead. Rather than destroy or re-secure the forbidden lore, Anakara had betrayed the Order and made use of it to raise an army of walking corpses. Led by the spectre of her dead protector and lover Trazeri Ni'Dharranoth, slain by Anakara's own hand, the skeletal legions had swept across the North conquering all in their path until the entire region lay under Anakara's dominion.

Glancing about the table Tal observed that the Councilmen's expressions were predominantly a mixture of shock and incredulity, with a healthy measure of fear atop it all. Among the mutterings Tal picked out the frequent utterance of the word "impossible."

King Garant seemed to catch the repeated usage of the word, as well. He gestured for silence. "Before we judge the plausibility of Guardian Damarrian's claim, perhaps we should hear his evidence." The King looked back at the Guardian "Proceed."

Unruffled, Kyril bowed his head acquiescingly and went on in an unhurried, businesslike voice. "You are all probably aware that following Anakara's death at the hands of the Godtouched Warrior Korven Zherrane, the secrets of Felmorinen were entrusted to the descendants of her family, that by such service they might atone for the deeds of their ancestor. House Amoran served this charge and the throne admirably until fifteen years ago, when Felmorinen was attacked and fell to unknown forces. There were few survivors of that night, and those who escaped brought back tales of retribution by the ghosts of Felmorinen's troubled past. This Council commissioned an investigation of those events."

"That investigation discovered no bodies left behind by the attackers, no clues as to who might have perpetrated the heinous attack. The body of Marquess Emereen Amoran was found in the vault containing Anakara's writings with large quantities of ash scattered about the room. The investigation concluded that knowing the fortress was about to fall, the Marquess destroyed the writings rather than fail in her family's guardianship. The tales told by the survivors were tentatively accepted as credible based on a lack of evidence to the contrary."

"In light of our ties to Valeran's founding, House Amoran, and the knowledge they kept secure, we in the Order undertook our own investigation. It has been a time-consuming and difficult affair, but we now have our findings, and it would appear just in time."

"And what did your investigation uncover that ours missed, Jhessaillian?" Archduke Zharkus asked with a raised eyebrow.

"A great deal," replied Kyril. "Although it's true that large-scale and extreme incidents of bloodshed and trauma can alter the Sephira in an area and produce violent ghost-like manifestations on occasion, we determined that the survivors' accounts were inconsistent with such an incident. This was, in fact, a very well planned and orchestrated military strike complete with enough trappings of the supernatural to distract attention from the identities of the attackers. It has been the task of discovering those identities that has taken us so long as we had no clear trail of evidence to follow, but we now know that the beneficiary of the attacks was then Prince, now King Kherzul Meravos of Bhellus."

The Guardian's announcement was met by troubled silence. Frowning, Duke Vernus was the first to speak. "This is a serious accusation to make of a sovereign King, even if he *is* the son of a rebel."

Haorn Orman nodded in agreement, his long moustaches swaying with the movement. "King Kherzul has never shown any ill intent towards Valeran. In fact, tensions between our nations have eased greatly since he took the throne of Bhellus. He has consistently reduced the military presence on our border and trade has begun to flow between us again."

"Still, let us not forget that the 'hunting accident' that killed King Shebedar was almost certainly arranged by Kherzul," interjected Talaren's father. "The motives of a man who comes to power in such a fashion must always be in doubt."

"I agree," murmured the King. "Guardian Damarrian, what proof do you have of these claims?"

"The proof of my own eyes, Majesty," replied Kyril. "I have seen some of the minions Kherzul has created. But I get ahead of myself. You see, we suspected for several years that the attack on Felmorinen originated from somewhere in Bhellus. Proving those suspicions was complicated greatly by King Shebedar's untimely demise and the fact that all the soldiers who seemed likely candidates to have taken part in such an operation had the unfortunate habit of dying or disappearing unexpectedly. This suggested that we were on the right trail, but we still had no proof. It was determined that more invasive measures would be necessary, so the Eye dispatched one of our best operatives to take over the investigation. With all due modesty, I am the one who was sent. I chose to focus on Kherzul because the deaths among the soldiers continued even after Shebedar was removed from the picture and, as Duke Daron pointed out, the circumstances by which Kherzul assumed the throne were questionable. I spent a great deal of time and effort securing an agent inside the palace at Bhel Meravos and once I had, long months passed by while I waited for my man to find anything of interest. Five weeks ago I received a communication from him that he had caught word of a meeting between King Kherzul and his top Generals, and that he was going to try to listen in. He gave me a time and place to meet him afterwards so that he could give me a full report of what transpired."

The Guardian's face hardened. "He never came, though I waited until well past the appointed hour. I can only assume that he was found out and a confession wrung from him, for when I returned to the Jhessaillian Chapterhouse that night it was already in flames. My brothers who were assigned there had been slain to the man, Guardians and Godtouched alike. It was there, in the fire-lit street, that I first saw them: dark, mist-like creatures with burning coals for eyes, as though a black fog had been poured into a human shell. Creatures very like what the histories tell us of Trazeri the Accursed. They wore armor with the marks of rank of the same Generals whom Kherzul had met with earlier that day. I fled on the spot after having counted at least six of the creatures, knowing I had to get word out of Bhellus, but I was seen and pursued. Two of the spectres hounded me all the way to the Felmorr Gap, flickering in and out of the shadows so I never knew if I was safe or not. After I crossed into Valeran I didn't see them for a long while and believed I had eluded them. I was tired from the chase and relaxed my guard, much to my regret. Three nights out of Val Jerak I was ambushed by the same creatures and took a bolt from a crossbow before I realized I was under attack. Luckily I was able to craft a Sephiral Illusion to fool the spectres into believing that they'd slain me and made good my escape. I treated my injury to the extent I was able and made straight for Val Zherrane, where I encountered Lord Solus last night on the outskirts of the city. He saw me to the Chapterhouse here, my brothers treated my wounds, and now I have relayed my information." Kyril fell silent, awaiting the response of the Council.

King Garant sat back in his chair, thinking deeply. He looked about the table at the men gathered there. "These are dire tidings indeed. What does my council think?"

"It seems a safe assumption that the creation of creatures like the Accursed is a prelude to hostilities," Baron Remarr rumbled. "We should muster our armies for war."

"Is not a situation like this more the domain of the Order and their Godtouched?" Asked Archduke Zharkus with a pointed look at Kyril.

"Typically yes," the Guardian admitted, "but this situation is far from typical. We have the same problem here that we had with the Undying centuries ago in that Kherzul has an army to defend him. Godtouched are protected from those who wield the Sephira and able to strike down spectres, but they are relatively few and faced with an army they are little more than well-trained warriors."

"And yet Korven Zherrane was able to single-handedly bring down Empress Anakara three hundred years ago," observed Baron Orman with a sly smile.

Hezig, the Minister of State, frowned. "True, but Korven himself credited his victory to Trazeri the Accursed forsaking his mistress at the last. That's why their crossed blades hang in the throne room, why those blades are the symbol of our nation."

"Yes, yes," said Duke Vernus impatiently, "we all know our history, but we need to focus on the present situation, gentlemen."

"It occurs to me that the evidence we've heard is all circumstantial," noted Baron Arvin. "While it appears clear that someone in Bhellus wields Anakara's old powers, we still have no conclusive proof that that someone is the King."

That provoked several grumbles around the table, but Tal noticed a few of the Councilmen nodding thoughtfully.

"Regardless of whether or not the culprit is indeed King Kherzul," said Daron, "we will certainly have to respond somehow. Diplomacy probably isn't an option at this point, which leaves the military. The question, then, would appear to be whether we should adopt a defensive stance or take the fight to the Bhellans." He didn't look at all pleased with his own words, but then he had always told Tal that it was the job of a Duke to always face the truth even if that truth was unpleasant.

The Jhessaillian spoke up right after Daron. "The Order is inclined to agree with Duke Solus's analysis. I would point out that it may be in your best interests to attack Kherzul at the soonest opportunity. The more time he has, the larger his force of reanimated dead will grow. Permit him too much time and he will surely drown you in a sea of corpses."

The King turned his sharp gaze to the High Commander of his troops. "Uried, what say you to that? Would such a strike be possible?"

The hard planes of the military man's face were stony as he considered. At length he spoke in a voice more accustomed to barking orders than discussing political policy. "This late in the year, we could still probably manage to muster a respectable force for such an attack, but I doubt anything we could reasonably put together on such short notice would be large enough to penetrate all the way to Bhel Meravos. And with winter coming, the Felmorr Gap will become impassable which would leave any forces we commit without the possibility of reinforcement. That would very probably be a fatal mistake for us. I would say that until spring the only offensive action we may safely consider would amount to little more than a raid in force."

Baron Ghared shook his head emphatically. "Unacceptable. So small an offense would likely gain us little strategic benefit, and may even hurt us. If Guardian Damarrian's attackers truly believe him slain, then they have no reason to suspect we know about any of this. A rash attack would only serve to show our hand prematurely."

King Garant sighed deeply. "Although I'm uncomfortable with allowing Kherzul the entire winter to grow stronger, I must agree. We'll likely need every advantage possible and right now the only one we have is that our enemy doesn't know us to be forewarned. It appears that we must adopt a defensive posture for the time being. Does my council agree?"

Murmurs of assent echoed around the table.

"Very well. I want you all to take advantage of the winter to build up your forces as much as possible and see that they are ready for the spring. See to it that the Houses under you do likewise, but for the time being let's keep the reason to ourselves. We don't want to cause a panic." Garant's eyes were like pale blue steel as he turned to the Archduke of Val Jerak. "Zharkus, I want you to return home as soon as possible and tend to your city's defenses. Should the Bhellans attack, Val Jerak will undoubtedly be the first city hit. We can't let them find us unprepared."

Zharkus bowed his head respectfully. "It shall be as you command, Majesty. My retinue and I can depart in two day's time. My son will ride on the morrow to go ahead of us and begin the arrangements." Beside him, Joren nodded once in acknowledgement of his father's implied command.

"Just be discrete. Too obvious a military buildup will give us away as surely as mounting an attack will." King Garant surveyed the table one more time. "Is there anything else?"

"Just one thing, Majesty," Kyril said, "something to bolster your hopes. I've already sent word to Cardon requesting the assistance of Order forces for Valeran. Assuming my request is approved, and I can see no reason why it wouldn't be, we will dispatch as many Guardians and Godtouched as we can spare to join in the struggle. You won't have to face this threat alone."

With a nod the King replied, "Thank you, Guardian Damarrian. The support of the Jhessaillian Order will no doubt prove invaluable in the coming struggle." He paused for a moment to allow anyone else to speak up with any other business. When none raised their voice Garant announced, "The Council is dismissed."

5
Crisis Upon Crisis

Tal felt like his head was spinning when he returned to his rooms after the surprise Council session. So much had happened so quickly over the past couple days, it felt as if nothing he had taken for granted in his life held true anymore. War was coming just as he had told Rania, but instead of the struggle over secession the noble Houses had seen coming for so long, it was to be a war against the resurgence of the greatest evil the North had known since Maeroth the Ruiner had burned away half the world in the Harrowing and brought about the Second Fall. Nightmares of the past were reawakening, and it appeared Tal would sooner or later have to face them. Everything had been thrown into turmoil from the moment he'd encountered the injured Guardian Kyril Damarrian. No, he reconsidered, it had all actually begun when he felt Rania's eyes on him. Battleborn, after all, were said to be harbingers of strife. Upon thinking of her, Tal found that he wanted very badly to go and discuss what he'd learned with the alluring Shevestra'ka, but all he'd heard in the Council was privileged information and sharing it with her would be a severe abuse of his position. So instead he paced restlessly in his apartments, wondering what the future would bring.

Tal had stopped Kyril in the hall following the Council meeting to ask the Guardian a few questions of his own. "You didn't mention anything about the Jhessaillian Prophecy," he'd observed, "yet last night you told me what you were doing was a matter of prophecy. How is this all involved?"

The Guardian had given him a disingenuous smile. "To be honest, I'm really not entirely sure," Kyril had replied. "But when Felmorinen is involved, you can usually assume that the prophecy is as well. The lines of fate tend to converge on that place. Little happens there that wasn't meant to, one way or the other."

"What do you mean, you're not sure?" Tal had asked incredulously. "Isn't the Order supposed to know these things?"

Kyril had chuckled. "Even we don't have all the answers, Lord Solus. Prophecy is more often a series of questions than anything else. We can make educated guesses, yet often we don't truly understand the significance of prophesied events until well after the fact, if at all. I'm sure that once my report arrives in Cardon, there will be entire teams of scholars within the Word of Jhessail analyzing it for significance. Maybe they'll find some answers in it, or maybe not. We'll just have to wait and see, and make do the best we can in the meantime."

On the whole, the brief conversation had done little to reassure Tal and much to unsettle him.

Perhaps an hour, certainly no more, after Tal returned to his apartments there was a surreptitious knock at his door. Not expecting anyone at this late hour, he looked quizzically at the door as he said, "Come in."

The door opened and the Seneschal bowed his way into the room. "Good evening, Talaren."

"Gyles," Tal replied with a friendly smile, "what can I do for you?"

"His Majesty asked that I fetch you," Gyles said. "He desires to speak with you in his private quarters."

That piqued Tal's interest. What could the King want with him? "Well then, I'd best not keep him waiting."

The Seneschal led Tal up several floors to the Royal suites. Once this floor had accommodated the King's entire family, but now its only inhabitant was Garant himself, the last living member of House Zherrane. That knowledge lent the quiet hallway a melancholy air, as if the spirits of Valeran's past Kings wept for the closing days of their dynasty. One door, leading to Garant's private apartments, was flanked by a pair of guards who bowed wordlessly to the Seneschal and the young Lord as they approached. Gyles knocked softly on the door.

"Enter," the King's voice said from beyond.

Gyles opened the door and ushered Tal in.

The room beyond was large and sumptuous, the floors covered with rugs bearing interlocking geometric patterns. The furniture was all made of dark, highly polished wood, intricately carved and chased with gold. A rich tapestry hung on one wall, depicting Val Zherrane as seen from a distance, covered in a pristine white mantle of snow. Surrounded by all this finery, the King himself stood in stark contrast, having removed his crown and ornate robes of state. Instead he sat comfortably in simple earth-tone tunic and breeches that wouldn't look out of place on a farmer.

"Ah, Talaren. Excellent." King Garant turned his eyes to his faithful old retainer. "Thank you for fetching Lord Solus for me, Gyles. I shouldn't have need of you for the rest of the night. Why don't you get some sleep, old friend?"

"Thank you, Your Majesty. I shall." Gyles bowed and let himself out.

The King gazed at the door and shook his head sadly. "Over fifty years Gyles has served me and my House, and still he only rarely calls me by my proper name." He looked back at Tal and his face creased in a smile. "I won't have any of that from you, Talaren. You're the heir to one of my most loyal noble Houses, the son of my dear friend Daron, and now my Champion besides. In private, I want you to call me Garant. No titles. That's an order from your King."

"Yes, Your... Garant." Tal smiled at his near-slip.

Garant waved a mockingly chiding finger at Tal before motioning to a nearby chair. "Please, sit down. I can see that you're curious. Probably wondering why I sent for you?"

Tal settled down in the offered seat. "Actually, yes, I was."

The King nodded. "Guardian Damarrian has done us a great service in bringing us his news, but I fear that it may yet prove of little benefit if we don't act on it swiftly and decisively. Knowing what Kherzul is about gives us a chance, but if his attack should come before we've been able to adequately prepare, it will only mean that we'll have seen our doom coming before it claimed us. To help prevent that fate, I have a task I need you to do for me, Talaren. I'll not lie to you, it's very likely to be dangerous. It's unfortunate that I have to put those I trust in harm's way, but that's one of the sad truths of my position."

"I understand, Garant," Tal replied. "That's what I've trained for. What would you have me do?"

"The Felmorr Gap needs to be reinforced as quickly as possible. House Jerak will doubtlessly be recruiting more soldiers, but in the meantime I'm dispatching a thousand of my own guardsmen to Val Jerak to bolster their garrison." Garant's blue eyes glittered as he regarded Tal soberly. "I want you to command them. Your father has volunteered the three hundred men he brought from Val Solus as well."

Tal felt his pulse quicken. His first command! "I'd be honored to do this for you, Garant," he said wholeheartedly, nearly forgetting in his excitement to address the King casually. "Although I'm curious why you want *me* to go. Wouldn't someone more experienced be a better choice, under the circumstances?"

Garant shook his snowy-haired head. "Let me teach you a lesson about ruling, Talaren. One of the most important things one who wears a crown must do is learn to assess and balance the strengths and shortcomings of the people under him. Zharkus Jerak, for example, excels at negotiations and deal-making. His talent has served House Jerak and Valeran well by bringing in handsome trade revenues. What the Archduke lacks, though, is a head for military matters. He still feels quite keenly the shame he brought on his House at the outset of the Bhellan Revolution when he settled in for a siege on his city only to have the bulk of Shebedar's forces ride right past him, and it has made him pricklier about his pride than ever he was before. Were I to send someone like your father to oversee the defenses of Val Jerak and the Felmorr Gap, it would be a blow to that pride and I'd risk alienating one of my most powerful Noble Houses. By sending you, I sidestep that. Your father assures me that you've an excellent grasp of tactics and strategy, and coming from the Hero of the Gilden Hills, I don't doubt it. But because you're still unestablished as a commander, I can send you to advise Zharkus without ruffling his feathers overmuch."

"Except in that I'm still my father's son," Tal observed, "and I'm sure Archduke Zharkus will see the political benefits House Solus could stand to gain through my participating in the defense of his city."

"There is that, true," Garant conceded. "But balanced against the possibility of losing his House's holdings to a Bhellan invasion, the likelihood of a rival House gaining a bit more prestige by helping him hold Val Jerak against that invasion will no doubt seem a small concern to him."

Between words, Tal thought he heard a muffled thump from the hallway. As he turned to look curiously toward the door, he could have sworn he heard another.

Garant must have heard it, too. His eyes also went to the door, and he wondered aloud, "What's going on out there?"

Tal stood, intending to investigate. He was only halfway across the room to the door, though, when it swung open without so much as a knock. Four guards in the black and red stood in the hall, weapons bared, and two of them gripped bloodied daggers. They stepped through the door as soon as they opened it, but stopped short for just an instant as they laid eyes on the young nobleman right in front of them. Apparently, Tal's presence came as a surprise to them.

Tal didn't hesitate to question. His instincts screamed at him and he reacted, closing the distance between himself and the men with a few quick shuffling steps. The frontmost of them raised his blade as the King's Champion neared him. Tal kicked high, his foot striking out like a bolt of lightning to connect with the man's wrist with a sharp snap of shattering bone. Tal's own sword flew from its sheath, slashing through the man's throat in a spray of blood. The second man swung his sword at Tal as his two remaining companions broke to either side in an attempt to get around the nobleman. Around him, and to the King. Tal sidestepped the blow aimed at him and kicked low and to the side, tripping up one of the men circling him. He brought his sword down hard on top of the falling man and then reversed his strike, angling up towards his attacker. He caught the man low in the abdomen, carrying the blow through to cleave him nearly to the opposite shoulder. He let go of his sword rather than take the time to free it, and spun about. The last man was nearly to Garant, a cry on his lips and dagger raised high. Tal leapt across the room, careening into the assassin's back. The man's downward stab at the King, ruined by Tal's interference, went well wide of its target. Tal wrapped an arm about the attacker's neck and wrenched him back, throwing him to the ground with a savage twisting motion. With a sickening wet crack, the man went limp.

A space of mere seconds had passed, and Tal had slain four men. For all his acclaimed skill at arms, the long years of training he had endured, the tournaments he had participated in, he had never before taken a life. Now he breathed hard, not from exertion, but from the shock of what he had just done. His hands and face were spattered with blood and more seeped into his clothing, warm sticky patches that made his skin crawl. His head swam, and for a moment he was certain he was about to empty his stomach at what he'd just done. Struggling for calm, he forced himself to take slow steady breaths.

"Are you alright, Garant?" Tal asked once he had himself in hand.

"Yes. I'm fine," replied the King, gazing with wide eyes at the corpse lying at his feet.

Tal nodded and went to the door, darting his head into the hall to search for any more attackers. The hall was empty save for the bodies of the men who had been guarding the room, which lay in pools of their own blood with throats cut. Tal stepped into the hall and bellowed for more guards. Then he stepped back into Garant's apartments and retrieved his sword from the ruined corpse it still lay embedded in. He wasn't sure how well he would have been heard, but he wasn't about to leave the King alone to go fetch the guards personally. There could be more assassins still lurking in the Palace.

Within moments the Royal apartments were swarming with Palace Guards. Still Tal loitered until High Commander Uried arrived. He and the King recounted the assassination attempt to the stony-faced Commander, who immediately began issuing orders to tighten security around the Palace, and especially around Valeran's monarch.

As Uried gave his orders, Garant pulled Tal aside to speak quietly to him. "Talaren, I want to thank you for the service you've done here tonight. Had it not been for you, I've little doubt those men would have succeeded. But you should return to your quarters now. Uried has got matters well in hand, and I think you'll need your rest tonight. Tomorrow will doubtless be a busy day. I'll have you informed in the morning if anything is discovered about who these miscreants were or who sent them." Guards were just beginning to move the bodies, hauling them off to be examined for any hints they might carry.

Tal bowed his head acquiescingly. "Very well, Majesty. I'll see you in the morning."

As he walked back alone to his rooms, Tal's thoughts were bleak. Yes, events were definitely moving quickly, and they seemed only to be accelerating. He hoped he would be able to keep up with them.

6
Secrets of the Past

Tal was awakened early the next morning by a loud, insistent pounding at his door. Grumbling quietly to himself, he threw off his blankets and roused himself from bed. He donned a dark dressing robe that he plucked from a hook on the wall and blearily stumbled to the front sitting room, still wiping the sleep from his eyes. As soon as he had the lock on the door unbarred, it swung open and Guardian Damarrian breezed into the room.

"Sorry to wake you," the black-uniformed man said briskly, "but we've got trouble."

Tal blinked at him. "You mean the men I had to kill last night?"

The Jhessaillian was pacing agitatedly. He shook his head. "No, no. Or at least only partially. Maybe." He stopped and turned back to Tal. "The entire Palace is abuzz about your display of heroics last night, by the way. But I think that the assassins may have been only a diversion. It's too bad you got so enthusiastic and killed them all. It'd be helpful to be able to question one of them right now."

Tal walked up to Kyril, took him firmly by the shoulders, and sat him down in one of the chairs before flopping unceremoniously in the opposite seat. "Guardian. Please. It's early in the morning, I'm still half asleep, and you're not making any sense. Let's start this conversation again, from a point where I've the foggiest idea what you're going on about."

The Guardian took a deep breath and let it out with a huff. "A short while ago some of King Garant's household staff began their morning chores of cleaning the throne room and preparing it for the King to accept petitioners. They found that the room had been broken into during the night, and something stolen."

Tal sat up in his chair, suddenly attentive. "What? What was stolen?"

"One of the Swords of Valeran. The one that belonged to the Accursed." When Korven Zherrane had founded Valeran, he had adopted two crossed swords for the nation's coat of arms, one for his blade and one for Trazeri's as a symbol of the final sacrifice the Accursed had made in allowing himself to be slain that Anakara might be overthrown. The actual swords themselves had stood crossed on the wall behind the throne since the Palace was built.

Tal considered for a moment, but his sleep-clouded mind couldn't grasp the significance of such a theft. "Why? What would anyone want with that antique weapon?"

The Jhessaillian spy sighed deeply. "I don't know, and that's what troubles me. I don't like things that I don't know. I don't like them a very great deal." He grimaced, "But I can hazard a guess as to who's responsible for this theft."

"Kherzul." Tal suddenly remembered what Kyril had said when he entered the room. "What was that you said about a diversion?"

"Oldest trick there is, Lord Solus. Do something spectacular in one place, like sending assassins through the King's front door, so that while everyone is focused on that, you can accomplish something else unnoticed. At least you kept the attempt on Garant's life from succeeding. Had that happened, the entire city would be in chaos and we'd have no hope of getting anything accomplished. As it is, we have a chance to act on events in something like a timely fashion."

Tal's eyes narrowed as wakefulness crept up on him and he grasped the oddity of this conversation. "What does this have to do with me, Guardian, and why is it you who's come to tell me?"

"I came to the Palace this morning to consult with His Majesty in coordinating your military and the assistance the Order will provide," Kyril explained, "and I arrived shortly after the theft was discovered. I attempted to speak with the King about it, but he asked me to fetch you before we began any discussion. Exactly what he wants of you or how you fit into this, I couldn't say."

"All right, then." Tal looked ruefully back to the bedchamber. "I suppose a bit more sleep is out of the question."

"I suppose you *could* sleep a little longer," the Guardian replied with a grin, "but most men are usually anxious to comply when summoned by their King."

"Point taken." Tal frowned irritably. "Does that wit of yours ever get you into trouble, Guardian Damarrian?"

"Oh, all the time," replied the Jhessiallian blithely. "That's half the fun of it."

Tal dressed quickly in simple, sturdy clothes of black and gray and then left his apartments, meeting Kyril outside his apartments. Side by side the Guardian and the King's Champion marched down to a private dining room adjacent to the kitchens to meet with King Garant over breakfast.

When they arrived the Monarch was already at the table with a plate before him heaped with eggs and a hefty slab of ham. Tal was sure he detected the smell of honeycakes wafting up from a covered basket at the center of the short table. No sooner had Tal and Kyril seated themselves than servants laid before them their own heavily laden plates.

Garant didn't waste any time on formalities. "I assume Guardian Damarrian has informed you of this morning's news, Talaren?"

"He has, Majesty," Tal replied. "Has anything further been discovered about the attempt on your life last night?"

The King snorted in disgust. "Nothing of any real use. They bore no House insignia to link them to anyone, nor does anybody recognize them, at least not that'll admit it. All four appear to be Northmen, but that hardly narrows things at all."

"Considering the apparent coordination between the assassination attempt and the theft of Trazeri's sword," Kyril said, "I would be inclined to think the two incidents linked. In light of his interest in relics of the Undying's era, that would seem to point to King Kherzul."

"I agree, but that leaves the bothersome question of why he would want to steal the sword." Garant looked from Tal to the Guardian, waiting to see if either of them had any insights.

Tal's brow furrowed in thought. "Trazeri's sword is a powerful symbol, one whose history is intimately tied to the founding of Valeran. Perhaps he wished to strike at our morale by taking that symbol from us."

Garant considered for a moment, then shook his head. "No, I don't think that feels quite right. This theft is more likely to provoke outrage than demoralization. Even if that weren't the case, the risk would still outweigh the gain. No, I think he must have had some more compelling reason to risk exposing his intent."

"I might be able to provide an answer to that question," Kyril volunteered reluctantly.

Tal looked askance at the Guardian. "I thought you said you didn't know why the sword was taken either?"

"I don't, but I may know a way to find out." The Guardian frowned in distaste. "It involves a Sephiral manifestation that we in the Order utilize hesitantly, and only at great need. It seems we have no other option, though. We need answers, and we may not have the time to get them through more conventional channels." He looked soberly at Garant. "Your Majesty, I will need your permission to be allowed into the Royal Tombs beneath the Palace as discreetly as possible."

Garant arched an eyebrow. "I can arrange that, but what do you want in the tombs?"

Kyril took on a lecturing tone. "When Korven Zherrane founded Valeran, he honored the sacrifice of Trazeri the Accursed in two ways. One was making the fallen knight's sword part of the coat of arms for the new nation. The other was having Trazeri's armor, the only physical thing remaining of him, interred in the Royal Tombs beside his beloved, Anakara.

As we need information regarding Trazeri's sword, I intend to ask its former owner."

Tal gasped. "You're going to raise the Accursed?" He asked incredulously.

The Guardian grimaced. "Not raise, exactly. Conjure his shade, yes, but his presence will only last a short while."

"If you can speak to the dead, wouldn't it be better to ask those assassins I killed last night? You said you wanted to question them."

Kyril shook his head. "Trazeri is more likely to know what we need. Besides which, I have no way to compel an answer from a shade. The assassins probably would refuse to answer or worse, attempt to mislead us. Korven believed Trazeri saw the light before the end, and he could have no possible stake in our current situation. I'll trust an answer from him far better than I could one from Kherzul's lackeys."

Garant looked troubled. "I don't like this, Guardian Damarrian, but I believe that you're correct in that it's our only chance at a prompt answer to this troubling riddle. I'll instruct Gyles to let you into the tombs. We can trust his discretion."

"I'm coming, too," Tal decided aloud.

"I won't say you aren't welcome, Talaren," Kyril replied, "but are you sure?"

"Absolutely. It's not everyday one gets a chance to meet a three-hundred-year-dead historical figure. And I want to hear what he has to say for myself."

Garant had sent for Gyles and given his instructions to the Seneschal, who led Tal and Kyril deep below the cellars of the Palace to the tombs carved into the stone beneath. The two lit a pair of torches and left Gyles at the cavernous entryway. Walking through the echoing darkness, Tal decided to attempt diverting his mind from the morbid thoughts being in a tomb naturally provoked.

"Guardian, why do you need to come down here to do this? Couldn't you have just conjured Trazeri up in the dining room?"

"No, Lord Solus. The reasons are a bit complicated with this sort of situation. You see, the essential force of life, what you might call the spirit or the soul, is a thing of the Sephira. When we die, that energy returns to the greater Sephiral that pervades the world, but an echo remains with the body or sometimes certain objects closely associated with the individual. What I'm going to do is use that echo to reconstruct Trazeri's essence for a short while. It's vaguely similar to what Kherzul is practicing, which is why the Order prefers to avoid it in most cases. Besides which, common wisdom has it that it's best to let the dead rest." They were nearing the far end of the long hall of tombs, and Kyril glanced at the two doors in opposite walls of the passage. "I think it's this one," he said, choosing the leftmost door.

The hinges on the door screeched in protest at being opened once again after so long. Torchlight brightened walls that had known only darkness for three centuries. The chamber within was a small square room with two large raised blocks of stone. The top of one was intricately carved into the likeness of a woman in restful repose. So cunningly crafted was the stone that Tal couldn't locate the seam where the lid met the base. The other was flat and unadorned, but atop it lay an ornate suit of heavy plate and mail armor arranged similarly to the representation of Anakara, gauntlets resting upon the chest.

Kyril lightly touched a hand to the breastplate. "Yes, this should do," he murmured quietly. Reaching into a pouch on his belt, the Guardian produced a stick of charcoal and began carefully drawing odd, sinuous symbols onto the stone around the armor.

"What are you doing?" Tal asked curiously as he watched on.

"These runes," Kyril replied absently, "Are Sephiral script. It's a language that was old even when the ancients were young. It's said that these symbols were taught to man by the Lost Ones when they first arose. Whether or not that's true, each character is a sort of diagram for directing Sephiral energy. They're the tool that enables Guardians to control our Sephiral interactions. Usually visualizing the runes is sufficient, but for an operation this complex, drawing them out first will make things a bit less taxing for me." He straightened when he finished drawing, examining his handiwork while replacing the charcoal stick in the pouch. "Even with them, this is going to be very difficult. I'll have to concentrate for some time before we see any result. Please don't disturb me while I'm preparing." He closed his eyes and stood silently, face blank. He stretched forth an arm and passed it over the armor, and as he did the symbols on the stone bier began to pulse softly with a pale blue Sephiral glow.

Tal stood by silently, not moving a muscle except to glance occasionally about the room. Shadows danced fitfully in the flickering torchlight, and there was no sound save his own breath and Kyril's, which came in a slow and steady rhythm. Minutes passed by with no hint of anything further happening, not that Tal knew what exactly to expect anyway. He occupied himself with studying the likeness of Anakara beside him. She had been a stunningly beautiful woman judging from the artist's depiction, with delicate, graceful features and a gentle sweep of hair to the shoulder. The face reminded him somewhat of Rania. Her features were a bit more bold, but there was a general sort of resemblance there, especially about the cheekbones and nose. Tal shook himself from his study when he suddenly remembered whose face he was comparing his new friend's to.

62

He found himself looking up at a third man clad in armor, of middling height and strong build, with long hair such a light shade of blond it nearly seemed white. The man was watching him with a sad smile on his face.

"She was a wondrous woman, generous and kind as well as beautiful, at least before the lure of power and prophecy changed her."

"She... reminded me of someone I know." Tal murmured breathlessly. Was this truly the man history remembered as the Accursed? It seemed he must be.

At the words Kyril's eyes snapped open, and Trazeri turned his gaze to the Guardian, his lips twisting into a contemptuous sneer.

"Why have you disturbed me, Jhessaillian? Have I not already given enough for your Order's prophecies? I played the pawn for you, watched the woman I loved destroy herself, betrayed her to her death, and died myself twice over. Are you not yet done with me?"

Kyril straightened himself and spoke respectfully. "I apologize for calling you back, Trazeri Ni'Dharranoth, but our need is great and you are the only one who may aid it."

Trazeri chuckled. "Spoken like a true Guardian. Your need is always great and dire, it seems, and the greatest burden of it always carried by your unwitting pawns. And what of your companion?" His gaze settled once more on Tal. "He carries himself like a man of arms. One of the Godtouched, perhaps?"

"I'm not of the Jhessaillian Order," Tal spoke for himself, "I am Lord Talaren Solus of House Solus, Champion to the King and soon to be an Armslord."

A faint smile softened the stern face. "A man who makes his own fate, or so it would sound that you believe. Speak your need, Champion of the Throne, and if it is truly so great as the Guardian claims, perhaps my assistance will be yours."

"The knowledge your beloved left behind has been seized, the powers she used awakened again," Tal said, choosing his words carefully. "The man who did this has arranged, at great risk, the theft of the sword that you once carried. We need to know why he would want that weapon so badly, that we may properly gauge the threat it represents."

The shade nodded. "I can answer your question." He looked back to Kyril. "But my answers are not for the Order. Is your presence necessary to hold me here, Guardian?"

Kyril's face was crestfallen. "No. The energies I invoked will dissipate on their own in several minutes."

"Then leave us. I will speak only to the young Lord."

With a rueful glance at Talaren, Kyril bowed and exited the room.

Trazeri walked over to stand directly before Tal and studied his face closely, as if looking for something. He seemed so real it was hard to remember he had been dead for hundreds of years, and he behaved nothing like what Tal had expected from all of the stories. He met the shade's gray-eyed gaze, refusing to look away or demonstrate any hint of hesitation. The shade smiled ever so slightly and nodded to himself.

"First, a word of advice. The Jhessaillian is bound to your path somehow, that much I can see. Be cautious with the Order, they hide their aims behind the shadows of forgotten history, and a man can become lost if he delves too deeply. However much you trust the Guardian, remember that his Order is wholly devoted to their prophecy and if he needs to use you up in furtherance of it, he will not hesitate to do so. From his presence, as well as your question, I perceive that you've become entangled in it already. Be forewarned. Serving as a tool of Jhessail's prophecy can cost one greatly, as I learned much to my sorrow." Trazeri's jaw clenched and his eyes strayed momentarily to Anakara's resting place before returning to Tal's face. "As to why this man you speak of would desire my sword, the answer is twofold. He has created more such as I was?"

"At least six of them that we know of," Tal responded.

"Six," Trazeri murmured. "A formidable force. The first reason he would want it, then, is that the sword is a weapon of the Sephiral realm as well as the physical and can harm those creations, a feat few weapons save those of the Godtouched are capable of. The second, you should pray he does not know and I will require a promise of you before I share."

"What do you want?" Tal asked cautiously.

Trazeri's expression intensified, his eyes boring into Tal's like augers. "The blade of which we speak is an object of ancient power, and is bound to a purpose far greater than any it will serve in your struggle. That purpose must be met, or much more than just your nation will come to ruin. You must swear to me that you will recover the sword, and that once you have done so, you will become its bearer. Keep it, carry it, and guard it from those who would seek its power for their own ends. Will you agree to this?"

Tal pondered. He felt he should consult with Garant before he answered, but the King was not present and he saw no other way to secure the information they needed. "On the honor of my House and my name, I swear it."

"I accept your oath, Talaren of House Solus," Trazeri said gravely. "As I said, the origins of the blade you name as mine are much older than any claim I had to it. Anakara found it in Felmorinen, and the sword is as much a relic of the ancient world as that fortress is. It is none other than *Kallevamar*, one of the Blades of Unity."

The words hung there in the air between them. The Blades of Unity. The two swords destined to be wielded by the Unifier, the savior predicted by the Jhessaillian Prophecy. Tal could hardly credit that one of them had hung unnoticed and unsung in plain sight behind the throne of Val Zherrane for three centuries.

"You're sure of this?" Tal asked, his thoughts reeling from the enormous responsibility that had just been placed on his shoulders. Even a hint of doubt might help assuage the burden.

"I am certain."

Tal nodded. "Thank you, Trazeri. You may have helped to avert an unspeakable disaster."

"You should not be so quick to thank me. Bearing a Blade of Unity is an unenviable task, one that could easily lead you to your doom. I do hope that your fate is otherwise. May you fare better than I did."

Tal could detect no sarcasm in the shade's voice. The wish seemed sincere. "I have to admit, Trazeri, you're nothing like what I had anticipated."

"I doubt that history has been kind to me or Anakara for what we did," Trazeri said softly, eyes distant. "But it was all done out of necessity. We sacrificed our present for the future. Now you, Talaren Solus, have become a part of that future we gave everything for. Don't squander our sacrifice." He walked over and brushed a hand across the face of the stone image of Anakara, that sad smile coming again to his lips. "My time here grows short. Please permit me a moment alone with my beloved before I fade."

Tal bowed, but Trazeri's attention was wholly focused on the stone woman now. He quietly exited the room, sealing the door behind him.

Alone in the darkness beside Anakara's sepulcher, Trazeri whispered to the cold stone. "I wish you could have been here, Kara. I've seen the face of the future we set in motion, and set his feet on the path he must follow. I cannot envy him what lies ahead, but at least I don't think he'll have to face it alone. It feels good to know that the things we did weren't in vain."

7

A Hasty Departure

Tal and Kyril made their way back out of the tombs in silence. The Guardian seemed to be sulking at his peremptory dismissal by Trazeri's shade. Tal, for his part, was too wrapped up in concerns spurred by the fallen knight's warnings to attempt conversation. He felt trapped by all that was happening. Based on what Trazeri had told him, the smartest thing he could do would be to distance himself from it all as much as possible. Knowing what he did now, though, there was no way he could do so without abandoning his duty to Valeran and forsaking the oath he'd given the shade. He had become like a pebble carried along by the leading edge of a landslide.

Gyles was waiting for them outside the heavy iron-strapped door at the top of the stairs leading up from the depths below the Palace. He closed and locked the door behind the Guardian and young Lord and then looked at them anxiously. "Did you get what you needed?".

Tal nodded. "Yes, I got it," he said in a subdued voice. "We need to inform His Majesty immediately." Perhaps the knowledge would seem less troubling once he shared it. He would have to be cautious about who he trusted with what Trazeri had revealed, but if Tal couldn't trust his own King then he knew not who he could. He would tell Garant everything. What made him nervous was that doing so would probably mean informing Guardian Damarrian in the process. Part of him felt that such a disclosure would only be right; matters of the prophecy, which surely included the Blades of Unity, were the Jhessaillian Order's responsibility after all. But Trazeri's words still echoed in Tal's thoughts: *The Jhessaillian is linked to you. If he needs to use you up, he will not hesitate to do so.*

The Seneschal obligingly led them through the Palace, not to the dining room they had last seen Garant in but to one of the King's private studies. The guards in the hallway, six of them now in the wake of the attempt on Garant's life, thanked Tal for his earlier defense of the King before opening the door for him and the Guardian. Gyles politely excused himself to return to his normal duties.

Garant was conferring with Duke Daron when they entered the room. Tal's father nodded to his son as the King shifted his gaze to the two newcomers.

"Ah, there you two are. Did you manage to find our answers, Guardian Damarrian?"

Kyril masked his frown with a sweeping bow before speaking. "Trazeri was unwilling to speak to me, Your Majesty, and sent me away. Lord Solus is the one the shade entrusted with his secrets."

All eyes turned to Tal, who took a deep breath to steady himself. This was it. "The theft of Trazeri's sword is far more threatening than we could have imagined, Majesty. The blade was discovered by Anakara in Felmorinen, but was forged long before her time. It holds within it the power to strike down the spectral creatures Kherzul has created." He paused, half tempted to leave it at that rather than finish, "It goes beyond that, though. It's one of the Blades of Unity. Kherzul has stolen *Kallevamar*."

The King's eyes widened. Daron looked sharply at his son in amazed disbelief. Guardian Damarrian's eyebrows rose so high they seemed ready to disappear into his hairline.

Of the three, the Guardian was the first to find his voice. "We have to recover that weapon," he said forcefully. "Kherzul can't be allowed to-"

"There's more," Tal said quietly. Again the questioning gazes settled on him. He felt strangely as if he were about to confess some wrongdoing. "Trazeri required an oath of me before he would agree to tell me what I've just told you. I felt that I should consult with you first, Majesty, but..."

"But I wasn't there," The King finished for him in a sympathetic tone. "I understand, Talaren. What promise did you give him?"

"I swore that I would recover the blade," Tal said as if pronouncing sentence on himself, "and that once I had I would become its bearer, to keep and defend it from anyone seeking its power."

Garant and Daron exchanged troubled looks. Musingly the King said to his old friend and advisor, "I'm already having one of my weaponsmiths make a replica of the weapon to hang in the throneroom, I'd thought only until the real one was recovered. But considering its nature, it might be wisest to entrust it to a protector, and your son's Armslord training would make him an obvious choice anyway."

Daron nodded slowly in reluctant agreement.

Most interesting of all to Tal, though, was Kyril's response. The Guardian merely stroked his beard thoughtfully, watching the young noble with unreadable eyes. What could the man be thinking?

With no protest from Daron forthcoming, King Garant turned his gaze gravely to Tal. "Well, Talaren, it appears that the responsibility for tracking down the thief and retrieving *Kallevamar* is yours. I suggest you set out for Val Jerak with all haste. I ordered the harbor closed this morning, and no ship has sailed since the theft. Denied escape by sea, Kherzul's agent will doubtlessly be riding hard for the Felmorr Gap."

"I can depart by early afternoon," Tal replied. He'd have to rush to do so, but it seemed he had little choice. This mission was too important to delay for any reason.

"Excellent," said Garant. "Hopefully you can resolve this matter before the men I'm sending arrive. I still want you in command of those forces."

"I'll see to it, Majesty," Tal promised, placing fist to heart.

Guardian Damarrian cleared his throat. "Your Majesty, I would like to accompany Lord Solus to assist in his search. Keeping *Kallevamar* out of Kherzul's hands is at least as important to the Order as it is to Valeran."

"You're asking the wrong man for permission," King Garant replied with a deferential nod to Tal. "As I just said, this responsibility belongs to Lord Solus."

Kyril looked expectantly at the young noble.

Trazeri's cautionary words immediately came back to Tal again, but he saw no graceful way to turn down the Guardian's offer, and no way whatsoever if Kyril chose to turn the request into a demand. Besides, an extra pair of eyes would be useful, as would the Guardian's Sephiral abilities and experience at ferreting out secrets. He would just have to be careful, as the shade had advised. But he still didn't feel his smile as he said, "I'd be thankful to have your assistance, Guardian."

Their tasks set for them, Tal and Kyril bowed to the King before excusing themselves to go prepare for their journey. Just before Tal got to the door, his father spoke up. "Son?"

Tal looked questioningly back over his shoulder.

"Take care out there. I've done all in my power to see you prepared for a day such as this, but this isn't one of Malry's tales and the world we live in can be cruel and capricious, never more so than when the winds of war blow." Daron's voice grew gruff as he concluded, "Keep your wits about you. No foolish heroics."

"Don't worry Father, I'll remember," Tal replied. "I'll see you again soon, I promise."

Daron gazed at the closed door for long seconds after his son shut it.

"That's a very promising boy you've got, Daron," Garant said gently, "I think we can expect great things from him."

"Yes, I'm very proud of him," replied the Duke of Val Solus, "but very worried as well. I hadn't expected him to have to prove himself this soon."

"I appreciate your concern, old friend, believe me," the King told him sympathetically. "This whole affair is volatile and we've set him right in the path of the maelstrom, but I believe him capable of weathering it successfully. He's a fine warrior, with a good head on his shoulders."

"I just don't like the unexpectedness of this all." Daron shook his head irritably. "After all the plans we've nurtured for so long, to have everything thrown into chaos by this crisis."

"Admittedly, it does seem problematic," Garant conceded, "but it could work to our benefit yet. If Talaren performs well enough, he could garner House Solus enough additional prestige and notoriety for me to openly declare you my heir apparent. Your son could potentially stop a struggle of succession from even happening. Those plans wouldn't be needed, then."

"Using my own son for political gain," Daron muttered bitterly, "I'm glad Narene didn't live to see me scheming like this. It'd have broken her heart." Talaren's mother had been a kind, idealistic soul, traits that her son had inherited.

"I'm sure she would have understood that it's for the greater good of Valeran," Garant said gently, "As would Talaren if he knew."

"I know," said Daron, trying to calm his anger at himself. "I just wish I didn't feel like we're throwing him to the wolves. I wish none of this were necessary."

"So do I, Daron," murmured the King. "So do all of us."

The sun had barely slipped past midday when Tal arrived in the courtyard of the Royal Palace clad in his armor and with his saddlebags slung over one shoulder. He'd packed quickly and sent down to the kitchens for the provisions he would need on his journey to the eastmost reaches of Valeran before sitting down at his desk to take care of one last bit of unfinished business. Now he just had to hope Tazmin would be able to follow the directions he'd given.

The nobleman made his way across the courtyard to the stables and ducked inside, smiling at a young stableboy as he asked for Stormwind to be saddled and brought out. The boy rushed to comply with a breathless, "Yes, m'lord."

When the great gray courser was brought out, Tal out of habit checked the ironshod hooves for any loose nails or lodged stones and made sure all the straps on the saddle were cinched tightly. He was almost finished when Guardian Damarrian arrived from the nearby Jhessaillian Chapterhouse riding a restive white stallion.

The Guardian brought his horse up alongside Tal and climbed down from the saddle. "Ready to ride?"

"Just about, Guardian," Tal replied as he went over the last few straps.

The Jhessaillian spy made an inelegant sound in the back of his throat. "Talaren, if we're to be journeying together, this formality will quickly become cumbersome for both of us. Just call me Kyril and it'll be a lot easier." He offered his hand. "I'd like to think we can be friends as well as associates on this mission."

Tal considered the hand for a moment before grasping it firmly. "My friends usually call me Tal, Kyril."

Kyril grinned as they clasped hands. "Alright then, Tal. Shall we be off?"

"Yes," Tal replied, "let's."

Rania wondered if Tal would visit her again today. She wanted to congratulate him for his latest accomplishment. All day the city had been abuzz with word of the cowardly attack on King Garant and how it had been thwarted by the young King's Champion. Already she had witnessed at least a dozen toasts to Lord Solus's health in the common room. What wasn't clear from the chatter circulating through the streets was just how many assailants he had dispatched. Rania had heard everything from a single assassin right up to a squad of twenty armored knights. She very much doubted the latter, but was still curious to hear the true account from Tal himself. More than that, though, she was anxious to continue building on the fledgling friendship she had struck up with the handsome and determined young nobleman. Her other reasons aside, it had been such a very long time since Rania had dared name anyone friend.

Her attention was drawn to a young man stepping into the common room, blinking uncertainly as his eyes adjusted from the sunlight outside. His deep red coat, finely cut and tailored and painstakingly embroidered with silver thread, virtually screamed nobility. A matching wide-brimmed hat perched rakishly atop his head, and an impish grin rode on his face as he scanned the tables of the common room. Eyes alighting on Rania, he strutted over to her table and sat down across from her without bothering to ask permission. "Unless I'm mistaken, you would be Rania, yes?"

She nodded, raising an eyebrow. "And you are?"

"Tazmin Joseth," he replied with a tip of his hat. "We have a friend in common, Rania - Lord Talaren Solus, the hero of the day."

"And how is Tal today?"

"Busy," Tazmin laughed, "but that seems to always be the case with my dear cousin. As much as I like the fellow, I have to admit I find his preoccupation with duty a bit excessive." He paused to attract the attention of a passing serving girl. "A glass of your best wine, if you will." He looked back to Rania. "Anything for you?"

"The same," she murmured.

When the drinks arrived, Tazmin handed the girl two silver pennies. "One for the drinks, and one for your lovely eyes," he said extravagantly. He took a long sip of his wine, looking appraisingly at Rania. "So you're the one our Tal has been mooning after. Seeing you up close, I can't say I particularly blame him."

70

Rania smiled ever so slightly. "I'm afraid you're mistaken, Tazmin. Talaren and I only recently met, although I would certainly hope I can claim his friendship."

The foppish Lord chuckled. "I'm sure you could claim more than that, Rania. I've known Tal since we were both just boys, but I've never known him to show such interest in any woman, nobleborn or not. I could direct you to any number of Ladies who'd love to know how you did it."

"Are you here on their behalf? If so, I'm afraid I don't have any advice for them." Rania lifted her own glass to take a drink.

"Not at all," Tazmin replied, "I'm actually here to do Tal a favor. He's apparently been sent away by the King to handle a bit of pressing Royal business. Before he left, he came to me and asked that I deliver this to you." He reached into an inner pocket of his coat to produce a folded page of parchment which he handed across with a flourish. "I'll admit I'm impressed, Rania. Just a few short days and already you've got him sending you love letters."

Rania took the letter, her lips compressed primly. She glanced briefly at the parchment before setting it off to one side on the table. It was sealed with silver wax impressed with a sigil of a fox's head. "You seem quite convinced that Tal's involvement with me is romantic in nature," she observed.

Tazmin looked at her skeptically before rolling his eyes with a shake of his head. "If you want to deny it, that's all well and good but I know Tal," he said. "Ever since he was fourteen he's spent the bulk of each day training to become the celebrated warrior we know and love. When he wasn't busy with that, he was cloistered with his father learning political strategy and military tactics. The rare moments he found to socialize were usually spent with me. Then you show up and before Tal even *knows* you, he gets himself hit in the back with an axe because he's too busy staring at you to notice an armored man clanking up behind him. I can't find him to go drinking with because he's here talking with you, and he even takes time before rushing off on the King's orders to write you a letter. If Tal's not interested in you, I'll eat this hat." Tazmin finished his wine in one big gulp. "Besides, I saw you two dancing at the Feast, and I think you make a handsome couple."

"Thank you," Rania said for lack of any better reply coming to mind. Tazmin didn't seem to know that she was an Adept of Shevestra. Apparently Tal was keeping her secret for her, even though she hadn't actually asked him to. "I'm sorry if I've stolen your drinking companion from you," she added as an afterthought.

Tazmin waved the apology off. "It's quite alright, especially if it pulls Tal out of his shell. I've long felt that he needs to take more time to enjoy life. Besides, with my charm, drinking companions are easy to find." He smirked at his own quip as he stood. "Which reminds me, now that I've delivered Tal's letter I should be doing just that. It was a pleasure meeting you, Rania. Perhaps we'll talk again soon."

"Yes, perhaps," Rania agreed.

Tazmin swept her a deep bow before taking his leave. Rania smiled in spite of herself. The outgoing, seemingly frivolous young lord was the last thing she'd have expected of a friend and relation of the reserved and serious Talaren.

Rania took a couple leisurely sips of her wine before picking the letter up and breaking the seal with her thumb. It was written in a deliberate, precise hand that suited Tal perfectly. As Rania read, though, her face grew grim and stony.

> Rania,
> I apologize for not giving you a proper farewell before departing from Val Zherrane, but I must leave immediately on a matter of the utmost importance. An assassination attempt has been made on King Garant, and in the ensuing confusion the sword that once belonged to Trazeri the Accursed has been stolen. I have been given the task of recovering it. To that end I have gone to Val Jerak, where I have also been given my first military command. The night we met, I told you that war was coming to Valeran. It now appears that it will arrive sooner rather than later. I wish I could reveal more, but even as much as I am telling you comes dangerously close to violating Council privilege. Although I would not presume to ask you to follow me, should you choose to come to Val Jerak I have little doubt that you would find good use there for your skills. I confess, I would find your presence there reassuring as well. Whatever you may decide, it is my fervent hope that we will meet again.
> Talaren

As soon as she finished reading Rania stood, her half-full glass of wine forgotten atop the table. She went upstairs to her room and quickly packed what few clothes she had into her worn old backpack, atop the unmarked leather-bound book her mother had entrusted to her the night she fled Felmorinen. Her thoughts raced as she packed. What little doubt she'd still had about the veracity of the vision that brought her to Val Zherrane had just fled. It was all true, she was certain now, and Tal somehow stood at the center of it. For some reason that thought brought her comfort, despite the dire tidings she felt behind his letter. She took the time to pull on her mail shirt, settling the familiar weight on her shoulders before strapping a harness crosswise across her chest that carried a dozen daggers, balanced for throwing and all sharpened to a razor edge.

The innkeep looked at Rania oddly when she informed the woman that she was leaving and wanted to settle the bill for her room. "Departing on a journey this late in the day, my lady? Wouldn't you prefer to wait through the night until morning?"

Rania shook her head. "I'm afraid not. I've a long distance to travel, and no time to waste." *No time at all.*

8
A Shadow On The Future

Sitting upon his massive, gold-inlaid hardwood throne in the great hall of the Grand Citadel in Bhel Meravos, King Kherzul Meravos seethed to himself as he frowned at the slip of paper in his hands. The missive, written in a cypher known only to Kherzul himself and a handful of his agents, had just arrived by raven from the west. Its contents were brief but troubling: *A Guardian escaped your followers. Valeran and the Order are aware of your activities. I have advanced my timetable. The weapon has been taken.*

With the plans Kherzul had painstakingly nurtured for nearly twenty years so close to fruition, this deviation was most unwelcome.

Seeming to sense his King's irritation, the household servant who had brought the message shifted his feet nervously.

Kherzul was not a terribly imposing man physically; he was neither as tall nor as broad as most of the warriors who served him, his clean-shaven face smooth and free of any intimidating scars. A simple gold circlet rested upon his neatly trimmed, equally golden hair and he wore a crimson robe with cloth of gold embroidery heavy upon the shoulders, chest, and arms. He carried no weapons, wore no armor. He had little need of them. He carried his sword in his mind, honed sharper than any mere blade. No, he was not a very fearsome man to look upon, but his people were learning to fear him well. Observing the traces of that fear in the man before him brought the slightest hint of a smile to Kherzul's lips.

"You may go," he said, savoring the look of relief on the servant's face. "And tell the guards outside to bring my friend the Major to see me." Kherzul was glad he had resisted the urge to kill the man outright for bringing him the bothersome news. It was no use wasting a properly cowed follower, after all. Fear was the most flattering form of respect.

Three years now Kherzul had held the throne, despite the objections of those who had accused him of foul play in the death of his father in a hunting accident. Even after the assassin he'd hired had been captured and admitted to having been sent by King Garant of Valeran after two days with Kherzul's very best torturers, his accusers had persisted in their claims. Some people just refused to be satisfied. He had noted those who hadn't accepted the murderer's confession, and coincidentally enough, they had all met with unfortunate accidents over the next couple years. After all, one could not have such treacherous thoughts circulating among one's followers. Secure on his throne, most had assumed Kherzul's ambitions satisfied, but the truth was he had only begun. Ambition was a way of life for Kherzul, instilled in him from his youth by his father, Archduke Shebedar of Val Meravos. Shebedar's ambitions had led him to begin the Bhellan Revolution, but had then fallen short when he settled for half a kingdom instead of reaching for the world. Shebedar had died in his son's eyes that day, when he'd offered King Garant a truce. He thought he had attained a great victory, but he had only shown his son how limited his vision truly was. It had been that same day that Kherzul began making plans to pursue his own ambitions, resolved never to let himself fall as grossly short as his father had.

Clearly something must be done about the unfortunate turn of events in Valeran. Kherzul's long, elegant fingers gently stroked the black gemstone dangling from the golden chain around his neck as he considered. His treacherous little sneak in the Valerite Court had advanced the timetable without consulting him, and Kherzul saw little choice but to do the same. It was irksome, but perhaps the situation could still be turned back to his advantage. Yes, he would set the next stage in motion this afternoon. But first, he had this other matter to see to, one in which he would take a great deal of pleasure.

The immense bronze doors to the great hall swung slowly open, and two armored guardsmen clad in red and gold livery entered, dragging a third whose rumpled and dirty uniform bore the black bear's claw of the Bhellan elite guard on its chest. The man's hair was ragged and unkempt, his face stubbled from several days in the dungeons beneath the palace. The marks of rank had been torn from his shoulders, yet still when thrown to the ground by the guards, he picked himself back up to stand proud and upright before his sovereign, saluting smartly.

Kherzul sat and studied the man, steepling his fingers before his face as he did so. He let the silence drag on long enough to become uncomfortable, letting the officer's confidence begin to seep away, before he finally spoke softly. "Major Skalgrim, so nice of you to join us. I trust your stay down below wasn't too uncomfortable?"

The Major's eyes tightened just a bit. "No more so than was intended, I'm sure, Majesty."

Kherzul nodded amiably. "Good, good. Do you know why I had you brought here?"

Skalgrim's lips tightened just perceptibly. "I'm sure you had your reasons, sire."

Kherzul leaned back in his throne and adopted a casual tone of voice. "Indeed I did. I've had reports from some of your men that you've been expressing disturbing opinions about my recent additions to our military forces. Opinions that might be considered by some to be seditious."

Now a hint of nervousness began to creep into the Major's manner. His eyes cast about the throne room as though he sought some hidden means of escape. "Sire, the things I said I only intended in the best interests of Bhellus and her army." Admirably, he managed to keep his voice steady.

"Perhaps, then, you'd care to share these opinions with me? After all, if they're in the best interest of our nation, there should be no reason for me to object, and if anyone has the power to act upon such suggestions, it would be me." Kherzul gently drummed his fingertips against each other as he spoke, fixing a predatory gaze on the soldier.

Skalgrim would certainly know that he was trapped, that Kherzul would have already heard what he'd said, that he could hide nothing now or his King would know and likely punish him for his attempt to withhold. He swallowed and took a deep breath. "I don't approve of these legions of the dead you've been raising, Sire. We Bhellans should stand on our own feet, fight our own battles, not hide behind the charnel of wars past. Asking our men to fight alongside walking corpses, some of them even old comrades, can surely do nothing good for the morale of the army. Finally, and not to question your Majesty's better judgment, but none of us feel comfortable with the creatures you have leading us. They're unnatural things, creatures of nightmare and legend. They can't relate to or inspire the men, only terrify them. Discipline is sure to suffer." He bowed his head, obviously believing himself condemned by his own words.

Kherzul straightened on the throne, impaling Skalgrim with his cold gray eyes. "There. Was that so difficult to say, Major? Did you believe I would strike you down on the spot for saying these words within my hearing?" He stood, slowly walking closer to the man held by his guards. "Your concern for your troops and your nation is commendable, Major Skalgrim. I ought reward you." Kherzul reached deep into a pocket of his robe to produce what appeared to be a black gem on a chain, the twin of the one he wore. He'd spent months trying to unlock the secrets that had enabled him to make these two, now he just had to be sure that the results were as he desired. He carefully placed the chain around Skalgrim's neck.

The Major clearly noticed the similarity between the two stones, looking quizzically back and forth between Kherzul's gem and the one he now wore. A faint glimmer of hope flashed in his eyes. "You're not going to kill me?"

Kherzul turned his back, glided back towards his throne. "I'm promoting you," he said without turning around. He waved a hand over his shoulder at the guards holding the man. "Give him his reward."

The guards had been instructed beforehand, and needed no further prompting. Skalgrim realized what was coming seconds too late. He gasped desperately, wrenching his arms free from the guards' grip even as they drew the poignards from their belts. The narrow blades slipped quite handily between Skalgrim's ribs, a blade puncturing each lung.

76

Kherzul perched on the edge of his throne, carefully arranging his robes as he leaned forward to watch the dying man struggling for breath on the marble floor. Skalgrim's horrified eyes were fixed upon him.

"You see, Major, while I appreciate your concern, I simply cannot have anyone in a position of authority who will question my orders. I do so hate being questioned, after all." He smiled a thin, blood-chilling smile. "But look on the bright side. Though your body is dying, your awareness will go on, quite possibly forever if you serve me well."

Major Skalgrim's struggles began to weaken, his breath coming in watery-sounding gurgles, blood frothing on his lips. His hands closed around the gem, tried to yank it off from around his neck. Kherzul stood again and descended from the dais on which his throne sat to kick Skalgrim's hands from the stone.

"Can't have you doing that, now," He murmured quietly. "You should thank me. You'll have a measure of free will that I granted none of my Generals. You'll still be you." His gaze turned cold and hard as stone as he met the clouding gaze of the Major. "Just never forget that if need be, I'll be able to immerse you in a world of agony that'll make what you're going through now seem a pleasant memory." Noting that Skalgrim was clearly not much longer for this world, Kherzul took a single step back to watch. Now came the test he had been waiting for.

As Skalgrim's last breath rattled in his chest, the gem at his throat began to glow softly. Or perhaps glow was not the word; its black hue deepened, as though it were drawing light into itself rather than emitting it. The darkness crept out from the gemstone, covering Skalgrim's body in a cocoon of blackest night. It pulsed like a thing alive, although Kherzul knew that that was about as far from actuality as possible. The darkness seemed to sink into the body, and all seemed still for a few seconds. Slowly, and then faster and faster, Skalgrim's flesh began to melt away into a puddle of gore, laying bare the bones beneath which proceeded to crumble to nothingness. All that remained was his uniform draped around a dark, misty humanoid shape. Twin coals burst into being where the eyes should have been, and the creature that had been Major Skalgrim rose to its knees, looking about the room as if dazed.

"Skalgrim," Kherzul said, and the glowing eyes turned toward him. "As I promised you, you have remained with us. And, as I also promised you, I can bend you to my will if you make me." He concentrated, composing a rune in his mind to reach out to the energies that composed Skalgrim's form and shift them, disrupting their orderly pattern. The spectre wailed in unearthly agony. It was music to the King's ears. "Will you serve me?"

Skalgrim sank to his knees. "I will." His voice sounded hollow, dead. Defeated.

"Very well," intoned Kherzul, though he remained unsure of this new minion he had just created. Unlike his spectral generals whose wills were wholly enslaved to his, Skalgrim remained independent. That fact could make him a very useful follower indeed, but his disobedience in life was cause for considerable concern. It seemed a test of loyalty was in order. "I want you to go to Val Jerak, Skalgrim. An agent in our employ is bringing the only weapon in the North capable of harming such as you there. You're to find a man in the eastern side of the city, a shopkeeper named Turval. He will tell you when and where to meet our agent. Retrieve the weapon and bring it back to me."

Skalgrim bowed deeply. "As you command."

Kherzul made a shooing gesture with one hand. "Off with you now, then."

Kherzul watched the spectre leave with a triumphant smile on his face. The stone had functioned exactly as he'd intended. During the entire process, he'd not touched the Sephira once. The stone around Skalgrim's neck had reacted to his death, and performed the transformation for him. All was in readiness.

"You." Kherzul said, pointing at the guard who had held the Major's left arm.

"Sir?"

"Kill me."

The guard blinked in surprise. "Pardon, Majesty?"

"I said, 'kill me,'" Kherzul growled impatiently.

The guard shook his head. "I can't do that, sire."

Kherzul rolled his eyes and growled. He focused his mind on the guard, reading the Sephiral patterns of the man's body, and then thrust a tendril of the dark power he'd learned to wield into a critical junction of that pattern. The soldier's eyes went wide in surprise as his heart blackened and withered within his chest. He collapsed in a boneless heap on the floor.

"Perhaps he'll obey a bit better as part of my companies of the dead," Kherzul mused, then turned to the other guard. "Do you think you can obey better than he did?"

The guard nodded frantically, the fear plain on his face. "Yes, sire!"

Kherzul bared his neck. "Then kill me."

The guard looked torn for a moment, then looked again at the body of his fallen comrade. He drew his dagger and swiped the blade across Kherzul's throat, cutting deep. Blood fountained out of the wound, covering Kherzul and the guard in crimson. The King of Bhellus sank to his knees, laughing a mad gurgling laughter until his strength gave out and he toppled to the side.

78

Moments later, Kherzul reawakened. He felt… different. Lighter, stronger, colder. He sat up and looked at his own hands. They were made of the same ghostly mist that had replaced Skalgrim's body moments before. He allowed himself a moment to revel in his transformation, joyous to have at last cast off his fleshy mortal prison for a form of true, ageless power. Then he looked up at the frightened guard standing above him.

"You know," he growled, enjoying the menacing tone this new form lent to his voice, "That really hurt." He took the dagger from the guard's nerveless fingers and buried it to the hilt in the man's belly.

Alone at last, Kherzul surveyed the carnage in his throne room. He'd have to send for someone to clean up the place. No matter, though. An important part of his plans had been accomplished, and now he could rule eternally. Soon, his armies would sweep westward to bring the entirety of the north under Kherzul's dominion. Eventually the entire world would be his. It was only a matter of time, and time was something he now had in abundance. But first, there was one more matter to be taken care of.

Kherzul stretched forth his thoughts to ensnare one of his spectre generals. *Sunamar, come to me.* He knew that Sunamar would feel the summons as an irresistible pull drawing him to his master.

A few moments later, one of the shadows in the corner of the great hall seemed to ripple and swell as the spectral knight stepped forth from the darkness to genuflect before the King. "I attend, my King."

Kherzul looked down upon his minion. "You've failed me, Sunamar. The Guardian I sent you to hunt escaped, and now he has informed his damnable Order of my doings."

Without rising, the former general replied. "But Sire, I saw him die."

"Apparently you saw wrongly," snapped Kherzul, "because now Valeran is preparing to face my armies. This makes me very unhappy, Sunamar."

"I exist only to serve you, Master. How may I make this right? I beg of you, command me."

"Because you're useful to me, Sunamar, I will grant you an opportunity to redeem yourself," Kherzul allowed. "But should you fail me this time, I shall certainly have to destroy you. I'll brook no incompetence among my Generals."

"I will not fail you, Master. What would you have me do?" Sunamar's deathly voice sounded eager.

"You're to stand in judgment for me over your newest brother." Had he still possessed lips with which to do so, Kherzul would have grinned viciously. Instead he satisfied himself with a dark, rattling chuckle.

9
The Weight Of Understanding

Time seemed to pass at an agonizing crawl for Tal. He and the Guardian rode hard from dawn until dusk each day, as fast as they dared without risk of wearing their horses out. They were making excellent time by Tal's estimate, but he wanted to be in Val Jerak *now*, to get on with his search for the thief who had taken *Kallevamar*. Since learning the true nature of the blade, his sense of urgency had become overwhelming.

The pace Tal set precluded the possibility of much conversation in the saddle, so he and Kyril spoke for the most part in the evenings when they made camp. Even then, Tal was far too exhausted at the end of the first night's ride to do more than eat a sparse dinner of bread and cheese before seeking his bedroll. The next evening, his mind troubled with thoughts of the coming war, Tal decided to try to avail himself of the Jhessaillian's knowledge.

"Kyril," he asked as he set a small pot of water beside their campfire to warm for tea, "what can you tell me about Kherzul?" They had taken shelter for the night in a clearing within a grove of fir trees that swayed and creaked soothingly in the wind.

The Guardian frowned thoughtfully and began rummaging through his saddlebags as he answered. "Probably not a great deal you don't either already know or have the information needed to infer. He's ambitious and ruthless, as demonstrated by his probable assassination of his own father to assume the throne. The speed and relative ease with which he then secured his position and silenced his critics would seem to indicate forethought and good strategic planning. And the fact that he's learned to wield Anakara's old powers with only her writings to guide him shows that he has either a sharp enough intellect to accomplish such a not inconsiderable feat, or the resourcefulness to find someone to teach him the basics of the Sephiral Arts without attracting the Order's attention, or perhaps a bit of both." Finding what he was seeking, Kyril pulled a long-stemmed pipe from his bags along with a pouch of pipe herb. "All told, an extremely dangerous enemy."

Tal followed the Guardian's example, retrieving his own pipe and pouch. He filled the bowl by touch, keeping his eyes on Kyril. "That's not quite what I meant. I'm more curious about his Sephiral abilities. Do you know much about those?"

Kyril lit his pipe, gave it a puff, and eyed Tal appraisingly. "You've had at least some of the training once given to Shevestra'ken," he said, exhaling a cloud of blue-gray smoke. "What have you learned about the Sephira from that?"

"It's the basis of all existence," Tal replied around the stem of his pipe, "of everything that is or may yet be. It is the origin point of life from which our spirits are drawn, and to which they return upon death. Vast as it is, it's impossible for any one man to comprehend in its entirety, but because we are of it we can learn to interact with it."

"That's a beginning," Kyril said, settling into a lecturing tone. "The manner of interaction is what determines the nature of the abilities of a Sephirally active individual. A Shevestra'ka calling his battle aura into being interfaces with the Sephira differently from a Guardian performing a manifestation, or one of the Godtouched. Two other factors are also significant in dealing with the Sephira, and those are belief and understanding. In order to do something with the Sephira, you must first believe that you can, so the strength of one's convictions can enhance their power over the Sephira. Further, if enough people believe a thing fervently enough, the Sephira will tend to manifest that belief in reality." The Guardian paused to blow several smoke rings before continuing. "Understanding is vital in that knowing the mechanisms of what one is trying to accomplish makes the actual doing much easier. In a great many cases, it is understanding that makes possible what would otherwise be impossible. Sephiral Healing, for example, is largely governed by one's knowledge of the body's workings."

Tal took the pot off the fire and poured two cups of tea. "Go on," he urged as he handed one cup to Kyril.

"Kherzul manipulates the Sephira in much the same way we Guardians do," Kyril said after taking a sip of his drink. "The difference between him and us is one of understanding. Just as there is enormous variety to the reality manifested by the Sephira, so too are there a myriad of differing energies within the Sephira itself. Aided by Anakara's writings, Kherzul's studies will have focused on manipulating the energies of corruption and decay and harnessing the Sephiral residues of the dead."

Tal suppressed a shudder as he contemplated the Guardian's explanation. "Isn't that similar to what you did yesterday in the tombs?"

"So it is," Kyril agreed. "I should point out that there is nothing implicitly evil about such energies or using them. The Order usually eschews such workings because of the unsavory reputation they carry and the temptation presented by certain applications of them. The histories regarding the Undying are a prime example of why that prohibition exists."

Tal shook his head sadly. "I don't understand why Jhessail or anyone who came after him didn't destroy the record of such vile knowledge while they had the chance."

Kyril gave a melancholy sigh as he tapped the ashes out of his pipe, but he volunteered no answer to Tal's implicit question. Instead, he asked his own question of his young companion. "Why are you so interested in Kherzul's powers, Tal?"

"I'm trying to understand him better," the young nobleman replied. "Knowledge of an enemy can be a mightier weapon than the sharpest blade."

The Guardian raised an eyebrow. "Shevestra'ken adage?"

Tal nodded. "And my father said much the same thing while teaching me battlefield strategy."

"Wise words," Kyril murmured. "Maybe that's part of why Jhessail spared the writings of Maeroth that Anakara eventually used to augment her own powers. Maybe he couldn't bear to destroy any knowledge, even if it was dangerous. That he grasped the danger seems clear. Why else would he leave those particular writings in Felmorinen when he liberated the rest of the library, and then never reveal even to his own Order the path to the ancient fortress?"

Tal shrugged. The explanation didn't feel wholly right to him, but he couldn't quite put his finger on what about it seemed awry. A morose silence descended on the two travelling companions.

After several minutes, Kyril stood. "We should get some sleep. There's another long day's ride ahead of us tomorrow." He ducked into the small tent they had set up a short distance from the fire.

Tal slept uneasily that night, his dreams stalked by dark, indistinct threats. Clawlike skeletal fingers tore at him from a clinging, obscuring mist while a cold, cruel wind seemed to laugh at his vain struggles to find the faceless source of the terrors. He woke several times during the night and each awakening seemed a blessing, but when he went back to sleep the dreams were still waiting for him. Always waiting.

Still haunted by the dreams, Tal rode the next day in a black humor. When he and Kyril stopped for the night, he chose a less weighty topic of conversation in an attempt to lighten his mood.

"Tell me, Kyril, how is it you came to join the Jhessaillian Order?"

The Guardian flashed him a quizzical look before smiling sardonically. "Would you believe that I was once, like you, heir to a noble House?"

Tal raised an eyebrow.

"Oh, it's quite true," Kyril laughed. "Granted, House Damarrian isn't as powerful or influential in Cardon as House Solus is here, but it has the wealth and status nobility brings. Sadly, I didn't embrace the attendant duties of my position the way you have. Instead, I used my family's resources in the pursuits of wine, women, song, and other dubious pleasures. I became quite the notorious socialite in Cardon, much to the dismay of my father. Truth be told, he thought me an embarrassment to our House. My younger brother, Marek, took a much greater interest in what I considered to be the more boring and prosaic aspects of running a noble House, and shortly before my brother's eighteenth birthday my father told me he intended to declare Marek his heir. I was furious with him and mortified at the loss of face that I would suffer, so at Marek's birthday celebration I announced that I was deferring my claim to House Damarrian to join the Jhessaillian Order. Doing so let me salvage my pride and infuriated my father by robbing him of the chance to shame me publicly."

Kyril shook his head ruefully, a smirk twisting his lips. "I learned quickly under the Order, but my instructors despaired of ever being able to instill in me what they called 'the proper attitudes of respect and discipline.' With time, though, my promotion to Guardian was approved and I began my service to the Eye of Jhessail, where I found that my youth hadn't been wasted quite so badly as my father had thought. Gossip, rumor, and innuendo had been like my food and drink during my aristocratic dalliances, and my affinity for them proved invaluable in my work for the Eye. Thanks to that talent I rose swiftly through the ranks, and now ironically have more political clout in Cardon through the Order than House Damarrian has ever had. I doubt my father will ever forgive me for that fact."

"An odd path to take," Tal murmured.

Kyril shrugged. "I suppose it was, but at least I eventually found something worthwhile to do with myself."

"You really feel that way?" Tal asked curiously.

"Certainly," the Guardian replied without hesitation. "What we do may not always be pleasant, is sometimes downright ugly, but is absolutely necessary. With the Armslord training you've had, I'm sure you must understand."

Tal considered for a moment, weighing his own feelings about the path he'd chosen. He remembered what he'd said to Rania about fighting to save Valeran from the chaos of a bloody succession. He recalled the feeling of still-warm blood coating his hands and seeping into his clothing in King Garant's apartments, the sense of queasy sickness that had filled him as it sank in that he'd just taken four lives. But if he hadn't, the King would be dead and Valeran splintered by civil war, easy pickings for Kherzul. It had been necessary. Tal nodded slowly. "I suppose I do, at that."

Over the next several nights Tal and Kyril continued to grow acquainted as they regaled one another with tales of their respective pasts. Kyril was loath to talk about any specifics of his experiences as a Guardian, but freely told tales of his days before joining the Order that would have turned Tazmin's ears red with embarrassment. He'd once courted two prominent young women from opposing Houses simultaneously and after tiring of them arranged to meet both in the same place at the same time, while

Kyril himself had instead gone to a safe vantage to watch what he called "the fun" when the rival Ladies discovered the trick that had been played on them.

In another of his youthful escapades Kyril had attended a fete thrown by a powerful Baron known for his stern propriety, and in the course of the evening had managed to slip into the host's drink an herbal concoction with properties both aphrodisiac and mildly hallucinogenic. The resultant antics, which had involved two serving girls, a highly regarded Lady of the Cardon aristocracy, and a roast suckling pig, had permanently tarnished the Baron's reputation and nearly forced him to relinquish his title to his heir. By the time Kyril finished that particular story, he was laughing so hard tears were coming to his eyes. Despite himself, so was Tal.

For his part, Tal's stories tended at first to focus on his training. After a couple nights of hearing Kyril's wild tales, though, Tal began to talk instead of misadventures with Tazmin, like the time a very drunk young Lord Joseth had conducted himself entirely too familiarly with Lady Lizelle of House Goresh, especially for the tastes of Lord Baram Ghared to whom she was betrothed. Baram had then and there challenged Tazmin, who could barely stand for all the drink in him, to a duel. The challenge had been hastily withdrawn when Talaren, then five years into his Armslord training, stepped forward to champion his cousin. Waking the next day with a splitting headache, Tazmin couldn't even remember the incident and to this day still wondered why Baram so despised him. Kyril laughed heartily at the story, but Tal still couldn't help but feel that his own tales were tame in comparison to the Guardian's.

Tal found himself growing to genuinely consider his Jhessaillian companion a friend, and after a week of riding surprised himself by broaching a subject he'd been unsure about bringing to the Guardian's attention. "Kyril," he said after they lit their pipes following another uninspiring dinner that evening, "something's been bothering me since speaking with Trazeri. He didn't say it right out, but I got the impression that he believed that he and Anakara had acted in furtherance of the Prophecy. What they did had been necessary, he said, that they had 'sacrificed their present for the future.' You yourself used similar words the other night in regard to your service to the Order." Tal fixed a searching gaze on the Guardian. "Were Trazeri and Anakara actually acting at the behest of the Jhessaillian Order when they conquered the North?"

The jovial grin Kyril had been wearing dropped away like a discarded mask and his eyes grew suddenly alert and guarded. There was about him the feral sense of a cornered animal. The Jhessaillian stared at Tal in consternation for the space of several breaths before saying quietly, "What I'm about to tell you can never be divulged to anyone else. It has the potential to damage the Order, and I only tell you because of the extraordinary circumstances that led you to ask that question."

Kyril waited until Tal nodded. "Agreed."

"The Jhessaillian Prophecy predicted Anakara's Empire, both how it would come to be and how it would fall," Kyril said. "It is entirely possible that she was acting on instructions contained in the Prophecy, that she never in fact betrayed her loyalty to the Order and the future we are charged to bring about. There are many of us who believe this to have been the case. It is also a possibility that Anakara acted of her own accord, that she was born to her fate and the inclination to do as she did in fulfillment of the Prophecy was written upon her without her conscious knowledge. Such is often the nature of those whose roles are foretold."

Tal let Kyril's answer sink in. In a roundabout way the Guardian was saying he didn't know for sure, but that the implications Trazeri's shade had voiced were quite possible. Having actually spoken with the fallen knight and remembering the bitterness and mourning in his voice, Tal could have no doubts. Within his thoughts, his understanding of Valerite history lurched and shifted. Empress Anakara Amoran the Undying had been a loyal Guardian throughout her entire unnaturally long life, had been responsible for the murder of tens of thousands and blackened her name in history all in service to the Order. Tal's stomach churned at the thought. He shook his head disbelievingly, trying to deny the horror of it. "You knew what was going to happen," he whispered. "It was foretold, but you Jhessaillians could have stopped it before it began."

"Probably," Kyril admitted, "but we didn't, nor would we if given the chance again."

"But all those lives lost..."

"Were worth the sacrifice!" Kyril asserted heatedly. "I know it's difficult, Tal, but you have to remember that if we fail, nothing will survive. There is a force out there, an evil so implacable that Kherzul is kindness incarnate by comparison and so powerful as to be incomprehensible to us. The Shevestra'ken knew of it once and attempted to fight it, before the Great Purge shattered them as an organization and stole from us almost all our knowledge. Did you know that the Sephira is weakening? The Order has recorded it over the course of centuries. The ancient enemy is leeching it away, growing ever more powerful by feeding off of the life of our world. One day, when the Sephira has been drained enough, they will manifest themselves to hasten the devouring and leave our entire world a lifeless husk. When that day arrives, if we don't have the Unifier to defeat the enemy and restore the Sephira, all existence will come to naught. Compared to that, what is the loss of a hundred thousand lives? Or a million?"

Tal's mind shied away from the magnitude of what he was being told. "I never knew," he murmured.

"As it was intended to be," Kyril replied. "If we let this information become general knowledge it would devastate people's ability to hope for the future. We allow just enough to be known for the importance of our task to be appreciated, but the true depth of the threat we keep to ourselves. It's the burden placed on us by Jhessail's Prophecy, and now you share in it. Few outside the Order have ever been granted this frightful honor."

"Why?" asked Tal.

"Because Trazeri told you enough that I think you needed to understand our higher purpose to be able to trust the Order," Kyril said. "Monstrous things have been done or allowed to happen in keeping history on the path that will eventually produce the Unifier. Things that can only be justified if one knows the stakes involved. Now you do."

Sleep came with great difficulty for Tal that night. Thoughts echoed through his mind, refusing to grant him any peace. *So enormous an evil,* he thought, *and such horrible sacrifices the Order is willing to make in fighting it. And now by seeking* Kallevamar, *I've become part of their struggle. Trazeri and Kyril both said as much. What sacrifices might I have to make? Could I really make such a terrible choice if it came to it?* At long last, after exhausting himself on his worries, Tal fell into a deep and thankfully dreamless sleep.

10

The City On The Threshold

It was with considerable relief that Tal finally spied the city of Val Jerak nestled at the base of the Felmorr Mountains. All told, he and Kyril had been on the road for three weeks and a handful of days, and their mounts were beginning to show the fatigue from their long ride. For that matter, so were the riders. Neither man rode his saddle quite so straight as when they had departed. Their shoulders slumped and their eyes were weary, if still alert. Kyril's uniform was rumpled and dusty, and Tal doubted his attire appeared any better. *We both look like we've been beaten with big, dirty sticks.*

Tal paused for just a moment as the city came into view to marvel at how small and insignificant Val Jerak looked beside the hulking monstrosity of stone that was the Felmorr Range. To say that the Felmorr were enormous or massive would be an understatement. The mountains had first become visible on the horizon nearly a week prior, as the rolling hills and forests of eastern Valeran began to give way to steeper, craggier terrain. With every passing day they had loomed larger, until Tal could barely credit that anything could be so huge. This close, they seemed a titanic gray wall whose top reached into the heavens and then stretched beyond. Snow was plainly visible in the heights of the mountains, an uncomfortable reminder that the air had been growing colder as winter drew near. Tal shivered and pulled his cloak tighter before spurring Stormwind on toward the city.

Even with the city walls in sight, it still took a goodly ride to reach the gates, and by the time Tal and Kyril passed into the city the sun was dipping close to the western horizon. As they were waved through by a bored looking guard in a mail hauberk with a halberd leaning against his shoulder, Kyril turned to Tal with a tired grin. "Well, we're finally here. What's our first order of business to be?"

Tal ignored the tired protestations of his body as he replied, "First, we seal the Gap Gates. I don't want to give our quarry any chance to slip away if it can be avoided. Then we'll go to the Keep and tell Joren what we've done." He suppressed the spiteful satisfaction that rose up in him at knowing how irritated his self-styled rival would be upon hearing of the pass being closed. Tal knew that Archduke Zharkus's heir had departed Val Zherrane the same day as he and Kyril, though several hours prior. It had surprised Tal that they hadn't caught him up on the road, but apparently the other young Lord had been riding every bit as hard as they. His passing had been reported to them by the few travelers they had stopped to question, and fortunately he was the only one who had been seen on the road riding so hard. That fact helped mitigate somewhat Tal's worry that if they hadn't caught up with Joren, the thief might have escaped them as well.

A broad avenue cut straight through Val Jerak from western gate to eastern, and as he and Kyril rode down the well-worn cobblestone street Tal gazed about at the city. The buildings were predominantly of stone and timber construction, strong gray granite hewn from the mountains beyond. The streets were lively with people; due to being located at the only easily passable route through the Felmorr Range, Val Jerak was a major hub for trade and always had a great many travelers passing through. At the center of the city the two companions passed through the enormous central market square where travelling merchants stopped their wagons to hawk their goods and the surrounding buildings displayed signs for all manner of artisans, craftsmen, and shops: armorers, seamstresses, provisioners and more, virtually anything could be bought or sold here. Tal and Kyril rode on and out the eastern gate.

The mountains loomed up in front of them, filling Tal's field of vision. Their base lay ahead about two miles, where the road sloped up and into a great sheer-walled cleft in the stone that looked as if it had been hewn by a titanic axe: the Felmorr Gap. Forest lay perhaps a mile to each side of the road, but out to that distance the ground had been clearcut to deny any cover to an enemy emerging from the Gap.

A stone wall stretched across the road a short distance into the Gap, with five wide arched gates spaced evenly along its length. Guardsmen walked along the top of the wall and manned each gate, waving through the occasional traveler. This late in the day, there were few still on the road.

Tal rode up to a long-faced, dour looking guard who squinted up at the rider drawing rein before him. "I need to speak to the commanding officer here," Tal announced in a peremptory tone of command.

The guard studied Tal and Kyril closely, his mouth twisting up like he was sucking on his teeth. He clearly noted their travel-stained appearance, and from the way his brow furrowed when he set eyes on Kyril, he also recognized the Guardian's uniform. "And who might you be?" he finally asked Tal.

"Lord Talaren Solus of Val Solus, here on business of the Crown. My friend is Guardian Kyril Damarrian, assisting me in the interests of the Order."

The guardsman straightened and saluted Tal with fist to heart. "Yes, sir," he said. "Follow me, please." He led them to a low building built hard against the side of the pass. Standing beside the gatehouse was a row of wooden posts topped by iron rings, two of which Tal and Kyril tied their horses to after dismounting. The guardsman stood by silently while Tal retrieved from his saddlebags the scrollcase containing the writ of authority Garant had provided him with.

Once Guardian and noble both stood beside him, the guard knocked firmly on the door three times.

"Yes? What is it?" asked a voice from the other side.

The guard opened the door and stepped into the gatehouse with Tal and Kyril on his heels. He saluted a stocky, sour-faced man seated behind a cluttered desk, whose uniform bore on the breast the shield with three red slashes of a captain. "Lord Talaren Solus and Guardian Kyril Damarrian wish to speak to you, Captain Harzik. Here on Royal business, they say."

The Captain eyed the two newcomers and then nodded his head. "Very good. You're dismissed, Derrin." As the guard saluted his superior and departed, Harzik turned his eyes back to Tal. "What can I help you with, Lord Solus?"

"Captain," Tal said with an acknowledging nod, "I've come on important business of His Majesty. I need the Gap Gate closed. Immediately."

Harzik raised a bushy eyebrow skeptically. "I trust this order has been authorized by the Lord of the city?"

Tal shook his head. "Not yet. I'll be informing Lord Joren as soon as I'm finished here." Seeing the Captain about to open his mouth to reply and knowing from the disapproving twist of his lips that he was going to refuse the order, Tal cut him off by proffering the scrollcase. "I think you'll find, though, that this grants me all the authority I need." He kept his voice quiet, but firm.

The Captain took the case, carefully removed the cap and pulled out the document contained in it. His expression shifted to slack-jawed astonishment as he read. Garant had been very generous in the wording of the writ, Tal knew. It granted him sufficient authority to seize control of the city if he deemed it necessary, though he hoped very much that it wouldn't be.

"Just what sort of business are you on to carry that?" Harzik handed the document and case back, his voice wavering as he turned a searching gaze on Tal.

"I'll explain later," Tal replied curtly. "For now, all you need to know is that the gate is to remain closed until you hear further orders from me personally. I should return with those orders in the morning. In the meantime nobody passes, in or out." He rolled the writ back up as he spoke, replacing it in the case which he tucked behind his belt.

Captain Harzik stood, his back straight and rigid as he saluted. "It shall be as you command, milord."

"Excellent. I'll speak with you on the morrow then, Captain." Tal bowed ever so slightly before turning and leading Kyril back out of the office.

The Captain followed right behind them, and was bellowing orders before the door closed behind him. "Close the gates!" When several of his men glanced askance at him, Harzik added, "You heard me, you mangy curs! Close 'em up! Move!"

Guardsmen scurried about, hurrying to comply with the orders, and by the time Tal and Kyril had untied and remounted their steeds the gates were beginning to swing ponderously shut.

Tal sat and watched from the saddle until the last of the gates were fully closed before nodding to himself in grim satisfaction. At last, he'd done something about the task at hand.

"You handled that well," Kyril murmured. "I'd not have expected you to have so firm a hand when issuing commands."

"You forget I was taught by one of the most respected noblemen in Valeran," Tal replied dryly. "But this was the easy part. I doubt Joren will cooperate so easily."

The Ducal Keep of Val Jerak was situated atop a hill in the northern quarter of the city, a grandiose fortress constructed of stone blocks ten paces to a side. Towering over the rest of the city, its design seemed to have been inspired by the hulking mountains that in turn loomed over it. Talaren and Kyril entered the grounds through the southern gate in the wall that ringed the base of the hill and rode up to the flight of pocked and worn stone steps leading to the main entrance hall. They were met at the base of the steps by a contingent of mailed guards bearing spears.

Tal climbed down calmly from Stormwind's back, noting as he did so the markings of rank on the leader's breast. With both his feet on the ground again, he turned to address the man. "Lieutenant, I am Lord Talaren Solus. I have to speak with Lord Joren."

The Lieutenant, a young man just short of Tal's own age with pinched features and a hawklike nose, bowed his head before replying, "I'm sorry, Lord Solus, but Lord Jerak isn't giving audiences at the moment. If you come back tomorrow..."

"That isn't acceptable," Tal interrupted crisply. "I'm on an urgent mission under orders of the King, and my authority derives directly from him in this matter. I must speak with Lord Jerak immediately." He offered an apologetic smile to the Lieutenant. "I'm sorry if this causes you any trouble, but I'm afraid I must insist."

The guard studied Tal for a moment, noting the determined set of the nobleman's jaw and the unyielding gaze resting on him. He nodded, and motioned them forward. "If you'll come with me, milord," he said respectfully before turning to his men. "See to their horses."

"Don't take them too far," Tal added, "we'll be back for them shortly." He turned to follow the Lieutenant up the steps.

The officer led them into a small waiting room with comfortable looking chairs padded in red velvet just off the entry hall. "Please wait here, sirs. I'll go inform Lord Jerak of your request." He bowed and hurried out of the room.

Tal and Kyril seated themselves in two of the chairs. Kyril sighed happily as he settled himself into the padding. "This is a far sight better than that hard saddle."

Tal nodded in tacit agreement, his thoughts more focused on the impending conversation with Joren. That the other noble would argue with him, he had no doubt. He would have to be firm, perhaps even a bit heavy-handed. A Jerak would respond to no less, at least not from a member of House Solus. He fixed a stony scowl on his face in preparation for the confrontation.

Long minutes passed by, each seeming an hour. Joren was no doubt taking his time in order to rile Tal. He was inclined to such petty displays. At long last the Lieutenant returned, bowing as he entered the waiting room.

"His Lordship will see you now, Lord Solus. Please come with me."

He led them down echoing stone corridors toward the great hall. Everything within the Ducal Keep was built on a grand scale, as if it had been constructed for men of twice normal breadth and stature. *No doubt to accommodate the egos of House Jerak,* Tal thought with a sardonic inward grin.

The ten-foot tall doors to the great hall stood open, beyond them a cavernous room with vaulted ceiling and regularly spaced swords hanging upon the walls. At the end of the long room, atop a low stone dais flanked by a pair of guards, Joren sat in a stone throne built on the same monolithic scale as the rest of the Keep. The impressive effect was marred somewhat by the fact that so large a seat made Joren look like a child by comparison.

Archduke Zharkus's heir watched on with languid eyes as Tal and Kyril approached the throne. Joren's full lips smirked with a peculiar mocking twist. Calculating green eyes remained locked on Tal as he drew closer, all but ignoring the Guardian who walked beside him. Joren's freshly laundered black and gold doublet stood in sharp contrast to Talaren's dust-covered black and silver.

When Tal and Kyril came to the foot of the dais, Joren shifted to look down his nose at them. "Ah, Talaren, my old friend. So good of you to come by. I rather wanted to speak with you." The way he bit off the word 'friend' said clearly that he considered Tal anything but. "I just heard about the commotion you caused at the Gap Gate. Perhaps you'd care to explain yourself before I have my guards seize you?"

Tal shrugged and replied lightly, "What's to explain? I ordered that it be closed."

Joren gripped an arm of the throne tightly and leaned forward to glare at Tal. "That much I know already. What I want to know is why you didn't come to consult me first before ordering about House Jerak's soldiers."

"Because I was in a hurry. And because I didn't have to. See for yourself." Tal pulled the scrollcase from behind his belt and tossed it up to the livid-faced Lord.

Surprised, Joren barely managed to snatch the case from the air before it landed in his lap. He yanked the cap off angrily and pulled out the document within. His face blanched as he read. "This is an outrage!" he declared in a strangled voice. His hands tensed as if preparing to tear the offending writ apart.

"Joren!" Tal's voice was like a whip-crack. "I'll remind you that destroying a royal document is a crime. Don't force me to have you arrested."

"You wouldn't dare," snarled Lord Jerak.

"Wouldn't I?" Tal grinned wickedly. "Then go ahead and test me."

"When my father returns..."

"He'll cooperate with me meekly as a kitten," Tal interrupted, "rather than risk my invoking the full authority that writ grants me." He fixed a cold stare on the incensed Lord. "Make no mistake, Joren. I'm here to conduct an investigation for the King, and I'll not allow any irrelevant enmities between our Houses to interfere with the execution of my charge. I'd rather do this with your cooperation, but I'll do it without if you force my hand."

"And just what are you investigating that compels you to stop the flow of trade through our city?" Joren's voice quavered with suppressed rage. The hand with which he gripped the throne's arm was white, tendons standing out against taut skin. Tal half expected to hear the cracking and grinding of breaking stone under that deathgrip.

"The morning you left Val Zherrane," Tal said calmly, "it was discovered that the Sword of the Accursed had been stolen from the throneroom of the Royal Palace. In light of recent events, we're convinced the thief is one of Kherzul's agents. I'm to prevent the culprit from escaping to Bhellus, and to recover the weapon."

Joren sneered disdainfully. "So you're disrupting our income from tariffs on trade for a rusty old heirloom? Threatening to usurp House Jerak over a weapon that more rightfully belongs in a museum than a throneroom?"

"If Kherzul wants it badly enough to risk so much in stealing it, the blade is surely important enough that we must spare no effort to keep it from him." Tal didn't want to reveal what he knew of the powers of Trazeri's sword, for that disclosure would certainly lead to questions of how he knew of them, or even of why the weapon had such qualities. Neither were subjects that Tal wanted to explore with more people than he had to, and especially not with Joren.

"And what if your thief managed to outrun you?" Joren taunted slyly. "You may have already failed in your mission without knowing it."

"To manage that, he'd have had to stay with the road, and we questioned several travelers coming the other way on our journey here," Tal replied. "None of them had seen anyone riding fast enough to keep ahead of us but you." He feigned a look of realization, widening his eyes and pursing his lips thoughtfully. "Unless you're suggesting yourself as a suspect?"

Joren's face went absolutely white, and spittle flew from his lips as he retorted in a near-shout, "Don't abuse the trust His Majesty has put in you, Talaren. House Jerak will cooperate with your thrice-damned investigation, if only to be rid of you. If that's all, this interview is over!"

When he and Kyril were out of the great hall, Tal sighed mournfully. "I just didn't have the heart to tell him that I'll be staying here afterwards with twenty-five hundred men under my command."

Kyril glanced at Tal out of the corner of his eye. "You enjoyed that, didn't you?"

Tal put on a look of shocked innocence and gasped. "Kyril, how could you suggest that?"

The Guardian chuckled as they made their way out of the keep to reclaim their horses and find an inn to stay at.

11

Defender of the Pass

"Have you given any thought as to how we're going to conduct this search?" Kyril asked Tal as they handed their horses off to a stableboy. They had taken a room at an inn close to the eastern gate, a three story stone building with a sign out front depicting a resolute Valerite Guardsman with bared sword. The sign declared the inn 'The Defender of the Pass.' Tal thought the name a good omen in light of his purpose in Val Jerak.

"A few," he replied, "although I'd also welcome any suggestions you might have. I've little experience or training at this sort of thing."

Kyril grinned as he slung his saddlebags over a shoulder. "How very modest of you. I'll not speak a word of advice, though, until I've had a cool glass of wine and a warm bath."

Tal chuckled. "Then we're agreed on at least one thing." He had already asked the innkeep, a round balding man named Harnar, to draw a pair of baths for them when he had paid for their rooms. "Let's get our bags into the room and see what we can do about that wine."

They entered the inn through the stable door in the back and after passing the savory scents of the kitchen emerged into the common room. The Defender was a cozy, well kept place. The floors appeared regularly swept, the furniture sturdy and in good repair if somewhat worn. A fire burned merrily in a hearth set into the wall, shedding warmth and light into the room. Master Harnar stood behind the long bar, polishing away with an old rag while a pair of pretty serving girls moved about the room, bringing food and drink to the guests of the inn. The clientele was reserved, primarily well dressed merchants talking quietly among themselves whilst drinking or perhaps puffing leisurely at a pipe.

Harnar ducked his head to Tal as they entered, tucking the cloth behind his apron as he came out from behind the bar to meet them. "If you gentlemen will follow me, I'd be happy to show you to your room."

Tal and Kyril followed as the innkeep led them up the stairs at the side of the room and down a hall to a door. He waited by the door as Tal and Kyril entered, depositing their bags on the pair of beds that occupied most of the tidy little room. "Is everything to your liking, sirs?"

Talaren nodded graciously to the man. "Yes, Master Harnar, we feel quite welcome here. Are our baths ready yet? We've traveled a long way and are quite anxious to shed the dust and aches of the road."

Harnar smiled amiably. "Of course. A hot bath is sovereign for the pains of a weary traveler. They should be ready shortly. I'll send Ilse up to fetch you as soon as they're prepared."

Kyril reached into a pocket and produced a silver coin. "Excellent, Master Harnar. Could you have some wine brought to us while we bathe?" He flipped the coin across the room to the innkeeper, who caught it and tucked it into a pocket of his apron with a duck of his head.

"It shall be done, Sir Guardian. Let me say again what an honor it is to have two gentlemen of your stature staying at The Defender of the Pass." Harnar bowed a bit awkwardly and then ducked back out of the room.

Tal opened a saddlebag and began selecting out fresh clothes to put on after he had washed. "I suppose it *is* fairly unusual for a Lord to take a room at a city inn. Visiting nobles probably stay at the Ducal Keep most of the time. It's certainly large enough."

Kyril laughed lightly as he sorted through his own bags. "After the way you settled Lord Jerak, it's probably wiser for us to stay in the city anyway. I'm sure, though, that all Harnar meant is that he's pleased to have two guests who are generous with their coin. Just try to relax tonight. Our search doesn't begin until tomorrow."

They had only just finished choosing their change of garments when there was a polite knock on the door. Tal opened it to find a young woman with honey-colored curls and big blue eyes demurely downcast. She bobbed a curtsy to him, smiling shyly. "I am Ilse, my Lord. Master Harnar sent me to show you to your baths?"

"Wonderful," Tal said, picking up the bundle of clothes at the foot of his bed. "Kyril?"

The Guardian grabbed his folded, clean uniform and they followed Ilse out into the hall. She took them back downstairs and through another door, occasionally glancing back coyly at Tal. The room the door opened into had a stone floor, sloping gently toward the center where there was a drain set into the ground. Six copper tubs lined the wall, two of them filled with steaming water. Short tables sat between each tub, and the one between the two filled tubs held a bottle of wine and two glasses. Tal and Kyril each set their fresh clothes on an empty table.

Tal turned back from the table, beginning to unlace his shirt, to find Ilse curiously watching him. His hands froze on the laces, and she blushed at having been noticed. "Forgive me, my lord. I was just wondering if you'd come from the Harvest Tournament at the capital. I've always dreamed of seeing something so splendid, but a Lord who's been there would be the next best thing."

Tal gave her an understanding smile. "There's no need to apologize, Ilse," he said gently, "Yes, I was there. I even competed. I'd be happy to tell you about it later, if you wish. And please, call me Talaren, or Tal. It's so much easier than having to use my title whenever you speak to me, and I promise not to be offended."

Kyril was stripped to the waist and wearing a mischievous grin. "You'll have to excuse my friend, Ilse. His modesty sometimes gets the better of him. He seems to have forgotten to mention that he won the competition for King's Champion this year."

Tal gave the Guardian a sour look and then deliberately pulled his shirt off. Overly modest in front of women, was he?

Ilse's blush deepened. She curtsied again. "That's very impressive, Lord Talaren. To think I'd meet the King's Champion! If you need anything, let me know." Her look was now considerably less shy and a great deal more admiring. She turned and let herself out of the room.

Kyril shed his breeches and lowered himself into the hot water with a long sigh. "You should have asked her to scrub your back."

Tal followed suit, stretching back in the tub as he let the heat relax tense muscles. A contented smile spread across his face. "I knew you were going to say something like that."

Kyril reached over to the bottle and poured them each a glass of wine. Lifting his glass, he took a sip. "Of course you did. You saw how she was looking at you as well as I did. You should heed my advice. Life doesn't always have to be all duty and protocol."

Tal picked up his own glass. "It's the responsibility I was born to, Kyril." He took a sip of wine. "But I'll try listening to what you advise. Let's start with the search."

The Guardian rolled his eyes. "Your loss," he muttered. "To begin with, I'd suggest you pay a visit to the Pathfinder's Guild tomorrow." The Pathfinders were outdoorsmen, mountain rangers trained in Felmorinen to navigate the high passes of the Felmorr Range. Although some few others might know a route or two to the ancient fortress, a Pathfinder's knowledge was comprehensive. "If anyone seeks a guide through the mountains, or attempts to find a way themselves, they will most likely hear of it, and I think they should be relatively willing to assist us. What did you have planned for the Gap Gate?"

"I was thinking that I'd allow it to be opened and for traffic to pass during the day," Tal replied, "under the condition that everyone passing through toward Bhellus submit to a search. I'll have to supervise it personally, but I think such an action would go a long way toward mollifying House Jerak."

Kyril nodded thoughtfully. "You're probably right. I think it unlikely that the thief will try that route once he hears about the searches, but you should watch it just in case he gets desperate enough. I'll focus on the city. So close to Bhellus, there must be plenty of professional smugglers and such folk who our quarry would be likely to seek out. I'll beat him there and make sure that if he tries, I'll hear about it." He shrugged, taking the opportunity for another sip from his glass. "Aside from that, we just keep our eyes and ears open, and wait for our chance. Unless the thief decides to go several weeks south and try taking a boat around the Felmorr from Stonefang Bay, we'll have his escapes closed off. He'll make a mistake eventually, and then we'll have him."

"You make it sound so easy." Tal sighed.

"Yes, and no," Kyril replied, "It's all just a matter of thinking, planning, and adjusting, not very dissimilar to politics. Or a battle, I suppose." Kyril frowned. "There's just one thing that bothers me."

"What's that?" Tal asked.

"Even with the distraction of the assassination attempt, Kherzul must have known that we'd notice the theft of the sword and react. Maybe he expected the attempt to succeed, and planned on the resultant chaos to cover his thief's escape, but I can't help but wonder if he had planned on this eventuality. In which case, how much of what we're doing did he anticipate?" Kyril shook his head. "No matter. He could hardly have foreseen your intervention. I think that we're probably ahead of the game for the moment."

Once they finished their baths, they toweled off and donned their fresh clothes. Ilse met them at the door out of the baths and took their travel-stained garments from them, promising they'd be laundered and returned in the morning. She looked Tal approvingly up and down before leaving them, and murmured with a little smile, "Talaren, you're even more handsome clean."

As Ilse walked away, Tal turned to Kyril. "Don't say it."

Kyril smiled innocently.

They moved on to the common room and took a table in a corner. A young man at the far end of the room was playing a lute, and some of the guests were dancing in a clearing that had been made in the middle of the room. In short order Tal and Kyril were brought a warm meal of beef and potato stew with fresh baked bread. Tal set to his food with a will, and ordered seconds when the first bowl was empty. Kyril ordered them each another glass of wine. It was Ilse who brought them the food and drink, a disconcerting sway in her walk and an inviting look in her eyes. Tal stared at Kyril, waiting for the Guardian's glib comment, but Kyril just sighed contentedly and acted as though he hadn't noticed. Tal would have almost preferred the witty remark to the knowing silence.

As Tal ate his second bowl of stew, Kyril excused himself and went upstairs. He returned just as Tal was finishing, their pipes and his herb pouch in hand. "The crowning touch to the end of a long journey," Kyril smiled, handing Tal his pipe. "You should try this blend I've got. I picked it up in D'nar during my journey from Cardon."

Tal accepted the pouch after Kyril had filled his pipe, and took a sniff to judge the aroma of this blend of Kyril's. It had a clean, crisp, head-clearing sort of scent to it that he found quite appealing. He thumbed some into the bowl of his pipe and lit it with the burning splinter Kyril handed over to him. The herbs tasted much as they smelled, with a faint undertone of mint. "Very nice," Tal murmured appreciatively.

As they sat smoking their pipes, sipping wine, and listening to the music, Tal at last began to feel a sense of relaxation steal over him, as the weight of all he had seen and learned in the past weeks fell away for a time. He smiled happily, leaning back in his chair with his head nodding in time to the music.

The man with the lute was joined at the end of his song by a woman with a flute and after a brief exchange of words, the two began to play in unison. More guests got up to join the dancers.

Finishing his pipe, Kyril tucked it into a pocket and regarded his companion. "You're looking a lot less harried now, Tal."

"I think your advice about trying to relax just sank in," Tal replied lazily.

The Guardian stroked his beard sagely. "I've often found that one of the most useful talents when dealing with circumstances of great seriousness is the ability to step back from them for a time. It helps to maintain one's sense of perspective."

"Hmmm," Tal nodded as he casually let his gaze drift across the room. With so many patrons dancing the serving girls had little to do, and Ilse stood idly beside the bar. She noticed Talaren's eyes on her and smiled back at him tentatively. Tal pushed his chair back and stood.

"Where're you going?" Kyril asked with a knowledgeable glint in his eyes.

"To maintain my perspective," Tal said blithely. He picked his way across the room to Ilse, whose smile grew as he approached. "Would you care to dance, Ilse?"

She darted a quick look at Harnar, who smiled gently and gave a little nod. "I'd be delighted, Talaren."

Tal offered Ilse his hand and led her out onto the floor, where they joined the sweep of motion of the dancers.

"I can hardly believe I'm dancing with a Lord," Ilse beamed up at Tal with wide blue eyes. "And not just any Lord, but the King's Champion!"

Tal smiled kindly into those eyes and said, "For all of that, Ilse, I'm still just a man."

She shook her head in wonder. "You say that, but you're *somebody*. People know your name. Me, I'm nobody. People like you don't usually mix with people like me."

Tal chuckled softly as the tune continued. "I couldn't disagree more. I've been taught that the nobility exists to serve our people. We're entrusted to govern for their common good, make decisions to enhance their prosperity, and defend them in times of war, with our lives if need be. Why then would I want to hold myself aloof from the people I serve, especially when spending time with you reminds me how precious what I live to protect is?" He drew a finger gently down Ilse's cheek to her jaw. "How precious you are, Ilse. Don't ever let anyone make you feel otherwise."

Ilse blushed a deep red and cast her eyes to the ground as the musicians brought their song to an end.

The next song began. "One more dance?" Tal asked warmly.

Ilse looked back up and nodded eagerly.

When their second dance was done, Ilse put her hand delicately to the side of Tal's face. "Lord Talaren, you've made me feel like a princess tonight. Thank you." She smiled gloriously.

"You're welcome." As he watched her returning to her place by the bar, Tal marveled at the effect just a bit of kindness could have.

Tal returned to the table to finish his drink. Kyril was gone, dancing with a dark-haired young woman in a richly tailored burgundy riding dress, probably a merchant. After draining the last of his wine, Tal went upstairs and was asleep within minutes.

The night passed all too quickly. Tal rose with the sun what seemed mere moments after he had crawled into bed and set out while Kyril still lay sleeping. The Guardian claimed that his portion of the search would best be carried out late in the day and into the night. Tal suspected it was just an excuse to get more sleep. Though the sky was light when he left the inn, the city still lay in shadow. This close to the Felmorr Range, the sun had to be well into the sky before it cleared the peaks.

Tal's business at the Pathfinders' Guildhouse took surprisingly little time. He had only to explain the situation to the rugged-faced Guildsman who greeted him at the door, and the Ranger immediately pledged that he would see to it that his fellows put a watch on all the high passes. From the outrage he expressed upon hearing the tale, the Pathfinder seemed to take the theft of Trazeri's sword as a personal affront. Tal guessed that was probably due to the weapon's historical linkage with Felmorinen, where the Rangers learned the lore of the treacherous stone mazes that comprised the heights of the Felmorr.

The remainder of the day, which Tal spent at the Gap Gate, was a long, tedious, grinding affair. After he explained his orders to Captain Harzik and his men, the gates were reopened and the inspections began. Traffic passed through at a snail's pace, as Tal insisted on a thorough search of everyone and everything leaving the city through the Gap. As the majority of the travelers were merchants with wagons full of goods, many of the searches could drag on interminably before he was satisfied, and tempers grew short as the line of waiting travelers grew longer. All the effort uncovered a great many wagons with hidden compartments in floor or wall concealing smuggled goods, but no hint of the stolen sword. Hours passed, shadows lengthened, and at last nightfall came. Tal ordered the gates closed for the night and returned to the inn.

Kyril, he was told, had left some time ago and had yet to return. Perhaps he had meant what he'd said about searching through the night. Tal retrieved his pipe from his room and ordered a glass of wine. He sat in the common room for a long while, chatting idly with Ilse when she had a free moment, losing himself in thought when she was busy. The image of Trazeri's sword, which Tal now knew to be *Kallevamar*, lingered in his head as he had seen it countless times displayed behind Garant's throne: a heavy, single-edged blade suitable for cleaving through armor, with a single deep blood groove, forward-thrust quillons, and wire bound grip. Although he had examined a multitude of swords that day, none had combined all these attributes.

Tal decided it was time to seek rest shortly after the same musicians from the prior night began to play. Apparently Master Harnar had decided to hire on the woman with the flute. Ilse cajoled him into a single dance before he went up, of course. When he finally made it back to the room he shared with Kyril, he fell asleep almost immediately.

Tal was awakened in the predawn darkness as Kyril let himself in. The Guardian had shed his uniform in favor of rumpled and stained rust colored tunic and breeches. With a sword belted at his side and an exaggerated swagger, he looked quite the part of the ruffian.

"Any luck?" Tal asked sleepily.

"Yes, and no," Kyril replied as he sat on his bed and began unlacing his boots. "Nobody's heard anything about the sword yet, but your inspections at the Gate have the city's smugglers well riled. They're hardly talking about anything else."

"Nice to know they appreciate my efforts," Tal said dryly as he rubbed the sleep from his eyes.

A trace of a smile tugged at the corners of Kyril's lips. "A few have also mentioned that the high passes have become particularly dangerous of late. Strange creatures prowling the night and such. Granted, the Felmorr have always had more than their share of ghost stories, but something definitely has the smugglers spooked. Our quarry will have a difficult time convincing one of them to take him that way."

"Doubly good for us," Tal noted. "The Pathfinders agreed to increase their patrols and look for our thief."

The Guardian nodded once. "I never doubted that they would."

Tal glanced out the room's window and winced. The stars were growing dimmer as the night began to wane. He climbed out of bed and set to dressing himself. "Kyril, I've still got one concern that's bothering me," he said as he laced up his breeches. "I'm worried that the sword may slip past me despite the searches. Do you think maybe I should keep the Gap Gate closed after all?"

"No, I don't," came the immediate reply. "If we seal that route completely, we increase the likelihood that the thief will decide to try fleeing south, which only complicates matters for us. Always leave the rat one apparent means of escape, even if it's a difficult one. Your being there will give him pause and force him to contemplate his next move, which buys me time to track him down. As for missing the sword if he does try the Gap," Kyril smiled wryly, "see that you don't."

"I'll do my best," Tal sighed as he belted on his sword and turned to the door.

The Guardian yawned loudly. "Have fun. See you at the same time tomorrow."

The day passed with the same grinding tedium as the one before. The sole difference was that now the vast majority of hidden spaces that were found in passing wagons were empty. Word of Tal's actions was spreading fast, it seemed.

When night descended, Tal detoured on his way back to the inn to stop at the Ducal Keep. His conversation that morning with Kyril had raised the possibility in his mind of the thief trying the southern route, and he was determined to do what he could to make that path as difficult as could be.

The same Lieutenant was stationed at the door this evening. When Tal asked to see Joren, the officer bowed and replied respectfully, "Begging your pardon, Lord Solus, but would you perhaps prefer to meet with the Archduke? He arrived with his entourage earlier today."

Tal agreed, and after a much shorter wait than the last time he had visited the Keep was ushered once more into the great hall. Zharkus Jerak's muscular bulk filled out the massive throne considerably better than did his son's, and his flinty eyes did a much better job of being intimidating as he watched Tal approach. Joren was there as well, standing to the right of and slightly behind his father. The younger Jerak wore a smug smirk as he fixed a disdainful gaze on Tal.

"Lord Solus," rumbled the Archduke as Tal came before him.

"Your Grace," Tal replied formally as he dropped a deep bow. It would be best to observe the forms of respect with Zharkus. The man could be unbearably prickly where matters of protocol were concerned.

As if in confirmation of Tal's thoughts, the Archduke said, "I've been informed of your activities at the Gap Gate, Talaren, as well as the authority His Majesty has granted you and how you've been throwing your weight around in my city." He leaned forward, seeming to loom over the younger noble. "I should warn you not to push me too hard, or you may find that this 'kitten' is more of a mountain cat, and one with long claws."

"Of course, Archduke." Tal forced his voice to be smooth and reasonable. He held the bow just a few seconds longer than usual to placate Zharkus.

"Now that we understand one another, Lord Solus, what can I do this evening to assist your mission?"

Tal straightened back up and carefully composed himself. "Your Grace, I'd like to respectfully request that a contingent of men be sent south to the villages on Stonefang Bay. They're the only potential escape still open to the man I'm seeking, and I'd like to see to it that they're watched."

Zharkus nodded slowly. "We might be able to spare the men to do as you ask. How many would you like sent out?"

Tal considered for a moment. "One hundred men should be sufficient. They can split up to have at least a handful of guardsmen in each village in the area. Should they find the thief, he should be taken alive and brought back here for questioning. The sword itself is to be turned over to my custody, by the King's order."

"One hundred men." Zharkus drummed his fingertips on the arm of his throne. "I believe we can manage that. I assume this is to be a short term deployment?"

"Just until the Accursed's blade is recovered, Your Grace," Tal agreed.

"Very well then," Zharkus declared, "they'll depart early tomorrow morning. Will that be acceptable, Lord Solus?"

"Yes, quite." Tal bowed once more. "I thank you for your assistance, Your Grace. It'll be noted in my report to the King." He smiled to himself at seeing the look of gloating gone from Joren's face before turning to stride back out of the hall.

Once Talaren had passed out of sight and well out of earshot, Joren stirred. "Father, I thought you were going to put him back in his place. You went along with everything he said!"

The elder Jerak chuckled darkly as he fingered the message in his pocket that had arrived by raven shortly before Lord Solus had made his appearance. "Patience, my boy. It wouldn't do for us to raise any suspicions just yet." He shot a warning look over his shoulder at his petulant son. "You very nearly did just that when he first arrived. For now, we must let him go on with his futile efforts. Not to worry, though - events have been set in motion about which he can do nothing. Why, with just a little luck, you may even get to see the Solus whelp die."

The following days continued to pass with the same tedium as the first couple. As the merchants of Val Jerak became accustomed to the inspections, Tal would arrive in the morning to find that they had already lined up in anticipation of the daily opening of the gates. Kyril's nocturnal activities continued to yield rumors and whispers, but neither of them seemed any closer to finding the stolen sword. After nearly two weeks without results, Tal's optimism was beginning to fade despite Kyril's insistence that the weapon must still be in Val Jerak.

So it was that Tal rode back to the Defender one night with two swords hanging from his saddle in addition to his own at his side. The weapons had been close enough in design to the one he sought that he didn't want to allow them through to Bhellus, so he had bought them from their owners out of his own pocket. In tracking a thief, he had no intention of becoming one himself. Tal took the blades up to his room and set them in the corner with the nearly dozen others he'd bought by now, eliciting a number of curious looks as he passed through the common room carrying them. He went back down and took an empty table, sighing as he sat down.

Ilse brought him a glass of wine without being asked, and sat down opposite him. "Rough day?"

Tal shrugged. "Just long. Won't you get in trouble for sitting down with me?"

Ilse waved off the question with a little laugh. "As long as it's with you, Master Harnar won't mind. He likes you and Kyril. Just having a nobleman and a Guardian under his roof has increased his custom and the Defender's reputation. A lot of people are curious what you're doing here." She gave Tal a questioning look. "Talaren, what *are* you doing here? We've heard about the Gate, and rumor has it that the Archduke is displeased about whatever it is, but nobody seems to know why you're doing these things."

Tal took a long sip of wine and fixed Ilse with a steady look. "I'm afraid I can't tell you exactly why I'm here, Ilse. There are forces acting against Valeran, and I'm here to see that they don't succeed. That's as much as I can say." At Ilse's crestfallen look, he took her hand and gave it a squeeze. "I wish I could tell you more. Trust me, please?"

Ilse nodded. "Of course, Talaren. I don't know who I could trust, if not you."

Tal arched an eyebrow at her. "But you hardly know me, Ilse."

"I know you well enough." She extricated her hand from his and smiled at him. "I shouldn't stay here talking all night."

Tal watched her back in bewilderment as she returned to work. Women. The more he thought he understood them, the more wrong he proved to be.

He stayed in the common room for a couple hours, drinking tea after the first glass of wine. He took a few turns dancing, trying to banish the cares from his mind, but they lingered however hard he tried. Apparently finding relaxation just wasn't as natural to him as it was to Kyril. When he sought his bed, he fell asleep quickly again. Amazingly, there were no swords in his dreams.

He awakened a couple hours short of dawn as the door to his room cracked open. Sitting up to greet Kyril, he rubbed his eyes with the back of his hand. And was startled to see not the Guardian, but Ilse, pale and trembling in a short shift.

"Ilse? What's wrong?" Tal swung his legs out of bed.

Ilse's mouth opened and closed, struggling for words. Then she was shoved into the room from behind, and Tal saw behind her the source of her fear: a tall humanoid form, misty and indistinct, clad in a mail shirt and Bhellan military uniform. Baleful red eyes stared at him as Ilse bolted toward Tal to huddle in terror behind him.

12
The Fruits Of Betrayal

Tal reacted without even a heartbeat's hesitation. He dove across the room into the cluster of swords he'd taken in the previous weeks, creating a clatter of falling blades. He came up with a blade in either hand, the one in his left still in its sheath. Not that it mattered. Sheathed or no, he knew these weapons would be incapable of harming the creature before him. But he might be able to buy Ilse the time to get away safely.

With a start, he realized that the ominous creature hadn't moved since entering the room. Eyes like hot coals regarded him dispassionately. At least Tal thought they did; It was difficult to judge expression in a burning ember.

"You have no need for swords, Armslord. Not with me." The creature's voice was a hollow rasp, a sound utterly unnatural. It closed the door behind it, eyes never leaving Tal. "I'm sorry to have frightened you and the girl. I needed someone who could bring me to you."

"An assassin from Kherzul, then?" Tal asked grimly.

"Not yet," replied the spectre, "though you'll no doubt draw his wrath eventually. I wish, rather, to assist you in the task that brought you here."

"Talaren?" Ilse whimpered from the bedside where she still cowered.

Tal walked carefully over to her, keeping his eyes on the misty form, forcing his voice to calmness. "It's okay, Ilse. He's a friend. I think."

"An ally of circumstance, at least," the spectre said. "In another time, another situation, you and I would probably have opposed one another, Talaren Solus. But the present state of affairs gives us common purpose. There is a monster on the throne of Bhellus."

"I know," Tal said, "Kherzul has brought Anakara's madness back into this world. He's raising the dead, and making spectres like the Accursed. Like you."

"He's gone further than that, I'm afraid. Not only does he practice those dark arts, but he has transformed himself as well. King Kherzul by now wears a form similar to mine," the creature gestured toward itself, "and he seeks the one weapon in all the North, aside from those of the Godtouched, that can do him harm."

"Trazeri's sword," Tal murmured, "what else do you know of it?"

The spectre tilted its head curiously at Tal. "What I have told you is all Kherzul spoke to me of it. If there is more, he either does not know it or did not share it with me. But the fact that it can strike him down should be enough, certainly. Would you keep this weapon from him?"

"Yes," Tal said with a nod, "at any cost. Do you know where it is?"

"Indeed I do," came the reply, "I was sent to retrieve it for him. But I will take you to it, in exchange for a promise."

"What would you ask of me?"

"Death. As soon as the sword is in your hands, you must use it to strike me down."

"Agreed," Tal said, "but why?"

"In life, my name was Major Aldon Skalgrim. I made the mistake of questioning what the King was doing to our military, and for my disobedience I became the test subject for the device Kherzul used to effect his own transformation. Luckily I kept my own will when he changed me, but I am certain that he'll eventually break it. When that happens, I'll become just another of his unquestioning, unthinking minions. I've no desire for such a fate. I should have ended when he had me killed." The spectre, Skalgrim, shook its head. "No. This way is far better. I will have an end to my suffering, and with the sword you may have a chance to save both our nations. But we must not tarry. Those with the sword will be waiting for me already. We must go."

"Where?" Tal asked.

"There is a disused barracks on the edge of this quarter of the city, just off the grounds of Jerak Keep."

Tal looked quickly to Ilse. She seemed somewhat calmer, although fear still stood plainly on her face. "Do you know the place, Ilse?"

The serving girl nodded slowly, focusing on Tal's face. "I think so, yes."

Tal crouched beside her to look her straight in the eyes. "Listen to me, Ilse, this is very important. You must tell nobody what you witnessed here, nobody except Kyril. When he returns, if I'm still not back, you must tell him where I am and why. Can you do that for me?"

"I can."

Tal donned tunic and breeches, quickly selecting the plainest he had and carefully avoiding anything with his House insignia on it. He shrugged his mail shirt on atop his clothes, neglecting the reinforcing plates that would take longer to don, and strapped his sword to his hip. Ilse watched quietly, clearly wanting to stay as far as possible from Skalgrim, who still stood in front of the door. As Tal pulled his boots on, Ilse tugged plaintively at his sleeve. He looked at her questioningly.

She whispered, "Please, Talaren, be careful."

Tal smiled gently. "Everyone always tells me that. Don't worry, I will." It would be cold outside. He stood and put on his heavy black cloak, and then faced Skalgrim. "Let's go."

Ilse remained in Tal's room as he and the spectre left. The hall was dark and quiet, with no sign of anyone else awake. Tal briefly contemplated taking Stormwind, but decided against it. Best to draw as little attention as possible. He stepped out the front door into the chill night air, and Skalgrim followed.

"They will be expecting only me, so you must stand in for me at the meeting. I will shelter in the shadows of your cloak." The spectre reached toward Tal's hooded face and seemed to melt away before his very eyes. The cold around him seemed to grow deeper, and as if Skalgrim spoke right into his ear, he heard, "Do not speak once we arrive, it will give you away. I will do all the talking."

Tal gave a quick nod. "Right."

He started down the street, turning at Skalgrim's prompting. Little more than a mile away, the old barracks building loomed ahead of them, a long structure of wood with a pair of double doors on the end. Crossed axes were mounted to either side of the door, tarnished and rusted from lack of care, proclaiming the function of the building. A faint light could be seen flickering through the high windows of the barracks.

Tal heard Skalgrim's voice again. "One moment. Let me improve your disguise." The spectre's glowing eyes appeared before Tal's vision. They made it harder to see, but at least he might have a chance of passing for the dead Major. "Whenever you're ready, you may enter."

Tal took a deep breath, steeling himself, and pushed the doors open to stride into the barracks with all the confidence he could muster. A handful of torches guttered fitfully in sconces on the walls. A column of mailed soldiers stood along each wall, displaying no house colors. Two more closed and barred the doors behind Tal as he strode down the aisle between the two columns, anger and outrage swelling in him with each step.

At the far end of the barracks waited Joren, a smug smirk on his face and a sword Tal recognized cradled in his arms. He raised his voice. "You're late. I was beginning to think the message you sent a hoax." His voice was heavy with arrogance.

"Just being cautious," responded Skalgrim's voice from Tal's cowl, "There are searchers about. I've come to retrieve the sword for my master, traitor. Give it here."

Joren threw back his head and laughed. "You have the gall to name me traitor? I've served faithfully." His eyes took on an accusatory glare. "Better than you have, I think."

A form detached itself from the shadows behind Joren, resolving itself into another misty figure with flaming eyes. The armor it wore was heavier and more ornate than Skalgrim's, the marks of rank indicating a general. Joren looked casually over his shoulder at it, then back to Tal.

"Might I say, Major Skalgrim, that death seems to be treating you well? You're looking much more substantial than your colleague, General

Sunamar." Joren's grin was wicked. "Whose shadow are you hiding in? Is that you, Talaren?" The soldiers around Tal drew their weapons.

The second spectre, Sunamar, stepped forward to stand beside Joren. "Skalgrim, you've failed your test of loyalty. Your existence is forfeit." He reached over and drew the blade Joren proffered to him.

Mist swirled from Tal's cowl and the spots before his eyes disappeared as Skalgrim appeared beside him. "I am sorry, young Lord, it appears Kherzul anticipated me. The only way out for us now is to fight." He drew his sword and stepped forward toward his counterpart as the ring of soldiers tightened around Tal.

Tal's blade emerged from its sheath with a soft rasp. A voice in the back of his head whispered that he couldn't stand against so many. He quashed it down ruthlessly. *Doubt is weakness.* "By the sword, then," he murmured. He raised his weapon and hurled himself at the closing ring of steel.

He cut one soldier down on his way by, a man whose eyes widened in surprise at Tal's speed just before the blade ripped through his abdomen. Tal cleared the circle, pivoted, and struck off the head of the nearest soldier before he could turn. He edged back as the knot of soldiers closed in around their fallen comrades, considering looks on most of the faces before him. The first two had been given to him by surprise. He'd not be so lucky again. He kept his blade before him, waiting for the next attack. With two soldiers still guarding the door, there were still over a dozen focused on him. Behind them he saw Skalgrim and Sunamar hewing at one another, and Joren standing well away from the fighting, hateful eyes fixed on Tal.

The soldiers before Tal split up, coming at him in groups of four. They pressed hard, forcing the nobleman back. His blade flickered like lightning, pushing swords away from him. Before he had opportunity to counterattack each group would break away and the next would push in at him. For long minutes it progressed thus, Tal struggling to keep his ground but slowly being pushed back. Skalgrim was faring little better; his sword unable to harm his opponent, he was forced to take a solely defensive posture.

One of the soldiers pressing in around Tal failed to retreat quickly enough after an attack and he lunged, running the man through at the cost of taking a slash to his swordarm. He managed to twist himself away from the blow enough to miss most of the impact, but blood dripped from the shallow score just below his bicep. Again he stepped back.

Just then, Skalgrim miscalculated a parry and Trazeri's sword slipped in past his guard, parting the armor covering his chest. The spectre stood transfixed for the blink of an eye, and then the shadowy substance that composed him boiled away. Skalgrim's sword and now empty mail shirt fell to the floor.

Sunamar turned his attention to Tal, joining the soldiers that harried him. Tal saw his chances of survival, already slim, disappearing. Soldiers swarmed in around him, rallying to the spectre that relentlessly hammered on his defenses without fear of a retributive attack.

Against the onslaught Tal was unable to keep all the sword blades from him. The wound on his arm was soon joined by half a dozen shallow cuts where he had been unable to completely evade an attack. He fought harder than he had ever done before, but against so many even the most valiant effort was hopeless. The only option he could see was to sell his life as dearly as possible.

A hollow thud reverberated from the doors, as if they had been struck by a battering ram. The bar on the door shook, and the two soldiers guarding the portal looked at it in alarm. Another thud, and the bar made a splintering sound. More of the soldiers were taking notice, turning their heads to look at the door and permitting Tal the opportunity to break away from them. Still the general pursued him, the Blade of the Accursed seeking Tal's flesh.

With a third impact the bar snapped, and one door was torn from its hinges to fall into the room. With an unearthly shriek, a new combatant hurtled into the room, cloaked in an aura of such menace that the guards at the door involuntarily shied back, and holding in each hand one of the axes from the outside wall. In the flash of an eye Rania had buried one of those axes in the belly of one of the soldiers next to her while the other axe caught the second soldier's blade as he struck at her. Contemptuously, she swept his weapon aside and clear of his hands. Her backswing caught him in the neck, producing a gout of blood that spattered across her face, making her already threatening visage all the more menacing. She turned, letting the first axe fall with its victim's body, while the second she hurled at one of the stunned pack that had been attacking Tal. It caught him high in the chest, flinging the soldier backwards like a broken doll to crash against the wall a bloody ruin.

Rania glided forward, divinity in motion, utterly unconcerned with the soldiers turning to face her. Her hands flickered to a harness filled with knives strapped across her chest, casting them at the men confronting her with the force of bolts hurled from a crossbow. Thrice blades darted from her fingertips and three more men fell, knife hilts blooming in chest, throat, and an eye. With an easy motion she pulled her sword from its sheath, took one more step forward, and she was among the still standing soldiers. Rania danced among them, blade flashing as men fell around her. She melted away from their attacks as though she weren't there at all.

Tal grinned. All of the soldiers had turned their attention to Rania. He had no idea how she had appeared seemingly out of nowhere to rescue him, but he silently thanked Shevestra for the unexpected turn. Without all the soldiers to trouble him, Tal more closely matched the spectral general who was still trying to press him. He caught the next attack with his sword, and forced Trazeri's weapon downward with the force of the parry. He kicked hard, connecting solidly with the ancient sword on the crosspiece and grip. A bone-piercing cold passed through the kicking foot, but *Kallevamar* spun from the spectre's hand and across the floor. Tal dropped his own weapon and flung himself after the sword, hand catching it as he rolled and came to his knees. Without looking, he twisted and swiped Trazeri's blade in a long lateral arc behind him. He felt steel buckling at his attack, and as his eyes came around he saw Sunamar staggering back, armor already beginning to drop away as his form lost coherency.

Only six men still stood around Rania, and most of them were bloodied already. Rania herself was covered in crimson, but none of the blood appeared to be hers. There was certainly no pain in her maniacal grin. The soldiers around her were intent on the young woman, their faces tight and frightened as though they faced a demon. To judge by Rania's demeanor, perhaps they did. None of them noticed as Tal approached behind them.

Rania threw herself into them just as Tal surged forward to strike. Realizing far too late that they were caught between two superior foes, the soldiers were ground to dogmeat in a space of heartbeats.

The barracks now resembled nothing so much as a slaughterhouse. Shattered bodies lay strewn about, dismembered limbs and entrails resting in pools of cooling blood. Joren pressed himself into the corner, the grin wiped from his face and a pasty pallor spreading across his features. His jaw trembled as he watched Tal and the Shevestra'ka close on him.

Tal placed a boot casually on Joren's chest and pushed him back down against the wall as he brought the tip of Trazeri's sword to rest lightly against the nobleman's throat. "You carried this all the way from Val Zherrane yourself, didn't you, Joren?"

Joren nodded, eyes desperate, trying to press himself back away from the blade. "Yes! Yes, I did!" The panic was clear in his choked voice.

"So, who is this master you boasted to have served so faithfully? Who did your orders come from?"

"It was my father!" Joren sobbed, "He's been plotting with Kherzul since we were children. I was just following his orders. Please, Talaren, mercy!"

Tal grinned wickedly down at Joren. "You ask me for mercy where you'd have shown me none, Joren. I'm afraid it'll come only with a price. If I let you live, will you testify against the Archduke before the Royal Court?"

"Anything, just please don't kill me!" Joren's voice was a wail. Tal felt sick at witnessing such debasement, even from a traitor. He removed the sword from Joren's throat.

Rania pushed Tal roughly aside, her eyes burning with rage. "Kherzul is responsible for this? What other designs did he have? Was he also behind Felmorinen's fall?" Her voice was quiet, but death was written across her blood-smeared face.

Whimpering, Joren tried scrabbling back further into the corner.

"You said Zharkus has been dealing with Kherzul for years," Rania said, the aura around her seeming to crackle with barely contained fury. "Did he have anything to do with the attack?"

Joren looked up at her in unadulterated terror. His mouth worked wordlessly, tears streaming down his contorted face.

"Answer me!" Rania snarled, startling even Tal. She reached for the blade at her side.

"Yes," Joren whimpered brokenly, drawing the word out between frightened gulps of air. "Father helped Kherzul sneak his men into Valeran, and found them the guides to get them to the fortress. He told me the plan had impressed him enough that it convinced him that Kherzul would be a stronger, more cunning ruler than House Zherrane has ever given us. He said that we'd see the north reunited, that Kherzul would expand our holdings, maybe even give us governorship of all Valeran. House Jerak would thrive again..." Joren broke down at last, sobbing uncontrollably.

Rania's face had gone stony at Joren's words. She looked down on him silently as if looking at the lowest creature on earth. "Kherzul." She murmured quietly, hand clutching the dagger at her belt. She took several deep breaths, trying to rein her anger back in.

"Rania, what are you doing..." Tal began.

She turned on him sharply and cut him off. "Tal, I need you to give me that sword you're holding."

Tal shook his head slowly. "I'm sorry, Rania, I can't do that." The effort of denying her while she stood cloaked in her aura was almost unbearable.

Her back stiffened. "Please, Tal, don't make this difficult. You don't know what it is that you hold."

Tal squared his shoulders and spoke very firmly. "I know exactly what it is, and I'm sworn to carry and defend it."

Rania's eyebrows lowered as her eyes tried to bore holes in Tal's skull. "Sworn to whom?"

Tal hesitated, glancing down at Joren. The traitor seemed too busy sobbing to pay attention to the exchange. "Its last owner, Trazeri

Ni'Dharranoth. I spoke to his shade, and he told me what this sword is. As the price for knowing, he made me give him my oath to carry and protect it."

Rania couldn't have looked more shocked if Tal had slapped her. "You carry it by right," she murmured, "though I never thought I'd see it."

Tal's brow furrowed in confusion. "Rania, how do you..."

"There's a lot you don't know about me, Tal," Rania said regretfully. "Some of it you should be told, but we don't have time for that now. Justice must be done to Archduke Jerak first. For now it may help to know that my full name is Rania Amoran. Felmorinen was my home, many years ago."

Tal reeled. The lost scion of House Amoran, presumed dead when Felmorinen had fallen. He had begun to suspect from the hints he had picked up on, Garant's comments to her at the Royal Feast, the semblance he had noted between her and the carving of Anakara, and of course Rania's exchange just now with Joren. Still, hearing it confirmed came as a shock. And now she had within her reach two men who had helped keep the secret of who had attacked her home and slain her family and friends.

Tal fixed Rania with a steady gaze. "You may not like this, but we have to take Zharkus alive. There has to be a trial. And before we do that, we have to hide Joren someplace safe." He looked thoughtfully at the sniveling nobleman. "The inn. We'll take him there. Hopefully Kyril will be back by now."

Rania nodded and pulled Joren roughly to his feet.

Dawn painted the street in pale colors as they emerged from the barracks half supporting, half carrying Joren. The air had a sharp edge of cold to it. It wouldn't be long before the first snows. There were few people on the streets yet, which was to the good. Covered in blood and gore as they were, Tal had little doubt they would start whispers or worse if they were seen. He was suddenly thankful for the shadow of the mountains.

"You're lucky I came when I did, Tal. You looked like you were about to get yourself killed," Rania said as they walked furtively through the early morning.

"Thank you for the rescue, Rania, but it must have been more than just luck that brought you to me," Tal replied, "what're you doing here, and how did you find me?"

"I came for the sword when I got your letter. It took me a while to get here since I was on foot. Knowing that we were both looking for the same thing, I started searching for you first. It took me almost all night to find the inn you were staying at, and when I did a serving girl named Ilse told me where you were and who you had gone with. She seemed quite concerned. I think she might have taken a liking to you." Rania grinned at Tal across Joren. "Funny, I wouldn't have thought her your type."

"I've been trying to get Tal to broaden his horizons." Kyril stepped from an alleyway with an amused look on his face. "You two look like you've killed half the city. I take it I missed the fun?"

"Not all of it," Tal replied, "We've still got to arrest Zharkus, once we get Joren here nice and settled at the inn."

"My, my. Quite the busy morning you've got planned for us," Kyril flashed his grin at Tal. "Any particular reason, or are we pulling down the Archduke just for the fun of it?"

"He's in league with Kherzul." Tal said bluntly.

"Good reason."

They arrived at the Defender of the Pass without event, but as they pushed their way in through the door, all eyes in the common room turned to them. Silence settled on the room as patrons taking their breakfast stared at Tal and Rania, soaked in blood as they were, hauling Joren between them.

Master Harnar scurried up to them, concern writ large on his face. He nervously scrubbed his hands at his apron. "What's happened? Ilse has been worried to distraction all morning, but she wouldn't tell me a thing." He looked suspiciously at Joren, and his eyes widened. "That's the Archduke's heir," he whispered in a scandalized voice.

"Dark events are upon us," Kyril replied quietly. "We need to leave this man here while we deal with them. This is a matter of the greatest importance to both the throne and the Order. Will you trust us, Master Harnar?"

"Yes, Guardian, of course." Harnar's tone was mollifying. He looked more closely at Tal and gasped. "Master Talaren, you're wounded! I'll send for a healer right away!"

Tal shook his head and waved the man off with his free hand. "None of them are too deep, Master Harnar, and I've no time for sewing and bandages right now."

The innkeeper nodded and followed them up the stairs. He opened the door to Tal and Kyril's room for them.

Tal and Rania dropped Joren unceremoniously on one of the beds. Tal glanced around quickly. "We'll need some rope," he said to Harnar.

"No, we won't," Kyril said, and walked over to grasp Joren's head. Looking into his eyes, Kyril said gently, "You've had a difficult and troubling night, Lord Joren. Sleep, and rest." Kyril's fingertips glowed briefly with Sephiral energy, and the frightened nobleman went limp, chest rising with the long slow rhythm of deep sleep. "He should be out for most of the day." Kyril turned a questioning eye on Rania. "So who's your new friend, Tal?"

Talaren introduced them hastily as he exchanged his usual Sephirally-forged sword at his side for *Kallevamar*. "Guardian Kyril Damarrian, meet Rania Amoran, Shevestra'ka."

Kyril smiled oddly as he bowed. "A pleasure, Lady Amoran. We've been wondering for quite some time what became of you." He noted the questions implicit in Tal and Rania's expressions, but cut them off before they could be voiced. "Shall we get back to the business at hand?"

They all stepped back into the hall. Tal pulled Master Harnar aside. "Lock the door, and let no one in. Keep this as quiet as you can. It should all be finished before long."

The innkeep nodded. "Yes, my Lord."

Tal left the inn with Rania and Kyril flanking him. Rania cloaked herself once more in the Sephiral aura of the Shevestra'ken. They made straight for the keep, unmindful of the stares that followed them.

When they arrived at the outer gates to the Ducal Keep, the two guards there stared at them in consternation and then moved to block their path, crossing their spears between them.

"Stand aside." Tal grated at them. The guards wavered.

"Or be cast aside." Rania added, easing her sword in its sheath, her aura conveying a sense of horrific violence on a frayed leash.

The guards looked at each other, and then hesitantly lowered their spears.

The threesome passed them by. At the door to the keep itself, six soldiers waited, led by a Captain who glowered at the small group approaching him, then raised his voice. "I don't know how you passed the gates, but you are not expected this morning. Move along."

"No," Tal said, "You will take us to His Grace immediately."

"I think not," the Captain sneered, gesturing for his men to form up behind him. None of them stirred. The Captain stood defiantly for a moment before realizing he stood alone. The soldiers stood rigidly, expressions confused and frightened.

"No reason for hostilities out here." Kyril grinned.

"Your work?" Tal asked. The Guardian gave a quick nod in response.

Rania drew her blade. "Take us to Zharkus. Now."

The Captain looked about to attack by himself, then the air went out of him. "Follow me," he muttered.

He took them on the same path Tal knew from his previous audiences in the great hall, glancing apprehensively over his shoulder every now and then. When they arrived at the closed double doors, he gestured to them. "In there."

"Thank you," Tal said, and then cracked the Captain on the back of the head with the pommel of his sword. The man crumpled to the ground. Tal shrugged apologetically to Kyril. "He irritated me."

Resheathing his blade, Tal pushed the doors open. Zharkus sat on the great seat at the end of the hall, taking council with a number of his ministers and officials, judging from the dress and manner of the folk gathered with him. The Archduke started up out of his throne, opening his mouth with an angry rebuke. Before he could speak, Tal cut him off.

"Archduke Zharkus Jerak, by the authority granted me by King Garant ,I charge you with treason and relieve you of your duties. Val Jerak is now under my command." Tal announced. A wave of shocked whispering passed through the room.

Zharkus's face was livid. "This is an outrage, Lord Solus! What proof do you have?"

"This morning, your son Joren attempted to give this sword," Tal drew *Kallevamar* and held it before him, "stolen from the Royal Palace of Val Zherrane, to a Bhellan agent. We have his confession that he acted on your orders, and that you've been conspiring against your sovereign with King Kherzul of Bhellus."

"As a representative of the Jhessaillian Order, I corroborate Lord Solus's claims," Kyril declared, "and give his action our full support."

Not to be left out, Rania told Zharkus icily, "For House Amoran and the Shevestra'ken, I also support Talaren's charges." She drew her blade and the blaze of her Sephiral aura grew even brighter, the pressure it exerted against the mind even more pronounced. "You should thank him for protecting you from *me*, Archduke. I'm looking forward to learning what you know about the night Felmorinen fell."

Faced with the menace that radiated from the Shevestra'ka, Zharkus's face blanched and he pressed himself back against his throne even as he continued weakly trying to sputter his claims of innocence.

Tal turned and looked over his shoulder. "Guardian Damarrian?"

Kyril stepped forward. "Yes?"

"Would you be so kind as to escort the Archduke down to his dungeon?"

Kyril grinned. "With pleasure."

Kyril led Zharkus out, Rania following behind with bared sword, while Tal began trying to calm the room.

13

A Time for Truth

Rania was climbing up from the dungeons of Val Zherrane for the second time in one day. After accompanying the Guardian down with Zharkus, she had returned to the inn Tal had been staying at to haul the comatose Lord Joren down to the dungeons and a separate cell of his own. The Jhessaillian wanted to question the both of them, and he wanted Joren safely under guard as soon as could be arranged.

She had been more than happy to fetch the traitorous Lord just to get away from this Guardian Damarrian. The man was full of questions passed off as conversation, questions like how she'd survived Felmorinen's fall, where she'd been since, and how she became an Adept of Shevestra. As though she would share any of those things with someone she barely knew, let alone a Jhessaillian who seemed to assume he had the right to her life's story!

As Rania emerged from the lower levels of the keep, the mood in the halls was tense. News had spread quickly of the charges against the Archduke, and everyone was walking as though the floors were strewn with broken glass, eyes guarded and suspicious, especially toward strangers. Strangers like her. She couldn't blame them, not really. It had been a shocking morning for everyone. She herself had a hard time believing all that had happened so swiftly. A duty that had weighed upon her for a decade and more had been lifted from her without her even knowing until it was already done, and with that one change, everything was shifting. She was still the only one who realized it, but she was going now to share what she knew with the one person she hoped she could trust with it, indeed had no choice but to trust.

Archduke Jerak's audience hall had been cleared by now, and she had to ask one of the subdued household servants where Talaren was. The fellow looked at her silently a moment before quietly responding that Lord Solus was in the Archduke's study, and would she like him to take her there? She nodded her assent and the man led her through more of the enormous hallways of the Keep, up a set of stairs and to an iron-hinged wooden door. She dismissed him there after he murmured that the young Lord was inside, and opened the door without knocking.

Tal looked up from behind the desk, where he appeared to be sorting through a mountain of papers. The wounds he had taken that morning were gone now after having been tended by one of the Keep's Order-trained healers, but he still looked like he had been through a war, blood matting hair to his brow and dried into his dark clothing. His eyes looked tired. Oh, so very tired. "Ah, Rania. Hello." He dropped the stack of papers he was looking at on the desk before him and sighed. "It looks like Zharkus has been supplementing his forces with mercenaries. I've already sent orders that they're to continue to receive their pay if they acknowledge that he no longer commands them and support whoever ends up with the regency." His voice sounded tired too, strained to the breaking point.

"Wouldn't that be you, Tal?" She tried to make her voice soothing, though such a tone was unfamiliar to her lips.

He shook his head. "Only until this mess gets sorted. I've no desire to set up shop permanently." He looked in disgust over the mess atop the desk. "Right now, my biggest concern is figuring out how deep Zharkus's treachery went, and how to counter it. Hopefully Kyril will wring some useful information out of him soon."

"You've changed since I saw you last," Rania murmured, and realized the truth of it as she spoke the words. There had been a sense of innocence, an idealistic naïveté, in his speech and manner when they'd first met, but now there was a hardness in those cold blue eyes of his, a guarded tightness about the lips. House Jerak's treason must have hit him hard.

Tal chuckled humorlessly. "Yes, I suppose I might have. I've had a sobering dose of reality since then." His eyes stopped roaming the mess covering the desk and settled on her again as he forced a laugh. "Would you listen to me? Just a handful of weeks since last I've seen you, and here I'm talking like it's been years. I *am* glad to see you again, though. I hoped you'd come. Are you going to stay, or did you just come for the sword?"

Rania leaned over, face only inches from Tal's, eyes holding his, and said, "No. My place now is with you. And don't you mean *Kallevamar*?" His jaw dropped as she spoke the blade's name, and Rania held up a hand to forestall the questions she saw in his eyes. She pulled a chair over from across the table and sat directly in front of him, their knees almost touching. "I told you I had things to explain, and now seems as good a time as any."

"The first thing you'll be wondering is how I know the sword we rescued this morning is one of the Blades of Unity." Rania took a deep breath, mentally bracing herself for the recollection of unpleasant memories. "Fifteen years ago, the night Felmorinen fell, my mother sent me out of the city with a handful of her most trusted guards to protect me. Just before she sent me away, she gave me a book that she said I had to take with me. It was the biggest secret ever, she told me." A bittersweet smile crossed Rania's face at the remembrance of those last moments with her mother. "I did as she asked, of course, but I wouldn't understand why it had been so important until several years later when I finally worked up the courage to read that secret book."

"Everyone knows that House Amoran was charged to defend Felmorinen's secrets, and they assume that meant the ancient texts Anakara studied from and the notes she took on her own research." Rania shook her head. "While that was part of our duty, the secret we were really there to guard was the book my mother gave me. It was one of Anakara's personal journals, a place where she recorded her private thoughts."

"I'd imagine it reveals a very different woman from the one history remembers," Tal commented. When Rania cocked her head questioningly at him he explained, "I told you I spoke with Trazeri's shade. Kyril conjured the spirit when the sword was stolen because we had to find out why Kherzul wanted it so badly. Trazeri refused to speak to Kyril because he was Jhessaillian, and would only talk to me. He spoke of other things besides the sword, too. He talked about the Order, and their prophecy, and the things he and Anakara had done. He seemed regretful, perhaps a bit bitter, but nothing at all like the monster that the histories would have led me to believe him to have been. I'd not be surprised after what he told me to learn that Anakara was likewise very different from what was recorded of her."

"I'd been meaning to ask you how you came to speak with Trazeri," Rania murmured. "You would find that the contents of Anakara's journal confirm your suspicion, were you to read it. But even more remarkable is its last page, which she wrote to her descendants. One can't shake the feeling that she had some idea of what would eventually happen to her, and some of what would take place after she was gone. It explains what *Kallevamar* is, and charges us with protecting its secret. None of us, nor anyone else, was to lay claim to it until one came who would wield it by right. I never saw how that could be possible, but now here you are, and my family's duty is finally fulfilled. My mother would be proud of that, I think."

Tal shifted uncomfortably in his chair. "Rania..."

"Wait," she said, "there's more I have to tell you. After Felmorinen fell I waited outside the city, watching the men who'd attacked gather and burn their dead before leaving. I waited for a whole day after they'd gone to be sure none of them were still there. Then I snuck back in, hoping against hope to find that my mother or father still lived. That was when Muzash found me. He'd been living in seclusion in the Felmorr, and had come to investigate after noticing all the refugees fleeing out of the mountains. I told him my story and why I'd come back. He wouldn't let me go into the castle, though. He'd already been there, and found everyone dead. Such sights weren't for the eyes of a child, he said. I started to cry then. Muzash didn't say anything; he just held my hand while I wailed away my grief. When I was finished, he told me not to worry, that he'd take care of me, and he led me to the cave that he'd made his home. He fed me, clothed me, finished my schooling. He was like the grandfather I'd never known. From the moment I learned who he was, I begged him to teach me to be a warrior like him so I could avenge my parents. He kept saying that I was too young but that when the time came, he would teach me. Four years later, shortly after I turned twelve, he made good on that promise."

Rania's eyes grew distant as she continued, "Muzash pushed me hard. From the very first, we practiced with sharpened blades, and when I made the same mistake too many times he'd not hesitate to leave me a scar to remind me. 'Sharp swords teach sharp lessons,' he said. But no matter how hard he pushed, I always tried to push myself harder. During our practice he was always so stern and cold, but after he always seemed haunted, guilty. The reason for his moods remained a mystery to me until almost the very end. Finally, when I was nineteen, he told me I was ready to take the oaths and become Battleborn, and asked me if I was sure that I wanted to. When I replied that I was, he sat me down and shared with me the second terrible secret that I would have to carry."

"Muzash was the last bearer of an enormous responsibility passed from Shevestra'ka to Shevestra'ka since before the Great Purge. He'd agreed to teach me because he knew his time was growing short and he needed a protégé to pass the duty on to. Although he'd trained many an Armslord over the years, none of them had proven suitable to inherit the task that Muzash had been entrusted with. He apologized to me for having to lay this burden upon me, but he had no one else. After explaining it all to me, he passed on to me the entirety of the Warrior Soul he carried within him as has been done for every Shevestra'ka to carry this secret. He died in the course of that passing, just as he'd told me would happen. I made a pyre for his body and set it alight at the next dawn, fulfilling my Master's last request of me, and then I took up the burden that he'd left for me." Rania drew her sword and laid it across her knees. "Tal, this is *Edyamar*."

Talaren stared dumbfounded at the weapon in Rania's lap. "All this time," he said quietly when he could finally find words, looking up into her eyes, "you've known where both Blades of Unity were. I can't imagine how that must have weighed on you."

The Shevestra'ka nodded grimly as she resheathed *Edyamar*. "As far as I know, I was the first since they were forged. Now you're the second." She smiled hesitantly at him. "I'm glad there's finally someone else who knows. It was so lonely, Tal. Lonely, and more frightening than I'd care to admit."

"Because the Blades of Unity coming together could be taken as a sign that the Jhessaillian Prophecy is nearing culmination," Tal expressed what Rania hadn't spoken. "I think I begin to understand why you were so concerned about that earlier. Is it because of *Kallevamar* that you intend to stay with me now?"

"In part, though there's more to it than just that," Rania replied. "I think fate brought me to Val Zherrane when it did so that I could meet you. I believe we're meant to fight this fight together." Perhaps this wasn't the best time to tell him about the vision, judging by the skepticism she saw in his eyes. Better to try using reason to persuade him of what she saw so clearly. "Doesn't it seem odd that I should meet you just in time for you to be sent off after, and made protector of, the Blade of Unity whose secret my family was trusted to guard? That I should just happen to be the bearer of its counterpart? Or that in pursuing you when I found out about it, you led me to finally learn who it was that gave the orders that brought about my parents' deaths?" With that thought, Rania felt the pain and anger from that terrifying night stealing over her again, filling her. "Even if I'm wrong, even if all those things are just wild coincidence, that's still more than enough for me to want to stay by your side. Helping you fight Kherzul seems like my best chance to finally avenge their murder."

Tal shied back from the raw fury that blazed from her eyes, but his own gaze softened as he asked, "You never knew until now who was responsible for the attack?"

Rania shook her head. "Until today I'd thought it was Shebedar, and that any possibility of vengeance had been stolen from me when he was assassinated. The only clue I had was this." She drew the dagger she wore at her side and held it out. Stamped on the pommel was the bear's claw sigil of the Bhellan Royal Guard. "I took it from one of the soldiers who killed the last of my guards that night." It was too much. From deep within, Rania felt the stirrings of all the anguish that had been absorbed by the Warrior Soul in the past few years beginning to well up. *Gods, not now! I don't want him to see this!* She stood abruptly, intending to flee, but there was no time. Her grip tightened around the dagger as she tried desperately to fight the wave of suffering back down, to maintain her composure through the inner assault.

Tal noticed how her face paled, though, the glimmer of tears at the corners of her eyes. He got to his feet as well and laid a reassuring hand on her arm. "I'm sorry, Rania. You don't have to talk about it any more. I know it hurts. I... I'm sorry."

Rania felt herself losing her internal struggle, felt her resistance beginning to buckle. She wrapped her free arm around Tal's neck and sagged against him as the shuddering wave of pain and loss engulfed her, tore at her, tried to scour away her sense of herself. She clung to him as to life itself, burying her face in his shoulder and gritting her teeth trying now only not to cry out. The hand that still clutched the dagger hung limply at her side.

Tal put his arms gently around her. "For what it's worth, Rania, I promise that Zharkus will see justice for his betrayal and the secrets he kept for our enemy. I can't guarantee you'll get a chance at Kherzul, but if there's any way I can help make it so, I will."

When at last the blood-drenched attack on her senses subsided, Rania took several deep breaths before pushing herself back from Tal. She smiled abashedly at him, hoping the effect wasn't ruined by her reddened eyes. "Thank you, Tal. You're a good friend. It's been a long time since anyone has tried to help me, and that demands reciprocation. Is there anything I can do to help you?"

Tal looked at her cautiously, judging her state of mind, before wearily returning her smile with a nod. He gestured toward the document-strewn desk. "Sit down. Dig in. Help me figure out what we're up against."

14

Tidings Of War

"This may be something," Rania murmured, handing a page to Tal.

He took the sheet and studied it after taking a second to force his eyes to focus. They'd been poring over documents like this for hours now. The page Rania had found appeared to be a ledger of some sort, with columns of numbers written in a precise hand that they had come to recognize as Zharkus's.

"It appears that he was skimming from the city's tariff income. I think those are daily totals," Rania offered.

Tal nodded. If Rania was correct, then the Archduke had managed to stash away a handsome sum, indeed. "This is probably how he was paying for all his mercenaries." Based on what they'd found so far, as many as half the soldiers in Val Jerak right now were sellswords. That Zharkus had been so determinedly building up a military loyal to his coin rather than the sovereignty of Valeran troubled Tal deeply. It spoke of plots yet uncovered. It certainly explained why the soldiers at the barracks that morning had shown no hesitation in attacking a Valerite Lord.

Without so much as a knock of warning, the door to the study opened. Tal was halfway up out of his chair, hand reaching for *Kallevamar*, before he realized the newcomer was Kyril. As the Guardian carefully closed the door behind him, Tal settled back into his seat and exchanged a silent grin with Rania. Her reaction had been identical to his own.

Tal felt a sinking feeling deep in his gut at the solemn expression the Guardian wore. That Kyril didn't offer a joke at their jumpiness only compounded his concern. "You've learned something?"

"Yes," Kyril replied, "quite a bit actually. The son seems eager to ingratiate himself with me and is talking quite freely. I suspect that he hopes to avoid the headsman's block through his cooperation. Regardless of his reasons, he's providing me a useful lever to pry information from Zharkus, who has been trying much harder to keep information from me. I think I've managed to get the names of most of their co-conspirators in the city."

"But not all," Tal observed.

"No." Kyril shook his head. "Probably not all."

"That's not what brought you up here." Tal felt certain that the Guardian wouldn't have interrupted his questioning for a few names. No, this would be about something far more serious.

Kyril sighed heavily. "No. No, it's not. Zharkus's behavior has been all too confident for my tastes, and Joren mentioned some new plan is under way of which he apparently knew few details. I've been working on the Archduke

122

for the last couple hours to get it out of him, and I think I've got as complete a picture now as we're going to get."

The Guardian's gaze seemed to turn inward as he organized his thoughts. "Kherzul and Zharkus were relying on subterfuge and surprise to allow them to initiate a coordinated, multi-front attack on Valeran and bring her down in the space of weeks. When I brought news of Kherzul's activities before the Royal Council, Zharkus got nervous and initiated the first two stages of the plan. With your prevention, Tal, of the assassination attempt on King Garant and the recovery of the Blade of the Accursed, both have now failed. Zharkus's haste yielded us a significant benefit in that it ruined the synchronization between his own efforts and Kherzul's."

"And what was Kherzul's part in this plot to be?" Tal asked.

"Concurrent to Garant's assassination, Kherzul was to send an enormous force through the Felmorr Gap. Mercenaries loyal to Zharkus would be stationed at the Gap Gate with orders not to resist the Bhellan host. Kherzul's forces would bypass Val Jerak to strike deep within Valeran. With the King dead and a superior force on the field against a splintered resistance, they expected a swift victory."

"They'd probably have had it," Tal said grimly. "So we've ruined the first two parts of the plan. Is Kherzul still sending his forces?"

"His army is already on its way here," Kyril confirmed with a frown.

"How long?" Tal questioned flatly. "And how many?"

"Zharkus doesn't seem to know their exact numbers," Kyril replied. "'Overwhelming' is the only description he gives for their strength. They should be here in three weeks, maybe four if we're lucky."

"Three weeks," Tal murmured. Enough time that the men Garant was sending him should arrive first. That was something, at least. "Do we know how many men we've got in Val Jerak right now?"

"Based on the supply requisitions I've looked at, I'd guess three and a half to four thousand," Rania volunteered.

Tal mulled it over. He'd have around five thousand troops once the reinforcements from Val Zherrane arrived. He didn't know how many Zharkus's 'overwhelming' meant, but he suspected he'd be outnumbered by at least two to one. Best to plan for three to one, then. If fortune smiled and brought a smaller force against him, it would be easier to adjust his tactics that way. That they'd have to fight, he didn't even question, and he was glad that neither of his friends seemed to either. Rania, with a bloodthirsty glint in her eye, looked as though she might even be looking forward to it. Tal felt only resignation; whatever he accomplished, matters were only growing more difficult, the stakes higher.

He'd need assistance in preparing a strategy for the defense of the city. "Kyril, how much do we know about who we can and can't trust in the military command structure here?"

"Not as much as I'd like," the Guardian replied grudgingly. "I'm sure that I haven't rooted out all of Zharkus's cronies. There's a General and his assistant, Krovar and Jonfer, who the Archduke has mentioned having to work around. You can probably trust those two. Beyond them, I couldn't say for certain at this point."

Tal nodded. It was a start, at least. "Send a runner to find them and have them meet me here in two hours," he said. "I'm going up to the rookery. The King should be informed of what we've learned."

Kyril bowed his head acquiescingly. "Alright, Tal."

As the Guardian turned to let himself out, Tal added, "Oh, and Kyril?"

"Hmmm?"

"I don't mean to tell you how to go about your business, but squeeze Zharkus hard. I need to know what enemies may still be lurking about."

After the door had closed behind Kyril, Rania looked expectantly at Tal. "Do you need me to do anything?"

"Go take a bath."

"That's it? A bath?"

"Yes. I'll be paying my own visit to the baths as well," Tal replied. "We both look like we've spent the day in a slaughterhouse, and that's no way for us to meet this General."

"So I'm to join you for the meeting as well, then?" Rania raised a querying eyebrow.

"Of course. Krovar and Jonfer will be meeting me for the first time, and I want to take the opportunity to introduce them to my second as well." Tal grinned.

A wide smile bloomed on Rania's face. "You're making me part of your command?"

Tal shrugged. "If you're going to stay with me, you might as well make yourself useful. I need someone I'm certain can be trusted, and at the moment that means you or Kyril. Our shared training makes you the obvious choice."

A thoughtful frown darkened Rania's face. "Are you really sure the Guardian can be trusted? Remember, his first loyalty is to the Order, not Valeran."

Thinking back to his conversations with Kyril on the road, Tal replied, "I'm bearing that in mind. But for the time being, I think I understand his motivations. We can trust him."

"Then I'll just have to trust your judgment, sir." Rania gave him a mocking salute.

Tal rolled his eyes. "Don't you dare start calling me that."

"But sir, you're my commanding officer now." She blinked at him with an infuriating feigned innocence.

"And your commanding officer wants you to call him by name." Tal tried to keep his voice level.

"Is that an order?" Rania's voice was mirthful, her eyes twinkling with impudence.

Clearly, she wasn't going to let Tal win this exchange. He threw up his hands in an approximation of disgust before walking briskly to the door. "I'm off to the rookery now. I'll see you back here in two hours."

Rania's laughter followed him into the hall.

That two hours later found Tal seated behind Zharkus's hastily cleared desk in clean clothing, his finest black and silver shirt and coat with the Solus running fox bold on the breast. He was thankful for the finery, which he had found waiting for him in his saddlebags when he arrived at the baths. Apparently Rania had retrieved them from the Defender of the Pass for him. Tucked into the top of the packs he had found a note:

> Tal-
> I thought you might find these useful. Or had
> you been planning on attending the meeting
> in those bloody rags?
> -V

He'd chuckled upon finding it. Though it seemed to him it would ruin the fun if he let it show too much, Tal found Rania's impertinence refreshing.

She was right, though; clothing signifying his status, much as he usually preferred to eschew such, might prove useful as a subtle reminder to secure the cooperation of Krovar and Jonfer. Right now, more than anything else, Tal needed that cooperation. Planning and preparing for a battle required a staff and those two represented the only remotely trustworthy recruits aside from the Guardian and Shevestra'ka.

A short while after Tal had settled himself behind the desk, Rania let herself into the study. Gone was the frightful, blood-covered warrior woman from earlier in the day. She had exchanged her mail armor and harness of knives for the same simple gray outfit she had been wearing when they met. Her coppery hair, still slightly damp from the baths, had just the hint of a curl to it where it brushed the back of her neck. Her face, no longer streaked with crimson, had a healthy glow that complemented the brilliant green eyes marvelously. Tal's breath caught in his throat as he was struck all over again at how lovely this dangerous young woman was. The hints of her danger were still there, of course, for the alert eye to see: the familiarity with which she wore the ever-present sword and dagger, the lithe self-assuredness of her movements, the way her eyes scanned the entire room in a quick glance as she entered. Tal also noted that she wore her hair now with a single narrow braid on the left side tucked behind her ear, signifier of an Adept of Shevestra to those who knew the lore.

Rania noticed how his gaze lingered on her and gave him a slow smile as she crossed the room. "Yes, Tal?"

He cleared his throat in embarrassment. "I just wanted to thank you for getting my things from the inn. It was thoughtful of you."

"I had to go there anyway," Rania shrugged. "I left my own pack there this morning before going to find you." Her eyes sparkled as the smile grew to a grin. "And I'm still curious what you'd intended for us to wear in the absence of our bags."

"I'm sure that we could have had something dug up for us by the household staff, but this is decidedly better."

"I'm glad that my commander is pleased."

Tal glared at her. Rania giggled.

"And just what, pray tell, is so funny?" Tal smiled as he spoke to take the edge off his words.

"How easy it is to provoke you," Rania replied. "It's fun pulling your strings. Sir." She elbowed him playfully in the ribs as she sat down next to him.

"You're impossible, Rania."

"I try."

Someone knocked firmly on the door three times.

"Behave yourself," Tal admonished Rania.

She smirked impishly and stuck her tongue out at him. "If you insist."

Tal sighed and rolled his eyes before raising his voice to say, "Enter."

The first man who stepped through the door was massive and blocky like the mountains his city nestled under. Not an ounce of his bulk appeared to be fat. He had a bulldog face and the dark hair so rare in sons of the north peppered with gray. Following him was a tall, lanky man with a lantern jaw, a nose that appeared to have been broken several times, and a mane of reddish-blond hair tied back with a leather cord. Both wore military uniforms in the black and gold of House Jerak.

The big one bowed as his companion closed the door behind them. "General Krovar, milord," he said in a deep, resonant voice. "And my attaché, Lieutenant General Jonfer."

126

The lanky man bowed as he was introduced.

Tal nodded to each in turn before making his own introductions. "Lord Talaren Solus of Val Solus. My friend is Rania Amoran, formerly of House Amoran, now a sworn Adept of the Shevestra'ken."

Jonfer's eyes widened as Rania's name and family were spoken. Krovar gave a small start of surprise before turning to look at her more closely, his lips pursed thoughtfully.

"Rumor said you had a Shevestra'ka with you, Lord Solus, but can this be true? Does House Amoran still live?"

Rania returned the General's study with a grim smile. "If its having a single living daughter who doesn't claim the title of Marquess can be considered alive for a Noble House, then yes."

Krovar's eyes returned to Talaren. "Remarkable happenings follow you into our city, milord. Do you have any other surprises for us?"

"I'm afraid I do." Tal gestured to the two chairs opposite the desk from him. "Please, both of you, have a seat."

After they sat, Tal took a moment to look each man in the eye before speaking. "I assume you've both heard what happened this morning?"

Krovar nodded sadly. "It seems to be all that the folk in the Keep are talking about, probably in the city as well. I always thought the Archduke perhaps a bit overly ambitious, but never did I believe him capable of the base treachery he's charged with."

"Neither did I," Tal sighed, "even though our Houses have often been at odds with one another. I'm afraid the proof is incontrovertible at this point. My other companion, Guardian Damarrian, has been questioning Zharkus and he's as much as confessed his guilt by providing us with most of the details of his alliance with King Kherzul."

"Which means that Bhellus is hostile," Jonfer observed in a direct voice, his lowered brows lending him an angry mien.

"It gets worse," Tal said darkly. He fixed Jonfer with a stern gaze, then Krovar. "This information is not to be shared with anyone. I'll be forward with you: we don't know yet who can be trusted and who not, but we have reason to believe that both of you can be. If word of what we discuss here gets out, I'll have to assume I was wrong and throw you both in cells beside Zharkus. It's harsh, I know, but right now we can't be too cautious. If either of you have a problem with this, I suggest you leave now."

Tal paused for a few breaths, waiting. Neither man stirred a muscle. He nodded in approval. "Guardian Damarrian has uncovered some extremely troubling information in his questioning of the Archduke. In addition to orchestrating the theft of the Accursed's sword, he has admitted to arranging an attempt on the King's life which I prevented before being sent here. These crimes were part of a larger plot with the King of Bhellus, and though we've managed to foil Zharkus's efforts we must assume that Kherzul continues with his. The next part of their plan was for Bhellus to invade Valeran in force, and Zharkus tells us the armies are already on their way. We have three weeks to prepare a defense against them. I've called you here because I need help doing that."

Krovar's fists clenched angrily at the list of his Archduke's treasons. Jonfer frowned grimly.

"We've both devoted our lives to protecting Val Jerak," the General rumbled. "We certainly won't stop now because of a bit of political turmoil. Although I must ask," he bowed his head apologetically, "without intending any disrespect or insubordination, whether you have the authority to command Val Jerak's forces."

It was a reasonable question, and Tal had expected it. "No offense taken, General." He took the scroll case which he had once more tucked behind his belt and set it on the table in front of Krovar. "If you read this document, you'll find that King Garant granted me the authority to temporarily assume command of the city if I deemed it necessary in the course of my hunt for the stolen weapon. I invoked that authority upon finding that the Archduke was involved in the theft. Though this coming attack lies outside the mandate of the orders I was given, I've already dispatched a report back to Val Zherrane and am sure the King will confirm my authority. Additionally, I've got just over a thousand men on their way here under my command." Tal grinned wolfishly at the General. "And whether you accept my authority in the city or not, I offer their assistance."

Krovar gave a single quick bark of laughter. "Alright, milord, if you're so eager to draw steel with us I'll not stand in your way." He slid the scroll case back to Tal unopened. "I won't need to be looking at that. It sounds like you've got everything in order. Now, tell us about this Bhellan army."

"We don't know a great deal at the moment, certainly a lot less than I'd like." Tal carefully kept his voice neutral, a summation of facts and nothing more. *To command is to become the confidence of your army,* his father had taught him. *If the commander betrays any signs of uncertainty or anxiety, the morale of those he leads will suffer.* "We have an estimate of when they'll arrive, and know that they comprise a mighty host. It's likely that they'll be composed in large part by irregular troops. Beyond that, we're in the dark. One of our first courses of action must be to surreptitiously get some scouts into Bhellus for a better estimate of what we face."

"That would seem well-advised under the circumstances," Krovar agreed. "What other preparations do you want us to begin making, my Lord?"

"Supplies," Tal replied. "I want all of our men equipped as well as possible. No doubt we'll need plentiful stores of arrows, and we should begin stockpiling food and drink as much as possible in case it comes down to a siege. We also need to gather in lantern oil, pitch, anything that will readily take a flame, as much of it as possible."

"Flammables, my Lord?" Jonfer's question was shaded with confusion. "Why should we need those, beyond what's required for the siege engines?"

"I'll explain that later," Tal averred. "For now, I need you to trust me in that those could very well be the most important of the supplies we need to build up. We've little time, so we'll have to move quickly on this." Moving on, he turned his eyes back to Krovar. "It's my understanding that Zharkus had been transitioning the army over to a mercenary base."

The General grunted disapprovingly. "A decision I protested frequently, but the Archduke would hear none of it. I believed he felt that mercenaries would be more willing to fight the other Noble Houses in the event of a struggle over succession, although now his choice takes on much more sinister implications."

Tal nodded. "Mercenaries may be loyal only to coin, but now I control the purse strings. I've authorized their continuing payment so long as they recognize the change in leadership. What concerns me more is the soldiers they replaced. Those men could be a valuable resource to us. I want word circulated that any who want to re-enlist will be welcomed back with full restoration of their former rank and salary. Besides bolstering our forces for the coming battle, it'll be a useful step toward returning Val Jerak's forces to a more proper composition."

A slow smile spread across Krovar's face. "Lord Solus, I like the way you think," he declared. "We can have your offer announced on the morrow. If you like, I can also arrange for the men to carry word themselves to any former comrades they think might be interested."

"That sounds quite acceptable, General," Tal approved. "Those preparations should keep the both of you busy for a time. There's just one more matter I'd like to bring up tonight. I intend to go tomorrow morning and have a look at the field before the Gap and the city's fortifications to begin fashioning a battle strategy. I'd appreciate your joining me to offer any suggestions or insights you may have."

"It would be our pleasure," Krovar agreed.

"Excellent," Tal said with a nod. "I think that should be enough for us right now. Unless there are any concerns you'd like to raise, we should get some rest. Come the morning we'll have our work cut out for us."

"There's just one thing," Krovar said as he and Jonfer stood. He extended his hand across the desk to Tal. "I'd like to say that it'll be an honor to serve under the son of the Hero of the Gilden Hills."

Tal rose to his feet and took Krovar's hand in a firm grip. "Thank you, General. I only hope that I can live up to my father's name for your city."

"I'm sure you'll acquit yourself quite admirably, my Lord," Krovar replied reassuringly. "You seem to have a good head on your shoulders, and I daresay that your father's instruction shows in you." He nodded once, approvingly, before he and Jonfer bowed and let themselves out of the study.

Once the door had closed, Tal turned to Rania and raised an eyebrow at her. "You were certainly quiet," he observed.

Rania smiled. "I didn't want to interrupt when you seemed to be doing so well by yourself."

Tal shook his head with an explosive sigh. "Why does everyone have to be so bloody confident in me?"

Rania's lips creased downward at the corners in the face of his sudden outburst. "You don't think they should be?"

Tal shrugged. "I don't know. I have faith in what Master Malry and my father taught me, yes, but I've never led men into battle before. Until a few weeks ago I'd never even killed before! And now I have to lead men who don't know me in the defense of a city I'm barely familiar with against an army probably larger than mine, but the Gods only know how much larger! That's an awful lot of unknowns, Rania. Yet I seem to be the only one concerned by all of it." His shoulders slumped as he finished.

"It's true, these are troubling times," Rania replied gently. "The sort of times when people need to believe in something just to keep fear at bay." She captured his gaze with her depthless green eyes and held it. "You make it easy for people to believe in you, Tal. That's a rare and precious thing."

Tal gave her a wan smile. "But what am I supposed to believe in, Rania?"

"Believe in yourself. If you can do that then no matter what happens, you'll always have it to fall back on. If it helps, remember that Krovar has no doubt seen his share of battles, and he seems to have faith in you. I doubt that would be the case if you weren't doing something right." She gave him a warm smile. "I'm no fool either, and I believe in you as well. I believe that no matter what comes, you'll give everything you have to doing what you feel is best. As I see it, so long as you accomplish that, you can't truly fail."

"Keep fighting the good fight no matter the odds, eh?"

"Exactly," Rania nodded solemnly. "Just like the Shevestra'ka I feel in your spirit."

Tal smiled abashedly at what, coming from an Adept, he felt sure was high praise. "You're right, Rania. I'm sorry to have put my concerns on you like that. I think I just needed to share them with someone. Thanks for tolerating it."

"Not at all!" Rania laughed. "I'm glad you trust me enough to share your troubles. We each bear a Blade of Unity, and between us are the only people who know where both are. I think we're going to need to trust one another." She stood and took hold of his arm with a whimsical smile. "And right now I want to trust you to show me to the quarters I assume you've had prepared for us. Or do we have to sleep here? I don't think this floor would be very comfortable."

Tal chuckled at her shifting of the subject. With a playful twist to his lips he replied, "This way, my Lady," before leading her up to the rooms he had indeed asked be set aside for himself and his companions.

Tal stared silently at the field spread out below him from his vantage atop the city walls, envisioning masses of men maneuvering and clashing, killing and dying. Scenario after scenario played out in his mind, an entire campaign of battles all fought on the same field, as he pondered what tactics would serve him best.

Krovar and Jonfer had reported to his rooms early in the morning and after fetching Rania from the adjacent suite, they had set out to inspect Val Jerak's fortifications. Occupying the strategically vital point it did at the end of the Felmorr Gap, Tal was unsurprised to find that the city's defenses had been extraordinarily well constructed. The outer walls were tall and thick, built on a similarly large scale to what he had observed in the Keep. Rounded towers were spaced every couple hundred paces along the wall, and atop each one perched a squat, insect-like catapult. The gatehouses had both inner and outer gates along with portcullises, and murder holes lined the ceiling of each long arching passage through the walls. All to the good, by Tal's reckoning. Even against superior numbers, Val Jerak appeared to be quite defensible.

It was possible that they could hunker down in the city and let the assault break itself on the massive stone blocks of the wall. Tal shook his head with a frown, pushing the thought from his mind. Doing that risked a lengthy siege and the possibility of the Bhellan forces dividing to strike deeper into Valeran, as they had at the outset of the Bhellan Revolution. No, Tal would have to engage Kherzul's army and inflict enough damage that they would focus all their efforts here. Besides, hiding behind the walls to wait for the attack would be too predictable.

Unpredictability was key to winning a battle, Daron Solus had taught his son. *The instant an enemy can foretell your actions, you fight at a disadvantage. To prevent this, you must utilize surprise and deception. Use these to force your enemy to respond to you in a predictable fashion, and the advantage will shift to you.*

But how to do it? That was what troubled Tal. No matter the plan he came up with, there remained the lingering doubt of whether it would be sufficient to fool a more experienced commander.

He stopped on that thought, remembering another of his father's lectures: *The application of deception on the battlefield is itself deceptively simple. If you are near the enemy, appear to be far; if defending, appear to be on the attack. When your forces are weak, present the face of strength and when mighty show yourself to be meek and feeble.*

Perhaps Tal could take that principle one step further and actually turn his own greatest weakness to his advantage. As he began considering scenarios again in light of this idea, it felt as if a new and previously unexplored layer of strategy opened itself up to him. Yes, he believed it could work. A smile crept its way to his lips.

"General Krovar," Tal asked, "what's the maximum range of our catapults?"

"I'd say just a shade short of a hundred and fifty yards," Krovar replied after a moment's consideration.

Tal nodded. "Alright. When the Bhellans arrive, we'll meet them first at the Gap Gate." He'd spent enough time at the Gate already that he didn't need to see it this morning. It was good defensive ground, the wall almost as thick as the one around the city if not as tall, and the pass limited the number of foes who could attack at once. A small force would be able to hold their own there for a goodly amount of time and surely inflict far more than their own numbers in casualties on the attackers. "I expect that our positions there will eventually be overrun. Once the fight starts to go against us there, the men on the Gate will fall back and retreat to the city, and that's when the battle will truly begin."

Tal gestured to the field below. "When the Bhellans come through the Gap they'll find the bulk of our infantry waiting for them, just within range of the siege engines. I'm going to want as many men out there as possible, even if it weakens our defenses on the wall. We'll need to present them with a threat that can't be ignored and hopefully such a show of strength will convince them we've more men than we really do. We'll also need a strong presence on the field because the infantry's main purpose will be to hold the Bhellan advance as long as possible."

"While the catapults pummel their back ranks," Jonfer guessed with a wicked grin.

"Exactly," Tal confirmed. "If we can keep them from getting inside the arc of the catapults' stones long enough we should be able to bloody them badly. We'll hold the cavalry in reserve in the city to push the Bhellans back with a charge so the infantry can retreat if our losses become too great. They'll also be on hand if the enemy tries to flank us, then. When and if we're forced back into the city, we can reevaluate our tactics then."

"It seems a workable plan, my Lord," Krovar stated.

"Excellent," Tal said. "Have the orders sent to all our officers. I'd prefer they receive them within the day if possible."

Krovar's brow furrowed concernedly. "My Lord, are you..."

"Yes, I'm sure," Tal interrupted.

Rania frowned at him. "Tal, Zharkus and Kherzul almost certainly still have men in the command ranks we still don't know about. Aren't you worried they might get word of your plan to the enemy?"

Tal grinned. "No, Rania. I'm counting on it. The enemy will surely know that I'm in command here, and that I lack experience. They'll be ready to believe I could make such a mistake." He turned his eyes to Krovar. "General, what would you do faced with the situation I just described, assuming that you also knew the plan behind it?"

"The enemy will have the advantage of numbers?"

"Almost certainly."

Krovar thought for a few seconds. "Knowing that you'd overcommitted yourself and that your strategy hinged on inflicting maximal losses with the catapults, I'd probably exercise a lot less caution in attacking the forces in front of me. I'd throw everything at you all at once to obliterate your men and destroy your ability to defend the city. Chances are Val Jerak would fall swiftly after that."

"I agree," Tal said. "But wouldn't you be surprised to find that I had issued orders that morning for the cavalry to actually be waiting in the woods to attack your rear flank as soon as you did that?"

Krovar's jowls shook with a sudden burst of laughter. "Most devious of you, my Lord."

"Thank you," Tal murmured.

From the other side of the city, a horn issued a single deep note that echoed from the buildings. Tal and his companions turned to gaze in the direction of the sound.

"It's the western gate," Krovar said. "That was the alert for approaching soldiers."

"Hostile?" Tal asked.

The General shook his head. "They would have sounded two notes."

A broad smile appeared on Tal's face. "We can plan further appropriate responses for my little trap later. Right now, we should get back to the Keep. I believe my reinforcements have just arrived."

15
The Wages Of Treachery

Deep beneath the Ducal Keep of Val Jerak, Archduke Zharkus Jerak wallowed in misery at the turn his fortunes had taken. Once one of the most powerful men in Valeran, he could hardly credit that he had fallen so far so suddenly. *And it's all because of that wretched upjumped Solus whelp,* he thought bitterly. House Solus had been a thorn in his side for two decades, ever since Daron Solus, then but a Baron, had routed the Bhellan armies that had marched right past Val Jerak while their comrades laid siege to House Jerak's seat of power. In doing so, Daron had gained such prestige that his House had been raised from a Barony to a Dukedom, and the new Duke's political clout came to surpass that of Zharkus's own House. Ever since then Zharkus had struggled to regain his House's position of ascendancy against the seemingly ever-rising popularity of the Hero of the Gilden Hills.

To make matters worse, Duke Daron had in the use of his new political strength ignored Zharkus's guiding principle that the primary purpose of power was to perpetuate itself. He had advocated and voted for provisions within the Royal Council that strengthened the nation and throne even when they might harm his own interests and holdings, and incongruously in so doing had only deepened the respect he was held in by his peers.

Zharkus had believed it impossible for anyone to be as great a bother to him as Duke Daron Solus until the son of his political nemesis, that wretched Lord Talaren Solus, had proven him wrong. It had been bad enough that the young Solus's accomplishments in training to become an Armslord had gained him the adoring attentions of the Royal Court and eclipsed anything Zharkus's own son Joren achieved. But now Talaren had proven himself to be far more infuriating than his father by ruining years of careful planning and consigning Zharkus to this darkened pit and the treatment of a common criminal. No, worse than that; no mere criminal would have to endure the prying, questioning attentions of that damned Guardian.

Grudgingly, the Archduke had to respect the talents of Guardian Damarrian. The man was a consummate interrogator, pulling information from his prisoner with an ease that made Zharkus feel an infant trying to struggle with an armored warrior. The Guardian used no implements, no affliction of physical agony to provoke the responses he desired. When his patience was tried, he would conjure up visions of the things he *could* do, that he *might* do if cooperation wasn't forthcoming. The efficacy of such tactics was undeniable. Yet even that wasn't what made the Guardian so frighteningly efficient at his task. It was the uncannily knowing way his dark eyes looked on Zharkus, the way he made statements instead of asking questions, seeming to know everything already and only needing Zharkus to respond for the formality of confirmation.

The first interrogation session had set the tone for those to follow. Zharkus had languished in his cell for no more than an hour before the Guardian had returned wearing a sardonic grin as he entered through the barred iron door. "My, my, your Grace, you've been quite the naughty boy. Stealing state property, attempting the murder of your sovereign, and then there's that unpleasantness with Lord Solus this morning. You were worried he'd discover that you've been plotting with a hostile foreign power, weren't you? Ah, yes, that particular indiscretion has been going on for quite some while. Why, you even helped provide cover for the toppling of a noble House that never did a thing to provoke you at the bidding of King Kherzul! Although I suppose he was just the Prince of Bhellus at the time, wasn't he? Let's start at the beginning then, shall we?"

No matter how Zharkus tried to deny the Guardian's pronouncements, the Jhessaillian had plowed relentlessly onward with his "questioning" of things he already seemed to know until he battered down any hope of resistance. To his great humiliation, Zharkus found himself telling of how he had been approached by Prince Kherzul of Bhellus during the signing of the Felmorr Accords that had ended hostilities following the Bhellan Revolution.

Kherzul had been young then, young enough that the Archduke was at first unimpressed by the Prince's talk of alliance. He'd been persistent, though, and finally Zharkus had grown impatient and snapped at Kherzul, demanding to know why he should be tempted by alliance with a Prince who was barely grown.

"I may be young yet and my father may hold the reins of state," Kherzul had replied with a predatory light in his eyes, "but a wise man plans for the long term and my father won't reign forever. His rule may even prove to be quite short lived. An understanding for the future could reap profound benefits for the both of us. I have great plans, you see. Great enough that a few well-chosen others may be able to benefit from them as well."

Zharkus had been impressed by the audacious ambition that was oh-so-thinly veiled in that response. Intrigued, he'd decided to play along with Kherzul's proposition. If worst came to worst and this "ally" became a liability, Zharkus could arrange for Shebedar to be informed of his son's plans and reap the gratitude of the King of Bhellus.

He'd heard very little from Kherzul after that until four years later when the Prince of Bhellus, beginning to become a power in his own right, had come to Val Jerak to negotiate the normalization of trade between his nation and Valeran. During his visit, Kherzul had requested a private meeting with Zharkus. When his request was granted, he reminded the Archduke of their agreement and then explained a plan he had conceived of to smuggle a small force through the Felmorr Gap, sneak into Felmorinen through the lightly guarded western passes, and seize the secrets left behind by the Undying. To ensure it's success, Kherzul needed only for Zharkus to look the other way when his men, disguised as civilians, passed through Val Jerak. Though the plan was brash and spoke of an ambition beyond even what Zharkus had already attributed to the Prince, it had its merits from the Archduke's perspective. It was risky, true, but most of the risk would be assumed by Kherzul and if he failed, a bit of care early on would insure that Zharkus's part in the plot could be traced back to the scapegoat of his choice. And if the Prince succeeded, it could open the door to enormous power for him, power that would make their alliance far more useful to Zharkus. He agreed to lend his assistance, and thus had his partnership with Kherzul begun.

The Guardian had then turned his line of inquiry to the present, focusing on the details of the current arrangements between the Archduke and Bhellan King. Again Zharkus attempted to resist divulging any information, and for his efforts was rewarded with his first experience of Damarrian's ability to commandeer his prisoner's senses using Order-trained trickery. Assailed by seemingly endless visions of heart-stopping terror, Zharkus had finally capitulated and told the Jhessaillian of the army Kherzul's last communiqué had said was coming to Val Jerak. This disclosure had earned him a brief respite from his interrogation, but the Guardian returned again later intent on wringing out the identities of Zharkus's allies in the city.

In the two weeks or more Zharkus estimated he had been in the dungeon, Damarrian had secured most of those names. It had gotten to the point where each name Zharkus managed to hold back, every tidbit of information kept secret, seemed a major victory. Those few operatives of his who still remained unexposed represented his greatest hope. Perhaps one of them could stage a rescue attempt or even get word to Kherzul, that the King of Bhellus might assist him somehow. They were slim hopes, but they were better than having to accept that all of his efforts had come to naught.

The sound of approaching footsteps roused the Archduke from his self-pitying thoughts and filled him with dread. Had the Guardian come to pick his brain again? The prospect caused him to press himself back into the darkened corner of the cell, his eyes glued to the narrow grill in the door.

Zharkus nearly breathed a sigh of relief when the face that peered into his cell was that of a poorly shaven guard wearing a leering grin. "Dinner time, yer Grace," the man said mockingly, and his face disappeared from the grill as he bent down to slide a wooden bowl through a low slot in the bottom of the door. Zharkus could hear the guard chuckling as his footsteps receded back down the hall.

Once more the Archduke regretted not having put any of his people down here in the event of just such a situation as this. Instead, he had used guard duty in the dankness of the dungeons as a punishment for soldiers who displeased him. No, none of the men down here held him in any great esteem. Most of them seemed sadistically amused to have him as a guest in one of their cells.

Zharkus was crawling across the floor to the bowl of unappetizing gruel when he heard from down the hall a sharp exclamation from the guard: "Who's there?" He froze in place, straining his ears against the darkness for any sound.

A sudden, startled yell cut off with a groan. There was a scraping sound as of boots scrambling for purchase on stone and then a thump.

Silence.

His hunger temporarily forgotten, Zharkus dragged himself to his feet and pressed up against the door to his cell, trying desperately to peer down the corridor. He very nearly jumped out of his skin when the pair of burning coals appeared right in front of him.

"Hello, Archduke." The voice sounded a breathy, rasping whisper. The eyes faded and disappeared, and the darkness within the cell seemed for a moment to gather and congeal, swirling about with a wholly unnatural sense of viscosity until it began to resolve itself into a humanoid form. The fiery red eyes re-manifested themselves, and a spectre stood within the cell in front of Zharkus.

"It's about time you came," Zharkus said haughtily, drawing himself up straight with all the dignity he could muster in such squalid surroundings. Doing so required a considerable exertion of effort. This was the first time he'd encountered one of Kherzul's spectral minions face to face, and he had to admit that the experience was decidedly unnerving. *This is an ally*, he had to remind himself every few seconds. "I was beginning to think your master would let me rot here. Now, how are you getting me out?"

The spectre shook its head, a hideous wheezing laughter issuing from the depths of its shadowy form. "You are a fool, Zharkus," it said at last. "You've acted rashly, and failed in the tasks given to you. Your paltry efforts have made matters more difficult for our master."

"Be that as it may," Zharkus bristled, "I've faithfully upheld my bargain with Kherzul. I've risked greatly for his gain. It's no fault of mine that our plans were thwarted by Lord Solus."

Again that laughter from beyond the grave. "Poor Zharkus," the spectre taunted, "brought down in ignominious defeat by an untried fledgling Lord. An appropriate end for the ambitions of a fool, don't you think?"

The Archduke glared balefully at the tenebrous man-shape, his fear completely subsumed by indignation. "I remind you, you piteous ghost," he growled acidly, "that I am an ally of your King! Cease your prattling and free me as you were sent to do!"

"You mistake the reason for my presence, Archduke," the spectre rasped. "King Kherzul does not suffer foolishness or failure. He certainly doesn't ally himself with them. You've shown yourself to be a liability, Zharkus, a liability to be purged before you have the chance to become any more of a hindrance."

Terror welled up in Zharkus at the cold finality of the last statement. "You wouldn't dare!" he gasped, backing away from the spectre. Rough-hewn stone stopped his retreat within three steps. "Guards!" he bellowed at the top of his lungs. Where was that cursed Guardian now? Where was the young Solus with his spectre-slaying blade?

"The guards are dead," whispered the spectre with relish as it advanced slowly, inexorably. "But fear not - you'll be with them shortly."

A dark hand shot out to grasp Zharkus about the neck. The Archduke tried to gasp, but his throat constricted shut with the deathly cold that emanated from the grasping claw. His feet scrabbled desperately to carry him away from his assailant, but in vain. He reached out in an attempt to wrench the arm away from him, but his own hands found nothing to grasp, only the bone-numbing iciness of death that was even now spreading through the rest of his body. His mouth worked franticly, producing a croaking rattle and nothing more. Vision receded as if he were looking up from the bottom of a well, and at the top there was nothing to be seen but a pair of angry red stars. Then night swallowed even the stars and the void reached out to envelop Zharkus.

16
Though The Darkness May Overwhelm...

I should've known this would happen, Tal thought. *I should've sent him to Val Zherrane for trial after the first day.*

The cell was filled with a stomach-churning odor, voided bowels mingled with the cloying stench of death. Zharkus's passing appeared not to have been pleasant. The Archduke's glazed eyes bulged with the horror of his final moments, his swollen tongue hanging from a mouth frozen in a rictus snarl. The flesh of his neck was blackened, as were his hands. The bodies of the guards had been in much the same condition.

"And no sign of Joren?" Tal asked.

Beside him, Kyril sighed. "Aside from the snapped lock on the door to his cell, nothing."

Tal turned his eyes away from the ruin of the Archduke to look at his friend. "One of Kherzul's spectres?" he asked quietly.

The Guardian nodded. "That would seem to be the most plausible explanation."

Tal shook his head in bewilderment. "But why? Why kill Zharkus and save Joren? For that matter, how did they get Joren out? Can those things pull a man through shadows with them?"

Kyril's voice was troubled as he replied, "I'm afraid I don't know the answer to either question, Tal."

"Even if they can't, we don't have the resources to spare to search for Joren," Tal fumed, incensed at his feeling of impotence at this new development. And just when everything had seemed to be getting more managable!

"No, we probably don't," Kyril agreed.

"Well, nothing for it but to go on," Tal murmured. He turned to the guards who stood in the hall behind him and Kyril. "Have Zharkus's body removed and prepared for burial in his family tombs. Let his spirit face his ancestors with what he did to their name. That much justice, at least, we can give him."

The guards saluted as Tal swept past them with Kyril in tow. This had been a dark opening to the day. Hopefully the rest of it would get better.

Such hopes were not to be, Tal realized as soon as he saw the ashen look on General Krovar's face when he and Kyril arrived in the study for the morning briefing. Next to the General, Jonfer looked little more cheerful. Rania was also already there, seated at the desk, her stiff posture bespeaking irritation. Armslord Malry, who had arrived with the men from Val Zherrane two weeks ago, turned his head from perusing the books on a shelf against the wall to give his former student an acknowledging nod.

"Finally," Rania breathed as Tal entered. "They wouldn't say what was wrong until you got here." She took in the grim scowls Talaren and the Guardian wore and shot a sharp look at Tal. "What's happened?"

"Zharkus is dead," Tal replied, "and Joren has disappeared." He crossed the room and sat down beside Rania, looking Krovar in the eyes. "So what's your bad news, General?"

"One of our scouts has returned," Krovar answered in a voice that strained for calm. "He found the Bhellan army, and reports that they're no more than ten days away."

"And how many are they?" Tal asked, his guts tightening with dread.

"Our man said it was hard to estimate their numbers with so many, but he put them at upwards of twenty-five to thirty thousand." Krovar's voice cracked as he spoke the number.

Tal felt as though he'd been struck in the gut with a warhammer. He'd anticipated facing odds of two or even three to one and prepared the others accordingly, but five or six to one? How could they hope to stand against that?

"He also reported that the bulk of the army appears to be composed of the walking dead," the General continued. "You can smell them from over a mile away, he says. I take it those would be the irregular troops you told us about?"

Tal nodded. "I'm sorry I couldn't tell you earlier, but the information was restricted to the Royal Council." It required a monumental effort to keep the dismay that coiled about his heart from entering his voice. "Kherzul has acquired the Sephiral powers that the Undying once commanded."

"Gods save us," Jonfer uttered.

"Unfortunately, I don't think the Gods will be much help," Tal said as firmly as he could. "We're going to have to save ourselves. I grant you that our enemy is far stronger than any of us had feared, but we can't let that break our resolve. I sent notice to the Noble Houses that Val Jerak would be coming under attack, and I'm sure that they'll be sending us help. We just have to hold out long enough for them to arrive." Desperately, he tried to believe his own words.

"Where do we stand with our stockpiles of oil and pitch?" Tal asked. The best thing for everyone's morale now, his own included, would be to focus on preparing the city for the assault.

"We've brought in every spare drop to be found," Krovar answered. "There's enough to light the city for months."

"You still haven't told us what you want with it all." There was an accusatory undertone to Jonfer's statement.

140

"The histories tell us that one of the Undying's favorite tactics when besieging a city was to reanimate the dead of that city to attack the defenders from behind. Considering its effectiveness, I see no reason why Kherzul won't try the same." Tal forced a vicious grin. "When he does, I want to be sure that every graveyard in the city is piled high with oil-soaked wood so we can incinerate the corpses as they rise."

A startled look passed across the Lieutenant General's face before he laughed ruefully, raking a hand through his hair. "I thought at first that you might be mad for making such an odd request without explaining why, but I see now I was mistaken. You truly are your father's son, Lord Solus. With thinking like that, we just might be able to hold the walls long enough after all."

"I thank you for the complement, Jonfer, but all I've done is counter an advantage of Kherzul's. If we're to defend Val Jerak, we need to create some advantages of our own. I want everyone thinking about how to do that. We know more about the enemy today than we did yesterday. Let's build on that."

"We should be cautious in controlling the spread of this new information," Malry spoke quietly. "Where is this scout now?"

"We've taken that into account, honorable Armslord," said Krovar, "and given the man comfortable rooms here in the Keep, along with orders to speak to no one of what he's seen."

Tal nodded appreciatively to both men. He'd been so concerned with what to do next that rumor control had completely slipped his mind. "What's the state of the troops, Malry?" The Armslord had been drilling daily with the infantry since his arrival, occasionally with Rania's assistance.

"They're solid," replied Tal's old instructor. "Had we more time I could probably enhance their skills further, but as it stands I think you'll be quite pleased with their performance."

"Excellent," Tal said. He was grateful for Malry's presence. Long experience had made the Armslord a canny judge of troop strength, and Tal was well aware of his talent for bringing out hidden strengths in those he trained.

"Now, unless there's anything else we need to deal with this morning," Tal paused for a second and when nobody spoke he went on, "let's get the preparations at the graveyards underway. If anyone comes up with any new ideas for our strategy, bring them straight to me or to the next briefing session. We've much yet to do before the Bhellans arrive, but you've all been doing a superb job. I'm confident that when the time comes, we'll be ready." Whether that would be enough he wasn't sure, but he kept those doubts to himself.

Tal leaned against a parapet atop the highest tower of the Ducal Keep. A cold wind blew down from the mountaintops, whipping the bottom of his cloak about his legs. He shivered at the blast of icy air, but continued staring moodily down at the field between Val Jerak and the Felmorr Gap. All too soon that field would be flooded by a sea of the walking dead, a host like no other the North had seen since the Undying's time.

I wonder if this is how the commanders who fought Anakara's armies felt. The stories from that time romanticized those men, lionizing their bravery and heroism in fighting against insurmountable odds. *Will history say the same of me?* Tal didn't feel particularly brave or heroic. What he felt was trapped and disillusioned. He could still hardly bring himself to believe the depths of treachery House Jerak had fallen to under Zharkus, and all for nothing more than crass political gain. Was that all that nobility came to in the end – a cutthroat quest for ever greater power over others, principle and loyalty be damned? Couldn't there be a better way, a way that didn't purchase power with the betrayal of the ideals instilled in him by his father and Armslord Malry? But what use would honor and righteousness be to him now, faced with an army he dared not hope to defeat? They certainly hadn't altered the fates of those men who had so courageously faced the same circumstances against the Undying. Most of them had in death become part of the army they'd fought against.

Still, the part of his mind where Daron Solus's teachings resided refused to give in to defeat before the battle was even joined. There was no such thing as an unbeatable force, his father had said. The challenge lay only in determining how to effectively engage the enemy with the resources you had and from the most strategically viable position. Tal had struggled mightily to do that, but he was unconvinced that his efforts thus far would be enough. There had to be something more he could do, but what that could possibly be eluded him.

His eyes lingered on the mountains around the Gap, following the sheer slopes up to the ice-encrusted heights. If only the snows would come! Winter's deep drifts typically made the Felmorr Gap impassable until the spring thaw, and that would grant enough time to gather a more appropriate force to repel the Bhellan attack.

Tal shook his head angrily at himself. Such thoughts were a waste of hope. Though the first snowfall should come soon, it would take a near constant blizzard from now until the Bhellans' arrival to prevent their passage.

He heard the trap door behind him open and then close again without breaking his reverie. A few seconds later he saw out of the corner of his eye the black of Kyril's Guardian uniform. His friend stood quietly beside him for a long while before finally speaking.

"I think the Shevestra'ka is worried about you."

Tal turned his eyes to the Guardian's face, which was calmly composed and free of any telling expression, and then looked back to the mountains. "You know, Kyril, we're all probably going to die here."

"It's possible. Does that bother you?"

Tal shrugged. "A little bit. What really troubles me is what'll happen afterwards. If we fail here, Valeran will likely fall."

"Likely," the Jhessaillian agreed.

Tal spun abruptly to face Kyril again and fumed, "How can you be so calm about it? Do you know something I don't? I know I've become involved in your Prophecy by carrying this sword. Does it offer you some sort of assurance of our victory? If it does, please tell me."

"I'm afraid you misunderstand how prophecy works, Tal," Kyril replied. "It doesn't predict so much as it guides. Think of it as a map to the future, a set of conditions that must be met to effect a desired outcome. An event being predicted doesn't guarantee it's actuality. If it did, the Order wouldn't be needed to safeguard it."

"Then what does assure you?"

"You said it yourself. Bearing *Kallevamar* has drawn you into Jhessial's Prophecy. I believe that all of the prior conditions have been successfully met. I also believe that it would not needlessly confront you with a challenge you're not equal to."

Tal contemplated for only a heartbeat before accusing, "That's circular reasoning!"

Kyril grinned at him. "I know. Infuriating, isn't it? That's how they teach us to think in the Order."

Tal shook his head. "You're all madmen," he muttered. "But while we're on the subject, what has the Order taught you that might be useful to us in the battle?"

"Well," Kyril said, "my greatest talent lies in the manipulation of light and sound, the sort of tricks I used to convince the spectres hunting me on my way to Val Zherrane that they'd managed to kill me. I suspect, however, that you'll be more interested in my ability to use the Sephira as a weapon. Although I've not concentrated on that aspect as much as most Guardians who serve in the Hand of Jhessail, I've had the benefit of instruction in those arts that we restrict only to members of the Order and can call fire and lightning as well as more subtle forces to strike down our enemies. Such exertions will eventually exhaust me, but until they do I'll be able to inflict greater losses on our foes than all of our siege weaponry combined and with much better accuracy."

"How close do you have to be to use those abilities?" Tal queried.

"I can target anything I can see effectively," came the reply, "beyond that, any Sephiral act becomes progressively more difficult and taxing."

"So right here would be an ideal position for you," Tal mused, gazing out to take in the commanding view of the field again. Once more his eyes followed the mountains up to where they met the sky. "Light and sound," he murmured as he felt a new idea beginning to take shape. Excitedly he turned back to the Guardian and demanded, "How loud of a noise can you create?"

Kyril shrugged. "I've never really tested," he said, "but I would imagine thunderous. Louder than that, probably. Sound doesn't require a great deal of effort to produce." He narrowed his eyes at Tal. "Why would a loud noise be useful to you? Distraction?"

Wordlessly, Tal pointed to the icy heights of the mountains around the Gap.

Kyril looked to where Tal was pointing and drew in a sharp breath. Then he threw back his head and shook with delighted laughter, so hard tears came to his eyes. "Genius, Tal," he finally gasped out between laughs, "absolute genius."

Talaren's responding grin was vicious, and for what seemed the first time in a long while his feelings matched the expression. "We'll defend the Gap Gate as planned, only when we're finally overrun we'll have a surprise ready for the Bhellans. I'll signal you by horn when all our people are clear, and then you make the most thunderous noise you can among the peaks. We'll shake the mountains down on top of them and bury the bulk of their army before they even see our main force." Tal allowed himself a bit of laughter. "By Shevestra, we may even be able to make this a fair fight!"

Kyril slapped his friend on the back. "I think you just might live to be hailed the hero of Val Jerak after all, Tal."

"Maybe," Tal beamed back. Just maybe. "You said you thought Rania was worried for me?"

The Guardian nodded, unruffled by the return to his first comment. "It's the way she watches you, as if she wants to help but doesn't know if she can." With a considering gaze on the young nobleman, he asked curiously, "How long have you known her, Tal?"

"I first met her earlier in the same day I found you half-dead on the road into Val Zherrane."

"Really?" Kyril sounded surprised. "The two of you act like long-lost friends."

"Sometimes it feels like we are," Tal said wonderingly, recalling the feeling of Rania's watching eyes that first day. "Maybe it's because of the shared experience of our training. Becoming an Armslord leaves it's mark, and leaves it deep."

"Perhaps," Kyril said lazily, and then cut his eyes slyly at Tal. "Are you sure that's all it is? She's quite the striking young woman."

"Just what're you implying?"

"If you can't figure it out by now, I despair of your ever doing so," the Jhessaillian laughed.

"I really don't think now is the time to be thinking about that, Kyril."

"There's never any time but now, regardless of what else may be happening," Kyril replied sagely. "Think about that, Tal."

The young nobleman nodded slowly, mentally reviewing his brief acquaintance with Felmorinen's dispossessed heir. As he did, it came to him that the better way he'd been hoping for moments ago had been staring him in the face all along. He had only to commit himself to following it. "Do you know where she is right now?"

"My, that was fast." The Guardian's eyes twinkled with mischief. "I believe she and Malry are drilling with the fourth regiment."

"I think I'll go help them," Tal said, turning to the hatch back down into the tower. Let Kyril think what he would for the time being, he'd learn the truth once all was done. If Zharkus's selfish embrace of power over principle had brought them to this terrible point, Tal had it within his reach to balance the equation. He felt so clear in his purpose right now, his path laid out before him. He had to let Rania know which one he'd chosen.

Rania had been surprised to see Tal walk into the practice yard where she and Malry were working with the soldiers. Thus far he had always been too busy with strategic planning to involve himself personally in these sessions. With great relief and no small amount of curiosity, she'd noticed that the worry lines were gone from the corners of his eyes and his movements were far more relaxed than they'd been earlier in the morning. He threw himself wholeheartedly into practicing with the troops, and for their part the soldiers seemed to appreciate the attention from the King's Champion. By the time they stopped for the day with the setting of the sun, Rania found herself once more marveling at the loyalty Tal seemed so effortlessly to elicit from those he came in contact with. More amazing still was that he appeared genuinely unaware of what a natural leader he was.

As the soldiers were filing out of the yard and back to their barracks, Tal pulled Rania and Malry aside. "I'd like the two of you to come with me to my quarters," he said softly.

"What's this about, Tal?" Rania asked.

"I've decided to accept the offer you made me when we met," Tal replied, then looked at the Armslord with a smile. "I want you to witness my oaths, old friend. After all, it's thanks to you that I'm in a position to be able to take them."

Clearly, the old man understood what Tal was talking about. With brimming eyes he clasped his student's arm and said, "I'd be honored."

Silently and with an air of solemnity they entered the Keep and climbed up to the floor where their quarters were all located. Tal opened the door and ushered his companions in before following them.

In the sitting room, Rania turned to face Tal as Malry stepped aside to observe. "You're certain of this, Tal? Once done, it cannot be taken back."

He looked solemnly into her eyes. "Completely. This is the path I choose."

She nodded once. "You know the words?"

"I do."

Purposefully, Tal dropped to one knee and bowed his head. For several minutes he held completely still in contemplation, and then in tones of deep reverence began to speak the words of the Shevestra'ken Oath. "Today I consecrate myself to Shevestra and to the eternal battle as one of her children. Fear, despair, and tyranny: these are my enemies and against them shall I ever be vigilant. Never shall I flee before the wicked, for this is the way of fear. Never shall I admit defeat while still I draw breath, for this is the way of despair. Never shall I suffer the mighty to shackle the weak, for this is the way of the tyrant. Wheresoever I may walk shall I bring courage, hope, and freedom, for this is the way of the just. I am the candle that holds the night at bay. Though the darkness may overwhelm, never shall my light falter. To the battle am I born. I am Shevestra'ka." As he finished reciting the words, Tal raised his eyes to Rania's face.

Formally, Rania intoned, "I hear these vows, Talaren Solus, and accept them in the name of the Mother of Battles. To walk the path of righteousness one must banish all dreams of dominion. Though you may lead, always must you serve. Do you now renounce all claims of rulership to stand among the Children of Shevestra?"

"Without reserve, I do."

Rania reached down to take Tal by the hands and pulled him to his feet. "Then I welcome you to the Shevestra'ken and embrace you as brother." She kissed him lightly on either cheek. "May the Warrior Soul burn brightly within you and guide your steps through darkness and travail." Still gripping his hands she instructed, "Take up the Single-Edged Awareness."

Tal's face became blank and expressionless as he entered the state of free-flowing concentration he'd been taught in his Armslord exercises. Rania did likewise and stretched forth her will to draw upon the Sephira. The glowing blue aura sprang forth to radiate from her person. Tenderly, Rania extended her consciousness out through her hands seeking communion with Tal's. When she had received the Warrior Soul this connection had formed slowly and tenuously, but now as soon as she reached out to Tal, the Sephira seemed to surge and leapt out to link them in a state of perfectly shared awareness. Rania gasped at the strength of the bond that instantly solidified as the Warrior Soul began to flow from her to Tal seemingly with a will all its own. The Sephiral glow that enveloped Rania spread to enclose him as well.

The two of them drifted in a confusing welter of shared thought, an entire mental conversation passing between them in the blink of an eye: *Is something wrong? The bond wasn't this strong before. Is that bad? I don't think so. Why is this happening? Don't know I can't control it don't try to control have to trust each other trust trust trust trust...*

As suddenly as it had surged, the scouring flow reached an equilibrium and stopped without severing the Sephiral link. *What was that? I never knew the bond could be so complete. I gave you more of the Warrior Soul than I meant to. I know. It equalized itself between us. Why didn't you tell me it had been hurting you? I didn't want that to affect your choice. Is it okay that you gave me as much as you did? It doesn't feel wrong. Do you still trust me? How could I not after this? Trust saved us. Yes, I think it did. It's finished. We should return to ourselves now.*

The glow faded around both Tal and Rania simultaneously. They both blinked confusedly for a moment as their thoughts once more became wholly their own, and then shared a knowing smile between them.

"You're an Adept now, Tal. Congratulations," Rania said.

The following days seemed to pass with amazing swiftness. Preparations throughout the city moved on at a breakneck pace, turning Val Jerak into a buzzing hive of activity. Rumors of a coming Bhellan attack spread uncontrollably across the city, but with so much going on it was hopeless to avoid. Tal was just thankful that the size and composition of the approaching enemy wasn't leaked to the general populace; the last thing he needed on top of everything else was panic sweeping the city. As it stood, the same preparations that had sparked the rumors let people see that matters were being dealt with and gave them the confidence to go on with their lives as best they could.

For his part, Tal was as busy as any three people in the city. From waking until finally seeking his bed in exhaustion, he held to a packed schedule of strategy sessions, overseeing preparations, and helping Rania and Malry ready the troops. Tal found a strange calmness in the feverish pitch of his work, a soothing reassurance that he was doing everything possible to see the city through the coming crisis.

Krovar, Jonfer, and Kyril were predictably congratulatory at Tal's announcement that he had sworn the Oaths and become Shevestra'ka. The following explanation of the plan Tal had worked out with the Guardian had raised everyone's spirits, producing an awed silence and grins from the

General and his Attaché and a warmly approving smile from Rania. Malry declared that his former student had become all he could ever have hoped. Though embarrassed at the praise, Tal couldn't help but be warmed by the look of beatific pride on his old mentor's face.

On top of all his other duties, Tal set aside time every evening to spar with Rania in the practice yard, using the time to accustom himself to the new abilities his fealty to the Bloody-Handed Maiden had brought him. After the first few nights they began to attract a crowd of off-duty soldiers and servants from the Keep who watched with rapt attention as the two glowing Shevestra'ken clashed with intricate blade and hand-to-hand techniques at blinding speeds. Though they were nearly evenly matched now, Rania maintained an edge over Tal in experience and won their mock duels more than she lost.

Often Rania would lecture Tal while they fought, explaining the intricacies of the Battle Trance. Though Tal had heard much of it during his training with Malry, he appreciated the review as well as the extra insights and emphasis Rania imparted from her own experience.

"Union with the Sephira brings us many gifts, and each should be appreciated to maximize your effectiveness. Much is made of the strength and endurance we acquire because they show themselves so overtly, and the speeding of both body and reflexes are impossible not to notice. Less obvious yet undeniably useful is the fact that when we hold the Sephira we heal our injuries at a greatly accelerated rate. Most subtle of all is the awareness that we gain, but in the chaos of battle it can be argued that it is our greatest advantage, for it allows us to avoid blows that we can't physically see coming or accurately attack enemies whose guards are down because they believe themselves safe behind us."

"Never forget, however, that all these gifts come with a price. In the heat of battle, the Sephira grows violent and unpredictable. If you don't guard yourself carefully, it can overwhelm you and rob you of your self-control, carrying you along on its flow. It may carry you to your death if this happens. Further, there is a basic dichotomy within our nature in that we are meant to be defenders of life yet in service to life we are often called upon to bring death. Death is a constant companion to us, and you will find that it gives with one hand while taking away with the other. When we kill, the Sephiral essence of the taken life passes through us as it rejoins the energy of the rest of existence, and it brings with it the agony and sorrow of a life ended. Some of that energy stays with us and strengthens the Warrior Soul, enhancing our abilities, but some of the pain also lingers. If you kill too frequently, the loss you absorb can become too much for you and it will begin to erode your sanity. That was the mistake I made and I barely realized it soon enough to save myself."

148

Exactly how Rania had come to take so many lives that she risked insanity was a subject she seemed loath to raise, and Tal let it pass for the time being without comment. Compared to their immediate concerns it seemed relatively unimportant, and Tal could understand why she might be hesitant to talk about something that so obviously troubled her. He was sure she would tell him when she was ready.

Time continued on in its steady march, and almost before Tal knew it his scouts were reporting the Bhellan host encamped on the opposite end of the Felmorr Gap. Come the next day, events would show whether all the preparation and planning had been enough. Tal responded to the reports by ordering that the city's soldiers assemble for him to address them. The waiting was over, and now was the time to let the men know what they would face come the dawn and to rally their spirits for the imminent struggle.

So it was that Tal found himself standing atop the gatehouse on the eastern wall flanked by his friends and advisors, with Val Jerak's gathered defenders filling the field before him. All together like this, they made for an impressive spectacle.

Tal looked to Kyril, and the Guardian nodded. He was utilizing a Sephiral trick to ensure that Tal's words would be audible to even the farthest away of the soldiers. With the affirmation that the voice amplifying Sephiral web was in place, Tal stepped forward to speak and a hush fell over the crowd below.

"Over the past few weeks you've all been involved in readying Val Jerak for attack. From the orders you've received you all know that such an attack is imminent, and many of you have accurately guessed that it is the nation of Bhellus that sends its forces against us. Those forces are now upon us and will bring battle against us on the morrow. The enemy we will face is like none other seen in the last several centuries, for King Kherzul has resurrected the ways of Anakara the Undying. When his armies besiege our walls tomorrow, the dead will march with them. Their numbers are mighty, and their powers formidable. Yet I stand before you now and I say: Let them come!"

"Though the enemy we face is fearsome, we stand forewarned. We know what comes against us, and our strategies have been prepared accordingly. The Jhessaillian Order stands with us to counter Kherzul's Sephiral arts with their own. The Necromantic King's dark servants will find they must contend with Shevestra'ken. And the great cities of Valeran have been informed of our plight. Even now, reinforcements come to our aid. We are the shield which holds back disaster from the rest of Valeran. If we can blunt the Bhellan attack, it can be turned aside and shattered. I have worked with many of you while we've readied ourselves for battle, and I know that I stand among the finest soldiers in the North. I have complete confidence that you can and will do what must be done tomorrow. The enemy comes with all their strength, but they will find their attack shattered upon this field where you now stand. Know tomorrow, when battle rages about you, that through your efforts will our lands and our people be kept safe and a new darkness prevented. You are the best Valeran has to offer, and together we will find our way through struggle to victory!"

Tal drew *Kallevamar* and thrust it into the air as he finished his speech, simultaneously reaching out to the Sephira. As the aura sprung up around him the soldiers cheered thunderously, their applause and cries rolling on and on over the new Shevestra'ka.

Tal nodded to himself. *Yes, let them come*, he thought. *We're ready.*

17

Never Shall My Light Falter

The Felmorr Gap was lit by an eerie pale half-light, the air bitingly cold and heavy with the promise of snow. Gray clouds stretched across the sky overhead from horizon to horizon. *How appropriate*, Tal thought, *that the sun won't rise today.* He stood armor-clad atop the Gap Gate with twelve score soldiers, mostly men from Val Solus who had volunteered to mount this defense with him. Every eye gazed down into the depths of the pass, straining for the first sight of the coming Bhellan horde. The ominous distant thunder of thousands of feet echoed from the mountain walls, creating an almost palpable tension among these men who would fight in the opening movements of the coming battle. Their nervousness was understandable enough. The prospect of facing tens of thousands with just over two hundred, even on strategically advantageous ground, was a sobering one.

Tal took in a deep breath through his nose. *They're still a long way away. The scouts said we'll smell them long before we see them.* Restively, he snugged his steel-backed gauntlets tighter.

Beside him stood Rania, likewise garbed for war. To the mail shirt and knife harness Tal had seen her in previously she had added heavy steel greaves on arms and legs and an open-faced helm. She rested one hand lightly on *Edyamar's* pommel.

She had come to his rooms early in the morning, while Tal was busily girding himself for battle. After letting herself in, she'd watched him struggling with his armor for all of two heartbeats before observing, "That looks uncomfortable. Let me help."

Without waiting for a response, she'd walked over and set to adjusting plates and fastening straps.

"Thanks. It's a lot easier with someone to help."

"I've been thinking about our battle plan," Rania said as she worked on one of his pauldrons. "How's that? Not too tight?"

Tal checked his arm's range of motion to make sure the armor didn't restrict him. "No, it's good."

Rania moved on to the other side. "I think I should be at the Gap Gate with you."

"But I need you and Malry to command the main infantry force."

"Armslord Zhierren can do that just fine by himself. He's seen more battles than I ever have. Besides, I'm far more useful to you fighting on the front lines than waiting behind you." Rania's tone had been eminently reasonable. "Unless you're trying to keep me safe by holding me back from the most dangerous fighting." An overly sharp tug on a strap let Tal know what she'd think of *that*.

She'd trapped him with that last comment. Considering that Malry probably was capable of handling command duties alone and the undeniable benefit of having an extra Shevestra'ka on the wall, there was no way for him to deny her request without appearing overly protective. "Alright, have it your way then," Tal sighed with a rueful shake of his head. "Did you know that you don't argue fairly?"

"I argue the same way I fight," Rania had replied sweetly. "To win. And you wouldn't have it any other way."

"Because you wouldn't let me."

"Of course not. Now stop complaining. You'll feel better having me there and we both know it."

Tal smiled to himself as he recalled the exchange. The fact of the matter was that Rania had been right - he *did* feel better with her there. She was so implacably confident in everything she did that it was hard to imagine anything that could overcome her.

As though sensing that he was thinking about her, Rania turned to Tal. "I noticed this morning that you're wearing your hair in the Shevestra'ka braid," she said conversationally. "It suits you."

"Thanks," Tal replied with a quizzical look. "Why do you mention it now?" The braid over his left ear was concealed at the moment by the snarling fox's head of his helmet.

"Just making small talk to pass the time," Rania said with a shrug. "I hate the waiting before a fight. Once it's apparent that violence is inevitable, I prefer to get right to it."

"Is it always like this, then?"

"What, the tension before a fight?" Rania nodded. "You get used to it, but it never completely goes away. I think I'd be worried if it ever did."

"I suppose you're right," Tal agreed. "It should never be easy to go into war. The fighting would never end."

"It never does," Rania said distantly. "There's only the one battle, stretching through the ages. All that changes are the places and the victims."

Tal smiled grimly at her paraphrasing of the Shevestra'ken adage. "And we'll always be there to fight it?"

"To our dying breaths."

For such a fatalistic statement, Tal found it strangely comforting.

The clamor reverberating down the Gap had grown much louder. An errant gust of wind brought a faint burning sensation to Tal's nostrils. He sniffed at the air and detected the hint of a charnel house reek.

Rania eased *Edyamar* in its sheath. "They come."

Now that Tal had caught it, the smell grew rapidly stronger. Within minutes it was nearly enough to make him gag. Far down the pass, the lead elements of the Bhellan army came into view.

Tal raised his voice to bellow to his troops, "Remember, we're here to show them a good fight so they know we're no easy meat. When things get too hot we pull back. I don't want any needless attempts at heroism, and once I order the retreat none of you look back until you're behind the walls in Val Jerak!"

The men nodded, saluted, or yelled back, "Yes, sir!"

Tal kept his eyes intently on the advancing enemy. As they drew close enough to see clearly, a shudder of revulsion passed through him. Knowing he would face an army of the dead had still provided little preparation for the actual grisly sight. The walking corpses were in varying states of decay, their putrescent flesh hanging in ragged strips here, sloughing off an arm there, or completely stripped away to the bone in some instances. The dead didn't march so much as they shambled in an arrhythmic, lurching approximation of human movement. They carried a mishmash assortment of weapons, many of which looked to be in a similar or worse state of repair than the corpses that bore them. Many carried no armament at all. Tal could make out scaling ladders being brought forward among the front ranks.

He opened himself to the Sephira, letting its power wash through him. His awareness blossomed, bringing Tal a new insight into the animated dead before him. They were a sea of shattered and splintered essences, pitiful glimmers in comparison to the healthful flame of life emanating from the soldiers on the Gap Gate. The broken souls emanated a sense of hatred and suffering, and seemed to resonate with each other in expanding ripples.

Tal felt a strangely detached and yet unbridled fury slipping over him, and realized with some surprise that the feeling was not his own but was carried to him by the energies in which he partook. The Sephira itself raged against the very existence of these unnatural creatures!

An instant later Tal's awareness underwent a peculiar doubling as Rania took hold of the Sephira herself. Over the course of their practicing together the two of them had found that when they both held the Sephira in close proximity to each other they experienced a less pronounced form of the bond they had shared when Rania gave Tal the Warrior Soul. For all the lore of the ancient Shevestra'ken they had between them, neither had any idea why this happened, but its reality was undeniable. The odd dual consciousness had enabled some of their more spectacular sparring matches as they moved in perfect accord with one another, and they suspected that it would greatly enhance their effectiveness when fighting as a team. That theory would be put to the test today.

Tal raised his voice to order, "Archers, stand ready!"

All along the wall, arrows were nocked and bowstrings pulled back.

Tal held his hand out in the air before him, carefully gauging the distance of the enemy. Five hundred yards. Four hundred. Three hundred. Two... One...

Tal's hand slashed downward. "Release!"

The air thrummed as a hundred bowstrings launched arrows skyward. They arched through the air and into the advancing corpses.

Tal surveyed the damage done even as his archers were preparing their second flight of arrows. The dead seemed hardly to notice the shafts protruding from their bodies. Here and there a particularly well aimed or lucky shot had knocked a limb loose from its owner, but even those corpses kept limping on undaunted. Tal didn't think a single one had been felled by the initial attack.

The second flight hissed through the air. And the third. And the fourth.

The advance of the corpses didn't slow one whit. By the time half a dozen flights had been loosed they were at the wall and the scaling ladders were going up.

Tal pulled *Kallevamar* from its sheath. "Archers, draw steel! Everyone hold the wall!"

The dead were unevenly matched against disciplined, living soldiers. They were neither particularly swift nor especially skilled at fighting. Their strength was in their overwhelming numbers and their tenacity in pressing the attack. Wounds that would down a living man were shrugged off by the dead. A corpse might be run through and yet still savage its attacker, heedless of the fact that its heart had been pierced. The only truly effective ways to stop them appeared to be dismemberment or mauling the body so badly it could no longer move to attack properly.

As fighting broke out on the wall, fat wet flakes of snow began drifting down from the sky. Tal noted the snowfall only on the margins of his consciousness, the bulk of his attention taken up by the struggle.

All too often the dead would gain a foothold atop the wall, one of them lumbering up from underneath a rain of blows with its fellows following close behind while the surrounding soldiers were busy trying to bring down the first. It was to these trouble areas that Tal and Rania directed most of their efforts. They hurled themselves into knots of corpses, striking with hands, feet, and swords. The Blades of Unity, driven by the Sephirally magnified strength of their wielders, severed limbs and bisected bodies with equal ease, carving the dead to spare body parts.

Attacks hailed down on the Shevestra'ken with such frequency that even their lightning-fast reactions were insufficient to evade every blow. Tal quickly gained a new, deeper appreciation for the specialized design of his armor. The strategically positioned plates, when combined with the quickened reflexes of a Shevestra'ka in union with the Sephira, enabled him to catch and deflect with his body the worst of the attacks he couldn't dodge. Rania, he noticed, employed the greaves on her arms in a very similar fashion.

The top of the Gap Gate began to grow slick with a vile mixture of slush, blood, and viscera as the snowfall intensified. Defenders fell infrequently, but each man lost weakened the overall effort. What little strategy there was to the Bhellan assault seemed clear: grind away the defenders through a long process of attrition. What matter to Kherzul if he lost thousands in passing the Gap Gate? He would still have sufficient numbers to drown Val Jerak in a sea of the dead.

The fighting dragged on for an hour, and then two. Tal lost track of how many corpses he had cut down or hurled from the wall. However many he vanquished, more kept coming. Nearly a third of his men had fallen to the dead, screaming and writhing under blows from rusted sword and axe blades or the rending of cold, dead hands. The dead never stopped hewing at an opponent until all signs of life were extinguished. Every such death Tal witnessed made him want to retch at the mindless savagery of it. Breakthroughs were happening more frequently now, enough so that Tal and Rania were hard pressed to keep up. It was time to retreat before the situation got out of hand.

"Prepare to fall back!" Tal yelled at the top of his lungs. He and Rania began moving to opposite ends of the wall.

A young soldier staggered into Tal, howling and clutching at the bloody ruin of his face where he had caught the swipe of a skeletal claw. One of his eyes had been put out in the attack. With a sudden surge of anger and three swift blows with *Kallevamar*, Tal hacked off both arms and a leg of the thing that had maimed the soldier and then caught the reeling young man.

"With me, lad! We'll get you out of here." With death everywhere he looked, it suddenly seemed eminently important to Tal to save this one life. He hauled the whimpering soldier with him to the end of the wall, where he pulled back the two endmost men and stepped in to take their places.

"Get back to the city! Take this man with you and get him to the healers. Go!" The soldiers took up their fellow between them and bolted for the nearest hatch down into the wall. Tal scooped up a discarded sword from the parapet in his free hand.

With both Shevestra'ken fighting off the tides of dead that boiled over the undefended ends of the wall, the Valerite soldiers began an orderly retreat. Tal and Rania gave up ground slowly, every few steps back freeing another soldier to bolt for the hatches down through the wall and to the horses waiting below to carry them back to the relative safety of Val Jerak.

As Tal and Rania converged toward the center of the wall, the last of the soldiers fell back to withdraw into the final hatch. The Shevestra'ken stood nearly back-to-back defending the escape route.

"Bolt it behind you!" Tal yelled to the last man clambering down into the hole. The soldier began to shake his head and Tal commanded, "Don't argue! Just do it!"

The soldier disappeared into the hole, closing the door behind him with a loud 'snick' of the bolts being thrown.

Together, the pair of Shevestra'ken fought their way through the press of deteriorating bodies to the edge of the wall. "Jump," Tal shouted over his shoulder. "I'll be right behind you."

"I'm not leaving before you do," Rania called back.

Tal growled as he split an attacking corpse from shoulder to navel. She *would* have to choose a moment like this to be stubborn. "Together then, on three."

In unison they leapt from the wall, pitching themselves forward to roll with the impact of their landings. As soon as Tal had his legs under him again he was dashing for the remaining mounts. The horses rolled their eyes and whickered nervously, clearly sensing the imminent danger of their situation. Tal ran through their ranks cutting the lines that held them hobbled, taking the reins of the last two and handing one off to Rania as she caught up with him.

The last of the fleeing soldiers were galloping out of the mouth of the Gap and disappearing into the drifting snow as Tal pulled himself up into the saddle. He exchanged a brief look with Rania. "I'm going to slow once we're out of the pass to signal Kyril. When I do, Rania, keep going. I won't be in any danger."

The fiery-haired Adept frowned slightly but then gave a small nod before kicking her horse to a run. With a last glance back, Tal did likewise. The Gap Gates were beginning slowly to swing open.

Heads stretched forward and tails streaming behind with the speed of their passage, the horses flew as though fired from a ballista. The walls of the Felmorr Gap flashed by to either side, and then the Shevestra'ken shot out of the Gap and onto the field between city and mountains. Tal waited until he had put several hundred yards between himself and the feet of the Felmorr before hauling back on the reins with one hand while the other reached down to grasp the curled horn at his side. He raised it to his lips, drew in a deep breath, and blew.

No sound emerged. In alarm, Tal examined the horn in his hands. It had been battered and buffeted in the fighting, and a long jagged hole had been opened in its side where it had caught a blow. Tal clamped his hands down tightly around the torn section of the horn and tried again, but to no effect. The damage was too severe, and the horn would issue no sound.

Icy dread clenched Tal's guts. Bhellan forces were already pouring out of the Felmorr Gap, and Val Jerak was only an indistinct dark blur in the concealing snowfall. There was no way that Kyril, from his vantage atop the Ducal Keep, would be able to make out the army emerging from the mountains. If Tal couldn't alert the Guardian within the next few moments, the best hope they had of defeating Kherzul's army would vanish.

The cavalry concealed in the forests would have horns but it would already be too late by the time Tal was able to reach them, and such a move would likely reveal their positions besides. Little as he liked it, he saw only one opportunity to stave off utter ruin.

Tal jumped down from his horse's back. "No reason we both have to die," he murmured to the animal and then gave it a slap on the rump. As the horse started running back to the city, Tal turned grimly to face the army bearing down on him and drew *Kallevamar*. "Never shall I admit defeat while still I draw breath," he quoted to himself as he began to stride toward the enemy forces. *One man to hold back an onslaught of thousands. I'm insane for even imagining I could do this.*

Mounted Bhellan soldiers, the first living troops Tal had seen among the enemy all day, were moving into the vanguard of the army. With his Sephiral aura reflecting from the drifting snow to cloak him in an ethereal blue halo, there was no way they could fail to notice Tal. Surely enough, a group of horsemen lined up and charged forward toward their lone foe.

Their attention captured, Tal stopped and held himself poised. At a hundred paces, he could make out an officer's plume atop one of his attackers' helmets. *That's the one I want. My timing will have to be perfect.* Like a breaking wave, steel-tipped lances lowered as the Bhellans pounded toward Tal. Time seemed to stand still as the Shevestra'ka faced down his enemies, carefully judging their distance to choose his moment.

At the last possible instant, Tal took two swift steps forward and launched himself in a prodigious leap right at the charging officer. The lances passed under him by inches, and he crashed into his quarry with a bone-jarring impact. The horseman was torn from his saddle to land flat on his back with Tal atop him. Before the officer had an opportunity to recover, Tal viciously thrust *Kallevamar's* point through his exposed throat.

Looking over the body of the man he'd just slain, Tal felt a surge of exhilaration. Hanging from a leather cord around the dead horseman's neck was a brass cavalry horn. Tal grasped the instrument and yanked, snapping the cord. He raised the horn and sounded it, two long notes followed by three short ones. As the signal he'd blown echoed back to him from the mountains,

Tal stood and turned back toward Val Jerak. He'd done his part and alerted Kyril. Now he just had to get back to the city.

Already the remaining horsemen who'd attacked him were wheeling their mounts around for another pass.

Kyril paced restlessly back and forth across the tower, pausing now and then to gaze anxiously eastward, squinting his eyes against the wind-driven snow. He could make out the outline of the Felmorr range out there, but at such a distance that was all he could discern. The infantry formations standing before Val Jerak's gates were right at the edge of what he could make out with any clarity. The Guardian bristled at being essentially blind to what was transpiring in the Felmorr Gap.

Since midmorning, the distant sounds of battle had drifted across the field and up to Kyril's ears. The snowfall had begun concurrently with the clamor in the Gap, almost as if orchestrated by some distant malevolent hand. Even the speculation of such a possibility troubled the Guardian deeply. *This has to be a natural storm, no matter how unfortunate the timing. Kherzul can't have learned how to manipulate the weather.* Such training was restricted to the more powerful Guardians in the Order because of the havoc it could cause if misused. As much as the King of Bhellus had managed to learn, surely he couldn't have wrested away such inner secrets of the Order.

On several occasions already today, Kyril had been tempted to halt the snowfall himself, but every time had restrained himself. Any manifestation involving alteration of the weather required a great deal of strength, strength that Kyril would probably need for other purposes later. He could resolve the difficulties the snow presented in targeting his Sephiral destruction by moving to the city walls, but he dared not move until he had heard and responded to Tal's signal. Should he miss it whilst climbing down the tower, the consequences would prove disastrous. And so the Guardian continued to wait, pace, and watch.

Movement below caught Kyril's attention. The ranks of the infantry were parting to allow a pair of mounted soldiers through. The retreat from the Gap Gate had begun then, and had been underway for quite some time already for the first of the men to be arriving back at Val Jerak. Kyril leaned against the crenellated wall and focused a gaze of raptorlike intensity on the scene in front of the gates.

Soldiers continued to trickle back to the city, usually in pairs and sometimes bearing wounded comrades. As more and more of the city's defenders returned from the Gap, a gnawing sense of disquiet crept through Kyril. What was happening in the Gap? Surely Tal must have gotten himself and his men out by now, but why hadn't he sounded the all clear yet? The Jhessaillian strained his ears, hoping against hope to hear the call of a horn.

158

When a single gently glowing figure astride a horse emerged from the snows and joined the infantry, Kyril snarled a curse under his breath. Something must have happened to Tal. He couldn't be dead - he mustn't! Kyril had suspected from the beginning that Tal was the one he was looking for, and when the young noble had sworn his Oaths to Shevestra, he'd been certain. For him to die with his fate unfulfilled would spell doom on over a millennia of the Order's efforts.

Something had to be done, and right now, or everything was lost. Kyril steeled himself to call upon the Sephira.

Just then a horn sounded from the field. Two long blasts and then three short. The Guardian breathed a sigh of relief. Talaren was still alive! No time for rejoicing, though. There was work to be done.

Kyril reached out with his thoughts, drawing in the Sephiral energy he needed. His scalp began to tingle with the familiar feel of the power of raw possibility. He fixed his eyes on a point he estimated to be high within the Gap, and drank in all the power he dared to. The tingling crept down his spine and out along his limbs until he quivered with it, felt that it might tear apart his own existence just to attempt to wield so much. He focused it all on that point his gaze picked out, seeing in his mind's eye what he would do, letting himself *know* that it *would* happen. Doubt could be as deadly as lack of understanding. He envisioned the directing runes to shape the energy he'd gathered and poured it into them.

The results were visible even from where Kyril stood. The point in the air his eyes were fixed on seemed to blister, creating a swirling maelstrom of snow as it exploded violently outward in a rapidly expanding sphere. The mountains seemed to shudder as chunks of ice and stone were shattered and hurled away by the initial shockwave, and then parts of the slope began slowly to tumble earthward.

The sound Kyril had created hit him seconds later. It was an enormous cracking noise, as if every peal of thunder since time began had been condensed into a single instant. The tower shook with it and the Guardian was knocked backwards off his feet, ears ringing. As he picked himself back up and his ears began to clear, he could feel as much as hear the low rumble of the avalanche he'd triggered.

Satisfied that he'd performed his duty adequately, Kyril turned to dash down the tower and to the walls. He should have just enough time before the next stage of the battle began.

Kallevamar flashed furiously in Tal's hands, weaving a wall of steel to ward off attack. His body moved in time with the weapon, ducking, bobbing, and dodging, dancing on a razor's edge where death would come swiftly at the slightest misstep.

The horsemen had returned but this time they hadn't attempted to charge the Shevestra'ka, having learned the futility of such a maneuver from their first attempt. Instead they circled him in a wide ring, riding into the center two and three at a time to harry Tal. There was no way he could counterattack one rider without leaving himself open to the next. He was well and truly mired, and every breath brought the leading edge of the Bhellan forces another step closer. Once they overtook him, Tal knew, there would be no escape.

High above and back within the Felmorr Gap, Tal could feel the Sephira swelling as Kyril's work began to take shape. Whatever else happened, at least he could die knowing he had salvaged Val Jerak's chances for weathering this assault. A single life given to overcome such great odds would be a bargain by any reckoning. Tal ducked under an axe blow from behind even as he caught a sword stroke from the rider in front of him with *Kallevamar*. He was spinning to face the next rider when the Sephiral energy building overhead flared and dissipated itself in a sudden surge.

The Sephira brought Tal the impression of an enormous force barreling toward him at a speed he'd never have imagined possible. The sensation lasted only an instant, and then he was brutally smashed to the ground. For the briefest of moments he was aware of a colossal boom, and then the world went silent with a sharp pain in his head.

The first coherent thought Tal had was that he must be dead. But no, he still felt pain, and that suggested that he still lived. He willed his body to move and surprisingly it responded, his head rising to behold a scene of absolute chaos.

Men sprawled on the earth where they had been borne from their saddles. Most of the horses had been knocked over as well, and those that hadn't were stampeding about in a panic. Even the walking dead had been dashed to the ground by the blast, although they were already beginning to stand again, apparently little the worse for wear.

Still Tal could hear nothing as he got unsteadily to his feet, but he could feel a deep rumbling in the earth. He spared a glance for the mountains behind and saw cascades of ice and snow hurtling down from the heights, picking up mass and momentum as they fell.

Such astonishing good fortune was not to be wasted. Tal picked up *Kallevamar* from where it'd fallen from his hand and set out at a run for Val Jerak before any of the Bhellans could recover enough to attempt to stop him.

Once he reached a distance where he could sense no other creature within bowshot of himself, Tal paused one more time to observe the collapse of the Felmorr Gap. The mighty wave of the avalanche had almost reached the bottom of the pass by now, and the Bhellans had got enough of their wits back to realize their plight. All order had vanished among their ranks as living soldiers scrambled to escape the kill zone, and even the dead seemed to move with added urgency. Mounted troops trampled over scores of shuffling corpses in their haste to save their own skins. With a resounding crash that shook the earth, and that Tal even thought he could hear faintly, tons upon tons of accumulated snow, ice, and broken rock plowed into the forces still within the Gap, burying them in an instant. Excess snow flooded from the mouth of the pass in a great wave that swept up man, corpse, and horse on its crest like so much detritus.

In the stillness that followed, the Bhellans seemed to be in shock, directionless and confused. Right now it would just be sinking in that, in the space of a few minutes, well over half of their attacking force had been entombed in the Felmorr Gap. That fact alone would put most of the living troops on edge and force Kherzul's commanders to consider what other tricks Tal might have prepared for them. It would make them cautious, but hopefully not too cautious. If they held too much of their strength back in reserve when they attacked the city, Tal's hidden cavalry ploy would be much less effective. Hopefully, the facts that they still had the advantage of numbers and that Tal would appear to be following the strategy leaked to them would be sufficient to lure them in.

Time would tell, but now it was time for Tal to get back to his men.

Rania glared balefully toward the Felmorr Gap as though she could melt the obscuring snow with the intensity of her gaze alone. It had been a few minutes already since Tal's horn had echoed from the mountains, followed shortly after by the Guardian's air-rending boom.

The sound had hit the men gathered before Val Jerak like a physical blow, staggering some and causing others to cry out, their hands grasping at ringing ears.

"What in the screaming hells was that?" one had cursed.

"The Lost Ones take me if I know!"

"Listen! That rumbling in the mountains! Lord Solus is bringing them down on the Bhellans!"

"And just how do you figure he's doing that, dungbrain?"

"Remember, he's a Shevestra'ka now. They've got, y'know, powers and all."

The men around Rania had shifted uneasily with surreptitious glances from the corners of eyes. Yet another voice rose in ridicule, "Not no powers like that! That's Jhessaillian work, it is."

"Well, if that's not Lord Solus, then what's he doing out there that he hasn't come back yet?"

Rania very much wanted to know that as well but had stopped listening after the question was asked, for that was when the riderless horse had come galloping into sight. The same horse Tal had been riding when last she had seen him.

The Sephiral link between them had faded rapidly with the growing distance when Tal stopped to sound his horn. Rania had been concerned when she didn't hear him blow the signal right away, but had kept riding. Tal had told her to. He said he'd be in no danger, and she had trusted him.

If he's gotten himself hurt, I'm going to kill him.

The irony that she should worry so for Tal's safety when she had long made a habit of disregarding her own was not lost on her. Under other circumstances it would probably make her laugh, but she was in no mood to appreciate humor right now. She felt much more like slaughtering her way through the Bhellans to find Tal and throttle him for lying to her.

Something tickled at the edge of Rania's awareness. Her gaze shifted slightly to the right to focus on the source of the feeling. As it grew stronger, she felt her anger tempered by relief. Tal was close and drawing nearer by the second. Now that he could sense her, Rania felt him alter his course to come straight toward her. She detected in him no severe injuries, but there was an insistent pain in his head that hadn't been there before. As he drew closer she felt him stop running and slow to a walk. With a sudden flash of insight, Rania understood why.

He won't let the men see him appear to be running away from the enemy. He's letting them believe in him. And as though it were her own, Rania could feel his distaste at engaging in such a theatrical display.

Scattered murmurs and pointed fingers accompanied the first of the soldiers spotting the dim glow in the snowfall. It grew brighter as Tal approached, and soon he could be seen as a silhouette at the center of the Sephiral nimbus. By the time his slow and deliberate pace brought him near enough to be seen clearly, the murmurs were beginning to give way to cheers.

Rania caught her breath. It was like a scene from legend, crystallized from the ancient tales and for a fleeting moment made real. Talaren strode from the field of battle as a hero of old: indomitable, inspiring, otherworldly. His battered and dented armor spoke of valiant deeds and foes vanquished. The fox's head of his helm seemed a living thing as it caught and reflected the light from his aura. His stained and tattered cloak fluttered behind, tugged by the wind. He was the very image of victory in the face of insurmountable evil.

Rania stepped forward to meet Tal as he drew near the front lines. He stopped and clasped her warmly by one shoulder, drawing her in closer.

"I know you're cross with me and I'm sorry," he whispered, "but we'll have to talk about it later. I lost my hearing when Kyril brought down the Gap. It's coming back slowly, but if I let the men know I'm injured it'll dim what hope I can give them."

Rania nodded her understanding. Of course he would know she'd been angry - he'd have felt it himself through the strange bond they shared. With Tal standing before her now, she felt the last of that anger draining away to be replaced by embarrassment that she'd questioned whether she could trust him. He knew no other way to be besides trustworthy. She returned his gesture by grasping his shoulder and giving it a gentle squeeze, hoping he would understand that he was already forgiven. Then she stepped aside.

"My friends," Tal declaimed loudly, and the cheering of the soldiers died down. "The enemy has come, and now stands opposite us upon this field. A mighty host King Kherzul set against us of tens of thousands, yet I stand here to tell you that already this morning he has tasted the bitter fruits of defeat. Even now, the bulk of his army lies buried within the Felmorr Gap. Though those that remain still comprise a great force, we shall show that their might is insufficient to overcome the hearts and arms of the men of Valeran. They come for us now. Stand with me, and we will demonstrate for Kherzul that never shall the North again succumb to the vile darkness that once blighted our lands!"

The soldiers of Val Jerak roared, howling their defiance of the Necromancer King as they rattled swords and spears against their shields.

Rania smiled coldly. Now the real fight began.

18
The Siege Of Val Jerak

Kyril gazed down from the city walls at the pandemonium below. The Bhellans had launched their assault on Val Jerak with a huge force, about half again the size of the defenders and spearheaded by walking corpses so decayed the Guardian was amazed they could function at all. Admirably, the men of Val Jerak hadn't flinched from the macabre horde descending on them and even now held their ground with a determination that did them honor. Up and down the wall catapults bucked and heaved, lofting balls of burning pitch and sprays of cabbage-sized stones into the Bhellan ranks.

Tal and Rania were clearly visible and easily picked out, sheathed in the radiance of their Shevestra'ken auras. They moved through the fighting like a scythe felling wheat, cutting foes down with murderous efficiency. Kyril observed in them a preternatural degree of coordination, as if a single mind directed both their bodies. Blows aimed at one would routinely be parried by the other, and when one created an opening in an opponent's defense the other was always there to exploit it. Even when forced together by the press of bodies they never seemed to get in one another's way. The Guardian thought he had heard of such a phenomenon in some Adepts of Shevestra, but never had he expected he might one day witness it. It would merit further investigation, if possible, after the battle.

"By the breath of the One," an archer near Kyril murmured in awe, "I think those two could fight this battle all by themselves. Just look at them!"

"Even they would be quickly overwhelmed if the rest of the men weren't here to keep the enemy busy," Kyril observed dryly. "Be glad they're with you, but don't discount yourself or your fellows." Off to the left, he noticed the Valerite line beginning to bulge inward. "Excuse me a moment." He drew upon the Sephira, shaped a short string of runes in his mind, and called down a roaring column of flame among the attacking Bhellan forces there. The line solidified again as men rushed in to fill the gaps left by fallen comrades during the resultant pause in the assault.

The same archer shook his head at Kyril's handiwork. "I'm glad we've got you here as well, Lord Guardian."

"Why, thank you," Kyril beamed. He turned his eyes once more to watching Tal and Rania. The Shevestra'ken had withdrawn back behind the front lines while his attention had been elsewhere. Tal seemed to be in the process of giving orders. Runners were dispatched, and the Adepts of Shevestra returned to the melee.

Moments later a horn sounded from the back ranks of the defenders. Kyril had been wondering how long Tal intended to wait before giving this second signal. Right now the horsemen hidden in the woods to either side of the field would be breaking cover to charge the Bhellan flanks. The clamor of battle would swallow the sound of their advance until they were nearly atop their quarry. This time the masking snows would work to Val Jerak's advantage.

Presently the horsemen came into view, charging from the featureless white depths with lances and spears held ready. With just under a thousand of them converging from each side they made a daunting spectacle, and it suddenly looked to Kyril as if the Valerite forces had the upper hand.

Finally aware of the rapidly closing cavalry, the Bhellan ranks began to shift. Not enough time. Between their lack of warning and the absence of military discipline or proper weaponry among the dead, they were ill prepared when the armored riders slammed into them. With enemies suddenly on all sides, the Bhellan attack began to falter. The Valerite infantry, with their Shevestra'ken champions leading the way, started to move forward to press their advantage.

Kyril redoubled his scrutiny of the clashing armies. Tal had now played out all of the tricks he'd prepared for the battle's opening, and seemingly to great effect. Now it only remained to be seen if Kherzul's spectre generals had any tricks of their own. The Guardian was willing to bet that they did.

Concern gnawed at Tal. Although there had been a few unexpected difficulties, the opening movements of the battle seemed to be going very well for him. Too well, in fact. His father had oft warned him of such situations: *When your fortunes on the field appear too good to be believed, you're probably being set up for a fall. Always be cautious under these circumstances and avoid overconfidence, and you just may be able to dodge the axe when it falls.*

There was also the matter of numbers to be considered. Although it was hard to gauge such things from the front lines, Tal estimated that the force currently engaging Val Jerak's defenders couldn't be much more than half what he'd seen make it out of the Felmorr Gap. And then there was the glaring absence of living soldiers in this first wave of attackers. Perhaps they were being allowed to rest and recuperate after their ordeal in the Gap, though Tal had difficulty attributing such mercy to Kherzul's commanders.

Because of his concerns he'd been loath to summon the cavalry from their concealment, but to wait any longer would have risked their becoming trapped outside the city when the time came to withdraw back behind the walls. So he had given the order to have them attack, resolving to watch for any indication of that axe Daron had warned him about.

The cavalry's charge had effectively staved in both of the Bhellan flanks and now horsemen rampaged through the walking dead, trampling corpses under steel-shod hooves and laying about to either side with swords and maces.

The opportunity was there to do what this strategy had been intended to do and decimate the attackers. Tal raised *Kallevamar* high overhead and bellowed, "Forward, men of Valeran! Forward for honor and the King!" With Rania at his side, he leapt forward to lead the counterattack.

"Honor and the King!" roared the soldiers behind him as they surged after. Tal wasn't entirely sure whether the Sephira had finished repairing the damage to his ears or if he was hearing through the link to Rania, but either way he heard them with perfect clarity.

Tal struck off the upraised arm of a bloated corpse before the blow it was readying could fall. He followed up with a kick that sent the thing staggering back into two of its fellows. Before Tal's foot had touched ground again, Rania leapt forward slashing *Edyamar* in a broad arc that clove through all three.

Their bond had proven to be even more devastatingly potent than the pair of Shevestra'ken had anticipated. In the heat of battle it seemed to grow stronger, to the point that Tal had to wonder if he and Rania were actually sometimes acting through each other's bodies. Though they still didn't hear one another's thoughts as they had before, it felt that they were only a hair's breadth away from such a state of oneness.

With the Shevestra'ken leading them, the Valerite infantry bit deeply into the Bhellan lines. The catapults on the walls fell silent, halting their barrage to avoid accidentally striking any friendly forces. In disarray, the dead couldn't reform their lines swiftly enough to slow the Valerite advance. Had they been capable of fear, this engagement would have turned into a rout. As it was, it was slaughter, pure and simple.

Another horn echoed across the field, sounding a single deep bass note. Tal's head snapped around to gaze in the direction it came from. There was nothing for him to see, naturally, as the snows would have blocked his sight even if the milling chaos of battle didn't. Regardless, he was sure he knew what was happening. The remainder of the Bhellan army was coming, and their entering the fray would very probably turn the battle back against Val Jerak's defenders.

"Disengage!" Tal yelled. "Withdraw to the city!" No good. Too few of the men could hear him over the commotion of their struggle. He'd have to order the retreat sounded, and every second could be vital. He spun about and dashed back for the Valerite lines.

Tal could feel Rania following on his heels as he wended his way through the gaps in the fighting, *Edyamar* a blur of constant motion in her hands as she covered his withdrawal. A sudden stab of pain burned through the link as a spear struck home just under her shoulderblade.

Rania whirled, snapping the shaft off the spear and twisting its head agonizingly through muscle tissue. *Edyamar* followed, decapitating the corpse that had attacked her. She reversed the blow to strike down diagonally through the headless body.

Tal halted in place and turned back to help Rania.

"Don't stop," she growled. "It's not too deep. I'll be alright." Her left arm hung limp at her side.

Tal nodded, and they continued on. Rania kept wielding *Edyamar* with her good arm until they had left the fighting behind.

Spotting a bannerman bearing a horn, Tal pulled the man aside. "Sound the retreat," he ordered. "They're bringing in reinforcements."

The soldier saluted and raised his horn, blowing the signal. The rearmost troops formed a double line before the gates of the city as they started to yawn open and the front ranks began to fall back.

Tal turned to join the soldiers who would hold the gates while their comrades withdrew. When Rania moved to follow, he frowned. "Please, Rania, you're injured. You don't have to do this."

She locked eyes with him. "My place is with you," she said softly. "I can still fight. Don't send me away, Tal." Her tone was almost pleading, much more so than Tal could bear to hear from her.

"Alright," he assented, "but at least let me do this for you." He gently turned her around and grasped the splintered shaft protruding from her back, bracing his other hand below the wound. "Are you ready?"

She replied through gritted teeth, "Do it."

With a single quick tug Tal yanked the spearhead out of Rania's shoulder. She sucked her breath in sharply as it came free, but gave no other indication of pain at its removal. A flow of blood welled out of the injury before quickly slowing and stopping as the Sephira began regenerating the damage.

The gates finished opening, and as soon as they did a stream of heavy cavalrymen in armor of overlapping metal scales rode forth to protect the infantry's retreat. Within seconds of the last horseman's passing, the flow of footmen back into Val Jerak began.

"How long will your injury take to heal?" Tal asked as he and Rania took their position at the center of the men guarding the open gates. He had little feeling yet for how swiftly Shevestra'ken regeneration mended hurts.

"Probably an hour or so now that the head's out," Rania replied. "It'll probably ache a little for a few hours after that, but I'll be able to use the arm and that's what matters."

The retreat was proceeding smoothly, thanks in large part to how badly the animated dead had been savaged. Still, Tal was agonizingly aware of every passing second. Time was the enemy right now, and he didn't think they had enough of it before the Bhellan reinforcements arrived.

The last of the infantry were just passing through the gates when the first of the fresh Bhellan forces came into sight. At their head rode a spectre atop a nightmarish steed that must have once been a horse before being exposed to Kherzul's dark arts. Lines of cavalry three deep rode just behind the necromancer's General, and behind them untold ranks of foot troops both living and dead. There were fewer than a hundred paces between them and the closest of the Valerite cavalry, who were only beginning their retreat.

"Damn," Tal cursed, "this is about to get ugly."

"That's what we're here for," Rania said darkly.

The spectre drew its sword and held it poised in the air. Tal stared at the blade, dreading the moment it fell. He saw no way to avoid losing most of his cavalry once the fresh attack began.

The blade began its descent. And as it did, flame erupted from the ground just in front of the spectre to create a burning wall ten paces high and stretching hundreds of yards to left and right.

Tal's eyes felt as if they were about to pop from his head. This had to be Kyril's work! He'd had no idea that the Guardian could do anything this spectacular, but was grateful to learn it now. Had the Jhessaillian been right there, Tal would have hugged him.

Having seen what waited for them on the other side of the flames, the cavalrymen wasted no time in falling back to the gate. Anything that got in the way they simply rode over. Only so many could pass beneath the walls at once though, and they swiftly bunched up around the gate waiting to pass.

Those walking corpses that could still be seen were reorganizing themselves back into orderly formations. The infantry with Tal and Rania, forming a thin shield between the cavalry and the enemy, waited tensely for the dead to come at them again.

The wall of flame seemed to part for an instant and the spectre emerged, its mount steaming and blackened with flames still licking hungrily at bits of flesh. As the pair of ghastly creatures advanced, the dead formed up around them.

Tal stepped forward, *Kallevamar* held ready before him. He raised his voice to be heard over the crackle of flames and the drum of hooves. "This blade has already ended two of your kind, Spectre. Do you wish to face it as well?"

Kherzul's general stopped a scant fifty paces away. "You fight well, Shevestra'ka, but Val Jerak is a doomed city. Surrender now and it will be spared. Keep fighting and I promise you we'll slay every man, woman, and child within these walls."

"After the damage we've done, you haven't the strength!" Tal taunted, stalling for time.

The spectre laughed derisively. "You've hurt us, true enough, but not so badly as you seem to think. Or do you forget that my Lord is master of the dead?"

The Sephira shuddered and writhed, seeming to cry out in agony within Tal's head. He sensed scores of fragmentary essences igniting, tiny sparks of sorrow and suffering that spread like wildfire. All across the field fallen soldiers in the livery of Val Jerak and Val Solus began to get back to their feet, taking up again the weapons they had died holding.

Rage coursed through Tal, his own mingled with that of the Sephira at the creation of such obscenities. "You'll burn for this," he snarled, his grip tightening on his sword, "and your master will burn with you!" He was on the verge of hurling himself at the hateful creature when a hand grabbed his shoulder from behind.

"The cavalry are in and the gates are closing," Rania murmured in his ear. "I think we'd best follow them, yes?" As she spoke, the wall of flames Kyril had called up gave a fitful flicker and vanished.

Tal turned and followed the last of the infantrymen through Val Jerak's closing gates. As soon as they were through, the portcullis slammed down behind them. He ventured one last look back at the narrowing sliver of the field between the closing gates. The spectre still stood in the exact same place, not having stirred an inch.

"A doomed city, Lord Solus," it called to him. "Remember later that you were given the chance to prevent it."

The gates boomed shut and the portcullis began to rise again as it was winched back up.

Tal stood staring at the closed gate in consternation. The spectre hadn't even tried to breach it! It was as if the thing didn't care! But why not?

"Tal?" Rania's voice broke him from his reverie.

"Sorry, Rania. I was just trying to figure out what the Bhellans are up to."

"Preparing to commit mass murder, it seemed fairly clear to me."

"I guess so," Tal said ruefully as they started walking down the long arch under the wall. "It looks like we've finally got a moment. What were you mad at me about before?"

Rania's face flushed. "When it took you so long to signal Kyril and come back, I thought you'd lied to me about not being in danger. I shouldn't have been so quick to mistrust you. I'm sorry."

Tal gave her a sidelong look. "You're a very odd woman, Rania. I thought it was supposed to be me apologizing in this conversation. I really didn't mean to lie to you," he added, "but when I said there'd be no danger I didn't know that my horn had been ruined. I had to get a new one."

"And just how did you pull that off?"

"I took one from a Bhellan cavalry officer."

Rania stopped dead in her tracks. "You actually stood and fought? Tal, you're either the bravest man I've ever met or completely out of your mind."

"If I'd had any other option, I'd have taken it," he replied defensively. "Besides, I'm not the one who insisted she stay on the field despite having just taken a spear through the shoulder."

"Fair enough," Rania said blithely, "I guess we're both insane, then. It must come with the job." She jauntily linked arms with him and began walking again.

When they emerged into the courtyard before the inner gate they found several hundred soldiers gathered there. The men erupted into whoops and cheers at the sight of the Shevestra'ken.

Tal held his hands up for silence, and eventually the cacophony died down. "Thank you, truly," he declared, "but I remind you that the enemy is still out there. To your posts, men!"

As the soldiers began trotting off, Tal shook his head and said quietly to himself, "Honestly! The way they're going on, you'd think we already won!"

Up on the wall, a catapult lobbed a ball of burning pitch skyward. It was only then, in the light of the flaming projectile, that Tal realized the shadows were lengthening and darkness drawing near. Had the fighting really gone on all day? He'd barely marked the passage of time.

"Lord Solus!" A fresh-faced young archer emerged from the door to the gatehouse, quiver swaying at his hip as he ran up to Tal and saluted.

"Are the Bhellans attacking again?" Tal asked, carefully keeping any sign of worry from his voice.

"No, sir. They seem to be pulling back to get out of range of the catapults," the youth reported breathlessly. "It's the Guardian, sir. He's collapsed."

"Take me to him."

"This way, sir."

They didn't have far to go. Kyril was stretched out on the wall above the gate, sleeping by all appearances. Several archers were clustered anxiously around him, and one of them had covered the Guardian with his cloak. Tal was relieved to see that his friend's chest continued to rise and fall with steady breaths.

"He just fell over when the flames went out," one of the archers said as Tal arrived. "He was really pale and barely breathing at first, but he seems to be getting better fast."

Tal knelt beside his friend and put a hand to his brow. "Kyril?"

The Guardian's eyes fluttered open, taking a moment to focus. "Oh, there you are Tal," he said thickly. "I seem to have overexerted myself. Never tried anything that big before. Did you see it?"

"I saw," Tal smiled. "You saved us all. But are you going to be alright?"

"Be fine," Kyril mumbled drowsily, his eyelids drooping heavily. "Just need... a little... rest."

Tal stood. "You three," he said with a nod to the closest archers, including the one who had volunteered his cloak. "Would you take Guardian Damarrian someplace he can sleep? A barracks, an inn, anyplace he can rest undisturbed will be fine."

"Yes, sir!" One of the soldiers took Kyril by the shoulders, a second by the legs, and the third took the lead to open doors.

Within seconds of the archers disappearing with their charge, a bell began to toll in the city.

"What now?" Tal wondered with a sigh, casting his gaze across the rooftops.

"There, sir!" cried a nearby soldier, pointing off to the right. A ruddy glow rose from where he pointed, and flames could just be seen crackling up above the surrounding buildings.

"And there!" called another, gesturing to the south.

In rapid succession as they watched, patches of flame cropped up all over Val Jerak.

"The city!" a voice wailed despairingly. "The city is burning!"

"Not the city!" Tal yelled out to calm the men. "The graveyards! Kherzul is waking our dead! The fires are to stop them!"

That restored a measure of order. Tal could hear his declaration being echoed up and down the wall. He eyed the fires nervously, hoping that this safeguard would prove effective. Crossing the wall, he gazed out over the darkening field of battle. Of the Bhellan invaders there was nothing to be seen save the glimmer of campfires for the living troops. At least the snow seemed finally to be abating.

"Talaren!" called a familiar voice.

Tal turned to greet Malry as the Armslord hastened to his side. His old mentor bore the marks of battle, his uniform stained and bloodied, a bandage hastily tied off around one arm, and the links of his mail shirt parted in places where it had borne the brunt of an attack.

"What is it, Malry?"

"The infirmaries are under attack!"

"What? How? The Bhellans didn't get into the city!"

"They didn't," Malry agreed, "but not all of the men taken to the healers could be saved. They had dead among the injured, and those dead have started to rise. After the retreat, I escorted several of our men to the healers' and we found the place in turmoil. We managed to get the healers and the less injured of their patients out, but there weren't enough of us to contain the dead. They're killing anything they come across, and then their victims get up again and join them."

"Idiot!" Tal berated himself. "I should have anticipated this!" He took a moment to get hold of himself. Nothing for it now but to deal with the situation. "Malry, I want you to take over command here on the wall," he said more calmly. "We'll send a company of guardsmen to each of the infirmaries to protect the townsfolk and eliminate any dead they encounter. I'll lead one group, and Rania will go with another." Tal looked at the other Shevestra'ka. "I know you prefer we stick together, but this way is better. You and I can both sense the dead without seeing them, and that'll be immensely valuable if they start to disperse into the city."

Rania flashed him that innocent-seeming smile that always accompanied her sliest barbs. "Why are you explaining, Tal? I only argue with you when you're wrong."

Tal rolled his eyes. "Let's get moving, then. Time's wasting."

On their way out of the gatehouse, before they separated to go gather their men, Tal asked, "Rania?"

"Hmmm?"

"Do try to be careful. You're still hurt."

Green eyes sparkled at him. "I'll be every bit as cautious as you."

"That's not particularly reassuring."

"It wasn't meant to be. But take care of yourself as well, Tal, or I'll beat you senseless when this is all over."

Tal chuckled. "Okay, you've got a deal."

"Is that the last of them, sir?"

Tal nodded wearily. "I don't sense any more around here. This part of the city should be clean now. Have any of the other groups reported?"

The soldier bobbed his head. "We've just had a runner from Lady Amoran. She reports her section clear and that she's coming to join up with us."

"Let's meet her halfway then, and pray the other groups have similar reports soon."

Whereas the day had seemed to pass in the blink of an eye, this night had been interminable. Tal had seen horrors enough to last him a lifetime. He wondered if, after tonight, he'd ever be able to sleep peacefully again.

By the time they had been able to reach the first of the infirmaries, the risen dead had already done their grisly work and there was little left but to direct the few survivors to safety. All but two of the healers had managed to escape the carnage, but the men they'd been tending were far less fortunate. Only a handful of those, the ones whose injuries were relatively minor or whose wounds had already been mended, had been able to flee. The rest had been slaughtered in their sickbeds by the corpses of former comrades, only to rise again moments later and join their killers.

From that point, Tal's worst fears had come to pass. Rather than fight in ordered formations like those he had faced outside, these dead had immediately scattered to carry their violence to the streets of Val Jerak. They fell mercilessly upon anyone unfortunate enough to cross their paths, creating more corpses to rise and join the mayhem, spreading themselves through the city like a dark and virulent contagion. Tal and his men had little choice but to hunt down and destroy the clusters of marauding dead that resulted and hope that they could contain them all.

Having to fight the corpses of soldiers in the colors of House Jerak or his own House was agonizing enough in itself, but worse by far were those who wore no House colors at all. A soldier made a choice, and while it wasn't a choice to die, they at least knew the risks of their profession when they chose to pursue it. The townspeople and smallfolk, on the other hand, had made no such choice. They had sought only to live their lives and carry on their trades in peace. They had erred only by being in the wrong place, and for that error their lives had been ended too early, their remains made chattel for Kherzul's ambition. He had no right! This wasn't warfare; to call it a tactic would lend it a legitimacy it wasn't deserving of. This was cruel, malicious, and monstrous, and it fell to Tal to right the situation as best he was able.

Under the circumstances, Tal felt his best to be pathetically short of adequate. It was, in fact, barely even tolerable. Early in the evening, he had burst into a modest residence just as the three animated corpses that had attacked the place were casting aside the bodies of their latest victims, a pair of young children. With the rest of the family cowering in the corner, Tal had dispatched their assailants only to sense the telltale essence flare as the children's corpses got up to attack him, their ghastly wounds gaping at him mockingly. Without pause he'd turned *Kallevamar* against those young bodies, hacking them into quiescence while their mother wailed desperately for him to stay his hand.

Afterwards, through tear-filled eyes, he'd tried to explain to the poor woman why he'd had to do as he did even though he knew he couldn't ask her to understand. Her cries still echoed in his mind, tearing at his heart, forcing him to ask if he was truly any less monstrous than what he fought.

That was the way the entire night unfolded itself as they scoured the city, following Tal's Sephiral awareness from nightmare to nightmare: around every new corner, another tragedy waiting to be played out. At the end of every street, another vignette of loss, sorrow, and compromise. Every body that fell meant another family shattered, more friendships lost, further hopes dashed. Could there be any joy left in the world after being party to such tragedy?

And yet still matters managed to worsen, for Tal made a discovery in the midst of all that madness that he wished he could un-make, a discovery that made him feel dirty for the learning of it: those slain by a Shevestra'ka didn't rise again.

His name had been Jennar, a guardsman from Val Solus. In happier times he'd crossed practice blades with his Duke's heir and even on occasion joined Tal and Tazmin for a drink in the city's pubs. He had been among those who followed Tal to Val Jerak, had stood on the wall at the Felmorr Gap, and had answered the call for men when the infirmaries came under attack. While investigating a darkened stable that Tal had sensed foes in, he'd been taken by surprise when the corpse of a stableman that had gone unobserved in the shadows reanimated. His comrades had cut the creature to ribbons, but not before it managed to skewer Jennar with a pitchfork.

Tal had been busy at the other end of the stables dealing with the dead who had done for the stableman, but upon finishing them had immediately rushed to the stricken soldier's side.

Jennar had looked up at him with a world of agony reflected in his eyes, but he'd put on a bold face and said, "Sorry, milord. Guess I shouldn't have tempted death so many times today."

Tal had replied gruffly, "No talk like that, Jennar. Once we get you to a healer, you'll be..."

The injured man shook his head vehemently. "We don't have time. Doubt I'd make it that far anyway."

He was probably right, Tal had to admit. The stableman had struck upward from the ground with the pitchfork, and its tines were buried deeply at an angle in Jennar's body. No telling how many organs had been punctured. It was a cruel miracle he hadn't been killed instantly.

"I ask a boon of my Lord."

"Anything," Tal replied with a catch in his voice.

Jennar's body was wracked by a fit of coughing. Blood flecked his lips. "I hurt so much, Talaren. Don't let me linger like this. End it quickly."

Tal hesitated.

"Please!" Jennar wheezed.

174

The Shevestra'ka nodded hesitantly. "Alright." He held *Kallevamar* poised point downward over Jennar's breast in both hands. "Though this seems poor repayment for the service you've given my family."

"Kill the thing I turn into before it can hurt anyone and keep these bastards from Val Solus, and I'll call us even."

Tal forced himself to meet the dying man's gaze. "By Shevestra's name, Jennar, I swear I will." And then he drove *Kallavamar* down through the soldier's heart. The wave of grief that accompanied the taking of a life swept through Tal, carried along with Jennar's essence as it passed through him and back to the Sephira. A tear rolled down Tal's cheek.

But Jennar hadn't risen again. There was no fragment of him left in the body for Kherzul's necromancy to sink its tendrils into. In being killed by a Shevestra'ka, his energies had reintegrated completely with the Sephira except for the small part that joined itself to the Warrior Soul. At least, that seemed to Tal the most plausible explanation.

The significance of Jennar's stillness in death hadn't been lost on the men. From that moment on they turned to Tal to hasten the passing of their grievously injured, much to his horror. He had the power to grant a clean death, they claimed, one which the necromancer couldn't disturb with his foul touch. They invented a name for it, and spoke it with reverence: Shevestra's Mercy.

How many times that night had Tal been called on to administer this 'mercy?' How many dying men had looked in his eyes and begged him not to let Kherzul take them? How many friends and allies had added their life energies to Talaren's Warrior Soul? He wished he could forget, but their names were seared into his memory: Jennar, Wolram, Fulgar, Tomyn, Baran, and the list went on. Nineteen names in all, and each one a razor cut on Tal's conscience. *Friends should be given comfort and succor, not death!* But death was all he'd been able to give.

Now the night that had seemed it would never end was finally drawing to a close. Dawn would be coming before long. And Rania was close. Tal could feel her ahead of him now, could feel within her a sorrow so deep it etched the soul. Her pain echoed his own and called out to him.

They converged on the central causeway that ran through the heart of Val Jerak. If Rania's emotions hadn't been confirmation enough that she'd discovered the same thing as Tal, the way her men looked at her was. Both groups held back respectfully as their Shevestra'ken leaders stepped forward to meet one another.

For a moment Tal was aware only of Rania standing before him. Covered in filth and gore, with new dents on helmet and greaves, she'd obviously had as eventful a night as he. Through it all she still managed to appear proud and inspiring, her back straight and face a mask of determination. Only looking deeply into her eyes was any of the sadness Tal knew to be there apparent.

They stopped only a few feet from each other, and Rania put fist to heart in salute. She made as if to speak, but couldn't seem to make herself do so. All she managed was, "Tal..."

Some things couldn't be put into words. Tal nodded. "I know."

Rania stepped forward and hugged him fiercely.

Tal wrapped his arms tightly around her and for long moments they stood in silence, unmindful of the men around them, sharing the sorrow that only they could truly fathom.

"It was terrible," Rania finally whispered. "So much suffering. So little reason. How can we hold back such malignant evil?"

"I don't know," Tal murmured back, "but we will. I've promised too many dying friends I would for us to fail."

He felt her nod. "Me too."

And then the gong above the eastern gate began to sound, calling out an alarm.

19

To Wake From Madness

The square before the eastern gate was filled with a confused profusion of soldiers when Tal and Rania arrived. Some were being gathered into a group beside the gatehouse while others dashed off toward the south gate as quickly as they arrived. Malry moved through it all exuding a sense of calm command, barking orders at all newcomers, sending most of them south.

"What's our situation, Malry?" Tal asked before the Armslord even had a chance to acknowledge his arrival.

"They're coming through the south gate," Malry reported grimly. "Lieutenant General Jonfer is leading the defense there right now. He's trying to hold them in the square, and I've been sending him reinforcements as fast as I can."

"How did they breach the gate without the alarm there being sounded?" Tal demanded.

"The gate wasn't breached," the Armslord replied, "it was opened. Spectre in the gatehouse, it seems. The runner Jonfer sent us said that one man made it out to warn the Lieutenant General, and that the fellow was scared witless. Said that one moment everything was quiet, and the next one of the shadows came to life and started slaughtering everyone. He also said their weapons were useless against it."

"That sounds like a spectre alright," Tal agreed. "What were you planning for the men you're not sending to help Jonfer?"

"I'm leading them down the wall to retake the gatehouse."

Tal frowned. "They'll be expecting that. You could be walking into a trap."

"I know," Malry said resolutely, "but if we don't close the gates again, or at least get the portcullis down, we're done for. We can't hold the square for long, not against the numbers they're throwing at us."

"That's probably true," Tal sighed. "But we need to do something else, something unanticipated. If we let the Bhellans set the pace of this battle, we'll lose for sure." He had yielded that initiative last night by withdrawing into the city, and the consequences thus far had proven disastrous.

"Then kill the spectre," Rania suggested bluntly. "That would be the most crippling blow we could deal them."

"She just might be on to something there," Kyril commented cheerfully as he joined their little circle, absently adjusting a sleeve of his slept-in uniform.

"Kyril!" Tal declared in surprise, "You're awake!"

"You didn't honestly think I could sleep through this commotion, did you?" Kyril's expansive gesture encompassed the entire courtyard. "I take it we're in trouble?"

"Bhellans coming through the south gate," Tal replied curtly. "They've taken the gatehouse there."

The Guardian nodded. "Yes, I'd say that qualifies as trouble. What're you doing about it?"

"That's what we were just working out. Now what was this about killing the spectre?"

"Remember your history," Kyril said chidingly.

Rania sighed in exasperation. "This is no time to be coy with important information. Tal, when Anakara was conquering what's now Valeran, Bhellus, and Amberyl, she rarely accompanied her skeletal legions personally. But Trazeri was always present for every battle. She arguably owed her rule to his skill as a tactician as much as to her own Sephiral knowledge."

"Yes," Tal agreed impatiently, "I remember that, but what does that mean to us now?"

"Tal, think about it," Kyril urged. "Those unfortunate creatures Kherzul is using against us don't have anything inside their skulls except maybe some decaying jellied goo. And I don't fully comprehend how you Shevestra'ken perceive Sephiral forces, but you must have noticed by now that the motivating energies of the dead are dim and fractured compared to the living. In light of those facts, doesn't it seem odd that they should act with anything resembling intelligence or coordination?"

"No, because they're being controlled." Tal fixed Kyril with a probing stare. "Are you saying that eliminating the spectre will break that control?"

A thoughtful frown creased the corners of Kyril's lips. "I can't say for certain, but I'd think it likely. Anakara and Trazeri demonstrated to the Order that a spectre can serve as a Sephiral conduit for its creator. Destroy that conduit and Kherzul's ability to influence events here should be severely dampened, possibly even eliminated." He eyed Rania curiously. "Although I'm wondering how Lady Amoran knew about this."

Rania smiled devilishly at the Guardian. "I didn't. I made a guess based on what I do know about the Sephira and the Undying. Not every answer requires the vaunted knowledge of the Jhessaillian Order, you know."

Tal cleared his throat. "Let's stay focused here. What matters is that you've both taken us a step closer to a plan. We need to kill that spectre, now we just have to determine how."

"There may be a complication," Malry said. "There's more than one to kill. We've sighted at least two of those things."

Kyril added, "Let's not forget that without Godtouched, Trazeri's Blade is the only way we can hurt them. So you're the only one who can do it, Tal. I'm sure the enemy realizes that as well. That's probably why the spectre at the gate yesterday didn't attack when you challenged it. We can expect them to try avoiding a confrontation with you."

"So we set a trap of our own," Tal reasoned as the pieces began to come together in his head. "Malry, it looks like you'll be leading that attempt to retake the gatehouse after all, and Rania and I will be coming with you. Once we succeed, one of the spectres will have to come to keep us from closing the gate. And when it does, I'll deal with it."

"Tal, did you hear a word I just said?" Kyril asked. "If you're there they won't come. They're trying to avoid you."

"No," Tal corrected, "they're trying to avoid a Shevestra'ka in formal armor with a foxhead helm. If I change my armor and neither Rania nor I immerse ourselves in the Sephira, I doubt they'll realize that I'm there until it's too late. We can close the gate and kill one of Kherzul's generals in a single stroke. Unless anyone has a better idea?"

When no suggestions were forthcoming, Tal nodded. "Alright then, let's do this while we still can. Malry, the command is yours. Get the troops ready for our counterattack. Rania, will you help me with my armor?"

Wordlessly, Rania followed Tal into one of the nearby towers. Once they were alone inside, she set to undoing the straps on the plates covering his torso and shoulders.

"I wanted to talk with you about *Edyamar*," he said quietly while she worked. "Though it'll allow you to slay spectres as well, I think that I should be the one to deliver the killing blow to the ones here. There would be too many questions if you were to kill one of them, questions I don't think either of us want to answer."

"I agree," Rania murmured.

"Then I'll try to handle them all myself. The only exception is that I won't let Val Jerak fall to keep our secret. If it comes down to that, you'll have to do what's needed and we'll both deal with the consequences."

"I can accept that," she replied, "but there's one other exception. I'll also kill one of them if I have to in order to protect you."

Tal chuckled. "That's your choice, but I won't argue with you there."

"Good," Rania said, "because if you did I'd have to hit you."

Once Tal was down to mail shirt and greaves he donned a spare helmet from a rack inside the tower before they both went to join the men assembled there.

Kyril was waiting for them outside the tower. As soon as the Shevestra'ken emerged he asked, "Where do you want me, Tal?"

"Are you well enough to handle the Sephira again?"

The Guardian shrugged. "I'm still fatigued from yesterday's exertions, but I can manage a bit more for you if I'm careful."

Tal nodded gratefully. "Then go find yourself a safe vantage from which to assist our men in the southern courtyard. They probably need all the help they can get right now."

"I'll give them what I can," Kyril agreed. "Best of luck with the spectre."

"Thanks, Kyril. Try not to push yourself too hard. I don't want you keeling over from exhaustion again."

"I'll do what I have to," the Jhessaillian grinned, "the same as you two. Can't let you Adepts have all the glory, after all." And with that he set off for the south end of the city.

As soon as Tal and Rania had taken their places amongst the soldiers, Malry ordered the column up the tower and down the wall. They marched along the parapet three abreast with the Shevestra'ken side by side in the second rank.

When the southern square came into view, it was swarming with dead packed cheek to jowl. All of the connecting streets were blocked by Valerite soldiers fighting desperately to hold back the crushing advance, but step by step they were being pushed back as more and more of them fell. Arrows hailed down from the surrounding rooftops to little apparent effect. While Tal looked on in dismay, the paving stones of a section of the square erupted upward in a geyser of stone chips, dirt, and body parts. A second explosion followed right on the heels of the first. It appeared that Kyril was in place. Even so, it didn't look as though the defenders could hold out for much longer.

The gatehouse loomed ahead, an imposing blocky stone edifice whose only entrance from this level was a stout iron-bound door.

"Alright men, stop your staring," Malry said loudly. "We all know what a losing fight looks like. We're here to get those gates closed. Let's take the heat off our friends down there."

As their column drew closer to the gatehouse, arrows began to shoot forth from the slits overlooking the parapet. Tal stifled a surprised exclamation. Though those fortifications had been designed against just such an attack as this, he had yet to see any of the dead wielding bows or crossbows. Apparently there were real, live Bhellan soldiers among those inside.

Fortunately most of the Valerite infantrymen bore shields, which helped limit their losses as they charged toward the door. Still, several men were felled by arrows they caught with their bodies instead of their shields.

As soon as the armored column reached the door, six burly soldiers brought forward a small, steel-capped ram from behind Tal and Rania.

Arrows continued to be shot from the gatehouse, but none of the slits allowed a clear shot at the area right before the door. Six jarring blows from the ram was all it took to knock the door in.

Malry leapt into the room before the shattered door had even hit the floor. Tal and Rania were right behind. Directly ahead of them waited a line of eight swordsmen in the crimson and gold of the Bhellan royal guard.

Tal and Rania broke to the sides to deal with the archers covering the parapet. Malry went straight down the middle. The snowy-haired Armslord caught the blades that leapt for him without cutting his momentum and then twisted his body to dart between the two centermost men. On the way past he laid open the abdomen of one of the soldiers, spilling the man's entrails on the floor at his feet. The second received a swift slash to the back of the neck as Malry turned, nearly decapitating him.

Although Tal had been years in training with Malry, this was the first opportunity he'd ever had to see his old mentor in actual combat. The man was an unbelievable swordsman. Though he lacked the Embrace of Shevestra that had transformed Tal and Rania into Battleborn, there was no doubt in Tal's mind that in the skills of an Armslord he easily surpassed them both. So great was his ability with a blade, so blindingly fast and unerringly accurate his attacks, one could almost believe that he *was* Shevestra'ken despite his lack of an aura. Tal felt a swelling of pride to have been taught by so consummate a master.

The fight was over quickly. Besides the swordsmen and archers there were perhaps a dozen animated dead in the gatehouse, and Malry had brought along enough soldiers to overwhelm them easily. The men of Valeran, now used to the dead rising again, hovered over the bodies of those who'd only been slain once and descended with bared blades at the first hint of movement.

Malry pulled the lever that withdrew the catch holding the outer portcullis. With a steely hiss followed by a resounding thud, the heavy metal grating slammed down. The inner portcullis followed seconds later as one of the soldiers triggered its lever.

Malry began rapidly issuing orders, gesturing to groups of men as he gave them their duties. "You men, man the cranks and get those gates closed. You, go hold the stairs up from the square. We'll have company coming from there soon, no doubt. You six, down to the murder holes. If there's any burning pitch still ready down there, you know what to do."

The soldiers indicated saluted and dashed off to fulfill their assignments. Malry turned to Tal. "That wasn't too bad," he commented. "If you were right, we should have company any minute. What're you planning once we're finished up here?"

Tal replied, "I'm torn at the moment between going after the next spectre and clearing out the square."

"It's a big mess down there," the Armslord observed. "It'll take a while to clean up, but the men we sent should be able to handle it now that we've stemmed the tide of reinforcements. Especially with the assistance your Jhessaillian friend is providing. I should think you'd do best to stay on the attack before the enemy can make any more messes to confound you."

As Malry spoke, the shadows behind him seemed to writhe and then coalesced into a looming humanoid form clad in breastplate and helm, under which burned the dispassionate red eyes Tal remembered so well from his encounter with Skalgrim.

Malry must have seen what was happening reflected in Tal's expression, for one instant he was speaking and the next he spun on one foot, his sword whistling through the air. His aim was true and the blade flashed through where the creature's neck should have been, but caused only a swirling in the tenebrous mist of the spectre's body.

Tal sprang forward, the Sephira coursing into his body as he opened himself to it. Time seemed to slow.

The spectre raised its own blade in response to Malry's attack and thrust it between the Armslord's ribs. Tal howled in rage as his mentor staggered back, legs going limp under him. The spectre pulled its blade free and began turning to face Tal, but far too late. The enraged Shevestra'ka was already upon it.

Tal swung *Kallevamar* with all his strength. The ancient blade ripped a gaping hole in the breastplate as it clove through the spectre's body. The thing immediately began to lose coherency, dissipating into nothingness as its armor and weapon clattered to the floor.

"Master," Tal moaned in a stricken voice, dropping to his knees beside Malry's prone form.

"No tears for me, Tal," the old Armslord said faintly as his glassy eyes tried to focus on Talaren's face. "It was a life... well lived." He took a deep shuddering breath as if marshalling his strength. "To fall fighting beside a Shevestra'ka I helped create... I have no regrets."

"Save your strength, Master. I'll..."

Malry shook his head weakly. "Only one thing... left for you to do." His eyes seemed to clear for a moment as he continued to gasp for words. "Make me part... of your Warrior Soul."

Tal stared at the blade in his hands. "Master, I can't..."

"You can." Malry's voice was soft but firm. "It's what I want." A gentle smile touched his lips as Tal raised *Kallevamar* haltingly. "Make me... proud, Tal. I'll be... watching you."

When it was finished, Tal slowly got to his feet. He wished tears would come, but it seemed he had none left. All of the soldiers in the room stood with heads bowed in deference to his sorrow. Rania alone met his gaze, her green eyes sympathetic.

"I'm going up above," Tal announced dully, "to check the enemy's disposition and determine our next move."

The air was cold atop the gatehouse, and carried the fetid stench of death. That scent had become inescapable over the last day, seeming to sink into the stones of the city in mute commemoration of the horrific events that had transpired here.

The Bhellan horde was spread out on the field below, a sea of reeking dead encapsulating tiny islands of living men. They seemed to already be moving in response to the closing of the gate, their formations shifting to march. At their head sat a second spectre astride its charnel steed. Tal saw no hint of a third, but found himself puzzled when he noted the direction the Bhellans were moving in.

"West. Why to the west?" he muttered to himself. Surely they weren't intending to try the same tactic at another gatehouse? Had they decided to bypass Val Jerak and try striking deeper into Valeran?

He felt her coming up behind him. Tal gave no indication he noticed, keeping his stare intent on the moving army.

Rania laid a gentle hand on his arm as she reached his side. "Tal?" she asked softly, a deep concern evident in her voice.

"I'll mourn Malry later, Rania," Tal said. "Save your compassion for then." He met her troubled gaze earnestly. "I'll likely need it when that time comes. But until then I've got other worries. It's your sword I need right now."

"You have both, whenever you may need them." She gave his arm a squeeze. "What's next, then?"

"We attack," Tal said bluntly. "But I'm not sure how until I can make sense of what they're up to."

The hatch behind them crashed open, and a sandy-haired soldier scrambled up. "Lord Solus!" he exclaimed breathlessly with a quick salute. "I've run all the way from the west gate. There's another force coming down the road! Sir, they march under the banner of the red wolf!"

Tal found himself grinning, though he could hardly believe his ears. He hadn't dared hope that reinforcements would arrive in time to aid him, but the red wolf was the banner of House Joseth. Somehow, Remarr and Tazmin had managed to send him aid! The Bhellans' movement suddenly made sense. They were turning to face the new threat.

"How many are they?" Tal asked excitedly.

"When I left, our best estimate was two thousand, maybe more."

Tal nodded. Too few to overcome the Bhellans by sheer force of combined arms, but their arrival presented an ideal opportunity for a strike against the remaining spectre.

"I have orders for you to carry," Tal said, his voice edged with steel. "Assemble the cavalry at the western gate. All of them, as well as any infantry we can spare. And have my horse, Stormwind, made ready for battle. It's time to end this insanity."

The soldier beamed with obvious pleasure at being the bearer of such orders. "Yes, sir!" He dropped a quick bow and clambered back down the hatch.

"You really think we can finish it here?" Rania asked after he was gone.

"Assuming you and Kyril are right about the spectres, yes." Tal replied. "Shall we go find out?"

Rania grinned wickedly. "We shall."

Lines of horsemen filled the western square and stretched on for hundreds of yards down the central causeway. A charged air of excitement hung over the place and filled the buzz of overheard conversations.

Despite their lack of Sephiral auras, Tal and Rania's arrival didn't go unnoticed. A pocket of silence followed them as they crossed the square, every eye turning to the Shevestra'ken Adepts.

General Krovar waited atop a full-chested brown warhorse at the gate in a heavy shirt of scaled armor. With him were Tal's great courser and a mighty black steed that looked every inch Stormwind's match, both girded in mail barding. Krovar saluted to Tal and Rania as they approached.

"General," Tal said with a nod by way of greeting. "What's our situation?"

"The Bhellans and the forces from Val Joseth are closing on each other," Krovar replied. "They'll be joining battle shortly."

"No time to lose, then," Tal said. "Make ready to ride." He began climbing up into Stormwind's saddle.

Rania was eyeing the black warhorse curiously.

"A gift," the General explained, "for all you've done in defense of our city, Lady Amoran. He's one of the finest to come from the Keep's stables. May he serve you well."

"Thank you," Rania said, scratching the horse's muzzle before taking the reins. "He's magnificent."

"There's one more matter before we ride, if you'll both excuse my temerity," Krovar said with a self-deprecating grimace. He gestured to a pair of bannermen behind him. "With your permission, we'd like to take these with us."

At the General's signal, the bannermen unfurled the standards they carried. The one was jet black with House Solus's running fox picked out boldly in silver. The other depicted in gray a tower crossed by a jagged bolt of lightning on a field of deepest blue. The banner of House Amoran.

The muscles in Rania's jaw tensed as she looked at the banner, and she turned her head to General Krovar with a single word. "Why?"

"Most of the men feel that Zharkus's treachery has tainted his banner and to march under it would be a bad omen. And the whole city knows that when House Jerak dishonored itself by betraying us, it was the scions of Houses Solus and Amoran who took up the burden of defending Val Jerak. None would've been surprised if you'd left us to fend for ourselves, especially after we found out what Kherzul had sent against us, but you never seemed even to entertain the thought. Such resolve demands to be honored, and because of that, not a man of us here wouldn't rather fight under your Houses' coats of arms."

Rania gave a curt nod. "As long as it's understood that in allowing this I'm not seeking to restore House Amoran. My oaths forbid me from doing that, even if I wanted to."

"I'm flattered by the gesture, General Krovar, and have no objections to the use of House Solus's standard," Tal said. "Bring the banners, but do so quickly. We ride!" He raised his voice and bellowed, "Open the gates!"

Slowly, the gates swung wide. Tal rode out through them, the remainder of Val Jerak's military strength following behind.

House Joseth's forces had veered south from the road to confront the Bhellan army moving to intercept them. The two groups were almost atop one another now, facing off with several hundred yards of clear field between them as they shifted formations in preparation for battle.

Tal chose a course to bring his men up alongside House Joseth's. He noted with incredulity that they seemed to be assuming an offensive posture despite being outnumbered at least three to one. Instead of covering the flanks, their cavalry stood in the front ranks where Tal would have expected to see pikemen. Behind them were rank upon rank of heavy infantry positioned to charge in after the horsemen. It was a style of formation one would expect to see employed to crush an inferior force, not attack one several times the size of one's own.

Before Tal and his men had crossed half the distance to the two armies, horns began to sound from Val Joseth's formations. They surged forward to attack and the Bhellans responded in kind, the remaining spectre leading their charge. As the Bhellans committed themselves, a dozen horsemen pulled ahead of the rest of Val Joseth's cavalry.

Tal sensed a massive shifting of energy in the Sephira, so pronounced that his skin seemed to tingle with it.

Within less than a second of that sensation, multiple columns of flame erupted skyward among the charging Bhellans. Strokes of lightning flashed down among them from the cloudless sky. Huge, jagged shards of ice manifested from nothingness and then hurtled into their army, tearing with ease through armor and flesh alike.

Tal's jaw dropped. The sheer destructive power he was witnessing defied belief.

How could even the dead withstand such bombardment? Apparently they couldn't. The Bhellan charge foundered under the withering assault. Tal saw the spectre emerge from a column of flame, trying desperately to cut its steed's forward momentum. A heartbeat later, a bolt of lightning blasted the unnatural mount into smoldering chunks of meat, throwing the spectre to the ground.

Kherzul's general picked itself up just in time to be overtaken by the horsemen leading House Joseth's charge. Blades flashed and when they had passed, there was naught remaining where the spectre had stood but an empty suit of armor falling to the ground. Those riders were Godtouched!

The effect on the animated dead was pronounced and instantaneous. All semblance of order among them disintegrated without the guiding will of a spectre to command them. Like feral animals they immediately fell to attacking whatever was closest to them, which predominantly meant each other.

A roaring cheer went up from the men behind Tal. For his part, the young Adept of Shevestra had to wonder if he was dreaming. For House Joseth to have sent troops in time to help was unbelievable enough, but their having enough Jhessaillians in tow to do as Tal had just seen was beyond the pale.

He rode on to greet the men who had come to the rescue of Val Jerak. They were pulling back from the fighting now, apparently content to let the enemy tear themselves apart.

As Tal approached House Joseth's banner, a grinning Tazmin clad in plate and mail armor rode forward from a cluster of black-uniformed Guardians.

"Hello Tal," Tazmin said cheerfully. "It was terribly thoughtful of you to leave some Bhellans for us. I was so looking forward to seeing our Jhessaillian friends here in action. I must say it made all of the nighttime riding worth the ordeal. Have you ever seen such a thing?"

Tal shook his head disbelievingly. "Tazmin, I swear you'll never change."

"Probably not," his friend chuckled, "but you seem to have. It must be working well for you, though. Your healthy glow is almost blinding." He glanced up at House Amoran's banner. "Now there's something I never would

186

have expected to see here and now." His quirked eyebrow seemed to take in both Tal and Rania. "I suspect you've got quite the story to tell me. One that'll require a good many drinks to go with it."

"Later," Tal said seriously. "I promise. But we're not quite done here yet."

"Tal, those repulsive things you've been fighting are tearing each other to pieces. What else could there possibly be to do?"

"There are still live soldiers in there among them. We need to get those men out."

"You can't be serious."

"I won't leave anyone to a death like that." Tal gestured at the corpses mindlessly rending and flailing at anything nearby. "Not even an enemy. We'll take the survivors prisoner. I won't force anyone to come with me, but I'm going even if I have to go alone."

"Not alone," Rania murmured, drawing *Edyamar*.

Tazmin stared in consternation at the two Shevestra'ken for a few seconds, and then shrugged. "Why not? I could do with a bit of exercise anyway."

Tal watched solemnly from atop the wall as another wagon heaped with dead rumbled up to the gates, bearing its grisly cargo to the pyres being erected on the field before the collapsed Felmorr Gap. The fighting below in the southern square had been some of the most intense, the losses staggering. Lieutenant General Jonfer had fallen down there, giving his life in ferocious defense of his city. Casualties were still being counted, but the current estimate was that nearly half of the men Tal had started the battle with had been slain.

No matter how he looked at it, Tal couldn't see the battle as having been anything but a grievous waste of life, not only for Valeran but for both sides. The Bhellan soldiers he'd attempted to save had been savaged when the dead turned on them, and only a few hundred had survived to be rescued. They had surrendered meekly, even thankfully at being extricated from their dire predicament. Tal only wished he had been able to get more of them out. He'd seen far too much death already.

Tal stood there watching, glowering at every wagon that passed beneath him, taunting him with the ruins of men. This was the price of war. He wanted to laugh bitterly at the irony that none of those passing under him were in the least responsible for what had happened in the past couple days. Not responsible in the slightest, yet it was they who had paid the price. By all rights, he himself should have been on one of those wagons. No, he chided himself, though he had ordered so many of those men to their deaths, he had done so in defense of life, theirs and countless others. The true responsibility lay on King Kherzul's shoulders, safe on his distant throne. So much blood for one man's ambitions. If Kherzul could die a thousand times over, it would only begin to settle the debt he owed so many for their own lives.

In stark contrast to the mournful scene Tal looked upon in the south end of Val Jerak, sounds of music and merrymaking drifted to his ears from the western and northern quarters. The soldiers he had not assigned duties to and the cityfolk alike were celebrating with reckless abandon, jubilant at simply having survived the madness of the last couple days. Part of Tal wanted to join them; part of him wanted to weep at the sights that assailed him.

"I thought I might find you here," Rania said quietly as she stepped up beside him. "You know, everyone's looking for you. Tazmin says you're moping, and Kyril claims that you just know that you can't keep up with them at drinking. I've lost track of how many people have asked me if I know where the Snowfox is."

"Snowfox?" Tal asked with a sideward glance.

"Apparently that's what they're calling you for saving their city. And I'm Rania the Resurrected." She laughed lightly. "Based on what I've heard so far, I was miraculously revived from death to avenge the plundering of Felmorinen's secrets. Some trick, eh?"

Tal grunted noncommittally.

"I think the name suits you," Rania went on, undaunted. "They mean it to be an honor, after all. You should incorporate it into your sigil. That foxhead you use would look even more striking with a snowflake in one eye, or something of the sort."

"I suppose so," he mumbled.

"For someone who just won a battle that was supposed to be unwinnable, you're frightfully morose. Is this that time you mentioned earlier when you'd need my compassion?"

Tal said nothing.

"I'll take that for a yes," Rania said after the silence stretched on several seconds. She put an arm tenderly around his waist and rested her head against his shoulder. "I understand your pain, Tal. I really do."

Irrationally, he wanted to contradict her, but held his tongue. Rania had lost her family and her childhood to the same enemy they'd fought here. She probably understood the loss he felt better than he did.

Instead Tal said quietly, "So many dead, Rania. How many of them might still be alive if I had made different choices? How many died for my mistakes?"

"You can't think like that." Tentatively, almost shyly, she stroked his arm with her free hand. "You did the best you could. Under the circumstances, you did far better than anyone could have hoped." Her voice dropped a bit lower as she added, "I know Malry didn't blame you."

There it was. Tal worked his jaw, trying to speak, but the words wouldn't come. He shrugged away from her touch, continuing to stare sullenly off into the night.

"Tal, I know how the deaths of people you care about can scar you," Rania murmured, the hurt in her voice making the truth of her words undeniable. "They can gnaw at you, harden you, even drive you to madness if you hold them too close. I made that mistake myself, and it nearly cost me everything. I don't want to see the same happen to you. Honor Malry's life, mourn his passing, but remember that he told you himself that he had no regrets. Don't carry any of your own for him. I don't think he'd approve of that."

Tal glanced at her briefly and then nodded slowly. "That may be so, Rania, but what really bothers me is that I just don't know what it was all for. So many men died here, and what did we really accomplish? We fought off

Kherzul's army, true, but they'll be back come the spring thaw and no doubt next time he'll send an even stronger force against us. And the dying will start all over again. This isn't a victory, it's just a temporary respite."

Rania's expression hardened to a disapproving frown as he spoke. She took hold of his arm again, roughly now, and said with an angry edge to her voice, "Come with me, Tal. You've been brooding over the dead for too long. I need to show you something."

He began to protest, but a single look at Rania's face was all it took to realize that she'd brook no argument.

She led him along the top of the wall toward the western gate, the sounds of merriment growing to a pervasive buzz as they walked, the streets below more and more populous. At length they reached the western gatehouse. The square and central causeway were thronged with people, soldiers in House colors and gaily garbed townsfolk mingling together. A roaring bonfire stood at the center of the square, with people singing and dancing around it in blissful abandon. Vendors with barrels of ale and wine stood on the street corners, the drink flowing freely. It was difficult to conceive of this square and the war-ravaged southern one existing in the same city.

"Look carefully, Tal," Rania said beside him. "Look at what you've protected. All of these people are still alive because of what we did. If every last one of them isn't a victory, then I don't know what we fought for. This is life. Don't turn away from it."

Tal wanted to smile. He really did, but he just didn't seem to have it in him. "You're right, Rania, this *is* what we fight for. Maybe I was wrong to say this isn't a victory. But that still doesn't lessen the price we paid, or my concerns over Kherzul and the rest of this war. It'll take a lot more to do that."

Rania glared at him. "Do you think I don't share those concerns, Tal?" she asked heatedly. "I do. I promise you, I want to see Kherzul dead more than anyone. It's the only way I'll ever be able to fill the empty place in my heart left by my family's murders. But people need to let go of their concerns for a little while sometimes, even me. And even you. There's nothing we can do about Kherzul tonight, so you and I are going to go down there and have a drink. And another. And another after that, until you bloody well stop acting like we lost the battle!"

In the face of such vehemence, Tal could think of no response to calm Rania aside from giving in to her demand. Besides, there was a certain amount of sense to her argument. He followed her without argument down to the street.

Their passage through the crowds was anything but anonymous. Within their first ten steps into the square, they were each handed a full mug of ale by a grinning tradesman who refused payment for the drinks, claiming they'd already paid in full by keeping his business standing. As Tal and Rania passed, commoners and soldiers alike would raise their mugs with cries of, "Val Jerak's saviors!" or "The Snowfox and the Resurrected!" or "The Fox and the Tower!" After all the toasts being drunk around them and to them, they were both well into their third mug of ale by the time they'd crossed the square.

Soldiers heartily slapped them on the back, declaring loudly that they would follow either of them to any battlefield, anywhere. Cityfolk thanked them for defending their homes, their families, and their lives. Many asked for their blessings. One prettily blushing young woman even told Tal she intended to name her firstborn after him! Although Tal's worries remained at the back of his mind, they began slowly to be swallowed up by the mirth that came from seeing and experiencing all he had kept from ruin.

As he and Rania made their way through the celebrants, Tal was surprised when a blonde streak of a woman leapt right at him to enfold him in a great hug. "Talaren Solus! I've been looking for you all night!"

Tal looked down in amazement, trying not to spill the drink he held in one hand, and the grim mask he'd worn was finally shattered by a smile as he recognized the blue eyes looking up at him. "Ilse! I'm glad to see you're well." He reciprocated her hug with his free arm.

"Of course I'm well, silly," Ilse giggled at him. "How could I not be with you protecting my city?" Her cheeks reddened as she laid eyes on Rania, and she disentangled herself from Tal to curtsy to the other Shevestra'ka. "You have my gratitude as well, my Lady."

"You're welcome," Rania replied. "I still owe you my own thanks for helping me find Tal that first night. I don't think I remembered to at the time. As a matter of fact, I recall being rather abrupt and ungentle with you. I apologize for treating you like that. I was just worried for Tal."

"I understand." Curiously, Ilse's blush seemed to deepen as she lowered her eyes. "I hope you didn't mistake my friendship with him for something else. I'd not want to come between you."

Tal's jaw dropped at Ilse's apparent assumption, but before he could correct her another familiar voice called out to him.

"Tal, you scoundrel! There you are, keeping all the loveliest ladies to yourself as usual!" Tazmin swaggered out of the crowd with Kyril in tow. Both men wore mischievous smirks and carried partially emptied tankards.

"Hello, Tal," Kyril grinned. "I've been getting acquainted with your friend Lord Tazmin here. What a fine, upstanding young fellow! I have to say I'm both surprised and impressed at your good taste in associates."

Tal stared at his friends in consternation. Trying to explain to Ilse now would doubtlessly set Tazmin off and hopelessly confound the matter.

For his part, Kyril probably wouldn't be much better. And why was Rania grinning at him with such obvious amusement?

Tazmin was eyeing Ilse curiously, a look she was returning with interest. Tazmin prompted, "Tal, you *were* going to introduce us, weren't you?"

"Yes, of course," Tal recovered. "Tazmin, this is Ilse, a friend of mine who I met while staying at the Defender of the Gap here in the city."

"A pleasure, my lady," Tazmin declared with a bow.

"And Ilse, this is Lord Tazmin Joseth, my cousin, friend, and heir to the Barony of Val Joseth."

Ilse curtsied with one of her shy smiles. "You're the one who brought all those extra men this morning, aren't you?"

"Indeed I am," the rakish nobleman replied brightly, "although I must confess that it's usually Tal who pulls my fat from the fire. I was happy to be able to return the favor this time around."

"Well, now that that's all taken care of," Kyril announced, "you've been shirking your duties, Talaren Solus!" He waved a finger at Tal. "You won the battle, now you've got to come get smashingly drunk with us. I'm afraid you've got some catching up to do already." With that, he drained the remaining ale in his mug.

"You honestly think you can go toe-to-toe drinking with Shevestra'ken?" Rania asked in an outraged tone that belied the amused twist to her lips. "I'll have to disabuse you of that belief, Sir Guardian, if Tal won't."

"Oh, I will," Tal grinned. It appeared his concerns could wait until morning after all. "If it's a duty, I can't very well turn it down, can I?"

"I should leave you to your friends then, Tal," Ilse said demurely. "I just wanted to thank you. All of you."

"I'll hear nothing of it!" Tazmin interjected. "We'd be delighted to have you join us."

"Yes, Ilse," Tal agreed, "you're one of my friends as well, after all. You're welcome to come with us if you'd like."

"Well in that case," Ilse said cheerfully, linking arms with Tazmin, "let's go find another drink for Guardian Damarrian."

Tal awakened the next morning in his bed in Jerak Keep with a throbbing head. He tried opening his eyes, but thought better of the idea when the light streaming in through the window bored into them like twin augers seeking his brain. He groaned quietly and contented himself instead with lying still, eyes closed, and opening himself to the Sephira. He had no idea if the healing it brought him would work on a hangover, but he could hope.

To keep his mind occupied, he began rummaging through his memory, trying to part the haze that seemed to have settled on the events of the night. He recalled roaming the streets arm-in-arm with Rania, each of them matching the other drink for drink. It had become something of a contest between them the night before, and they had both put down enough to astonish Kyril. Kyril. Yes, he had been there, along with Tazmin and Ilse. The whole lot of them had made good on Kyril's demand that they get "smashingly drunk." Vaguely Tal recollected standing on a street corner with his friends, swaying against each other and singing at the top of their lungs with a crowd of drunken soldiers around them joining in. An odd memory; Tal didn't usually sing. The rest seemed truly to be a blur. He could bring to mind no other specific images of the evening, only the impression that he'd had a very good time. Far too good, judging from his current state.

With a start, he realized that among the sensations carried to him by the Sephira was another presence, in his room and close to him. He rolled over and cracked his eyes open ever so slightly. Rania lay sleeping peacefully on the other side of the bed.

Tal sat bolt upright, struggling fervently to remember how they had come to be here. His memory stubbornly refused to cooperate. Had he and Rania...? No. No, there were their boots and weapon belts, discarded haphazardly in the corner, but otherwise they were both still clothed as they had been last night, he in his House colors and she in the gray that was her custom.

Awakened by his movement, Rania's eyes fluttered open. "Good morning, Tal," she murmured, and then winced. Her Sephiral aura flickered alight, and with it came their state of linked awareness. Rania's lips twitched into a little smile. "Something startle you?"

"I don't... How did you..." Tal floundered for words.

"You asked me to stay last night," Rania murmured with a devilish smile, "and now you can't remember it?"

He shook his head mutely.

She reached over and patted him on the cheek, eyes dancing with mischief. "Oh, you poor, poor boy."

Hesitantly, he asked, "Rania, did we..."

"What matter if we did?" she replied with a laugh. "Would you want me to describe the bits you can't recall?"

Tal blushed at the suggestion. "Regardless of how you or I feel about this, people will gossip..."

"Let them," she said casually as she arched her back, sighing contentedly at the stretching of muscles. "If they've so little to concern themselves with besides imagining escapades between us, I say leave them to it."

"But do we really need to encourage them?"

"Who's to encourage? I don't see anyone else here." There was a polite knock on the door in the sitting room, and Rania raised an eyebrow. "I stand corrected. Does anybody ever leave you alone?"

"No," Tal replied in a long-suffering voice, "they don't seem to." He got up and walked out to the sitting room, trying on the way to tug his slept-in clothing into a semblance of presentability. It was a futile struggle. "Yes, yes," he called irritably when the knock repeated itself, "come in."

"Tal," Tazmin said in greeting as he entered the room, then paused when he got a look at his friend. "You look awful."

"Thanks," Tal replied dryly. "Tazmin, of all people I'd think that you'd know better, after a night like last night, than to disturb me so early in the morning."

"Morning?" Tazmin chuckled. "You did drink a lot. It's midday." He craned his neck to look over Tal's shoulder and grinned. "Oh, I see."

"You'll have to excuse Tal," Rania said, casually adjusting her rumpled shirt as she crossed the room. "He seems to be having difficulty remembering last night, and it's got him rather flustered." She responded to the sour look Tal gave her by poking him teasingly in the ribs.

"Is that so?" Tazmin laughed with an approving nod for his embarrassed friend. "I hate it when that happens. If you'd prefer, I could come back later. I was just hoping to catch up with you since we didn't get around to it last night, at least not that I can recall. It can wait."

"No, it's fine," Tal muttered. "We're already awake. Come in and have a seat." Fitting actions to words, he flopped himself unceremoniously into one of the sitting room chairs. Rania settled herself beside him with considerably more grace.

"Well then," Tazmin said once he was seated, "let's start with this remarkable young woman who appears to have stolen you from us." He turned his eyes to Rania. "Are the things I've been hearing true? Are you really House Amoran's lost heir, risen from the grave?"

"Yes and no," Rania replied. "I *am* Rania Amoran, but I survived the fall of Felmorinen."

"That's a relief. All of this business with creepy mystics and the dead coming back to life gives me chills."

Rania told Tazmin her story then, of the night her home and family were taken from her and of meeting Muzash and training under the last Adept of Shevestra. She left out certain parts that she had shared with Tal, like the book her mother had given to her and anything having to do with *Edyamar*.

Then it was Tal's turn. He recounted for his cousin all the events since his departure from Val Zherrane, from the search for Trazeri's Blade to

Zharkus's treason to his taking the Shevestra'ken oaths. He kept to himself the fact that Trazeri's sword was actually *Kallevamar*, as much as he hated to keep secrets from Tazmin. He also failed to mention the bond that the Sephira had forged between himself and Rania. Aside from his still not understanding its nature, it just felt too much a personal and private matter to share.

"So what about you, Tazmin?" Tal asked when he finally reached the end of his tale. "How did you manage to get here so quickly?"

"I'm afraid that my story is a lot less exciting than yours, Tal," Tazmin said. "After you left Val Zherrane, I returned to Val Joseth to mind affairs in the city for my father while he dealt with Council matters. When your message about the Bhellan army arrived, it sounded like you were in a bad enough spot that I mustered all the men I could and came running."

"What I'm really curious about," Tal commented, "is the Order. How did you manage to bring those Jhessaillians all the way from Val Zherrane?"

Tazmin grimaced. "That's the odd part. I wish I could take credit for that, but the truth is I had almost nothing to do with it. They arrived in Val Joseth the same day as your message, and they were already coming this way. When I asked them what their business was, they told me they'd been ordered to Val Jerak. Wouldn't say who by, though, only that they had reason to suspect Kherzul might attack the city. I was wondering if maybe Kyril, your Guardian friend, had given that order."

Tal exchanged a long, troubled look with Rania. "He didn't say anything to me about Jhessaillian reinforcements," he said slowly. "I can't see why he'd neglect to mention such an important piece of information." His brow furrowed with concern. "Besides, for the Jhessaillians to have been marching and in Val Joseth by the time my message arrived, Kyril would have had to have given such orders well before we knew Kherzul's forces were coming."

"So much for solving that mystery," Tazmin sighed. "Anyway, I showed the Jhessaillians your message and that got their attention. They were quite agreeable when I asked them to accompany our army in riding to your rescue. And that's about all there was to it, aside from what happened when we arrived. I believe you saw most of that yourself."

"Yes," Tal agreed, "I did. It's not easy to forget such a spectacular demonstration of the Order's capabilities."

"It certainly explains why nobody ever goes to war with Cardon," Tazmin chuckled as he stood. "Well, Tal, I hope you'll excuse me now. Ilse insisted that I go visit her at that inn she works at. She's a real charmer, that one is."

"Of course, Tazmin. Say hello to her for me."

"I will, assuming I remember," Tazmin grinned, and then stopped dead in his tracks just at the door. "Speaking of which, I almost forgot - that

General, Krovar, wanted to know if you'd deliver the eulogy at the burning of the pyres from the battle. I told him you would."

"Thanks for volunteering me," Tal sighed.

"We both know you'd have done it anyway. You've never known how to say no to anyone, except the Ladies at Court." Tazmin winked at Rania and added, "Though one Lady seems to be changing that. I'll see you later, Tal." And then he slipped out of the room.

After a long silence, Rania murmured, "It sounds like there's more going on than we know about."

Tal nodded. "It seems that way."

"I don't like it."

"I'm not so sure I do either," he agreed. "We may have to figure this out on our own."

"Just us?" Rania asked.

"I trust Tazmin," Tal said, "but there's always the worry that he'd inadvertently let slip something he shouldn't. He talks too much sometimes."

"Yes, I'd noticed."

"And while I consider Kyril a friend," Tal continued, "he's still a Jhessaillian. Though their assistance saved us yesterday, I'm starting to feel unsettled about the circumstances surrounding their arrival. It sounds that they may be up to some scheme of their own, and we've no way to tell what their goals are or if Kyril is a part of it. For the time being it looks like we can only rely on each other."

"Have I ever mentioned that I really hate all this plotting and distrust?" Rania asked rhetorically. "I prefer a good, honest enemy I can see. But I suppose I should at least be thankful that I've got good company."

It had taken three days' preparation, but today Val Jerak was finally ready to bid farewell to her dead from the battle that the city's folk were now calling the Battle of the Falling Snows. Between its coinciding with the first snowfall of the long winter to come and the avalanche in the Felmorr Gap, Tal supposed the name had been inevitable.

He had dreaded the arrival of this day, when he would have to put words to an entire city's grief. His own as well, for Malry and Jennar and all the other men whose lives he'd had to take were among those who would be given to the flames this morning. Laying eyes on the ten great mounds of bodies awaiting their final honors on the field, Tal felt the sorrow at their loss rise up anew within him, unblunted by the short space of time that had passed. Yes, this was going to be a difficult morning.

In another sense, though, Tal had also been anxiously awaiting this day. Once this ceremony was completed, once he had spoken his piece for the men who had given so greatly for Valeran's safety, the last of his duties here in Val Jerak would be discharged. *Kallevamar* had been recovered, the city successfully defended. He could not be expected to take over the rule of the city now, thanks to his Shevestra'ken oaths. Tazmin's arrival had been doubly fortuitous for that reason, for he also understood how to handle the daily affairs of one of Valeran's great cities and didn't share Talaren's constraints. Tal had spoken with his friend about it yesterday, and Tazmin had agreed with a grin and a laugh to assume the Regency of Val Jerak until the King decided who the city's new Lord would be.

After today, Tal would be free to leave. He would be free to do what he knew had to be done.

The start of it had been the casualty reports. Having commanded Val Jerak's forces in the battle, Tal had felt obligated to go over them, and doing so had provoked a swift resurgence of the melancholy Rania had pulled him out of during the victory celebration. That was how she'd found him a couple nights ago, poring fretfully over the reports.

"You look like you need a friend right now," she had observed immediately upon laying eyes on his frown.

"It's these cursed numbers," he'd sighed, exasperatedly throwing the sheaf of pages he'd been perusing down on the desk in front of him. "To look at them, you'd think we suffered a crushing defeat."

"But we didn't. We destroyed Kherzul's army and preserved the city."

"Exactly, and there's the problem."

The look Rania had given him then was equal parts bewilderment and irritation. "You're not making sense, Tal. How could that be a problem?"

Because she was easily his match in single combat, it was easy for Tal to forget that Rania hadn't been instructed in large-scale strategy as he'd been. So to explain himself, he'd chosen to answer her question with one of his own. "What's the most basic objective when facing an enemy on the battlefield?"

"To kill the enemy," she'd answered without hesitation.

"Most would think so, but no." Tal shook his head. "It's to break his will. The killing is just a means to that end. Once the enemy's resolve is shattered, the day belongs to you."

Rania nodded slowly, and Tal had been able to see the comprehension in her eyes. Then she'd proven she understood what he was getting at by observing, "But Kherzul's armies of the dead don't break."

"No, they don't. They keep fighting however outnumbered they are, however poor their ground, however injured they may be. Until we eliminate the spectres controlling them, they'll never stop short of their own destruction."

"You don't think we can win this war?"

"I don't know. We might be able to with the Jhessaillians behind us, but even then the cost will be atrocious. The battle we fought went very well for us, all things considered, but you've seen the losses we took." Tal had sighed, gazing sightlessly at the discarded pages of casualties. "Now imagine an entire war composed of battles like that. However long it lasts, a season, a year, or several years, the dead will keep piling up higher and higher. Any we don't burn will likely rise up against us. We'll bleed from every victory, and every defeat..." He shook his head. "I shudder to even think what a defeat would look like, but we can be certain we'll suffer at least a few. Even if in the end we manage to triumph, I very much doubt what's left behind will bear much resemblance to the Valeran we know."

They'd sat for several minutes in silence then, the shadows in the room seeming to press in against the candlelight. Though she said nothing of it, Tal was certain that Rania had been thinking of the same thing he was: the tear-soaked night they'd had to purge the walking dead from the streets of Val Jerak, and the horrifying prospect of having to face more such nights. More slaughtered innocents. More shattered lives. More friends begging for death, that their corpses not rise again.

It was Rania who'd finally broken the stillness with a whisper. "There's another way. Kherzul's armies won't come again in the spring if he doesn't survive the winter."

"You think we should send Godtouched to assassinate him?"

"No. I think we should send Shevestra'ken. We can strike swifter than Godtouched, and the guards Kherzul will surely have will be less of a problem for us. With the Blades of Unity we can slay him, spectre or not. I can guide us over the Felmorr and into Bhellus undetected. I know the high passes as well as any Pathfinder."

"Rania..."

She'd cut him off before he could object. "It's the best way, Tal. If we try to fight Kherzul army to army, we're fighting him his way. You just explained how that will end. Let's fight him our way instead. The two of us, alone and unexpected, may be able to accomplish what countless deaths and fighting without end won't. It's what we're supposed to do. It's who we are."

Tal had stared into her unflinching gaze for what seemed an eternity before nodding. "Alright. We'll see to Kherzul ourselves."

They would depart tonight. Rania had quietly gathered together the supplies they would need for the journey. They needed only wait for night to fall, then they could slip unobtrusively from Val Jerak. By morning they'd have already begun their ascent of the Felmorr Mountains.

But first they had to get through these funerary rites. Even were it not a matter of honor to attend, their absence would surely have been noted by any spies Kherzul still had in the city and raised suspicions. Besides, they needed this ceremony as badly as anyone else in the city to help put their sorrows behind them.

Talaren and Rania stood together upon a raised dais along with General Krovar, Tazmin, Kyril, and the twenty Guardians who had come from Val Zherrane. The fourteen Godtouched who had also come stood armored before the dais as an honor guard.

Tal had spoken briefly with most of the Jhessaillians to thank them for their assistance. Though they had all been both gracious and courteous, he still found the Godtouched a bit disconcerting. The training that hardened their Sephiral essences into a barrier against malign sorcery and a weapon against immaterial foes also rendered them undetectable to Tal's Sephiral awareness. It was a very peculiar feeling, speaking to a man who one of your senses told you didn't exist.

Behind the dais were the piles of the dead, with the collapsed Felmorr Gap beyond. Tal hadn't been thinking of symbolism when he ordered the dead gathered here, but now felt the backdrop to be a poetic summation of the Battle of the Falling Snows: victory and ruin, hope and despair, all together. All the same.

The crowd gathering on the field was enormous, and growing by the second. Hardly a man, woman, or child in Val Jerak had failed to have their lives touched by the strife that had descended on this place, and now the whole city was turning out to recognize the sacrifice of the fallen. It was tragic, but all to the good. These dead deserved all the honor that could be given them.

When the swelling of the crowd slowed to a trickle, Tal flashed a quick hand signal to Kyril. After a moment the Guardian nodded to indicate that he had finished his runeworking to amplify Tal's voice. Not that Tal needed any signal; he was growing more adept at distinguishing such things in the Sephira.

Tal stepped forward, head bowed as he composed himself to begin speaking. An expectant hush fell over those watching, many bowing their heads mournfully with him. He allowed the silence to stretch on, letting the somber mood settle in. At last, he raised his eyes along with his voice.

"We have come here today to honor our fallen heroes, whose sacrifice protected us all. We have come to sing their praises, that they might hear and know they were loved. We have come to face our own sorrow at their loss, that it not tarnish our happy memories of them.

"In times beyond the recollection of history, Shevestra taught us that there is a battle that never ends. It is the battle of light against darkness, of life against death, and of hope against despair. All that truly changes about this battle is where it is fought and who fights it.

"Five days ago, the Eternal Battle came to Val Jerak. Darkness descended upon us at the bidding of its emissary, King Kherzul Meravos. He unleashed against us a host of the dead, torn from their slumber without even the benefit of their own wills. They were a force fearsome enough to fill even the strongest of us with despair.

"But these were courageous men of Valeran. They had the bravery to turn away from their dread and instead embrace their hope. They chose to face the darkness even though doing so meant risking that the light of their own lives might be extinguished. But from where did that courage come? What hope could be so great that one would face death itself to preserve it?

"Look around you. Every person here, this land, this city, all that you behold is what these men fought and bled and died to preserve from destruction and desecration. We are all the embodiment of their hopes. They fought to give us the gift of a future. It is the most precious gift imaginable, and one sanctified by the sacrifice these men made.

"A gift so dearly bought, however, does not come without its responsibilities. We all now have a duty to the men who paid with blood for our future to make it what they would have wanted for us. We owe it to them to face each coming day with compassion, understanding, and courage. We must dare to dream of a future in which further such sacrifices need not be made, and strive each in our own way to make that dream a reality. That is how we may honor the memories of the loved ones we have lost."

Tal paused for a few heartbeats, and when he spoke again it was in a more contemplative tone. "We all bid farewell to friends today. Some of us have lost husbands, or sons, or fathers. All life is connected, and we are all lessened by the loss of these great men. But we must temper our sorrow with the knowledge that they are not truly gone from us. Their spirits have joined with the Sephira and are part of the life of our world now. One day, in other lives, they will walk beside us once more and the bonds we have forged may be renewed. Until that day, we will hold them dear in our hearts and remember them in times of joy. We will go on, and carry their hopes forward with us. We will not forget."

Tal bowed his head silently, letting the quiet stretch on a few final moments for the people of Val Jerak to bid their dead farewell. At last, he looked up again.

"Guardians!" Tal turned crisply about to face the pyres, and all those gathered on the dais turned with him. He put fist to heart in salute.

Seconds later, ten pillars of flame leapt in unison from the piled bodies, roaring upward hundreds of feet in tribute to the dead. Hotter and hotter the flames burned as the Guardians fed them more Sephiral energy, going from red to yellow to nearly white. Tal could feel their heat on his face even though he stood at least two hundred strides distant. After about a minute, the flames vanished as suddenly as they had begun. Nothing remained where they had been.

"Goodbye, Malry," Tal whispered. "I promise I won't fail."

When Rania knocked on his door late that night, Tal opened it immediately. He'd been waiting for her.

"All ready?" she asked as she entered.

Tal looked once more around the room before nodding. His Shevestra'ken armor stood on its rack in the corner, where he'd left it. He'd have liked to have it on this journey, but it would stand out too much for the purposes of his undertaking. He'd asked Tazmin to watch after the armor for him in the letter he was leaving for his friend to find. That letter, along with several others he'd written this evening, sat atop the desk in the study. Aside from those letters and the armor, there was little indication he'd ever been here.

"It's a funny thing, Rania," Tal said as he settled his pack onto his shoulders. "Considering what we intend to do, I should be feeling nervous, but I don't feel that way at all. I think it's because you're coming with me."

"I feel the same, Tal." Rania smiled. "Just you and me and the enemy ahead of us. It feels right."

"I'll take that as a good sign." He turned to leave. "Let's go finish this."

Mission Report - 17 Norvem, J.Y. 1038

Sir,

I apologize for the unusually long delay in the filing of my first progress report. Events have progressed far more rapidly than was anticipated and my full attention has been required to stay abreast of them. A full summary follows.

I have confirmed that our intelligence with regard to the activities of Kherzul Meravos was accurate. During my observation of him one of my watchers was compromised, resulting in a retaliatory strike on the Bhel Meravos Chapterhouse. All associated personnel were lost. In this attack Kherzul demonstrated capabilities far surpassing our projections, consistent and potentially in excess of our end-stage scenarios. It is my recommendation that his risk assessment be elevated from high to extreme.

In response to these developments, I exercised my authority as primary overseeing operative to initiate late stage measures. After escaping to Valeran (and being seriously injured in the process) I disclosed to their Royal Council information regarding Kherzul's activities. I also made contact at this point with the Solus heir, Talaren, and began my evaluation of the viability of our expectations for him. I will detail my findings later in this report.

Once more the King of Bhellus proved better prepared than expected, having secured an ally within the Valerite Royal Council. Resultantly, my disclosure to the Council triggered the premature execution of one of his plans. An assassination attempt was made that night on King Garant Zherrane which only failed due to the intervention of Lord Solus. Concurrently, the sword which once belonged to Trazeri Ni'Dharranoth was stolen from the Royal Palace.

As I had no information on which to base a judgment of the significance of this theft, I secured permission to enter the Royal Tombs in the company of Lord Solus and performed a Recollection of the Essence on Trazeri's remains. Though the shade refused to speak with me, it did reveal to Lord Solus that the stolen weapon was, in fact, *Kallevamar*. Significantly, the shade demanded as the price for its information that Lord Solus recover the weapon and thereafter bear and defend it. To my knowledge, these facts are known only to myself, Lord Solus, King Garant Zherrane, and Duke Daron Solus. I do not at this time believe that containment procedures will be required.

Considering the obvious importance of these events, I volunteered to assist Lord Solus in his recovery attempts. Doing so additionally afforded me the opportunity to continue my observation of him. We proceeded to Val Jerak, where Lord Solus had orders following the recovery of *Kallevamar* to take command of military reinforcements being sent from Val Zherrane. At this time I had serious misgivings regarding Kherzul's demonstrated power and the unexpectedly advanced state of his planning, and thus prior to my departure made my request of which you are no doubt aware that Order forces be mobilized to assist Valeran. I deemed this a prudent precautionary measure as well as one that would strengthen Valerite goodwill toward us should our brothers' assistance be required.

Following our arrival in Val Jerak, Lord Solus and I spent twelve days in our search for *Kallevamar* before he was approached by a spectre calling himself Major Aldon Skalgrim. Skalgrim claimed to have been the test subject of a vested manifestation developed by Kherzul to create an object that reacts to its wearer's death with spectral incarnation of the departing essence, the intent being to allow Kherzul to convert himself to spectral form. I have not confirmed these claims personally, but consider the information to be reliable.

Seeking retribution for his condition, Skalgrim offered to lead Lord Solus to the place where *Kallevamar* (the spectre was apparently unaware of its true nature) was to be exchanged for transfer to Bhellus. In the ensuing conflict Skalgrim and another unidentified spectre were destroyed and *Kallevamar* recovered. Lord Solus also discovered that House Jerak had been responsible for the theft, and had been working with Kherzul since approximately the time of Felmorinen's fall. He immediately imprisoned the Archduke and his heir and assumed control of the city.

It was during these events that I first encountered the last descendant of House Amoran and became aware of her association with Lord Solus. It would seem that following her disappearance she became the apprentice of the Shevestra'ka Muzash Finallin, for she is now an exceptionally powerful Adept.

My interrogation of Zharkus Jerak revealed that my concerns with regard to the state of advancement of Kherzul's plans were well-founded and a massive military force was already inbound toward the Felmorr Gap. Though vastly outnumbered, Lord Solus took charge of organizing the defense of the city and in two days and a night of combat emerged victorious, with the final engagement decided by the arrival of our Val Zherrane Chapter in the company of reinforcements from House Joseth. I will forward a detailed account of the battle for analysis by the tactical division of the Hand of Jhessail.

Throughout these happenings I have been repeatedly impressed by the capabilities of Talaren Solus. If our prophetic projections for him have erred at all, it has only been in underestimating him. He is unusually well-disciplined and responsible for his age, and has shown himself to be a natural leader of men. His training at the hands of Daron Solus and Malry Zhierren have rendered him a formidable strategist and masterful warrior. He has demonstrated to me a keen and flexible intellect, and from the first I have been amazed at the strength of his Sephiral presence. This latter has only grown more accentuated with his swearing of the Oaths to Shevestra and investiture of the Warrior Soul from Rania Amoran in the days leading up to the battle at Val Jerak. Considering also that he now carries *Kallevamar* and is already being hailed as a hero in Valeran, I cannot emphasize strongly enough my belief that he is indeed one of the individuals we seek.

Although her reappearance was unexpected, I feel I must suggest the possibility that Rania Amoran may be the other. Her attunement to the Sephira appears to match Talaren's, and there seems to be some manner of bond between them the nature of which I do not yet fully fathom. Despite having known each other for no more than three months, their speech, manner, and coordination in combat situations would lead one to believe them long-time intimates. Their synchronicity in battle is particularly notable, being so pronounced that I must wonder if they have rediscovered some lost discipline of the Shevestra'ken. Any information the Word of Jhessail might be able to provide from the archives regarding such talents would be greatly appreciated and potentially vital to the completion of my mission. Even if Rania proves not to be the second prophesied one we are searching for, she could be useful as a vector to influence Talaren.

Winter is now beginning in the North, rendering large-scale military deployments impractical. It seems reasonable to expect that this will result in several months of quiet here, during which I will continue my observation of both subjects. Any significant findings will be noted in forthcoming reports.
In Guardianship and Vigilance,
Effarim'Zor Kyril Damarrian

Kyril sighed and gently rubbed at his temples after setting the quill pen aside. Writing reports like this always gave him headaches. He had not only written the whole thing in the ancient runic script known to few who hadn't studied under the Order, but also coded it so as to be understandable only to his superiors within the Eye of Jhessail. One had to be cautious with information as sensitive as this.

A minor headache was the least of his worries, though. This mission was coming more and more to leave a bad taste in Kyril's mouth. There had been signs from the outset that he wasn't being told everything, but at the time he'd taken it as simply a matter of course. An operative was rarely told the entirety of the design he was participating in, only the part he had to play in it. And Guardian Kyril Damarrian had been honored to be chosen for this particular role; Few ever received the opportunity to be so closely involved in the fulfillment of such crucial events in the Jhessaillian Prophecy.

But now the luster of that honor was beginning to wear thin, and questions Kyril had previously brushed aside were beginning to assert themselves more forcefully. Why had he been detoured from his primary assignment into Bhellus to confirm what the Order already essentially knew? How had the contact he'd been given within the Royal Palace been exposed, and with such inconvenient timing? Kyril had thought the whole thing reeked of the influence of other agents, and now he was certain.

The clincher had been the timely arrival of his brothers from the Val Zherrane Chapterhouse. He'd placed a request for the intervention of Jhessaillian forces, true, but the timelines just didn't match up. For his brothers to have reached Val Jerak from the capitol when they did, the mobilization orders must have been sent prior to Kyril's request. More to the point, they'd have to have been sent before Kyril had even uncovered that a Bhellan attack was imminent.

It seemed apparent now that there was more to the Order's machinations in the North than Kyril had been made privy to, and that fact distressed the Guardian to no end. Those unknowns could easily prove to be a danger to his operation, his new friends, even to his own person. Inquiries would have to be made, but obviously not through the conventional channels and chain of command. Fortunately, Kyril had access to his own network of contacts beyond those he was given for specific assignments, and a good many of those contacts were back in Cardon, within the Order itself. He'd particularly focused on building ties within the Word of Jhessail for the access they could gain him to the archives, and those would be the people he'd need to direct his questions to now. If his need was desperate enough and he called in enough favors, he could probably even manage to dig into the secrets contained in the Shadow Record, though hopefully that wouldn't be necessary in this case. Getting the information he wanted should just be a matter of time, waiting for ravens to carry messages back and forth between Valeran and Cardon.

At least he'd have something to keep his mind on as the winter passed besides the dreadful thought of what the spring would be like. Kyril suspected that the Battle of the Falling Snows had been just a taste of the suffering to come, and a small one at that. That thought inevitably led to other, even more uncomfortable ones. When Kyril had told Tal that the Order's work was worth the enormous sacrifice it sometimes demanded, that without paying the price there would be no Unifier and without the Unifier all life would end, he'd believed it. But back then "the price" had been an abstract, a set of numbers without faces, a sanitized euphemism. After standing on the battlefield and bearing witness to the carnage and suffering, after seeing so many men put themselves in the path of certain death in defense of their homeland, after walking among the stacks of bodies left in the aftermath, it became impossible to be so cavalier with human lives. Was this hope of the Unifier that his Order held out, drenched in centuries of blood, really the only way? Would Tal be any less heroic without thousands of corpses to mark his rise, any less capable of what prophecy would ask of him? Couldn't there be a better way?

The ink on Kyril's report had dried while he sat brooding. He began folding it to be sealed, but before he finished the first crease the door to his rooms crashed open.

Trained reflex had the Guardian out of his seat in an eyeblink, Sephiral energy gathered and the rune form half-visualized to immolate the doorway before he recognized that the man standing in it was Tazmin Joseth.

Val Jerak's new Regent was clad in the dandyish crimson finery that appeared to be his usual attire. What wasn't usual was the seething anger that contorted his face and colored it nearly to match his clothing.

"Regent Tazmin," Kyril breathed as he released the Sephira. "You should be more careful about barging into a Guardian's quarters. I nearly seared you to a cinder. I assume there must be some sort of problem?"

"They're gone," Tazmin declared as he stormed across the room. "That great fool must be starting to believe what they're saying about him in the streets. Or maybe it's her doing. He hasn't been quite right since he met her." He virtually hurled a sealed letter onto Kyril's desk. "Here. He left one for you, too."

Kyril eyed the foxhead seal in white wax on the letter before turning his eyes back to Tazmin. "What has Tal done?"

"You can read it for yourself in his own words," Tazmin grumbled, "but let me paraphrase for you: 'Kyril, becoming an Adept of Shevestra seems to have gone to my head. Between that and my overly sensitive conscience about everyone who died in the battle I commanded, I've decided that the only acceptable way to deal with this war is for me to commit suicide in spectacular fashion. So I'm taking my fancy sword to Bhellus, where I'll try to sneak up on Kherzul and smack him in the back of the head with it. And don't worry about all his bloody guards, I've got Rania with me to deal with them since she's got an even bigger axe to grind than I do. Don't tell anyone what we're doing, and we'll see you when we get back if we don't get our idiot selves killed.'"

Kyril shook his head slowly through Tazmin's tirade, and found himself laughing quietly by the end of it. "Tal, Tal, Tal," he murmured. "You brave, noble, brilliant fool."

"What?" Tazmin demanded incredulously. "Doesn't this worry you? Shouldn't we try to stop them?"

206

"And how would we go about stopping them?" Kyril asked. "They almost certainly left last night, and knowing those two they'll keep moving all day today. If we try to pursue or contact them once they're in Bhellus, we risk revealing them to Kherzul. I assume they're going over the Felmorr, which means we've only got a handful of days before they get that far. Not enough time for us to catch them with the lead they have. We can get a message to the Pathfinders to have their Rangers look for them, but I doubt that even the entire Pathfinder's Guild could stop a pair of determined Shevestra'ken. And it's not likely they'd even try once they realize who Rania is. Her ties to House Amoran technically make her their leader."

"But what they're doing is insanely dangerous! They could both die!"

"That's a possibility," Kyril admitted soberly. "It's also a possibility that they could succeed. The part of me that's a Guardian of the Jhessaillian Order agrees with you that they're taking too great a risk, especially considering that we've something of an interest in the pair of them. But the part that's Tal's friend thinks he may be right. If he manages to kill Kherzul, it'll prevent an enormous amount of bloodshed. Either way, the fact remains that we can't do anything but increase their danger. Tal and Rania made their decision, and all we can do is respect it and hope for their well-being."

Tazmin's look was crestfallen as the anger went out of him. "That's all?"

Kyril shrugged. "That and see to it that Kherzul doesn't suspect that they're coming for him. I assume that Tal left some sort of instructions to that effect?"

Tazmin nodded. "He wants me to announce that they've gone to consult with Duke Daron on strategy for the war, and that they left without fanfare to avoid any possibility of overshadowing the honors given the dead yesterday. It sounds like the sort of gesture Tal would make."

"Yes, it very much does. You'll follow his suggestion?"

"I guess so," Tazmin agreed sourly, "if there's really nothing else I can do."

"You could pray, if you feel so inclined."

"Not usually," Tazmin laughed, and then looked sheepishly at the floor. "But I suppose speaking a few words to Shevestra and maybe the One wouldn't kill me."

"And there are a few people who should be informed of Tal's actions," Kyril added. "His father and the King, for starters."

"He left letters for both of them as well," Tazmin said. "I'm sending couriers to deliver them."

Kyril chuckled softly. "That boy has the most unhealthy habit of doing everything himself."

"I just hope this time he hasn't taken more on himself than he can handle," Tazmin said quietly.

"So do I," Kyril said consolingly. "We have to remember that Talaren and Rania are both extremely capable. If anyone can accomplish what they've set out to do, it's those two."

"That's true," Tazmin said with a grimace, "although that still doesn't help with the fact that it's my best friend out there risking his neck. Still, thank you, Kyril."

After Tazmin had left, Kyril looked irritably at his report. He'd have to rewrite it now to account for this new development. The Jhessaillarim'zan wouldn't be pleased, but there truly was nothing to be done. Even the Jhessaillian Order had limits to what it could influence. Everything now rode on the shoulders of a pair of young Shevestra'ken somewhere in the Felmorr Mountains. Kyril just prayed that Tal would have the sense to avoid needless danger.

23

A Passage Through The Heavens

Tal's feet were cold. Despite the thick leather boots he wore and the even thicker woolen socks beneath, still the cold seemed to try to seep into his bones as he and Rania trudged through knee-deep snow along the incline of the narrow path that twisted its way up the rock face of the Felmorr. As they gained altitude the snow slowly grew deeper and the cold more biting. Already the difference was noticeable, and they had only begun their ascent a few hours before when the sun finally crested up over the mountains.

Rania led the way confidently, choosing their path without hesitation whenever the stone walls around them presented a crack or branch. Tal was astonished at how frequently it did so, and he found himself thankful for Rania's presence at each choosing. At one point she veered off of the obvious path to scramble up over several large snow-covered rocks and through a narrow crevasse that Tal hadn't even thought passable.

"The path we were on ends at the top of a cliff a couple miles further on," she said by way of explanation as she waited for Tal to catch up. Her breath turned to mist in the frigid air.

"It's amazing how well you seem to know these mountains," Tal commented as he squeezed himself through the opening between the two facing rock walls.

Rania glanced at him with a peculiar twist to her lips and then gazed off northward, where the path they were on now switched back on itself and disappeared around a lip of stone. "I've spent most of my life up here," she replied. "There's a map of all the paths in the war room at Felmorinen, and I used to spend hours staring at it as a child. It seemed impossible that anyone could ever find their way through such a vast and twisted maze, let alone memorize the routes. But years of navigating the paths eventually ingrains them in you. The map in my head might be more accurate than the one in Felmorinen now."

Tal pulled his cloak close against a gust of wind. He had a hard time imagining spending years up here. "So do you believe the stories about the mountains having been raised by Felmorinen's builders?"

Rania looked back at him again with a quick nod. "Without a doubt. When we get closer to the top of the mountains you'll begin to understand. Seeing Felmorinen will help, too. We'll pass by close enough for you to get a look. It's clearly man made, but just as clearly part of the mountains."

Tal gave an impressed whistle. "The amount of power it must have taken to do such a thing..." It was so mind boggling he couldn't even find the words to express it.

"Yes," Rania agreed, "The ancients had knowledge that would make the Jhessaillian Order blush. Most of what the Order knows was recovered from Felmorinen by Jhessail when he slew Maeroth, after all, and I'm sure the fortress still holds other secrets. There are parts of it that nobody has ever been able to get to. Hallways that end in doors that don't open, stairways that go nowhere. I sometimes wonder what will be found there when somebody finally figures out how to open one of those doors." She shook herself from her musings. "We should keep moving. Daylight's wasting, and the nights up here can be deadly cold."

Tal fell in behind her as she started off again. He was very much looking forward to the sight of the fortress at the heart of the Felmorr Range. It sounded such an intriguing place, figuring heavily in so many major historical events, yet always a mystery whose origins lay long before any of the histories remembered.

Hours more they continued their march, ever upward and generally northward. The air continued to grow colder and colder, but at least the snow remained about the same depth. More disturbing were the changes that came over Rania as they climbed ever higher. Her eyes grew cold and glassy, her back stiff and her movements more furtive and guarded. She hardly spoke except to give Tal directions. It would have been obvious that something had her deeply troubled even without the jumble of emotion that Tal sensed in her through their Sephiral bond.

As the shadows began to lengthen across the slopes, Rania turned to speak again after well over an hour of silence. "There's a spot just ahead where we should be able to make camp. Be careful. The footing can be treacherous in the dark."

The location Rania spoke of was a wide stretch of path overshadowed by a jut of the mountain face that appeared to shield the path from the worst of the snow. Tall crags of rock provided some shelter from the gusts of wind that blew in from the west, as well.

Tal and Rania set to clearing a patch of ground for their tent. Within a few minutes they had the canvas structure up and ducked into its relative shelter. Bedrolls and blankets were unrolled, and then they sat down knee-to-knee for a brief dinner of cheese and dried beef. Rania produced a small oil-burning stove to heat some water for tea.

As they waited for the water to heat, Tal smiled gently at Rania. "Something is gnawing at you, and I hate to see you like this. Is there anything I can do to help?"

She eyed him warily for a moment before replying so softly Tal had to lean in close to hear. "There are things you still don't know about me, Tal. Unpleasant things. Things I did up here that I'm ashamed of. I know I should tell you about them before you find out some other way, but I'm afraid."

"Whatever it is, I think you've sufficiently disavowed your actions," Tal said soothingly. "I doubt anything you did then will substantially change my opinion of you."

Rania's smile was as sad and distant as her voice. "Oh, it might. You have to remember, Tal, that I saw everything I'd ever known or cared about swept away in one terrifying night as a child. The scars left behind by something like that don't heal quickly or easily. All that kept my desire for life from withering away was my need to exact vengeance for that one night. It was what kept me dedicated enough to finish the Shevestra'ken training. It was all I wanted."

"When I became an Adept four years ago, I thought I was finally ready to avenge my parents. Based on the evidence of the dagger I'd taken that night, I was sure my home had been destroyed under King Shebedar's orders, and I intended to put my ghosts to rest by killing him. But when I came down out of the mountains, I learned that he'd been assassinated only a few months previously. I felt lost. My mentor was dead, the only thing like family or a friend I'd had in over a decade, and I was alone again. I thought my vengeance had been stolen from me, but the thirst for it remained. I believed that thirst could only be quenched with blood, and decided that if I couldn't spill Shebedar's I'd have to satisfy myself with the next best thing."

With haunted eyes, Rania drew a quavering breath and continued. "It was Bhellan soldiers who'd attacked Felmorinen, and I knew that they regularly patrolled the other side of these mountains, so I came back up here and started hunting their men. I would come on them in the night. There were rarely ever more than a dozen of them in a group, never more than two sentries out. Once I'd killed the watchers, the rest were easy. They were half asleep, unarmored, and disoriented. I'd leave them to be found, after branding every soldier's body with the signet ring of House Amoran heated over the remnants of their campfires. Eventually, the brand began rumors that the mountains were haunted by Anakara's vengeful ghost. When I caught wind of the rumors, I took to dying my hair black to heighten my resemblance to the Undying."

She shuddered, dropping her eyes in shame. "As I grew more confident, I came to relish the terror I inspired in them. Sometimes I would let one of their watchmen raise the alarm so they could be all the more aware of the slaughter I was bringing to them. Towards the end I would let the last one beg for mercy and send him back to Bhellus, always with the same message for his superiors and fellow soldiers: 'Felmorinen remembers.'"

Rania looked up again, meeting Tal's horrified gaze with a tear-filled one. "I killed so many men in those few years, Tal, so many that the energies absorbed by the Warrior Soul began to overwhelm me. Instead of filling the empty place in my heart, all that blood I spilled only made it grow larger and

211

emptier. I took myself to the verge of insanity, and it was only while I was teetering on the brink that I understood what I'd done. In my obsession with the monstrous acts that took my family from me, I had become a monster myself. I had betrayed the ideals Muzash taught me with indiscriminate slaughter. What I'd been doing wasn't vengeance, it was murder. And it was an utter betrayal of my oaths and my master's memory."

The tears were streaming down Rania's cheeks now, her words punctuated with broken sobs. "I've been trying to put that all behind me, to believe that everything changed when I met you. It really seemed for a while like it had, but I'm not so sure now. Despite everything that's happened, all those men are still dead. Nothing I can do will wash their blood from my hands. However much people may call me a hero for the things I've done since meeting you, it won't make what I did in the years before any less wrong. I still know the horrible truth of the lives I've taken, the terrible acts I'm capable of. A monster in disguise is still a monster."

It was finally too much for her. Shoulders slumped, face a mask of self-loathing, Rania began to cry so hard she trembled with each wracking breath. Despite his shock at the acts she'd confessed to, Tal couldn't help but feel for her. He'd never imagined that Rania could break down this completely, and now having seen it, he never wanted to again. Wordlessly, he reached across the space between them and pulled her to him. She came without resistance, leaning into his shoulder and grasping at the front of his shirt. He held her silently for long minutes while she cried herself out, gently stroking her hair with one hand.

When at last Rania's tears seemed to subside, Tal spoke softly into her ear. "Rania, I don't know the woman you're telling me about. What I do know is that people can change. The woman I know is a devoted and loyal friend, capable of great compassion and personal warmth, and is a comfort to be with in dark times. I've seen her selflessly throw herself in harm's way in the defense of strangers. I've seen her wounded by the horrific things she's witnessed. I've felt her spirit, and nothing can convince me that what I felt was the soul of a cold-blooded murderer. You may have done terrible things, but you can't give up on yourself for the mistakes of your past, however awful they may have been. You're better than that. There's still plenty of hope for you, you just have to be willing to learn from your errors and seize it. From what I've seen, I'd say you've been doing just that."

Rania looked at him with tear-reddened eyes. Her smile was tenuous, but held the first genuine warmth Tal had seen from her since they entered the mountains. "You're too good to me, Tal," she murmured. "You have been from the beginning. You've shown me so much in the short time I've been with you. You've reminded me what Shevestra'ken are supposed to be, helped me to live by that standard, even taken from me the torment that the

212

Warrior Soul was causing me. I think I'm starting to understand what my mistake was now. I was letting my pain define me. I need to find a new way to live, and you're the one who makes me feel that I still can. The madness is still in me, though. I can feel it lurking in the shadows of my mind, waiting to drag me into darkness and dishonor again if I give it the chance. That's why I have to see Kherzul die. Knowing what I know now, I'll never be completely free of my past until I do. I want that freedom, Tal. I want it so desperately."

"We'll get him, Rania," Tal whispered, "I promise."

"I know we will," she agreed quietly. "But I'm glad you're here with me to remind me that there's more to life than hurt and vengeance. Thank you, Tal. Thank you for helping me remember myself."

"I'm happy to have helped, but I didn't really do much," Tal replied with a smile. "I just tried to be your friend. The rest you did yourself."

"You cared," Rania said. "That makes all the difference." She turned her face up towards him, gazing earnestly into his eyes.

It was all Tal could do not to kiss those still slightly quivering lips. He felt himself losing the internal struggle as he tilted his own face towards her. *You'd use Rania's grief like this for your own selfish desires? What kind of beast are you?* Getting a grip on himself with that thought, he instead kissed her chastely on the forehead.

"Of course I cared," he said softly, and then playfully tousled her hair. "Now, if you're done trying to convince me of what an awful person you aren't, I think our water is more than hot enough for tea."

After they finished the tea they both sought their blankets, still fully clothed. Though the tent was better than outside, it was still bitterly cold, and getting colder as night drew on. Tal gave a start of surprise as Rania snuggled up close beside him.

"Body warmth," she said simply when he looked at her. "Besides, it's nice to remember that I'm not alone anymore."

Tal nodded, settling himself under the blankets. Rania rested her head on his shoulder. He put his arms around her hesitantly. *Just for warmth,* he reminded himself. He almost wished he didn't enjoy her closeness so much. Rania had enough to deal with already without him getting foolish notions in his head.

Rania sighed sleepily, closing her eyes. "Good night, Tal."

Tal watched her sleeping face beside his for a long time. All traces of the hurt that had been there before were gone now. He wished he could see her at such peace all the time.

"So many wishes," he sighed quietly to himself, "and so little I can do. I hope it's enough for you, Rania."

She stirred ever so slightly in her sleep, murmuring something soft and unintelligible.

Tal pulled her protectively closer to himself before closing his own eyes.

Sleep took him.

They awakened the next morning shortly before dawn. Tal was loath to leave the comfortable warmth of the blankets with Rania, but he reminded himself that he had a purpose waiting at the end of the journey and forced himself to rise. Rania did so as well, yawning and stretching before pulling her boots on. They struck camp and were once again trudging through the snow by the time the sky began to grow light.

"We should be able to make it to the heights by tonight," Rania said as they set out, "and then it will be another two or three days to cross before we begin the descent down the eastern side."

"Two or three?" Tal asked.

"Depending on how cooperative the path is. Once we get high enough, the Sephira will start distorting space. It's part of the defenses left behind by the ancients. It makes it much harder to pass the heights unless you're familiar with the routes beforehand."

The day stretched on, a long continuous march up the snow-blanketed slopes. They paused briefly early in the afternoon for another meal of dried beef and some bread. Tal took the opportunity to find a good vantage atop an outcropping of rock to gaze back to the west. The view was breathtaking, the gently rolling hills of eastern Valeran so far below stretching off to the horizon like a sea covered in snow. Villages and townships speckled that sea, barely visible for the great distance. When he turned away from the sight, Rania was smiling up at him.

"It's amazing, isn't it?" she asked.

"Like standing at the top of the world," Tal replied as he jumped down beside her. "You seem to be in much better spirits today."

"I am," Rania smiled. "It feels good not to be hiding any dark secrets from you anymore."

"None? How boring." Tal smirked.

Rania punched him in the arm. "I suppose I could make some up if m'lord so desires."

Tal cringed. "That shouldn't be necessary, as long as you stop calling me m'lord."

Rania laughed gaily and joined arms with him. "Come on, Tal. We could waste the whole day bantering here if I let you."

True to her prediction, the ground began to slope less and less as night drew closer. By the time darkness was settling in, it was nearly level, and less closed in to boot. Peaks and crags still broke up the landscape and lent it a mazelike quality, but after two days of climbing up the narrow cuts in the mountainside it seemed very open indeed. They set up the tent on the leeward side of a great jumble of loose boulders that afforded them a fair degree of shelter from the wind.

Once the tent was erected, Tal set off to find some wood for a fire, nodding absently at Rania's advice not to stray too far from the camp. He found some scrub brush a relatively short distance away and cut enough to make a modest campfire. As he was cutting he noticed that the Sephira had an odd feel to it up here that he hadn't paid much attention to during the day's climb. It seemed slippery, almost. No, that wasn't quite it. It just shifted and slid about oddly, as if reality here wasn't entirely stable.

When he turned to return to the camp with his arms full of wood, he had to stop and look about for a moment to find the boulders they were camped beside. They were farther left and considerably more distant than he had remembered. As he made his way back, he observed that the footprints he had left in the snow on his way out were spaced as if they had been made by someone with a pace half again as long as his own. Rania hadn't been exaggerating about the land changing here, it seemed.

Arriving back at the tent, he looked around curiously for Rania as he dropped the thin branches in the clearing he had made for the fire. There was no sign of her.

A tickle at the back of his mind warned him that something was hurtling toward his back. He twisted and ducked, and a snowball flew past him to splatter against the side of one of the boulders. Tal turned toward the snowball's source and had just enough time to see a grinning Rania before the second one hit him square in the face. Rania shook with hilarity as Tal wiped the snow from his eyes. She stopped laughing when Tal picked up a double handful of snow, crushed it into a ball, and hurled it at her, striking her right at the neckline of her mail shirt.

The fight was on. The two Shevestra'ken dodged, rolled, and dove, all the while throwing snowballs back and forth, both laughing gleefully the whole while. The Sephira flowed freely through them, giving the snowball fight an unusually frenetic pace. It was inane, ludicrous, and the most fun Tal remembered having in months. After a great many exchanges of snowballs, Rania charged and pounced on Tal, bearing him to the ground. They wrestled back and forth, each trying to rub the other's face in the snow, although in actuality they both became so covered in the white flakes it was hard to tell who was winning. Finally they wound down, lying side by side in the snow and laughing uproariously.

Rania punched Tal playfully in the ribs. "Now look what you've done," she giggled, "You've gone and mussed me."

Tal gave her a sly look. "Might I remind you that you started it?"

"What does that have to do with anything?" Rania leapt to her feet and offered Tal a hand up, which he accepted. "That fire is starting to sound like a wonderful idea right about now."

Tal couldn't agree more; now that he wasn't moving around so much the cold seemed deeper, especially in his wet, snow-encrusted clothing. He turned his attention to the wood he had carried back to camp, and in a short while had a merry little blaze going. He and Rania huddled together beside the fire to take their evening meal and lingered there while the flames burned themselves out, enjoying the warmth and gazing at the stars. He wasn't sure if it was just him, but Tal thought they seemed brighter this high up. At last, as the flames were dying down, they retired to the tent.

Rania stripped off her boots, followed by her mail shirt, and dropped them in the corner. She started pulling her shirt up over her head, and Tal whirled to face the tent wall.

There was a rustle of clothing, followed by a long silence. "Are you enjoying yourself?" Rania's voice asked from behind him.

"Just let me know when you're done," Tal replied.

Rania sighed. "If we're going to be traveling together, it just won't do if every time I have to change you're going to go studying the weave of the tent. I certainly won't when you do, and there's no way you're sleeping beside me in those sodden clothes you've got on. You don't have to be such a prude around me, Tal, unless it would really bother you that much to see me."

Her accusation of prudishness brought to Tal's mind memories of other voices, of Tazmin's endless teasing and of Kyril telling Ilse that Tal's courage vanished around women. Always, it seemed, his attempts to be polite and proper were mistaken for shyness or worse. Well, no more. If Rania wanted him to look then he'd oblige, propriety be damned.

Tal turned back toward Rania as casually as he could manage. "No, it doesn't bother me."

She was on her knees watching him, arms crossed beneath her breasts. The corners of her lips twitched up in a tiny smile. "Good." Very deliberately, Rania unbuckled her sword belt.

Tal tried hard not to stare, to keep his eyes focused on her face and eyes. It was difficult though, and every time his eyes strayed Rania would respond with a mischievous grin and her movements would grow slightly more languid and provocative, as though she were trying to divert his gaze from hers again. Once all her clothes were gone, she stretched with a contented sigh before going through her bags to find new ones, and then seemed to take her time doing so.

Rania seemed to be making a game of this, Tal thought, but he couldn't for the life of him tell if her goal was to make his jaw drop or to see if she could spook him into retreat.

216

There was no chance of the latter. Tal was transfixed by Rania's lithe unclad form, the long shapely expanse of her legs, the ripple of muscle beneath smooth skin as she moved. Memories of the feeling of her body close against his the previous night set his skin atingle, and there was no way he could exorcise them even had he wanted to. Remembering even to breathe seemed a titanic effort.

When Rania had finally finished putting on shirt and breeches of a mottled grey and white, she settled herself across the tent from Tal, resting elbows on knees as she eyed him boldly up and down. "Your turn," she murmured with a grin he could only describe as wicked.

He blinked twice before getting enough of a hold on his thoughts to realize what she meant. "I suppose fair is fair." Lazily, Tal grasped his shirt and pulled it off, stretching out his shoulders before tossing it aside, trying his best to play at Rania's game.

"Very nice," she purred, "do go on."

She wasn't going to make this easy for him, it seemed, but this was no time to shy away. Tal unbuckled his swordbelt as deliberately as she had moments before.

Tal found it extremely hard to sleep that night, with Rania snuggled up close beside him. If she could see the thoughts that flickered through his head she would probably drub him halfway back to Val Solus. Or would she? Based on her behavior earlier tonight, she might just laugh them off, or maybe even entertain similar ideas herself.

Confusion and indecision warred within Tal at that latter possibility. Could Rania truly have an interest in him similar to the one he was having a more and more difficult time denying he had in her? And if so, could he act on it in good conscience? After all, she had been through a lot and the past couple weeks had clearly recalled in her the pain of old and deep hurts. That he had seen her break down before him twice now, something he would otherwise have imagined impossible, made that undeniable. Would it not be unfair of him to make romantic overtures to Rania while she still stood on such shaky emotional ground?

Tal spent most of the night staring at the taut canvas above, painfully aware of every breath Rania took beside him while his thoughts ran in circles. After hours, he felt the only way to calm them would be to get away from her for a few moments, let the thrill her nearness brought fade and allow clarity to rule. He squirmed out of the blankets, gently easing himself away from her.

Rania's eyes cracked open at his movement. "Tal?"

"I'm just going out for a bit of air," he whispered back as he pulled his boots on. Almost as an afterthought, he strapped on his swordbelt.

The cold air hit him like a slap in the face as he crawled out of the flap at the front of the tent, stooping to tie it back down after he exited. Standing again, he took a deep breath of air. Yes, this would help.

Unconsciously, he opened himself to the Sephira. It truly was becoming habit for him now.

All thought of Rania was forgotten when the rush of sensation carried on the flow of existence brought him the feel of not one, but two other presences near him. He whirled to face the second one, *Kallevamar* springing from its sheath.

Tal hadn't noticed the man crouching alongside one of the boulders when he emerged from the tent, so well did the stranger's clothing blend into his surroundings. It was a blend of grey and white, so close in coloration and pattern to what Tal had watched Rania put on earlier that it might have been cut from the same bolt of cloth. The man didn't move from his crouch as Tal drew the blade, only raised his empty hands before him.

"There's no need for steel, Shevestra'ka. Even if I bore you any ill intent, I've no doubt you'd vanquish me swiftly enough."

"Who are you?" Tal asked, "And what do you want?"

"My name is Toven Ahren," The man replied as he stood slowly and with great care not to make any threatening moves. "I am a Pathfinder." He bowed to Tal. "As for what I want, I'm here looking for you, actually. A raven arrived yesterday afternoon in Felmorinen advising us that you might be headed this way." His eyes darted over Tal's shoulder, and Tal spared a glance behind him. Rania was emerging from the tent.

"Well met, Marquess," Toven said respectfully.

"And a good morning to you, Toven," Rania replied, "I'm a bit surprised to see you."

"You know him?" Tal asked with a raised eyebrow.

Rania shrugged. "It's hard to spend your life in the Felmorr without running into a Pathfinder every now and then. I'm known to them."

Toven chuckled. "I should say you are." He turned to speak to Tal. "Marquess Amoran here is something of a legend among us. None know the Felmorr better than she. You travel in good company."

"I'm certainly in agreement," Tal said amiably. "Now, why is it you were looking for us?"

"Not to try and turn you back, as I was advised you might be concerned," the Pathfinder said reassuringly, "but to bring you a warning. Our people ranging the eastern sides of the mountains report that the Bhellan patrols all seem to have been withdrawn. They've not caught sight of any soldiers in weeks, but they also report that something else is out there now. Odd sounds, tracks that seem to be neither human nor animal, that sort of thing. Nobody has seen whatever it is yet, or at least nobody has lived to tell about it. We've lost a lot of men out there lately. Sometimes the bodies are found, mauled beyond recognition. Whatever has taken up habitation in our mountains, it seems to have a bad temper."

Tal rubbed his jaw thoughtfully. "Probably some new trick of Kherzul's. Thank you for the warning, Toven. We'll keep our eyes open. Maybe we can take care of this little problem of yours on our way through."

Toven nodded graciously to Tal, and then turned a questioning eye back to Rania. "If I may ask, Marquess, are you going to stop at Felmorinen?"

Rania shook her head. "I haven't set foot there since I fled fifteen years ago, nor will I until I can stand before my parents' tomb and tell them that they've been avenged." Her voice was hard and cold. She glanced at Tal, and then said more gently, "Perhaps that will be soon."

"I look forward to the day," the Pathfinder said, and then bowed to the both of them again. "Is there anything I may assist you with?"

"No," Rania replied, "we can manage just fine."

"Of course you can," Toven smiled. "Then I will be on my way back to Felmorinen."

"We're headed in that direction as well," Tal said, "if you wait for us to break camp, we'll accompany you until our paths diverge."

Toven agreed cheerfully, even going so far as to help Tal and Rania break down the camp. In short order everything was packed up again, and the three of them set out together toward the east.

They walked in silence for the most part. Tal spent most of the time looking about in wonder at his surroundings. The slippery feel to the Sephira was one thing, but the way the landscape shifted and distorted was quite another. Distant points of reference would grow nearer or more distant, or sometimes slide along relative to each other. It was disconcerting in the extreme. Impressively, neither Rania or Toven seemed put off by it in the slightest. Eventually, the wandering landmarks began to make Tal feel a bit queasy, so he turned his eyes downward and concentrated on putting one foot in front of the other.

Early in the afternoon they arrived at a branch in the trails beside a particularly enormous peak. One branch snaked its way up the peak, the other disappeared around the base.

"Well, it looks like this is where we part ways," Toven declared. "I wish you both luck on your mission. May you succeed and return safely."

"Thank you," Tal murmured, "we'll try."

He and Rania watched the Pathfinder walk off down the lower path.

"Why does he call you by your title?" Tal asked curiously.

Rania rolled her eyes. "Tradition holds that the Marquess of House Amoran is the Pathfinders' leader. It's more an honorary title than anything else. But they insist that since it doesn't involve rulership, it doesn't conflict with my oaths. So they call me by the title they've always called their leader."

"I take it that outfit you're wearing is one of theirs?"

"This?" Rania plucked at her sleeve. "Yes. I had a number of them made while I was up here. They're useful in these mountains. I suppose that honorary title has a few uses." A trace of a smile graced her face. "Shall we be on our way?"

They wound their way up the face of the peak. Once they were near the top, the path curved around the northern face.

As they rounded the bend, Rania pointed off down below. "There it is," she said, a hint of sadness in her voice, "Felmorinen. My home."

At the base of the peak was the end of a long and narrow valley. Incredibly, within the bounds of that valley it still appeared to be late autumn. Not a trace of snow was on the ground, and the trees were brightly colored with red and yellow and orange. Full-grown trees, at this height! There were fields down there as well, most appearing fallow although a handful looked to have been recently harvested. The air was suffused with a soft Sephiral glow that was no doubt responsible for the unusual weather. At the center of the valley was a small city of uniform stone buildings surrounded by a perfectly circular wall. The streets seemed strangely quiet and empty. Although it was still home to the Pathfinders' Guild and a small contingent of Valerite Guardsmen, Felmorinen had never been truly resettled after the disaster a decade and a half ago. Too many people still believed that it was cursed, haunted, or both. At the exact center of the city rose a great grey spike, reflecting the sunlight as if the stone of the fortress had been polished to a mirrorlike sheen. Up and up it climbed, far higher than any of the surrounding mountaintops, as though it were meant to pierce the heavens themselves. Astonishingly, it seemed to have no joins in the stone. It was all of a single piece, as though it were a part of the mountains themselves. Just like Rania had said.

Tal tore his eyes from the awe-inspiring sight to look at his companion.

Rania stood gazing down at the city, jaw clenched. A hint of wetness glistened at the corner of an eye.

Tal wrapped an arm gently about her shoulder. "I'm sorry, Rania. I wish I could take your pain from you."

She eyed him peculiarly. "It isn't yours to take, Tal, though I do appreciate the desire. If you can give me happiness, that's enough."

"How can I do that?"

She leaned into him, putting an arm around his waist. "You already do."

24

Howling in the Darkness

After turning away from Felmorinen to continue the journey to Bhellus, Rania found herself feeling strangely content. Usually the sight of her childhood home provoked in her such sorrow that it threatened to swallow her in its bleakness. It had begun to do so again this time, but being able to turn to Tal had helped her fight off the despair and rage that remembering that bloody night a decade and a half ago inspired. She was no longer alone in the world, fighting a personal battle that could never be won, and it felt wonderful, like the first rays of sunlight after years of darkness.

The world about her seemed so fresh and new as she led Tal through the twisting paths of the Felmorr, it felt almost as if she were seeing them for the first time. The Sephira seemed to sing in her as she walked, full of the joy of life and endless possibility. For far too long she had let herself be blinded by her pain, driven by her desire for blood and vengeance to the point that she had forgotten everything else. She wouldn't make the same mistake again. Yes, she had suffered deep hurts in her life, but she was still alive. She saw that now. More importantly, she felt it. She was still alive, and she could retrieve herself from the abyss she had cast herself into.

Night fell soon after they had put a handful of miles between themselves and the ancient fortress. They were making excellent time; the passes were being unusually cooperative. Another day of travel would probably bring them to the other side, and then they could begin their descent.

Once the tent was up, Tal went looking for firewood again. Now that Rania was resolved to pick up the pieces of her life and start anew, she knew she was going to have to find a way to deal with him. Her feelings for him had been growing undeniable of late, but Tal seemed to remain frustratingly unaware of them. When he was usually so sensitive to her emotions, how could he manage to be so oblivious of this one? Couldn't he sense how she felt through their bond?

Maybe not. Rania had tried using the bond to tell if her feelings for Tal were reciprocated, but had found that he kept too tight a reign on his emotions for her to be sure. He cared about her, of that much she could be certain. She felt it like an undercurrent in his emotional state whenever they talked. That much she could have told without the bond, though. What she wanted to know was how deep that current went.

She had been sure that he had felt it too when they met, that instant and compelling attraction. Even had Tal not been the most talented warrior at the tournament, Rania doubted she would have been able to take her eyes off him. When he had sensed her watching, when their gazes had met from a distance, and when he had chosen her as his Queen of Roses despite her being a complete stranger, it had seemed confirmation that he had felt the same thing. Tazmin had certainly thought that Tal had an interest in her, indeed he seemed to take it as granted. Why then, did Tal's attitude toward her now seem so... chaste?

Rania wished that the night she'd spent in Tal's room back in Val Jerak had been half as interesting as she had implied in her teasing of him. The truth of the matter was that they'd both succumbed to lethargy, brought on by the same alcohol that had emboldened Tal to ask her in, before anything of note happened.

The events of last night had bewildered her as well. She admitted to herself that she'd hoped to provoke some sort of reaction from Tal when she changed in front of him, but didn't know what to make of the one she'd received. She'd been surprised that he didn't seem more embarrassed by the situation, had even appeared to enjoy it to some degree. And the way he'd responded certainly suggested that he found her desirable, but then why hadn't he taken any action on that desire? If he was attracted to her and cared about her, could there be something else holding him back? What else could there be? Was there something wrong with her?

Rania'd hardly been able to get any rest over the night, feigning sleep so as not to disturb Tal while she tried to work through those nagging questions. She had a sneaking suspicion that he'd also remained awake, and if so, she would have given her swordarm to know what had been going through his mind. Had he been thinking of how uncomfortable he'd been with that night's episode, or had he been recollecting the sight of her as fondly as she had been hers of him?

The issue could no doubt be clarified by Rania's having a straightforward talk with Tal about it, but the very thought made her unbearably nervous. If her interpretation of the vision she'd had in these very mountains was correct, her fate was now tied to Tal's. Even were it not for that, between their carrying the Blades of Unity and the inexplicable link between them, they were essentially stuck with each other. Not that any of that was at all a bad thing, but if such a conversation didn't go well it could make a good situation suddenly very uncomfortable. Was that a chance she should take?

Rania sighed and shook her head, gazing off into the darkness where Tal had gone in search of fuel for the fire. "After all the painful things I've told you, Tal, why is it hardest to tell you that I love you?"

The next day's march brought them to the eastern edge of the mountains, where the trail began to slope downward again. By dusk the clouds had begun to drop a light snowfall. Rania found them shelter under an escarpment of rock, and they once again went through the routine of making camp.

They took their dinner beside the fire, drinking in the heat. As they were finishing the meal, a mournful howl echoed up the mountains from the trail ahead.

Tal looked off in the direction of the sound and then back at Rania. "Wolves?" he asked.

Rania shook her head as another howl reverberated up to them. "Too deep. I'm not sure what that could be."

Tal stood, unsheathing *Kallevamar* and gazing off into the darkness. Rania joined him, *Edyamar* in hand.

The howls drew closer, taking on a more dire note. Not mournful, but hungry. At least they came only one at a time. Whatever was making the noise, it was alone.

Tal glanced thoughtfully back at the fire, and walked over to pick up a burning branch in his off hand. The howling was almost on top of them, now.

A shadow moved in the darkness down the trail, giving an impression of great size, perhaps as large as a horse or maybe a bear. Surely no bear ever made a sound like that, though. It moved slowly toward them, quiet now. Rania heard a deep snuffling sound, like something sniffing the air. Two sickly green points appeared on the shadow as it swung what was apparently its head their way.

"It looks like it *is* some of Kherzul's work," Tal muttered.

Still closer the shadow crept, and now Rania could begin to make out what she was looking at, even though she could still put no name to it. In form it seemed to resemble a great wolf, but it was a bit larger than a horse, and instead of fur it had a scabrous grey hide covered in festering boils. Thick limbs corded with muscle were tipped by bone-white claws as long as daggers. Its long muzzle bristled with teeth and dripped slaver that steamed in the air. A low snarl rose from deep in its chest as it crouched at the edge of the light.

The Sephira began to seethe with the anticipation of struggle.

The creature surged forward, bearing down on Tal. He leapt from its path as jaws snapped at him. Rania lunged in at the thing's rear flank with a swift slash, scoring the tough hide with her blade. A putrid stench rose from the wound, almost causing her to gag on its foulness. The beast rounded on her, lashing out with a huge claw, and she danced back from the attack even as Tal hurled himself into its other side. He hit it with a quick series of strokes, drawing a guttural roar from its throat. As it turned its head back toward Tal, he thrust the burning end of the brand he held at its face and the creature shied back. Rania cut deep into the shoulder above its foreleg as the unnatural thing leapt away, circling them and growling.

"Injuring it probably won't slow it down much," Tal said through clenched teeth. "We'll have to find some way to cripple it."

Rania gave a tight nod, keeping her eyes on the beast.

When it came at them again it chose Rania as its target, pouncing at her with redoubled fury. She threw herself clear, but felt claws rake across her mail shirt as the thing hurtled over her. Tal charged in with a swing at a rear leg, failing to hamstring it but carving off a small chunk of heel. The creature spun around with supernal swiftness as it landed and launched itself at Rania before she had her feet under her again. Tal stepped in directly between it and her, laying open part of the thing's brow with *Kallevamar* before thrusting the burning branch into one of the ghastly green eyes. The beast twisted its head in pain and snapped its jaws closed on Tal's left arm before he was able to pull it clear. He screamed as the teeth sank into his flesh and hewed at it with his free hand, lopping off a paw at the ankle as it rose to strike at him.

With Tal's agonized cry and the flood of pain through their bond, Rania's world was swallowed by a red haze. She sprang to her feet as the thing tossed Tal about like a rag doll and threw herself at its blind side with a howl of her own, rage beyond words. She brought *Edyamar* down atop its neck with bone-jarring force, cleaving through hide and muscle to leave a hideous gaping wound. It let go its hold on Tal, casting him aside to turn its attention back to Rania. She was ready for it, and met the turning of its head with the edge of *Edyamar*. The blade bit through the muzzle and clove the thing's jaw off, but Rania wasn't done yet. She rolled under an awkward swipe of the remaining front claw, and hacked off the remainder of the leg Tal had injured as she came to her knees on its other side. The thing foundered as it lost the leg, and Rania spun as she rose again to hack savagely at the thick neck. Finally the beast was being slowed by its injuries, and it couldn't move fast enough to keep her from finally hewing head from shoulders on her third stroke. The body toppled sideways, limbs twitching spasmodically as if refusing to admit it had been slain. Rania had forgotten about it already. She dashed to Tal's side where he lay in the snow, desperately hoping his injuries weren't too severe.

Before she even reached him she could tell that he still lived. She could feel the Sephira flowing through him, which meant he was not only alive, but still conscious. He lay still, though, sprawled in the snow, hair fanned across his face. A crimson stain was slowly spreading in the snow around his savaged left arm. Rania knelt beside him and gently brushed the hair from his eyes.

Tal's gaze focused on her, and she could see his pain in the tightness of his face. "That really bloody hurt," he groaned through gritted teeth.

"At least you're alive," Rania replied with relief. "What did you think you were doing, attacking it head-on like that?"

"It was almost on top of you," Tal groaned, "I couldn't let it hurt you."

Rania didn't know whether to be touched by his concern for her or mad at the foolishness of his frontal attack. Rather than decide, she moved her attention to Tal's wound to see how bad it was.

She winced as she inspected his arm. The teeth had pierced the sleeve of his mail shirt and penetrated deeply. Being tossed about by the arm had both deepened and widened the gash, and shattered links of mail had been ground into the broken flesh. Blood still welled from the wound.

The first thing to do was stem that flow of blood before Tal lost too much more. Rania gripped the sleeve of Tal's armor, drank in the Sephira deeply to bolster her strength, and yanked. Links popped and snapped, and she ripped the arm of the mail shirt free. She then tore off a wide strip of cloth from her cloak and tied it tight around Tal's upper arm. He watched her work in silence except for a grunt as she pulled the makeshift tourniquet tight.

Rania tore up more of her cloak and set to bandaging the wound.

"It burns," Tal said weakly as she worked, "I think the bite may have been venomous."

"Don't talk," Rania soothed him, "Just concentrate on holding on to the Sephira. It'll help you fight the poison, if there was any." He would already know that, of course, but stating the obvious made her feel a little less worried for some reason.

Once she had the bandages in place, Rania considered her options. She was too concerned about Tal for them to stay here overnight. Even with the accelerated healing of the Sephira, he probably needed to have his wound properly tended, and that meant getting him down out of the mountains and to a healer.

"Can you stand?" Rania asked.

"I think so." He started trying to struggle to his feet, and Rania bent over to help pull him upright. Once standing he wavered a little, but seemed for the most part steady.

"We need to start down the mountains now, Tal. Be careful, and if you've any doubts about being able to go on, let me know. I'll carry you if I have to."

"The tent?" Tal questioned.

Rania shook her head. "We'll have to leave it. I don't intend to rest until I see you safely to a healer, anyway."

Tal nodded, and Rania ran to the tent to grab their packs. Fortunately Tal's was considerably smaller and lighter without the tent in it. "Okay, let's go," she said breathlessly as she returned to him.

It was slow going, picking their way down the steep slopes in the dark, and Tal's injury slowed them further. His left arm hung limp at his side, hindering his balance. Rania stayed hard and fast on his right side so she could catch him by the good arm whenever he slipped. Sweat covered his face after only an hour, and he looked frightfully pale. Rania didn't know what to do but keep pushing on, murmuring encouragement to Tal every few minutes. He would smile at her each time she spoke, a spark of his usual self briefly showing through the grim mask he wore. He had long since stopped trying to speak.

Rania's concern grew deeper with every step, just as Tal's condition continued to worsen. At last he was having such a hard time going forward that Rania stopped to allow him a few moments of rest. He slumped down against the stone face of the mountainside, and Rania crouched beside him to have a look under the bandages. What she saw stopped the breath in her throat. The skin around the wound had swelled and turned an angry red, and that beyond the red was a pale, deathly grey.

Tal seemed to catch her expression as she settled the bandages back in place. "I knew it was bad," he mumbled thickly.

Rania felt the Sephira leaving him and the blood drained from her face in fright. "Talaren Solus, don't you go passing out on me!" she yelled at him. If he lost the Sephira, death would likely follow soon after.

Tal roused himself a little, weakly lifting his head from where it drooped against his chest. He seemed to have a hard time focusing his eyes on her. "Rania," he croaked, "Beautiful Rania. I wish..." He lost focus again, looking past her.

Rania slapped him in the face. "Don't you dare die on me, Tal! Kherzul has taken everyone I've ever loved. If he takes you, too, I might never be able to crawl back to the light again!"

The slap combined with her yelling in his face seemed to pull Tal back. "Yes you can. You're strong enough." His eyes sharpened a little, and he reached up weakly to touch her cheek. "So strong. I'll try to stay with you, if I can."

"You'd better," Rania replied roughly, her throat tightening with emotion. She pulled his right arm up around her shoulder and began to half carry, half drag him with her down the path. "Just remember the Sephira, Tal. Hold on to it, and you'll live." She hoped.

Rania lost track of the time as she struggled downhill with Tal. He tried to help her, tried to move his legs of his own accord, but his strength was almost gone. The sky slowly grew brighter, and then dawn was upon them. In the daylight, Rania became aware of just how terribly pallid Tal's face looked. He struggled simply to keep his eyes open, and his breath came with obvious difficulty.

226

"I'm sorry, Rania," he rasped in a hoarse whisper a short while after the rising of the sun, "I can't..."

Rania felt the Sephira flee him as he suddenly turned to dead weight on her shoulder. She teetered under the sudden shift in weight, then stopped and carefully lowered Tal to the ground. She cupped his face gently in one hand. "Tal, don't do this. Come back to me, Tal. Taaaaaal!!!" The uncaring wind whipped her wail away.

She felt bile rising in her throat, and fought it down with great effort. She couldn't lose her head now. Tal's chest still rose and fell slowly, she still had time to save him, if only she could find a way. Desperately, she cast about her mind for an idea, any idea.

Only one thing came to her, and she wasn't sure it would work. The bond. If it seemed to carry Sephiral energy between the two of them, just maybe it would let her hold the Sephira for Tal to afford him the resilience and healing it brought. She laid her hands gently against the sides of Tal's head and tried reaching out to him, to the life energy that *was* him far more so than his body. She immersed herself in the Sephira as deeply as she ever had, fueled by her rage at Tal's injury. She concentrated with single-minded determination on the love she felt for him, on the kinship she felt between their souls. Something was there. She could feel it like a membranous barrier separating them. She pushed, and the barrier swelled, stretched, and finally shattered. The Sephira rushed through her and into Tal.

His breathing grew just perceptibly easier. His brow burned with fever, but at least he might still have a chance. Not wanting to squander whatever time she had, Rania hefted his unconscious form up onto her shoulders and started staggering down the mountainside once more.

Time seemed to flow by sluggishly, an unending repetition of one careful step after another. Rania paid only enough attention to her surroundings to keep herself on the right path, the rest of her concentration devoted wholly to maintaining her Sephiral link to Tal. He would groan or mutter incoherently as she struggled along, and she was grateful for the sounds. It was his falling silent that terrified her beyond belief.

Darkness came again as the sun dipped down below the peaks behind her, and still Rania plodded on, unwilling to stop for fear that fatigue would finally drag her down. Tal's life depended on her keeping going. She repeated that thought to herself over and over, a litany to keep her moving. She was nearly out of the mountains now, and from their base it would only be a few miles to the city of Bhel Femoryan. She knew a healer there who had tended her more serious wounds on occasion during her years in the Felmorr.

Every breath burned in her lungs. Her arms and legs felt like they were molten lead, heavy and blazing with white-hot pain in protest at still being worked. Exhaustion clouded her thoughts, the familiar surroundings of the Felmorr dredging up old memories unbidden and weaving them into her present. She found herself listening warily, ears straining for footfalls besides her own, snatches of distant conversation, any sign of the Bhellan patrols that Toven had already told her had vanished from the mountains. She tried to shake herself from the haze, to force her eyes to focus on the here and now rather than half-remembered apparitions from her past. And as she did so, recognition hit her like a hammer between the eyes: this was where it had started, where everything had begun to change for her. Rania was, at that very moment, carrying Tal past the place where she had experienced the vision that first led her to him.

It had been a late summer night, and this low in the mountains the air had still held enough warmth that she'd required scant protection against the cold that prevailed higher up. Earlier in the evening Rania had found a group of Bhellan soldiers, nine men strong and boasting confidently among themselves of the valor and prowess they'd show should they encounter the shadowy Ghost of Felmorinen. From the way they spoke, it seemed they thought the accounts they'd heard of slaughtered patrols to be mere myth, campfire tales told to frighten raw recruits. And then one of the soldiers had declared scornfully that he'd been at Felmorinen fifteen years prior and seen nary a sign of the avenging spirit. Upon hearing his words all restraint had fled Rania, consumed by crimson rage. The orgy of violence that followed had been unusually excessive, as the wrath-filled Shevestra'ka had not been satisfied with merely slaying her foes; she had, to the man, literally cut them to pieces before their bodies hit the ground.

At that point she had been experiencing her bouts of Sephiral torment for a few months, but the one that came over her later in the evening as she was making camp had made all the others pale in comparison. It had brought her to her knees, shrieking in agony, clawing bloody tracks around her eyes as she tried desperately to make it stop. After it finally subsided, she'd laid quivering prostrate on the cold ground, gulping lungfuls of air as the Sephira began knitting skin back over the self-inflicted gouges on her face.

When Rania had at last raised her head again, she'd been startled to find that she wasn't alone.

The woman standing over her had been tall, her ageless face lined with sympathy as she gazed down upon the Shevestra'ka. She had also been clearly something other than human. Her hair had been of flame, dancing about head and shoulders without seeming to burn her. Her flesh had shimmered with a soft silver sheen beneath the skin, and the eyes that beheld Rania were solid black, paired orbs of deepest night. She'd been clad for battle in armor of segmented overlapping plates that glistened the crimson of freshly spilled blood, and paired blades of exquisite workmanship had been sheathed at either hip.

228

"My poor, dear, broken child," the woman had said sadly, in a voice that seemed to reverberate through the mountains and inside Rania's head. She'd reached down to cup Rania's chin softly in one hand and gently drew the Shevestra'ka up to her feet. "So terrible a fire has been kindled in you, but it need not consume you. The time has come for you to turn this page, to step forward and shed the darkness that clings to you. You are meant to shine like a beacon to light the world."

"I don't understand," Rania had protested, still as confused by the woman's presence as by her words. "Who are you? What do you mean?"

"You must leave this place," the woman answered. "Follow the sun's path to the seat of power. There you will find that which you need, and which in turn needs you. But make haste, time will not wait for you."

"How will I know when I find it?" Rania asked, desperate for an answer that made sense. "What am I seeking?"

"You should know that better than I. Hope. Redemption. Purpose. The Future, for you and countless others. You will know it when you find it. The road to these things begins here. Follow it."

And with that, as though she'd never existed at all, the woman had been simply gone. Rania had wonderingly put a hand to where the apparition had touched her face, and it had come away warm and sticky with fresh blood. But had it come from her own wounds, or from the woman's hands? She felt rather than knew the answer, but was even more sure of it now, months later, than she had been at the time.

"You forgot to tell me another thing I would find, Shevestra," Rania murmured as she continued trudging with Tal's unconscious form down the mountains. "You never told me I'd love him. Even were it not for everything else you did say, I'll save him for that alone." She steeled herself with her words, determined not to make a liar of herself, and put another foot in front of the other. Time continued on in its steady march, and so too did Rania.

She nearly stumbled and fell when the ground leveled out underneath her, and she had to look about, blinking in confusion, before it registered in her mind that she was out of the mountains. Fighting down a yawn as she got her bearings, she turned further southward to make for the city.

The going was a little easier on flat ground, and that was perhaps the only reason Rania was able to keep pressing herself forward. That, and the iron determination not to lose the man she loved without his knowing the depth of her feelings for him.

Step after step, and the walls of Bhel Femoryan loomed before her as the dark of night began once more to give way. Step after step, and she stood before the gates. A watchman in a leather breastplate looked at her in puzzlement at the gates and asked her a question she didn't really hear.

"We were attacked by a beast in the wilderness," Rania gasped, "I need to get him to a healer."

Apparently her answer satisfied the guard, for he yelled up for the portcullis separating them to be raised and waved her through.

As Rania staggered through the gates another watchman came up beside her and tried to take Tal from her shoulders, but she growled at him and the armored man backed off. Instead he walked beside her as she made her way to the place she remembered. So close, now.

The sun had just broken over the horizon when she at last stood unsteadily before the little shop with a sign portraying a neatly tied bunch of herbs. Before she could free a hand to knock on the door, the guardsman stepped forward and rapped on it for her. She gave him a wan smile of thanks.

The door opened to reveal a stocky old woman with grey hair in a tight bun at the back of her head. She wore a leather apron covered in pockets and pouches.

"Mistress Ferrin," Rania greeted her in a dry rasp.

"Child!" The woman declared in surprise. "I haven't seen you in ages! Come in, come in. It looks like your friend needs help badly. Hurry, now, no time to waste!"

Rania felt a great surge of relief as she crossed the threshold of Mistress Ferrin's shop. Everything would be alright now. It had to be.

25

An Unexpected Visitor

No sooner had Rania laid Tal gently down atop the cleared table Mistress Ferrin led her to than the healer set to work on him. The older woman placed a hand to Tal's brow and tsked irritably. She thumbed open an eyelid and muttered inaudibly to herself at whatever she saw. She looked up past Rania to the guardsman who still lingered at the door, watching on curiously.

"Thank you for your assistance, young man," Ferrin said briskly, "I think I can manage things now." The tone of dismissal in her voice would have done any noblewoman proud.

The guard shrugged and left, closing the door to the shop behind himself.

Mistress Ferrin began tenderly unwinding the strips of cloak from Tal's arm, grumbling about improperly washed bandages. Once she got a look at the wound, her eyebrows rose sharply and she shook her head before turning her eyes to Rania again. "What did this to him?"

"A beast in the mountains. It wasn't a natural creature." Rania suddenly realized that she was still carrying the packs. She dropped them in the nearest corner, her eyes never leaving Tal's ashen face. Sephiral energy still flowed through her to him.

The healer nodded. "Aye, I thought that might be it. Whatever the brute is, it's been attacking anything or anyone that strays too close to the mountains. Has the farmers in the countryside hereabouts scared out of their skins. I've seen a few of its victims, and even tried tending a couple. Of the ones I've seen, this boy is the most whole yet. How did you get him away from the thing?" She rummaged through some earthenware jars on her shelves as she spoke.

"I killed it." Rania said simply.

"That's quite the trick," Ferrin replied as she selected out several of the jars and set them on a corner of the table. "Then again, you always were good at getting yourself into trouble." She looked wryly at Rania for a moment before taking up a mortar and pestle from the front of another shelf. "You should get some sleep, child. Looks like you should have fallen over from exhaustion long ago. I've a few beds for patients in the back room. You can use one of those." She waved the pestle vaguely toward a door.

Rania shook her head. "I have to keep channeling the Sephira to him. It's the only thing that kept him alive on the way here."

Ferrin began judiciously mixing herbs from the jars into the mortar. "Well, that explains what you're doing in the city with that aura of yours. It may not glow much, whatever you're doing , but I can sure feel it there. Lords, girl, its making *me* tired, just feeling the fatigue rolling off you from that thing. Weren't you worried that the guards might have noticed it too?"

"That didn't matter," Rania said around a jaw-cracking yawn. "Only keeping Tal alive mattered."

The healer smiled knowingly as she began grinding up the herbs. "So it's like that, is it? Don't worry, child, I think he's through the worst of it. He looks to have come close enough to death to spit in its eye, but if he made it this far, he'll not expire on my table. Some clean bandages, a warm poultice, and..." She looked up and blinked at Rania. "Did you say Tal? As in Talaren, that young Valerite Lord everyone has been nattering on about?"

Rania drew herself up proudly, or tried to at least. "The same."

Mistress Ferrin shook her head amazedly as she continued to grind away. "So much trouble for an old woman you are, child. You'll land me on the headsman's block, soon or late." She set aside the mortar and bustled over to the hearth to fetch a kettle of water already warming beside the fire.

"I do hope I haven't brought you any trouble," Rania said. Truly, she hadn't even thought of it, so intent had she been on finding aid for Tal. She would hate to bring any sort of tribulation to the kindly old woman.

"Phaw! If anyone asks, I'll just pretend I didn't hear what you just told me. The lad's name is well known, true, but not so much his description. Besides, you know that I wouldn't turn away King Garant himself if he came injured to my door." Ferrin mixed a dribble of the hot water with the ground herbs and set to mixing, a considering look on her face. "Our own King Kherzul, though, him I might turn away. That one's not right in the head, you ask me. Actually makes me wistful for the days of his father, pompous puffed-up ass that he was."

Rania smiled in amusement, but didn't dare say anything.

A pungent aroma began to drift from the mortar as Mistress Ferrin mixed her poultice. "So, child, what brings you back to Bhel Femoryan again after so long, aside from your injured friend?"

Rania frowned hesitantly. "I probably shouldn't tell you. It could be dangerous for you to know."

The old woman fixed her with a knowing eye as she applied the red-brown paste she had created to a clean bandage. "Looking for trouble again, then. Ah, the impetuousness of youth!" She began wrapping the fresh bandage around Tal's wounded arm. Once it was snugged down, she glanced back at Rania. "If you're going to insist on watching over him, you could at least pull up a chair. Sit down, before you fall down."

Rania pulled a ladder-back chair across the floor and sat down beside Tal. She took his good hand in hers and stroked it gently.

Meanwhile, Mistress Ferrin had taken out three cups from yet another of her many shelves. "I was just about to make some tea when you arrived," she said, "would you like some?"

Rania nodded, the question suddenly bringing to mind the fact that she really was terribly thirsty.

The grey haired woman poured one cup full of hot water before throwing a handful of tea leaves into the kettle. She moved back to the shelf of jars and began searching through them again. "Something a bit different for him," she murmured, "Something to help him rest and mend." She selected a jar and pulled from it two leaves, which she crumbled into the cup of water.

While they waited for the tea to steep, Rania said, "Thank you so much for your help, Mistress Ferrin. I don't know what I'd have done if not for you."

The healer gave her a motherly smile. "None of that, child. It's what I do. It was worth it just to get that frightened look from your eyes. But now you know how much trouble it can be, tying your heart to a man."

"For him, I'd go through the same again and worse." Rania grimaced at the words as they left her mouth, realizing how besotted she sounded.

Mistress Ferrin gave a hearty laugh. "I hope he's worth it, child. I'd hate to see you end up with a good-for-nothing." She gave Tal's unconscious form a considering look. "He's certainly pretty enough, and if half of what they say is true, he might be quite the catch. Assuming he treats you well, that is."

"Very well," Rania replied, returning to stroking Tal's hand while Ferrin poured their tea, "In him I've rediscovered the joy in life I once thought lost."

"That's a strong recommendation," Ferrin said as she picked up a wooden funnel. She walked over to Tal and worked his jaw open, inserting the funnel between his teeth. She began to slowly pour the cup she had prepared for him into the funnel, taking care not to choke him. "Just don't go losing it again."

"I don't intend to," Rania murmured, and then took a sip of her tea. It was slightly bitter, but sovereign for her parched throat.

After emptying the cup into Tal, Mistress Ferrin removed the funnel and studied him carefully, again checking his brow and under his eyelids. She gave a satisfied nod. "That should do for him." His breath *did* seem to be coming easier, Rania noticed, and his face was getting back some of its color. "I think you can stop doing whatever it is that you're doing now, child."

Rania released the Sephira, and a weariness such as she had never known slammed down over her. She nearly slid right out of her seat under its weight. Muscles that had felt tired and weakened from her ordeal moments ago now seemed to scream at her with agony at the slightest movement. She sighed and slumped in the chair. "Maybe some sleep isn't such a bad idea after all." Her head felt like it was stuffed with wool, her thoughts muffled and slowed.

"It's a very wise idea, is what it is." Ferrin came around to help Rania rise from her seat, but before she got to her, the front door swung open without so much as a knock.

The man who strode into the shop was tall and slender, with dark blonde hair and beard trimmed neat and close. There was a hawklike curve to his nose that lent him a predatory look, and he carried himself with confident dignity. His burgundy coat and breeches were well tailored, his black boots polished to a glossy dark shine. Four guardsmen in leather armor followed him in, including the one who had followed Rania to the shop.

"Lord Brant!" Mistress Ferrin exclaimed at the newcomer. "You honor my humble household with your presence."

The man nodded graciously to her. "I understand another victim of the mountain attacks was brought here, good lady."

Ferrin ducked her head with a surreptitious cautionary glance at Rania. "Indeed, my Lord."

The Lord sighed. "I suppose it's too much to hope that the unfortunate fellow survived?"

The healer shook her head. "On the contrary, my Lord, this is him here." She motioned toward Tal's prone body. "As you can see, he is quite alive. I expect he should eventually make a full recovery."

A great smile spread across the Bhellan Lord's face. "Excellent!" he declared, "I've been looking into these attacks personally, but this is the first survivor I've heard tell of." He shook his head in exasperation. "You've no idea how hard it is to gather information about a beast nobody has seen and lived to tell the tale about. I'd like to see him." He walked over to the table Tal was laid out on. Rania watched him guardedly.

"You can look all you like, my Lord, but I doubt he'll be telling tales anytime soon. He'll sleep for quite some time after what he's been through, I think."

The Lord seemed to ignore Mistress Ferrin's statement. "Got him by the arm, did it?" He mused as he looked Tal over. His eyes lingered on Tal's face, and slowly widened. Under his breath, Rania heard him mutter, "Take me for a fool if this isn't..." He turned his head sharply toward the healer. "Can he be moved safely?" He asked Ferrin.

The healer's brow furrowed with concern. "Yes, my Lord, but..."

Brant gave a quick nod to the guards behind him. "Do it." He turned back to the old woman. "Don't worry, good lady, we'll take good care of him. I want him in the manor, to question when he awakes." His eyes settled on Rania. "You're the one who brought him in?"

234

Rania saw no other choice. This Lord Brant had clearly recognized Tal. Their mission could not be stopped here, no matter the cost. She leapt to her feet, reaching out for the Sephira and her sword at the same time. At least, that was what she tried to do. Her exhausted mind fumbled for and failed to grasp the Sephira, and muscles pushed beyond endurance shrieked at her in protest and pitched her forward to the floor, *Edyamar* not even halfway out of the sheath.

"Well, that was unexpected," Brant commented as two of the guardsmen came over and hauled Rania to her feet between them. She wanted to wail in shame as they carried her to the door as easily as they would handle a child.

Before being hauled out the door, Rania managed to twist her head around to look at Mistress Ferrin. The healer wrung her hands in consternation and mouthed to Rania the words, "I'm sorry."

26
One Man's Struggle

Tal awakened to a dull throbbing in his arm. He was more than a little surprised at the fact that he did wake; in his last memories of the long trek down the mountain, he had been sure he was done for. Rania must have found some way to save him. There was strength in that young woman's spirit, far more than she gave herself credit for, and somehow her strength had sustained him when he'd even given up on himself. He wondered where she was now.

There was no sign of her when he opened his eyes. He lay in a huge feather-stuffed bed with posts carved in a spiral pattern. The room about him was similarly well appointed, from thick rugs to velvet curtains to carved tables and chairs. He hadn't the foggiest idea where he might be.

"So, at last our sleeper awakens." The speaker was a tall man with short blonde hair and beard seated at one of the tables. Tal didn't recognize the man, but the weapon lying on the table before him was certainly familiar. *Kallevamar*. The man idly tapped his fingers on the wire bound hilt as he considered Tal. "I have a great many questions for you, my friend. Almost enough that I don't know where to start." He flashed his teeth wolfishly. "Almost."

"Who are you?" Tal asked, his voice rough and dry.

The man at the table raised an eyebrow. "I thought I said I was the one with the questions." He made a dismissive gesture with the hand not on *Kallevamar*. "But I'll gladly answer your questions if you will answer mine." He waited for Tal to nod, and then added, "You sound like you could use a drink. There's water on your bedside table."

Tal managed to wriggle his way to the edge of the bed and found sitting on it a pitcher of water and a cup. Using his right arm he managed to pour some water, which he gulped down immediately, and then poured another cup.

After Tal had downed the first cup of water, the man spoke again. "In answer to your question, I am Lord Brant Femor of Bhel Femoryan. And you, unless I miss my guess, are Talaren Solus." He grinned at the expression on Tal's face. "Don't look so surprised. I make it my business to follow the goings on in our neighbor to the west, and I frequently attend the more notable of Valeran's festivals and tournaments to stay up to date. Recognizing the King's Champion up close wasn't terribly difficult. Now, it's my turn." He lifted *Kallevamar* a couple inches up off the table. "Is this what I think it is?"

Tal frowned for a moment, but decided it would be useless to deny what the Lord seemed to already know. "That depends on what you think it is. It's the blade of Trazeri the Accursed."

Brant nodded. "Good. You're being truthful. That will make this much easier." His raised eyebrows emphasized his point. "Your next question?"

"I had a friend with me. Where is she?" Tal didn't want to give away Rania's name if he could help it. Her face wasn't yet as well known as his, but her name might be recognized.

"The girl? She sleeps in another room in this wing of my manor. It seems she was quite exhausted. I wasn't even able to question her when we brought you two in before she fell asleep." Brant pointed at Tal's bandaged arm. "What did that to you?"

Tal suppressed a shudder. "I don't know what to call it. It was a creature created by your King, a thing of death and corruption."

"Whatever it is, it's been plaguing travelers and outlying villages within my lands. Many of my people have died as victims of its depredations."

"You needn't worry about that anymore. We slew the beast." Tal berated himself for volunteering the information, then thought better of it. It would help to build the man's trust for when he would eventually have to mislead him. He considered his next question. "Why have you brought me here? What do you want with me?"

"Is that one question, or two?" Brant's eyes danced amusedly and then his expression flashed back to sobriety. "They say that a wise man keeps his friends close and his enemies even closer. I'm still trying to decide which you are. What is the battle leader who defeated us at the Felmorr Gap doing in Bhellus, carrying the sword he must surely know our King desires so much?"

It was the question Tal had been waiting for, and he had been thinking this whole time of how he would respond. "After seeing the forces King Kherzul has at his disposal, I came to the conclusion that Valeran cannot win a war against Bhellus. Knowing how badly he wants that sword, I came to offer it to him in exchange for turning his eye away from my nation."

Brant shook his head sadly. "You were doing so well, too," he murmured. "If I believed that, Talaren, your present quarters would not be so comfortable by half. Do you really expect me to believe that a Shevestra'ka, sworn to fight until his dying breath, would surrender to a creature such as our King has become? I may be a fool, but not that big a fool." He lowered his brows angrily. "Try again."

Tal sighed. "What I said about my appraisal of our chances is true, or close enough. I brought the one weapon that can harm Kherzul with me because I intend to kill him." He glared challengingly at the Lord, preparing to launch himself at the man. He hoped his body was up to it.

Brant clapped his hands together and smiled broadly. "Much better. I told you this would go easier if you were truthful with me. What would you say if I told you that I might be willing to lend you some assistance?"

"I would ask you why," Tal replied, relaxing ever so slightly.

"A reasonable question, under the circumstances," Brant said smoothly, "but one with a long answer."

Tal gave the Lord an amused grin. "I don't seem to be going anywhere."

Brant nodded. "Alright, then. I consider myself a patriot, Lord Solus. To me, that means putting the interests of your people above your own and taking the long view, especially if you're in a position of leadership. I learned this from my father. He personally opposed Shebedar's revolution, but the Duke had ignited a fire in the hearts of the Bhellan people with his rhetoric of liberation and regional pride. With his people fervently supporting Shebedar and the other lords this side of the Felmorr likewise pushing for rebellion, my father had the hard choice of following a cause he didn't believe in or being the first to be attacked. In the end, he joined with the revolutionary forces to spare our people the suffering that a siege on the city would bring. He rode with Shebedar's armies, and sadly fell at the Battle of the Gilden Hills." Brant quirked an eyebrow at Tal. "Just so you know, I don't hold that fact against you, or your father for that matter. He was simply doing as he had to, much as my father was."

"I was only thirteen at the time, and found myself suddenly the Lord of my city. Ruling under King Shebedar wasn't an easy thing." Brant sighed. "There was very little to him but ambition and greed. Kindness and wisdom held no sway over that man. He levied backbreaking taxes on the people and forced conscription into the army in the hope of one day finishing what he started in the revolution. To try to take some of the strain from my people, I cut the taxes my House asked of them to almost nothing. It cost House Femor greatly in power and influence, but kept the loyalty of those under me."

Brant began drumming his fingertips on the sword again. "I thought that Shebedar was bad, but little did I know that the true abomination was his son. Kherzul had ambition to match his father, a keen intellect, and an utter lack of scruples. He would shy away from no act that would gain him power, and he proved it when he had his own father assassinated so he could assume the throne."

"Of course, Kherzul denied any involvement in Shebedar's demise. Those who persisted in their accusations had an amazing tendency to have unlikely and fatal accidents. Over the years, the same has happened to most nobles who expressed any sort of criticism toward our King. Between silencing his detractors and the policy changes he made in stark contrast to those of his father, Kherzul began to garner a certain amount of respect and admiration." Brant's face grew angrier with every word. "It was ever his way to work from the shadows, using trickery and deceit to build his power and revealing his intentions only once it's too late for anyone to stop him."

"Yes, he quite fooled us in Valeran with his apparent goodwill," Tal said in commiseration.

Brant shook his head disbelievingly. "The sad part is how easily and conveniently everyone forgot how he came to power. I never did. There was little I could do against him, but I watched and listened and waited. When he began talking as his father had about the power and glory of the Bhellan nation, I began to fear the worst, but my fears fell far short of the truth. The powers Kherzul has unleashed threaten not only your nation, but ours as well. He has convinced most of Bhellus that the unification at last of the north in its entirety justifies the use of any means necessary, including those he employs, but I remember my history. Kherzul will conquer the north if left unchecked, but in doing so he'll turn it into a land of the dead. By my reckoning, that serves nobody but Kherzul himself."

Brant fixed his eyes seriously on Tal's face, a grave turn to his lips. "The greatest threat Bhellus faces is her own King, Talaren. It's beyond my power to prevent what I see coming without allies, but the very act of seeking them out could land my head on the block. I had begun to despair of ever having any opportunity to save my nation from this fate, and then as if in answer to my prayers, you fall into my lap. In my position, I'm willing to take my allies where I find them, and so I would assist you if you're willing to accept my aid."

Tal nodded slowly. Brant's reasoning seemed sound enough, and if he intended any harm, he had already had ample opportunity to inflict it. "I believe I can trust your motives. How did you intend to help me?"

"I can provide you with a way to travel to Bhel Meravos with minimal risk of discovery." Brant spread his hands before himself and smiled self-deprecatingly. "It isn't much, true, but that's about as far out as I can safely stretch my neck without having it stretched for me by a noose."

"Even so, it'll be a welcome aid to my mission," Tal said gratefully.

Brant made a restraining gesture with one hand. "There is one other thing I need before I'll help you. A promise."

"It seems lately like everyone I meet wants me to swear some oath or other to them," Tal sighed with a long-suffering look. "What promise would you have of me, Lord Femor?"

Brant chuckled at him. "Nothing you'll find too odious, I think. I'm willing to betray Kherzul, but not Bhellus. I just want your word that after you slay Kherzul, you'll not use the opportunity to place a Valerite puppet on the throne."

"Then you have it." Tal grinned. "I only want to eliminate Kherzul's threat, not build an empire."

"A healthy attitude," Brant laughed. "I'm glad we're able to understand each other, Talaren. Gods, it feels good to have an ally finally, even if he technically should be the enemy." His eyes glittered in amusement.

"Glad I could help," Tal said dryly. "Now, how do you plan to get Rania and I..." His eyes widened. "Rania! Quickly, we need to go let her know you're a friend before she wakes up and tears this place down looking for me!"

"The girl? I wouldn't worry about her. She tried to attack me when I took you from the healer's shop and seemed far more of a threat to herself than anyone else. Besides, I had her disarmed and put under guard." Brant looked perplexed by Tal's sudden urgency.

"That'll only make things worse. She must have been beyond exhaustion when you saw her. You've no idea what she's capable of normally." Tal realized he was standing across the table from Brant, looming over him.

The Lord raised an eyebrow. "Is she really that dangerous?" Incredulity filled his voice.

Tal reached out to the Sephira and let it flow through him. "I'm that dangerous," he said softly as the aura of power enfolded him, "Rania is more like a force of nature. She's the one who killed the beast once it got its teeth into me. What do you think she'll do if she thinks you've got your teeth in me?"

Brant's face paled and he shied back in his seat, unconsciously raising a hand defensively before himself. The control in his voice was strained as he replied, "Alright, if it's that big a problem..." He broke off as a loud crash echoed down the hall outside, and then looked questioningly at Tal.

Tal nodded. "That's probably her. You should let me go first."

With two long strides, Brant was at the door. He opened it, and Tal leapt into the hall.

Not twenty paces away, Rania stood amid the wreckage of the door she had just obliterated, cloaked in the full glory of her battle aura and with a sword in hand. Two guards who had apparently been watching over Tal's room while Brant was inside were between them, rushing at Rania with blades raised.

"Rania, stop!" Tal yelled.

Her eyes met his, and then the guards were on her. She flowed out of the way of their blades with no apparent effort, and then kicked one of them in the face so hard that the man spun full round with the force of her blow

240

before collapsing limp on the floor. The other swung at her again and she caught him by the wrist before the blow could land. She twisted hard and a sickening pop came from the guard's wrist. His sword dropped from nerveless fingers and Rania let him go. She walked up to Tal as casually as could be.

"Are you ready to go? We'll need to find our swords." She sounded like she was suggesting a noonday stroll.

"We're not going, Rania. Lord Brant is going to help us." He gave her an irritable look. "Didn't I just say to stop?"

Rania glanced over her shoulder at the guard nursing his wrist and the motionless one on the floor. "They were between us, and they were attacking me. I won't let anyone or anything come between us, Tal. Besides, I didn't kill them."

Brant peered out of the room Tal had emerged from. "Talaren, I see what you meant," he said as he took in the wreckage and incapacitated guards. "Your friend here *is* quite impressive."

Tal pointed at the sword in Rania's hand. "I don't suppose the guard you got that from is still alive?"

"I thought we were being held prisoner, and he was in my way." Rania shrugged. "He should live, if he gets help soon."

Brant winced. "I suppose I can't really blame you under the circumstances. I put you into this situation." He started down the hall toward the wrecked door, saying over his shoulder, "I'll see to having this mess cleaned up. You two stay in your room, Talaren. I'll come and explain my plan as soon as I've taken care of everything."

Tal nodded and led Rania into the room he had awakened in. He had barely closed the door behind him when Rania leapt upon him and enfolded him in a rib-cracking hug.

"I was so worried about you," she said breathlessly.

Tal stroked her hair softly with his good hand. "I'm alright. Thanks entirely to you, unless I miss my guess."

Rania reached up with both hands to grasp Tal by the head and forced him to meet her gaze. "I said I wouldn't let anything come between us, and that includes death," she said fiercely.

Tal blinked at her in shock. "Rania..."

"I love you, Tal. You had the nerve to go and almost die on me before I could find a way to tell you, so I'm making sure you don't get another chance."

Tal opened his mouth, but speech fled him. So instead he pressed his lips to hers, kissing her deeply, lingeringly, as he'd longed to so many times before. "I love you, too," he said when he pulled back, and then laughed, "but hearing you say that, I can't help but wonder if I'm still feverish and delirious."

Rania put a hand to his brow. "I'm no expert at these things, but you feel fine to me," she grinned. Then more seriously, "How's your arm?"

Tal chuckled. "Feels like it's been bitten through by a giant wolf. It hurts, but I think it should heal."

"Good," Rania said with an impish twinkle in her eye. "I want you sound of body."

Tal's ears reddened, and Rania laughed. "Have I ever mentioned that you embarrass too easily, Tal?"

"As a matter of fact, you have," Tal replied. "As I recall, you were naked at the time."

"Oh, so you did notice after all."

"Notice? Gods, Rania, I couldn't get it out of my mind! I thought you said you knew how you look?"

"You say such nice things sometimes," she said fondly. Tal noticed, though, the hint of a blush in her cheeks.

"I thought I was supposed to be the one who embarrasses easily," Tal teased.

Rania smiled and widened her eyes entirely too innocently. "But I'm only a humble swordswoman. I'm afraid that I don't have the benefit of all the social exposure at court that m'lord has."

"Let's not start with that again," Tal sighed. "What did I ever do to deserve this?"

"I don't know," Rania laughed, "but it must have been wonderful."

Tal tried to keep a straight face, but confronted by Rania's grin he found himself laughing along with her. Their mirth was cut short by a single knock at the door, and without waiting for an answer Lord Brant stepped into the room.

"You'll be glad to know that all three of those guards will survive," he said without preamble. "It would have made it much more difficult to conceal you if we'd had any sudden unexplained fatalities here in the manor." He spared a glance for Rania and then turned his eyes to Tal. "I assume that you've told her about our little understanding?"

"I actually hadn't really gotten to it yet," Tal replied, "but Rania will behave herself." He shot her a wry grin. She punched him in his good shoulder.

Brant suppressed a laugh as Tal sighed ruefully and rubbed where Rania had hit him. The Lord looked back to the red haired young woman appraisingly. "I'd heard rumors from our watchers in Val Jerak, but wasn't sure I believed. Tell me, are you truly Rania Amoran of Felmorinen?"

Rania rolled her eyes. "Why does everyone keep asking me if I'm really me? Yes, I'm Rania Amoran, the Ghost of Felmorinen returned from the dead or whatever bloody story you've heard."

"I apologize if the question offends, my lady. Please let me be the first noble of Bhellus to apologize to you for the atrocity our King perpetrated on your city. None of us knew that he had done it until recently, but his actions were and are unforgivable. They stain the honor of my nation." Sincerity lined Brant's face.

Rania's green eyes had gone cold and hard, and so did her voice as she spoke. "My quarrel is with Kherzul, not Bhellus. I'll have retribution for his slaughter of my friends and family soon enough." Tal took her hand consolingly, and she gave him a little smile of thanks.

"Yes, and that's exactly what I've come to discuss with you two," Brant said seriously. "I've promised Talaren that I can get the both of you to Bhel Meravos unmolested. I thought you might like to know how I intend to accomplish that."

"That might be useful," Tal agreed.

"With his war begun, Kherzul has been building up the military as fast as he can. He's emptied nearly every graveyard in Bhellus with his dark sorcery and conscripted so many commonfolk that it'll cripple our economy before long, but still he wants more. He recently issued a call for mercenaries, and is promising such pay for them as would turn any man's head. The announcement was made little over a week ago, but already we've had a fair number answer his call." Brant scowled and shook his head in disgust. "They're mostly ruffians looking to make what they think will be an easy fortune off of pillage and plunder. We've got just over seventy of them in the city right now, and an unpleasant lot they are. In a few days I'll be sending them off to the capitol, where the King wants to personally take their pledges to serve him. They've been arriving in small groups, so few of them know each other. I doubt two more faces would be noticed amongst the rabble."

Tal mulled it over. Brant's plan would give him and Rania a crowd to hide in, an excuse to be on the road to Bhel Meravos, and possibly even an opportunity to get within striking distance of Kherzul. It was far better than any other course Tal had been able to conceive of so far. "That sounds like a workable plan, Brant. Thank you."

The Bhellan Lord shrugged awkwardly. "I'm doing it for my people, not for you, even if you do seem a likable fellow. Perhaps we could strike up a friendship once all this unpleasantness is behind us." His brow furrowed in concern as he glanced at Tal's bandaged arm. "Will you be healed enough to travel, though? You've only got three, four days at most before you'll have to leave."

"I'll be fine," Tal assured him. "That should be time enough for the Sephira to heal me. Enough to travel, at least, if not entirely."

"Good," Brant said, satisfied. "Although I wouldn't advise leaving your room while you're doing that. It makes you both very hard to miss, and I'd prefer word not get out that I'm sheltering two Shevestra'ken. That would draw Kherzul's eye to me, without a doubt. I've already promoted the guards who saw you come into the city to ensure they keep quiet, but I can't do that for the entire manor staff. I only have a use for so many Captains, after all. You can keep this room, and I'll have a new one made up for Rania, since her door seems to be in several pieces at the moment."

"No need," Rania said. "I'll stay with Tal."

Brant smiled indulgently. "Alright, then. Is there anything else you'll need?"

Rania glanced at the table, where the Lord had left *Kallevamar* when he rushed out to the hall with Tal. "The sword I was wearing when you brought me here," she said. "It's an heirloom, and I'd very much like it back."

"I'll have it brought up for you, then. If there's nothing else, I have affairs to tend. A city doesn't run itself, after all. I'll see you both again later." Brant clasped hands with each of them before letting himself out of the room again.

"He's pleasant, for a Bhellan," Rania commented after the door closed.

"He's an honorable man," Tal agreed, "not at all what one would have expected to find in Kherzul's backyard."

"Evil knows no boundaries," Rania said, quoting a Shevestra'ken saying. "It's refreshing to be reminded now and then that neither does goodness."

"You're right about that." He put his right arm warmly around Rania's shoulders. "So now that we both know how we feel about each other, where does that put us?"

"Together," Rania said contentedly, leaning into him. "Does anything else matter?"

No, Tal thought, it really didn't.

27
Death's Servant

The messenger hung suspended in the air, toes mere inches from the ground. Dark, nebulous energies swirled about him as an animal shriek of terror and torment was torn from his lungs. The cry went on and on, until every last glimmer of life had left his body. The cloud around him dissipated, and the desiccated husk of a human being tumbled to the floor and crumbled to dust atop the scattered stack of papers he had been carrying.

"No," Kherzul rasped from his throne, "I wouldn't like to see the reports from the battle. I already know what happened." At least, he knew everything up until the last of the spectres commanding his forces had been destroyed. It wasn't difficult to surmise the remainder from that point. His glorious army, a force that should have crushed Val Jerak in mere hours, defeated and obliterated because one young and untested battle leader had proven far more capable than was reasonable. Even two weeks later, Kherzul was still furious.

Harath and Tobar, the two Generals who'd led Kherzul's army, had in life been Bhellus's finest military commanders, yet still they had been bested by Talaren Solus. Special attention would be required for that one. His victory would turn him into a symbol in Valeran, but that could be turned to Kherzul's advantage. Tearing down such a symbol could produce marvelous demoralization in the ranks of an enemy. Though the Solus youth was Shevestra'ka, the son and protégé of the finest military mind in the north, and appeared to have the Jhessaillian Order behind him, he was still flesh and blood and therefore suffered from the greatest weakness of all: mortality. Remove him from the picture, and the resolve of the rest of Valeran would surely crumble.

There would be ample opportunity in the coming months of winter to devise a suitable means for the elimination of Solus. Right now, Kherzul was more concerned with the other side of the equation that had lost him the battle at Val Jerak. His Spectral Generals had displayed little of the initiative or flexibility that had once made them effective commanders. Perhaps there was a downside to leashing their wills to his own. It was an irksome possibility, but not one that was beyond solution. Creating free-willed spectres was a risk, as the late Major Skalgrim had shown, but an appropriately malleable and weak-willed candidate should be manageable enough, and Kherzul had an ideal subject in mind.

He raised his voice to address the pair of guards at the door to his throneroom. "Why don't you go fetch my friend the Archduke? I think I'd like to have a few words with him."

The guards hurried out of the room without bowing or saluting. Most of those in the Palace were finally beginning to grasp that their ruler preferred swift obedience over hollow ceremony.

They returned several minutes later dragging between them a disheveled and wild-eyed Joren Jerak. They cast him unceremoniously to the floor before the throne, where Joren cringed on his knees like a cur dog expecting a beating. With his grimy clothing, sunken cheeks, and pallid skin, it was hard to believe that this wretched creature had been until recently a powerful nobleman.

"Ah, Joren. There you are," Kherzul rumbled. "I trust your journey here wasn't too much more unpleasant than warranted. I understand that traveling through shadow is quite distressing for the living. I do hope the experience hasn't shattered your mind, as that would make you quite useless to me. Can you talk without gibbering at me?"

"I can... speak," the miserable bundle of rags answered tremulously.

"Good. I may not have to dispose of you just yet, then." The King of Bhellus allowed himself a short laugh when Joren recoiled as if struck. "I must say, Joren, you and your cretin of a father managed to botch things up spectacularly. Thanks largely to your ineptitude, my army was defeated at Val Jerak. I had your father punished for his incompetence, now I just have to decide what to do with you. Do you know why I had you brought here instead of sending you to feed the worms with Zharkus?"

Joren quailed and, eyes on the floor, answered in a barely audible mumble, "No."

"I didn't think you would." Kherzul was taking enormous pleasure in the disgraced nobleman's discomfort. "You must see, Joren, that though I may be vindictive and intolerant of failure, I also have a certain sense of fairness. I appreciate that for the most part you simply followed your father's instructions, and are therefore less culpable for the unwise decisions he made. Am I not merciful?"

"Yes, Your Majesty," Joren groveled.

Yes, Kherzul decided, this one should work nicely. "Of course, there is still the matter of reparations to be made for the trouble you helped cause me. Fortunately I have an idea for how you can repay your debt to me that I think you might find to your liking. You see, you possess a quality I find most attractive in certain of my followers. Do you know what that would be?"

The glint of hope was unmistakable in Joren's eyes as he raised his head. "I don't know, Majesty."

"Then let me give you an example," Kherzul said, leaning forward to loom over Joren. "When General Thedor came to the dungeons of Val Jerak to punish your father and bring you to me, he tells me that you tried to hide quietly in the corner of your cell and avoid notice. Even though your father was in the next cell and you could hear everything that transpired, you made not a sound while he was being strangled by my spectre. No cries for help, no pleas for mercy, nothing. Your only thought was to save yourself."

"You are a coward, Joren. That's what I like about you. A coward doesn't betray his Lord, for fear of discovery and punishment. A coward doesn't seek to supplant his Master, for fear of failure and death. A coward follows orders. A coward can be trusted. Can I trust you, Joren?"

"I would never dare to displease you, Majesty." Such marvelous obsequiousness!

"I didn't think you would," Kherzul agreed. "I have an offer to make you, then. I've need of a good coward to be chiefest of my minions, and I believe you would be excellent for the position. I offer you power, eventual reinstatement of your title under my rule, and immortality in exchange for your eternal service to me. Make no mistake, if you cross me I can and will destroy you, but I will also reward your successes if you remain faithful. Does this opportunity agree with you?"

"Yes, Majesty, it does." Were Joren truly the dog Kherzul thought of him as, he would have been enthusiastically wagging his tail.

"There is, of course, one catch." Kherzul pointed at one of his guards. "You there, would you give Archduke Jerak here your dagger?"

The guard drew the blade from its sheath and walked up to Joren, handing him the dagger hilt first. Joren looked in puzzlement at the weapon in his hand.

"If I'm to grant you the power and agelessness of a form like mine," Kherzul intoned, savoring every word, "you'll have to be dead first. Go on then, Joren. Kill yourself. Think of the power and position you can gain. All you have to do is open your own veins and it will be yours."

With shaking hands Joren raised the dagger to his breast. He held it poised over his own heart, entire body trembling. Thrice his arms tensed to plunge the blade in, but every time shied back as soon as the tip began to dig into his flesh. Failing at that, he took the dagger in one hand with the blade resting against his other wrist. For long seconds he stared at the weapon as if willing himself to cut. Tears of frustration leaked from his eyes. Finally, the blade dropped from his hand and he hung his head shamefully. "I can't!" Joren wailed. "I can't do it!"

Kherzul had had a difficult time not laughing through the entire display, but now he allowed himself his mirth. "There, there," he chuckled. "You've passed the test. If you'd actually had the steel in you to do it, I'd have let you rot with the rest of the corpses in my armies. I'm convinced now that I was right about you. I will honor our agreement." He stood and descended the steps of his dais to stand over Joren's kneeling form. "I should warn you, the process is rather painful."

He reached down and grasped Joren vicelike by the head with both hands, lifting him up off the floor. The nobleman howled at the chill of the spectre's touch sinking into his skull. Kherzul paused a moment to relish the cries before releasing the energies that would transform Joren. When he did, black fog billowed from between his hands, writhing down and around Joren's body to form a cocoon around him. His screams gained a new intensity, an extra edge of desperate agony, as the fog began rapidly to decompose his flesh. Soft bits of gore sloughed off to the floor at Kherzul's feet while the transformation ran its course. Joren's cries lost their intensity but none of their fervor, degenerating into a series of wet slurping and gasping noises as his throat and lungs dissolved away. Finally there was nothing left for him to scream with and the room was suddenly silent. The fog cocoon contracted inward, gradually resolving itself into a humanoid shape. Red eyes opened within the mist.

Joren the spectre raised a smoky hand before his eyes, waving it back and forth. Then he looked down at the rest of his body. He began to laugh quietly.

"I left your will intact," Kherzul said, "because it affords you certain advantages I need. But I want you to know the one restriction I did place on you as a safeguard, Joren. Your continuing existence depends upon my own. See that I am well protected, and you may well go on forever. But the day I fall the forces binding your consciousness to this form will fail."

"Then I will serve you well, Majesty," Joren's dead voice replied. He laughed again, flexing his arms. "This is incredible, Majesty! But you understated when you said it would be painful. That was beyond excruciating."

"The price of immortality." No need for Joren to know that Kherzul could have transformed him almost painlessly, but had chosen not to for his own pleasure. "Now, for your first duty. Tell me everything you know about Talaren Solus."

The next few days in the manor were peaceful ones for Tal and Rania. Not wanting to do anything to bring suspicion on Lord Brant, they remained in the room he had given them, enjoying the pleasure of one another's company and exploring the feelings they had finally been able to share with each other. Servants brought them their meals and Brant stopped in to converse occasionally, but his visits were of a necessity short as he didn't want to draw undue attention to them by being too friendly.

The city's Lord explained that he had told his household that Tal and Rania had been part of a larger band coming to answer the call for mercenaries, but had run afoul on their way of the beast that roamed the mountains. According to Brant's cover story, the rest of their group had fallen in the struggle before Rania managed to wound the creature badly enough to drive it away, possibly to kill it. Brant, naturally, had granted them shelter in his manor while Tal recovered from his wounds in thanks for the tale they had brought with them of the mysterious creature that threatened the countryside, and the blow they had dealt it. It was all a very tidy lie. Brant thanked Tal with a toothy grin when he observed as much. "Being a good liar is one of the most important advantages you can have in politics," he had responded with a chuckle, "especially in Bhellus these days."

Tal kept the Sephira flowing through him every waking moment to speed the healing of his arm. The effect was little short of remarkable. He still hadn't become accustomed to how the energies of the Sephira could quicken the mending of injuries, especially one as severe as his had been. By the time he went to sleep the second night, the wound had closed itself, leaving only a tender patch of skin and an occasional dull ache to mark it. He was even able to use his left hand again, although it still seemed a bit weaker than he was accustomed to.

Rania told him the tale of her journey to Bhel Femoryan following his losing consciousness, and explained how she had held the Sephira for him to preserve him through the arduous trek. It seemed that the strange bond that had been forged between them still held a few undiscovered secrets. Tal wondered if they would ever learn exactly what had happened between them in those few moments when their minds had been joined. Passing the time with a bit of experimentation based on Rania's discovery though, they did learn something new about the bond: they could use it to shift the Sephiral power they held back and forth between themselves, weakening one to fortify the other.

So it was that on the third night, when Brant informed them that the mercenary column would leave in the morning, Tal actually felt a pang of regret at leaving behind the peaceful existence he had led for the past few days. The Lord also brought them supplies for the journey: provisions, a tent to replace the one they had left behind in the mountains, and several changes of clothes for each of them. The garments he gave them were rough things predominantly in earthen tones. Brant claimed that what they had brought with them would stand out too much in the company they would be keeping. At his suggestion, Tal and Rania also unbound the braids above their left ears that night. After having worn it for several weeks now, it felt odd to Tal to have the lock of hair loose again.

The next morning they were fetched by a bored-seeming guard in the plain leather armor that appeared to be standard issue in Bhel Femoryan. He led them out of Brant's manor and through the stone-paved streets of the city to a square on the east end that was host to a milling crowd of rough-looking men. The occupants of the square wore a mishmash of different styles of armor in assorted states of repair, or in a few cases no armor at all. Most bore swords at their sides, but here and there Tal caught sight of an axe or mace, and even a few bows. Despite Brant's best efforts to help them blend in, Tal and Rania still stood out from the rest. With their well-kept arms and mail shirts, they looked more like the professional mercenaries they were posing as than the rest, especially Rania with her harness of knives. They received a number of considering looks as they left the guard behind to join the crowd, but most eyes turned away in disinterest, or in haste when Rania directed a challenging glare at any who looked for too long.

The townsfolk seemed to be steering clear of the square this morning, and those few who passed close darted uneasy glances at the gathered men before hurrying on their way. Mounted soldiers in chainmail and livery in the red and gold of Kherzul's own House Meravos waited idly in pairs at the four entrances to the square, watching the assembling "mercenaries" with hard eyes.

Tal and Rania moved to the center of the throng, trying to fade into the crowd. It wasn't difficult; there seemed to be no organization to the gathering, and the men mostly occupied themselves with loud boasts to any of their fellows who would listen of how many men they would kill, the glory they would cover themselves in, and the wealth of spoils they'd claim. Tal very much doubted what he heard. From what he could see, this group wouldn't have the discipline to stand up to the first cavalry charge that they faced. These weren't soldiers - they were little more than an armed mob.

After a short wait, no longer than twenty minutes or so, the soldiers at the eastern entrance bellowed for the mercenaries to form up in a double column. The result was chaos as the men in the square hurried to comply. Tal and Rania ended up side by side about two thirds of the way down the line. Once all the jostling was over and the men were neatly lined up, one of the soldiers at the head of the column shouted, "Move out!" and they began their march toward Bhel Meravos.

The air that morning was chilly, but not uncomfortably so. Tal found he didn't even have to keep his cloak closed against the cold once he started walking. It was actually pleasant compared to the frigidity of the Felmorr. Of course, winter had only begun and it would get much colder before spring returned to the north. Snow covered the ground in a shin-deep layer, but that on the road they followed had been trod down by traffic and the footing was surprisingly firm. Tal found himself smiling as he walked. On more than one occasion he had to resist the urge to reach out and take Rania's hand as they walked. From her glances at him and occasional rueful smiles, she was engaged in a similar internal struggle.

The soldiers who accompanied them rode with three at the head of the column and three behind, with the remaining two ranging up and down the double line of walking men. They looked disdainfully down their noses at their charges, as though gazing upon something unclean and uncouth. Tal supposed that they were, but still their behavior irritated him. They were acting more like their charges were prisoners than fresh recruits.

For their part, the men who had come to answer Kherzul's call seemed perfectly content to plod along, many talking quietly with the man beside them. Any voices raised too high, though, received curtly barked orders from the mounted soldiers for quiet. Before too many miles had passed, many of the men on foot were glaring balefully at the soldiers' backs whenever they weren't looking.

Tal and Rania walked in silence for the most part. The few words they did exchange were hollow pleasantries, talk of the weather or how Tal's arm was feeling. Truth be told, it was completely healed, but he still wore the bandage for show. Brant's tale had included his injury, after all, and he didn't want to cause any suspicions over how swift his recovery had been. That was why the conversation was so flat, as well. Any topic of genuine interest to Tal or Rania would no doubt seem out of place and could potentially spoil their ruse.

They stopped at midday for a brief rest and a hasty meal before setting out again. The column kept marching well after dark, as the daylight was growing shorter and shorter as winter deepened. When they finally did stop for the night close to a stand of trees, several men with axes descended on the copse and returned with enough wood to build several sizable fires. The soldiers retired to their tents almost as soon as they were erected, leaving a single of their number outside to watch over the men who gathered around the fires to eat and talk.

Tal and Rania, still conscious of their need to blend with the rest, went to the closest of the fires to take their evening meal. The others around the fire glanced curiously at the pair now and then as they ate. Finally, after several minutes, one fellow across the fire from them spoke up loudly. "What I don't understand," he drawled, "is what a woman is doing here. Everybody knows a woman's place is by the hearth, not in a fight." He was burly, with unkempt dark hair and a mean cast to his features.

Rania graced him with an irritated scowl and replied icily, "I've as much reason to be here as any of you, and more than most."

The man sitting to the speaker's left nudged the other man in the ribs. "Careful, Tarm, I hear she's the one what chased off the beastie that'd been haunting the mountains."

The burly man, Tarm, barked a quick laugh. "I heard she only managed it because the thing was too busy using her friend there for kibble." He nodded toward Tal.

Rania's eyes narrowed dangerously. "I promise you, I'm as good in a fight as any three of you." There was no hint of anger in her voice, only certainty.

Another man, this one short and broad of shoulder with a scruffy beard, laughed even louder than Tarm had. "That's mighty confident of ya, little lady, but boasts is easy to make. What would ya do if we asked ya to prove it?"

Rania stood slowly. "You, you, and you," she said, pointing in turn to each of the men who had spoken. As they stood, Rania unbuckled her sword belt and handed it to Tal. "And to give you a chance, I won't use any weapons."

The men laughed heartily at that, and Tal took advantage of the noise to whisper, "Are you sure about this? Those aren't practice weapons they're carrying, and we'll be noticed if you use the battle trance."

Rania flashed her teeth at him. "I know," she whispered back. "I'll be fine."

She led the three men about thirty paces out from the fire. Once she stopped, they spread out to surround her.

"You don't have to do this," the man who had nudged Tarm said. "Nobody expects you to really fight three armed men without nothing but bare hands."

"Frightened?" Rania asked with a raised eyebrow.

The man sighed. "Have it your own way then. We'll try not to hurt you too much." He said the last with a meaningful look directed at the glowering Tarm.

The gathering was attracting a fair amount of attention from the other fires, and several men made their way over to watch. The soldier who was watching them all spoke into one of the tents, and he was joined by two of his comrades, all looking on from a distance.

"Well, are we going to wait all night?" Rania growled impatiently.

Two of the men around her wielded swords, while Tarm clutched a wicked-looking battleaxe with a broad blade. They began closing in around her. Rania stood completely at her ease as if she were unaware of them. When the first man, the one who had challenged her to prove her boast, came at her with sword raised, she suddenly exploded into motion. She stiffened her hand and struck viperlike at the man's arm as he swung halfheartedly at her, stopping his attack dead. The same hand darted forward, following up along her attacker's numbed arm to grasp him behind the neck. She pulled him forward and down while bringing her knee up sharply into his abdomen, and he dropped into the snow gasping for breath. The other swordsman swung at her back, but she dropped down under the blow and kicked his legs out from under him. While he scrambled back to his feet, Rania darted away from a series of swings from Tarm's axe that were far too forceful for Tal's taste. If one of those connected, the results could easily be fatal.

As the second swordsman regained his footing and rejoined the axe-wielding brute, he eyed Rania warily, clearly reassessing her skills. The two circled her cautiously, until Rania surprised them by suddenly charging at the man with the sword. He was so taken aback he didn't even have the opportunity to attack before Rania pounced on him, gripping him by the shoulders and coiling her legs up against his chest. She unwound her legs forcefully, leaping off of the man into a backflip and at the same time sending him flying back several yards to land hard on his back with a grunt. Tarm howled and hurled himself at Rania, axe swinging wildly. She gave no ground, calmly dodging out of the way of each blow. With every swing that missed, Tarm's rage seemed to grow and he pushed at her harder and harder. After several missed blows, he drew too close, and Rania sidestepped a mighty overhead swing to bring her behind Tarm's bulky frame. She snaked an arm around his neck from behind and squeezed. Tarm struggled against her for several seconds, but there was no breaking Rania's grip. His struggles weakened quickly, and when he finally went limp, Rania let him drop.

The first swordsman, having finally regained his breath, ran to Tarm's side as Rania walked nonchalantly back to the fire. "He'll wake up in a few minutes," she said over her shoulder, "I didn't want to hurt any of you too much, after all." She paid no mind to the whooping and cheering from the onlookers as Tal handed *Edyamar* back to her.

Tal glanced over to where the Bhellan soldiers had been watching from. Seeing that they wouldn't have to break up a riot, they were returning to their tents.

253

True to Rania's word, Tarm came to again moments later and returned to the fireside in the company of his compatriots. Tal was surprised to see the large man, who had been inches away from foaming at the mouth in rage during the fight, grinning broadly.

The big ruffian slapped Rania on the back heartily as he came up to her. "You fight like a demon, woman. You're my kind of girl!" He declared.

Rania smiled indulgently. "Glad I could change your mind," she said, laying a familiar hand on Tal's knee, "But I'm afraid I'm already spoken for."

Tarm flashed a dirty, gap-toothed grin at Tal. "You'd better be careful no one tries to take her from you, boy."

Rania laughed. "I'd feel sorry for anyone who did," she chuckled. "They'd have to deal with me as well as him, and he's as good as I am when he's not injured."

The burly man thumped Tal on the back much as he had Rania. Tal was amazed the blow didn't knock his teeth loose. "After what I've just seen, I'll take your word on that. What are you called, friends?"

"I'm Jerwyn and she's Camelle," Tal replied, giving the names they had decided upon with Brant.

"Good to know you," Tarm said. "These are my mates, Keswick and Haddar." He pointed in turn to the two swordsmen who had fought Rania with him. "And these useless sacks," he gestured to the men still sitting around the fire, "are Robar, Worrin, Gadmer, and Dworik." Each man nodded as he was named. "We've seen our share of scraps, but we ain't never seen anyone can fight like you, Camelle. You two can share our fire anytime."

"Thank you," Rania murmured.

"Aw, it's nothing," Tarm said with a wave of his hand. He went to where he had been sitting earlier and retrieved a bulging wineskin, which he handed to Rania. "This is what you can thank me for sharing. Have a bit and pass it on. It's the good stuff." He winked in a conspiratorial manner before taking his seat again.

Rania uncapped the skin and took a long pull from it before handing it to Tal with a hint of a grimace as she swallowed.

As soon as Tal took a sip, he understood why. Whatever was in the skin, it tasted like fermented lantern oil and kicked like an angry warhorse. He barely managed to keep from gasping at the taste as he took the skin from his lips and passed it on to Robar.

The skin was passed around the fire several times, although each time it came to Tal, the sip he took was smaller. The last couple times, he didn't even drink at all, just raised the skin to his lips and pretended to. He didn't relish the way his head would probably feel in the morning if he drank too much of Tarm's foul brew.

As the men drank more and more, their tongues loosened and they spoke freely, recounting stories of fights they had been in and laughing raucously. From what Tal could gather, they were a band of brigands who had made their way raiding merchant wagons, and had decided to sign on for Kherzul's war not only for the opportunity to loot, but because the King of Bhellus was offering full pardons to any man who answered his call for mercenaries.

"No longer a wanted man and with all that Valerite gold, I'll be a Lord in no time, just you watch!" said Gadmer at one point to the laughter of all the others.

"So what's your story, Jerwyn?" Asked Keswick. "How did you and Camelle end up here?"

"Our band was working for the Archduke over in Val Jerak," Tal said. He and Rania had worked out this story in Bhel Femoryan. "But he got himself put in irons by some Lord named Solus. This Solus, he offered to keep paying us to stay on, and in the same breath said he wanted us to fight a battle at six or seven to one odds." Tal laughed. "Well, we weren't being paid well enough to die for it, so we came to Bhellus to look for work, figuring that those odds meant this would be the side to be on. The first few nobles we talked to weren't too interested so we worked our way north, and then we heard that the King was looking for folk who knew one end of a sword from the other, and headed to Bhel Femoryan since it was closest. Too bad that beast caught up to us before we got there. We lost a lot of good men to that thing." Tal sighed.

Keswick nodded sympathetically. "I hear tell that it's a terror. Did you get a good look at it?"

Tal rubbed the bandage on his arm ruefully. "It had big teeth, I can tell you that." The other men around the fire roared with laughter.

As the night wore on and the effects of Tarm's draught began to wear off, the men started seeking their bedrolls. Tal was among the first to leave, Rania following him when he stood. They had several days of marching left yet, and Tal didn't want to wear himself down by missing too much sleep. He'd likely need the energy when they arrived in Bhel Meravos.

The second day's march passed much as the first, except that Tarm and his friends joined the line behind Tal and Rania when they formed up in the morning. They talked as they trudged on, of course, and involved the pair of Shevestra'ken in their conversation. There was such a rough honesty and sense of humor to the men that Tal couldn't help but like them a bit in spite of knowing that they had made their way in the world by killing and looting. These were strange times indeed, that he should find himself rubbing shoulders with and befriending the likes of them.

Late in the morning their column passed a village that lay alongside the road, a small collection of farms and homes. While the buildings were still distant, Tal noticed that a large patch of ground outside the village appeared to have been churned up recently, several rows of piled dirt mounding up the snow beside recessed pits in the earth. He pointed it out to Rania before looking over his shoulder to speak to Worrin, who marched next in line.

"Are those what I think they are?" Tal asked.

Worrin frowned at the mounds and spit loudly. "Yeah, most like. That'd be the work of King Kherzul stinking Meravos. I've heard stories 'bout it. Been happening all round the countryside. Folk wake up in the middle of the night and find the dead digging theirselves out of the ground. Ain't seen it myself, but it scares the peasants all but good. Can't say as I blame 'em, either. The dead got no business getting up and walking around."

"If what Kherzul is doing frightens you so, then why are you going to go fight for him?" Tal carefully kept his voice low so as not to carry. The soldiers escorting them might not appreciate his question.

Worrin shrugged. "I don't run the world, just try to live in it. Kherzul scares me, but not so much as being against him does. This way we don't have to worry 'bout him coming after us. Besides, the gold he'll give us spends as good as any other."

Tal forced a laugh. "True enough. I was just wondering."

As they drew closer to and passed through the village, Tal noticed that the streets seemed unusually empty. Most of the houses were dark and vacant. One family was busily loading their possessions onto a cart pulled by an old swaybacked mare. They paused and watched with frightened eyes as the column passed by, the plain dressed farmwife with her tired face comforting one of the two dirty-faced children when he started to cry. Tal shook his head sadly.

"It's the same everywhere," Haddar said from where he walked beside Worrin, "everyone's scared, and they's all running to the cities hoping to find safety there. Terrifying days, these."

Anger and disgust roiled within Tal. Even now, well within Bhellus, everyone he met seemed concerned and disturbed by Kherzul's acts, yet they remained silent and even followed him out of fear. That fact alone was more terrifying than anything Kherzul did himself. Never before had Tal considered how completely such uncontrolled fear could drive away all reason and capacity for self-determination.

As the days and miles passed by, Tal saw more rows of upturned ground, more villages and even some small towns that stood mute and abandoned. Here and there were the stubborn holdouts who wouldn't let fear overcome them, but they were few and far between, and seemed to have even less hope than they had fear. They held on to their lands and homes and lives because they didn't know anything else to do but keep going. With every hopeless face he saw, Tal came more and more to crave Kherzul's destruction, as much to restore that hope as to save Valeran. He had said it before, but now he came to truly understand that he was fighting not only for his own land, but for all the lands that might yet fall to the necromancer's ambitions.

Two weeks they marched from sunup until long after dark, and as the time passed by the days continued to grow shorter and the air colder. Twice snow fell in the night, but fortunately none of the snowfalls were great enough to substantially slow their progress. Tarm and his friends remained relatively upbeat through it, even if their moods were somewhat dampened when they ran out of drink after the first few nights. The soldiers leading them would not allow them to stop for a night in one of the towns along the way, so they had no opportunity to replenish their supply of alcohol.

Every step of the way a sense of expectation mingled with dread grew within Tal as the end of the road loomed closer and closer, along with the confrontation that would come soon after. It was in such a state of mind that Tal, on the afternoon of the second day into the fourth week of marching, crested a hill and found himself looking for the first time ever upon the city of Bhel Meravos.

29

The City of the Dead

Tal's first impression of the capitol of Bhellus had been the smell. He first noticed it before the city even came into sight, a faint odor underlying the crisp scent of snow that seemed to burn in his nostrils. It grew with each passing step, and by the time Bhel Meravos came into view, the smell was strong enough that Tal had been able to recognize it. He knew it from the Battle of the Falling Snows. It was the stench of death.

When at last the city lay spread out before him from his vantage atop the last hill, it presented Tal with an odd sight. All around the outer walls of the city there had been constructed just over a dozen enormous barn-like buildings. Another five that Tal could see appeared to still be under construction and in varying stages of completion. In the spaces between the barns and away from the roads, rank upon rank of unmoving humanoid forms stood cheek by jowl with each other. Tal's jaw dropped at the sheer number gathered around the city. At least now he knew the source of the corrupt stench of decay that assaulted him.

Beyond the barns stood Bhel Meravos itself, one of the great cities of the north, with broad streets running between its stone-faced buildings with their roofs of slate. The city was built around a hill, climbing higher and higher as one went deeper into the city until at the center, atop the crown of the hill stood the great Citadel of House Meravos, its towers thrusting up to the heavens high above the rest of the city.

The roads leading into the city were thick with folk fleeing from the countryside. Sprawling encampments of those unable to find space within lay outside the ring of barns and well away from the grisly congregations of the dead. Most of the newcomers moving down the road seemed to be filtering into the encampments, swelling their size even further.

The soldiers who had escorted the column called a halt atop the hill and herded the men following them off to the side of the road.

"This is as far as we take you," one of them bellowed. "From here you can try to find accommodations in one of the city's inns. If you can't find the space or don't have the coin for an inn, you can sleep outside the city with the other vermin." His mouth twisted in spiteful satisfaction. "In two days at dusk, you shall gather with the other mercenary swine at the great square before the Palace, that the King may take your oaths to follow him. Be thankful that he will deign to hear them from such a group of scoundrels and thieves as you. Once you've sworn to serve, you will be provided with barracks." As soon as he finished speaking, he and the other soldiers turned their horses and rode away, pursued by the jeers and taunts of the men they had insulted.

Soon after the soldiers left, the men they had brought out from Bhel Femoryan began to disperse, breaking off in small groups to seek rooms or campsites. Tarm waved Tal and Rania over to join him and the others, who stood in a rough circle.

"Camelle, do you and Jerwyn know where you're going?" He asked as they came closer.

Rania shrugged. "I imagine we'll end up staying in the camps, but I think we'll have a look around the city first."

The bulky man nodded. "You do that. Me and the boys'll be staying somewhere around there." He pointed toward the camps on the southern side of the road they were next to. "You should come and drink with us. There's got to be something fit to get drunk on in those camps, and I mean to find it." With a last leering grin he and his companions started down the hill.

Tal stood gazing at the city.

"Are we waiting for something?" Rania asked him quizzically after a moment.

Tal shook his head. "I was just thinking. There it is." He waved his hand toward the city. "We've come to the end."

Rania took him by the hand and began down the slope. "Not the end, Tal. A new beginning."

If the roads into the city were crowded, the streets within the walls could only be described as mobbed. People pressed in against each other, and the scent of fear and stale sweat was almost enough to overwhelm the reek of the legions outside. A constant buzz of talk filled the streets, giving the city a single insistently babbling voice. Tal and Rania pressed through the masses, their swords and armor earning them hardly an inch of elbow room. They had to hold hands just to avoid being swept away from each other by the vagaries of the crowd.

Tal wanted to laugh bitterly at the irony of the crowds. People were fleeing their homes in droves because they were scared senseless by their dead getting up and shuffling off in the dark of night. That they would then choose this place to take refuge, the place from which all the trouble and fear was emanating, seemed both incongruous and insane. Perhaps some of them hoped that there would be calm at the eye of the storm, but he saw little in the crowds to indicate calm of any sort.

Although Rania had claimed they would stay in the encampments outside, Tal very much wanted to get a room so they would have some sort of base of operations. After the weeks of continuous marching, he wouldn't have found a bath out of order, either. After a brief whispered consultation with Rania, she agreed and they set out to find a room.

Such an undertaking was, of course, far less easily accomplished than it sounded. The innkeeps at the first seven inns they tried protested that they were already full up, sleeping three to a bed, and even their haylofts were full. When Tal asked for a private room for himself and Rania, they were often laughed out of the inn. When at last the eighth inn was able to offer them a cramped little space in the attic under the eaves, with a narrow pad on the floor that made Tal glad he and Rania didn't mind sleeping close, the price Tal paid for it was well over what he'd normally expect to pay for the most luxurious of rooms. With the cost of two baths added, he could have sworn he was giving the innkeeper enough to build an entire second inn.

However much it cost, Tal decided as he settled into the steaming waters that it was well worth the price. He just sat, head tilted back to gaze at the ceiling, soaking in the warmth until finally the last of the chill from outside left his bones. Following the baths, Tal and Rania went down to the crowded common room for some hot stew and cold ale. Once he had finished his stew, Tal brought out his pipe and carefully filled the bowl. He sighed contentedly after puffing it alight, and shared a little smile with Rania across the table. For just the moment, everything was good. He had dire concerns ahead of him yet, to be sure, but they could keep at least until he had a pipe and a drink.

The common room was not only packed full but also so loud that Tal and Rania could only talk to each other if they yelled. They finished their drinks quickly and proceeded up to their tiny little space under the roof, Rania getting a stub of candle from the innkeep so that they could have some light.

As soon as Tal closed the door behind them, Rania turned to speak to him. "So, Tal, what's the plan now that we're here?"

Tal shook his head. "I didn't have one, except to look for a way to get close to Kherzul. This gathering for the mercenaries seems like a possibility, though. I think we should go have a look at the square it'll be in and see if the ground is favorable."

"Scouting the terrain?" Rania asked.

Tal nodded. "If it looks good, we'll plan from there. If not, we've theoretically got all winter." He chuckled to himself. "Although if the prices for board stay like this, I'll have spent the entire treasury of Val Solus by then."

Rania laughed. "Getting parsimonious on me, my Lord?" She asked, her tone teasing.

"No, just a little concerned," Tal replied, "I didn't bring *that* much coin with me. I hadn't expected to run into anything like this."

"Don't worry about it," Rania said, "if worst comes to worst, we can always sleep under the stars. I thought you liked keeping me warm." She grinned mischievously at him. "Did you want to go see the square tonight?"

Tal stifled a yawn. "No, in the morning. We've had a long march. I want to get to bed."

They awakened late in the morning with the sun well into the sky. After a quick breakfast of porridge and sausage in the common room, Tal and Rania set out to explore the city and find the square Kherzul would be receiving the mercenaries in. They found that there were, in fact, four squares in the city directly outside the Citadel gates, one at each cardinal direction. The "great square" as the soldier had described it seemed to be the southernmost of these, by far the largest. Three wide avenues ran into the open square, and where they would have intersected stood a statue twenty paces tall of King Shebedar in plate and mail armor, a stern scowl on its stone face and hand resting on the hilt of the sword at its hip. Like the rest of the city, the square was riotously busy with foot traffic, but at least the extra space in the square afforded a bit of breathing room. The wall separating the square from the Citadel's grounds had clearly been built to keep the commonfolk out rather than to repel any sort of attack; it was thick, but stood only a few feet higher than a grown man's head and lacked any real defensive fortifications. A narrow walk ran along its length, and above the gates this walk broadened out into a platform that was roofed over to shield from the elements but left open at the front.

Tal nodded toward the enclosure atop the gate. "I'm certain that that's where he'll be," he said just loudly enough for his voice to reach Rania's ears.

Rania nodded and then turned to point at the statue, as if she were commenting on it to Tal. "Probably. We could leap up to the top of that wall easily while in the trance."

"My thoughts exactly," Tal said with a wary glace around. Nobody seemed to be listening, or paying them any mind whatsoever for that matter. "We should finish this conversation somewhere else. I've seen what I need to."

They meandered out of the square and back through the city to the inn, taking time to familiarize themselves with the layout of the streets, which wound about with the landscape to make for a confusing tangle. By the time they got back to the four floor building they were staying in, though, Tal thought he had a decent idea of how to get around.

Rania led the way directly up to their makeshift room, and Tal got right down to explaining his plan, such as it was.

"From the look of things, it should be fairly simple, really," he began. "We'll show up as early as reasonably possible, so we can get places at the front of the square. Once Kherzul shows himself, we jump up to the wall and kill him." Tal raised a cautionary finger. "I'm sure he'll have at least a few of his generals with him, so we may have to deal with them, as well. I'll try to bypass them to get at Kherzul, so I'll need you watching my back." He looked her in the eyes to drive home his next point. "Rania, you're probably not going to like this, but I don't want you to kill any of them unless it's unavoidable, at least until Kherzul goes down. He still doesn't know about your sword, so that should give you the advantage of surprise if anything happens to me."

Surprisingly, Rania just nodded her acceptance. "Agreed, but if I have to kill one of them to save you, don't expect me to hesitate."

Tal chuckled. "I think I can accept that." He tilted his head at her curiously. "I expected you to fight me tooth and nail on that, and especially on my taking the lead and being the one to make the attempt on Kherzul. Why didn't you?"

Rania shrugged. "I've told you I don't argue with you when you make sense. We need every advantage we can get, and throwing one away just so it could be my hand to slay Kherzul would be foolish. So long as he dies, I'm satisfied. Just being there to witness it will be more than I've hoped for in a long time." She shook her head disbelievingly. "Even now, I find it hard to credit that by this time tomorrow, my family will be avenged."

Tal put his arms about her wordlessly, hugging her close. Tomorrow. The crisis would be over then. It could work. It had to work.

The next day seemed to stretch on forever. Tal and Rania both awakened early, but neither really felt like talking. Tal felt suffocated by the anticipation of the coming evening. He was a little afraid, he confessed to himself, but mostly he just wanted it to be over. He wanted the veil of fear that had settled on the North to be lifted. He wanted an end to the questions and doubts that came with the task he'd set himself. He wanted Rania's past laid finally to rest, and to be able to spend even a few minutes with her without the cares of the world riding on both their shoulders.

Rania sat crosslegged on the floor, carefully sharpening the blades of her knives. As she finished each one, she would test the edge and the balance before giving a satisfied nod and resheathing it.

The hours slipped by in silence. Tal was thankful that it was far enough into winter that the days had grown so short, else the wait would have seemed truly interminable.

As the sun began to drop toward the now distant Felmorr mountains, Tal and Rania both put their mail shirts on and donned the Blades of Unity. Rania fastened her knives on, and turned expectantly to Tal. "Are you ready?"

"Yeah," he replied breathily.

Rania turned toward the door, hesitated, and turned back to hold a leather-gauntleted palm against his cheek. "However this goes, Tal, I love you. Remember that."

Tal took the hand and squeezed it. "We'll be fine," he said. "Together, we can do this. I love you, Rania."

She smiled faintly, and led him out of the room.

They arrived in the square early as they had planned, the sun still a handsbreadth from the mountains. It had been cleared of traffic by soldiers who stood at all three entrances to the square, about a hundred to a side. As Tal and Rania approached they were hailed by a Captain, apparently the leader of the group guarding the street they were on.

As they approached the officer, he eyed their weapons, looking up to their faces once they drew within speaking range.

"Mercenaries?" He asked disinterestedly.

"That's right," Tal said.

The man waved them through.

The square was mostly empty, only eight men having arrived yet. Tal and Rania sat down at the base of the statue, watching more people arrive as they waited. When the square began to fill up, they started to migrate their way to the front, picking their way slowly so as not to cause a commotion or seem overeager to get close to the wall. By the time the sun was sinking from sight, the square was mostly full and the Shevestra'ken stood in the second rank back midway down the left side of the wall, with little more than ten feet separating them from it's base.

Men jostled each other with curses, but Tal ignored it when he was buffeted about, his eyes intent on the structure atop the gate. As the last rays of sunlight were fading from the sky something seemed to move within the darkness under the enclosure and, one after another, several pairs of malevolent red eyes burst into being. Tal took a quick count of them. Seven.

Six of the shadowy figures peeled off from the enclosure to take places evenly spaced along the wall, three to each side with the closest to the King standing just beside the short set of steps leading up to the platform. All six wore heavy armor polished to a mirror-like sheen.

Kherzul was distinguishable from the rest only by his position and attire. About the shoulders of his misty form he wore a robe the deep red of clotted blood. A simple golden crown rode on his brow just above the burning eyes.

A hush settled quickly over the assembled men as Kherzul glided to the front of the enclosure, sweeping the twin coals of his gaze across them.

"You have come here today in answer to my call for fighting men," a rasping voice emanated from the robed figure, "to give to me your undying loyalty. In exchange for this, I have promised to forgive all crimes you may have committed against Bhellus. I have offered to house you and see to your needs. And I have promised you all the spoils you could desire."

"Aye, that's what we signed on for!" yelled an insolent voice from the middle of the crowd.

An ominous chuckle rose from the King. "Then you shall have it." He cast back the robe and raised his hands dramatically toward the onlookers. "Someone should have taught you all that the spoils of war," Kherzul intoned, "are death."

Writhing tendrils of darkness snaked out from the shadows around Kherzul, reaching down to the confused men standing directly before him. The first few men touched by the tenebrous pseudopods fell boneless to the ground, and chaos erupted in the square. The crowd surged in a panic toward the streets out, where the soldiers who had let them in had formed up and drawn weapons. The shadowy tentacles stretched further, claiming more men, and Tal and Rania surged forward toward the wall, filled with the Sephira before they had finished their first step. They angled in alongside the wall, and after passing the first two generals they leapt. Tal kept charging forward, *Kallevamar* springing from its sheath, as Rania turned to hold off the spectres behind them.

Surprise was on his side, and the spectre Tal bore down on was only just beginning to draw his weapon when the Shevestra'ka reached him, *Kallevamar* sweeping in a glittering arc that passed right through the space between pauldrons and helm. He kept running, passing through the still dissipating cloud that had been the spectral General, and pounded up the stairs. Kherzul was turning to face him. He felt the Sephira coiling about the necromantic King, being readied to defend him.

Tal mounted the last step, *Kallevamar* coming up to deliver the killing blow, when his muscles suddenly froze. He struggled, or tried to, throwing every ounce of his will into trying to force his arm to move just far enough to cut the King of Bhellus. It was useless. His body stood rigid, unmoving. He could hear the clash of steel on steel behind him. Through their link, Tal could feel Rania fighting the two spectres behind him, felt her turn, felt the shock of dismay that ran through her when she laid eyes on him. He wanted to howl, but his body refused to cooperate even that much.

"Tal!" Rania yelled, and spun to sprint to him. She made it two steps, and then Tal felt her muscles lock up the same way his had. Despair bounced back and forth through their link, seeming to grow stronger with each echo.

"Well, well," Kherzul said softly, picking *Kallevamar* out of Tal's unresponsive hand. "I've been desiring for this for quite some time. Thank you." He craned around Tal. "I want these two alive, Joren. I believe I may have a use for them."

In the square below, the tendrils still scythed through the remaining men, who were being successfully contained by the soldiers as their back ranks were gnawed away. Kherzul turned his attention back to the square, and fallen bodies began to stir and rise.

Helplessly Tal beat against the insides of his skull as he felt a mailed fist smash into Rania's face, and then the link between them collapsed. A few seconds later, something hard and cold struck him at the base of his neck, and darkness swallowed his world.

30
The Endless Night

A dull, grinding pain squeezing around his skull greeted Tal as consciousness tentatively returned to him. His shoulders ached, too. He cracked his eyes open and found himself looking down at a pitted and cracked stone floor. He was dangling forward almost on his knees, kept from falling on his face by what felt like chains encircling his wrists and fastened to the ceiling above. He got his feet under him and straightened himself up, the room lurching woozily as he did so. Light flickered in through a grill in the iron door that stood before him, making shadows dance across the rough stone walls. Tal groaned with relief as the pressure on his shoulders eased up, but found that even standing, he couldn't lower his arms below his head. Looking up produced another wave of nausea and confirmed that he was fettered from above by heavy chains clamped about his wrists.

Tal concentrated through the pain in his head and took hold of the Sephira. Strength flowed into him, washing away the ache in his shoulders and steadying his head. He wriggled his way around so his arms were held upright above him and set his feet firmly, gripping the chain in his bound hands. He pulled, straining every muscle against the heavy steel links. They grew taut, but none gave way. He tried several sudden, violent jerks but to no more avail.

A loud scraping at the door announced that the bar was being drawn. The portal creaked open, and the mistily indistinct form of Kherzul, clad in crown and robe, glided into the cell. He stood before his prisoner, well beyond Tal's reach, watching with baleful red eyes as the Shevestra'ka glowered at him. "You're lucky I've hopes that you might be of use to me," he said at last in his rasping whisper of a voice, "or you'd be part of my dead legions right now. I take attempts on my life quite seriously, I'm afraid. Of course, you may find your way there yet, if you insist on being uncooperative."

"You might as well kill me now, then," Tal spat back. "I don't oblige madmen."

The spectral King chuckled, a menacingly hollow sound. "I give you my assurance, I'm quite sane. Just because you don't know the reasons why I do as I do doesn't mean that those reasons don't exist. Now, what is your name?"

Tal raised his chin stubbornly. "Jerwyn."

Kherzul shook his head. Tal felt him draw in the Sephira, and howled as blinding agony shocked through every inch of his body, driving away all rational thought and leaving him twitching and gasping, held up only by his bound arms.

"There's no point in trying to lie to me," Kherzul said, "I know you to be Shevestra'ka from the fact that the Sephira flows in you even now. I know that the weapon you carried is the Sword of Trazeri the Accursed. I even know that the girl who accompanied you is the Marquess Rania Amoran. From these things, and the fact that I have seen your face through the eyes of several minions of mine you have slain, I know you are Talaren Solus. If you persist in lying, it will bring you only pain. What is your name?"

Tal staggered back to his feet and with a defiant glare answered, "I am Talaren Solus the Snowfox, commander of the Valerite forces at the Battle of the Falling Snows, where I wiped your filthy army of corpses from the face of the earth."

Kherzul nodded, looming closer to stare Tal right in the face. "And yet here you are now, helpless in my power. Surely you must see that you cannot resist me. I ride on a storm of change, change that cannot and must not be stopped."

Tal leapt and twisted, swinging on the chain as he kicked up at Kherzul's head. His boot passed clean through, knocking the crown from the King's head and across the room. Numbing cold pierced through Tal's foot like a lance of ice. Kherzul simply walked over and picked the crown back up as Tal tried to regain his balance on the numbed foot. No sooner had he found it than another wrenching wave of pain shuddered through him, as though his body were trying to rend itself apart. He clamped his jaw shut, refusing to give Kherzul the satisfaction of his crying out. It was all he could do to keep from doing just that, and the muscles in his jaw were knotted and sore when the pain finally receded again.

"Surely you know that attacking me is futile. The one weapon in the North that can harm me is firmly in my possession now. Trying to injure me is beyond your abilities and contrary to your best interests." One more jolt ran through Tal, making dots dance before his eyes, before his trembling from the prior ordeal had subsided.

"What do you want from me?" Tal grated through clenched teeth when it was over.

Kherzul regarded Tal with crossed arms. "You are a Shevestra'ka. You have rare and useful talents, skills, and training. Moreover, you have Sephiral abilities that could serve me well. It would be a shame to just turn you into another rotting puppet when you could be so much better utilized alive. I want you to join my cause."

"Never," Tal spat.

"Oh, one way or another, you and the Marquess will both serve me," Kherzul laughed menacingly. "What we'll determine down here is in what capacity. We can take our time, though. We've got until the spring." He turned to the door. "Obviously, you're still feeling obstinate. I'll come back after your resolve has had a little more chance to weaken. Perhaps you'll be more prepared to listen then."

The door boomed shut behind Kherzul. Tal groaned quietly, feeling like a rag doll that had been fought over by a pair of mastiffs.

Rania stalked angrily about her cell in a tight circle, the widest range of movement her chained wrists would permit her. Had she been a cat, she'd have been lashing her tail in fury. All her attempts to slip or break her bonds had met with failure, no matter how deeply she pulled in the Sephira, and she had been angry enough to immerse herself in it as never before. She still was. Captured by her most hated enemy, robbed of the Blade of Unity she was sworn to protect, and unsure even if Tal still lived, blinding rage filled her, screaming for release.

She rounded on the door when she heard the screech of metal on metal. As soon as Kherzul's dark-shrouded form became visible, Rania hissed, "You'll pay for all you've done, monster."

Unblinking crimson eyes fixed on her. "I see the years have made you as defiant as your mother was. She said much the same thing when she was brought before me, but she gave me what I wanted by the end. I was in a hurry, though, and I'm afraid I wasn't gentle. She called out for you with her last words, you might be interested to know. An unfortunate business, but unavoidable. She stood in the way of something I needed. Is that what you so hate me for, or is it something else?"

"If you're so far gone in your own vileness that you can't even recognize all your crimes, I'm not going to catalog them for you," Rania snarled back, yanking at her chains to try to get at him. "All the lives you've crushed cry out for your destruction."

"How odd. I can't hear them. What are a few lives in comparison to the reunification and restoration of power to the North? If by crimes you mean the crime of ambition, then I am guilty. If by vile you mean willing to do what is necessary to achieve my goals, then I suppose I am vile. But I'm afraid I can't have a prisoner using such unkind words to describe me." Kherzul raised an admonishing finger before him.

Agony suddenly flared within Rania, all of her bones seeming to flash into molten lead searing through the rest of her body. She stood through it, shaking like a leaf in a high wind, glaring balefully at Kherzul, her hatred of him holding her up.

"I'm impressed," Kherzul rasped as the burning ebbed away. "You know, I always wondered what happened to you after our little raid. I long suspected that the notorious 'Ghost of Felmorinen' hunting my men in the mountains was you. When I learned that you had resurfaced and were now Shevestra'ka, I was actually quite proud of you."

"Why should you be proud of me?" Rania snarled at the Spectre King.

"Because I created you," Kherzul replied. "Had it not been for me, you'd have become the next guardian of Felmorinen, wasting away your talent protecting an antique fortress and never reaching your full potential. Without the anger I gave you, you might never have made it through your training. Without me, you'd be nothing. But now you have to put that anger aside, see that I made you strong, and understand that I can make you stronger yet if you will but serve me instead of futilely lashing out."

"I'll stand witness to your annihilation one day," Rania sneered.

Fire coursed through her nerves, an ocean of suffering pouring through her and filling her until she knew she must drown in it. She sagged forward against her bonds before angrily and awkwardly righting herself. Her knees wanted to buckle, but she refused to let them.

"You really shouldn't want that," Kherzul crooned, "when I'm the only individual who could return you mother to you. Or your father. I could, you know, if you only swear to obey me. Would you like that?"

"You mean you could give me twisted and corrupt mockeries of them," Rania panted. She was at the limits of her ability to shelter from the torment in her anger. "I'd only despise you all the more for doing so."

"You were able to transfer your hatred of me to this 'twisted and corrupt mockery' I now inhabit. Why could you not transfer your love for them likewise?" The spectre waved a dismissive hand. "But no matter. You'll change your mind eventually, I'm sure. You could have made it a lot less unpleasant for yourself by agreeing quickly, but I see that there's no hope of that. Think on what I can offer you." Kherzul opened the door and left. A few moments after his departure, the torchlight coming through the grate was extinguished, plunging her into darkness lit only by her own aura.

Alone in the tiny stone cell, Rania stifled a sob. Never since Felmorinen fell had she felt so helpless.

Tal stood in the darkness, struggling to keep his mind calm and to think. It had been several minutes after Kherzul left his cell before the torchlight from outside had gone out. That suggested that the Bhellan King had not left immediately. He had said that Tal and Rania both would serve him. Tal wasn't sure if that had been a slip on the spectre's part or not, but he clung to that statement and its implication that Rania was alive. Probably also held prisoner, but alive, and that gave him hope.

He got as close as he could to the iron door. The chains pulled his arms back painfully. He yelled Rania's name as loud as he could several times, and then stood in anticipatory silence, straining to hear an answer so hard that he didn't dare breathe for fear of missing it. Long seconds passed, and Tal heard nothing but the beating of his own desperate heart.

With a sigh, he returned to the center of the cell again to relieve the pressure on his arms. Clear thought. That was what he needed now. Regrettably, no matter how he looked at it, he could find no means of escape from his current circumstances. He would have to wait, and endure, and hope Kherzul made some sort of mistake, left Tal some sort of opening. For the time being, contacting Rania was where his energy would best be spent, but it seemed they were beyond each others' hearing. That left the possibility of the mysterious bond between them, but Tal had no idea how far they could reach each other from.

"Not like I've got anything else to do," he chuckled ruefully to himself. He was struggling to keep his spirits up, to nurture whatever hope he could. Despair yawned wide under him like an endless abyss and if he gave in to it, he wasn't sure he would be able to recover from the fall.

He reached out with his mind, focusing on every nuance of his surroundings that the Sephira carried to him, searching for any hint of Rania's presence in the currents. The Sephira seemed subdued and quiet in this place, although it carried a hint of tension, an undertone of menace and fear. Its flow was gentle, even sluggish as it eddied through the subterranean passages. Tal frowned to himself. Subdued and quiet wasn't what he was looking for. Rania was a woman of powerful emotion, and that emotion tended to stir up and insinuate itself into the Sephira. He focused on the stronger emotions coming to him.

Fear, suffering, and hopelessness were the dominant feelings that came to Tal as he concentrated ever deeper, lingering in the Sephira like echoes of the agonizing dramas that had been played out here over the years. There was none of Rania in any of it. A trace of anger, hot and barbed, brushed his awareness, and Tal immediately focused his attention there. He worked his way up the currents, and exulted as he felt fury mingled with frustration that minded him so much of Rania he was certain he had found her. He began trying to stretch his own Sephiral presence out to that sense of her, beads of sweat breaking out on his brow from the effort. He had to reach her. Just a little further...

Rania paced restlessly in the dark. The Sephira swirled and eddied around her, stirred from its lethargy by the rage boiling inside her. The range of motion allowed by her bonds wasn't great, but she had to keep moving or burst. She'd have much preferred having something to break or better yet enemies to kill, but she had to make do with what was available to her. Which admittedly wasn't much. Every time that thought came to her, it stoked her fury anew.

She held on to her rage like a talisman. Rania was no fool; she knew that the coming days would be difficult and filled with torment. She had to cling to her anger, to her hatred of Kherzul, to all that she was, or be broken. That was one victory she could never let the Bhellan King have. She would much rather die first.

Idly, Rania wondered whether Kherzul would conduct her torture entirely on his own, or if he would send some lackey to see to it.

Her thoughts were suddenly pulled away as a familiar presence in the Sephira tickled her mind, reaching out to her. With a relieved gasp, she stretched out to Tal's searching reach and as she touched it, awareness of him filled her. The relief she felt was echoed by his own as the bond solidified between them. He was shackled much as she was, it seemed, and from the muted ache throughout his body, it seemed he had experienced Kherzul's less than tender ministrations as well.

Rania wished she could speak to Tal through the link, but it carried only feelings and awareness, not structured communication. Still, it was enough. She could feel Tal's concern for her through it, and that served as yet another reminder of who she was, a much more pleasant one than those she had been focused on.

Rania stopped pacing in circles, absorbing herself entirely in her invisible connection to Talaren. It was like he was right there with her; in a very real sense, he was. The darkness seemed suddenly less empty.

The dark stretched on interminably. With no windows, no trace of sunlight, Tal had nothing in his environment against which to mark the passing of time. He had not yet felt the need to sleep, which told him it had been less than a day, but besides that he couldn't guess how long he had stared at the walls and door of his wretched prison. Sleep was not a prospect he looked forward to. Bound as he was, there would be no comfortable way to accomplish it, which was no doubt the intention. Deprive him of sleep, deprive him of food, deprive him of water, all to weaken him and wear away his will. The thought reminded him uncomfortably of how thirsty he was, and his stomach grumbled at him irritably.

Finding Rania had felt like a major victory, even though it seemed to put them no closer to escape. The bond between them still held firmly, and the sense of her in his mind was calming.

After what seemed ages, ruddy light flickered through the grating of Tal's cell door again, dim at first but growing brighter. A short while later the door scraped open, and one of the spectral generals entered the room followed by a soldier bearing a wooden cup, bowl, and funnel.

"You shouldn't have come here, Talaren," the spectre said in a cold voice, "but I'm glad you did. I've been waiting a long time for this. I finally get to see you humbled."

Tal's brow furrowed at the familiar way the spectre spoke to him. He remembered now, just before he had been knocked unconscious, Kherzul had addressed one of his minions as...

"Joren," Tal gasped disgustedly.

"Indeed," the spectre nodded. "In service to a new King and finally more powerful than you."

Tal shook his head. "I never sought power, Joren. My desire was always to serve."

"Oh, please!" Joren snarled. "For as long as I can remember, every time I've tried to gain standing and prestige, you were there to overshadow me and block my way. For someone who doesn't seek power, you've managed to attain quite a bit of it." He waved an arm at the soldier beside him. "You, feed the prisoner and then leave us."

The soldier stepped forward and took Tal roughly by the chin, forcing his head back and mouth open. The funnel was jammed in between his teeth, and then the soldier poured the contents of the bowl into it. Thin, tasteless gruel filled Tal's mouth, and he had to struggle to get it all down or gag on it. As soon as the bowl was emptied, the soldier set it aside and poured the cup into the funnel. The water was stagnant and foul tasting, but Tal gulped every last swallow greedily.

His jaw was released, and the soldier wordlessly departed from the cell.

"Before we continue, there's something I want to show you," Joren gloated. "A little trophy his Majesty allowed me to keep from your pitiful attempt to kill him." He drew the blade at his side and held it out so Tal could see.

Tal's eyes widened. Joren held *Edyamar*!

"I see you recognize the Amoran wench's blade," Joren purred. "I'm hoping you'll irritate Kherzul enough that he'll let me kill you with it." He extended the weapon, holding the point inches from Tal's throat, and chuckled. "Now wouldn't that be poetic? So tell me, Tal, is that red-haired little minx as entertaining a plaything as she looks?"

Tal glared with hate-filled eyes back at his old rival. "What's between Rania and I is no concern of yours," he growled angrily. *Edyamar* was close enough he could probably kick it from Joren's grip just as he had the crown from Kherzul's brow. With luck, the blade might even strike Joren and destroy him. But that would lose him the single advantage he now had and possibly the only chance he would have to escape, for only a moment's vindictive satisfaction. Still, the temptation was there. Tal tried to reign in his anger.

"It's too bad I don't have a body anymore to find out for myself," Joren mused. "Maybe I should order one of the guards to do it for me, and tell me what he thinks?"

Tal quivered with fury and outrage at the vile suggestion. "I should have had you executed immediately back in Val Jerak," he fumed. "You're an insult to everything decent, Joren. Now stop talking about Rania and get her sword out of my face before I throw myself on it and let you suffer the consequences. I doubt Kherzul will be very pleased with you if let me die before he has his fun. He knows I can't hurt you now, so you couldn't even claim you were defending yourself."

"Have it your way, then, if you're so anxious to get on to the rest." Joren resheathed *Edyamar* and took a barbed scourge from the opposite side of his weapons belt. He chuckled malevolently as he uncoiled it. "I think I'll enjoy this more than taunting you, anyway." He stepped around behind Tal, and a few seconds later it began.

The scourge lashed into Tal's back, barbs ripping into his flesh and then tearing out, over and over, relentlessly. He struggled not to cry out, but after the sixth or seventh lash the strain became too great and he howled in pain.

Tal twisted about on the chain as he twitched with each successive stroke, but Joren seemed not to care whether he scourged Tal's back or front. Both were viable targets, and both became crisscrossed with bleeding wounds. The Sephira raged through Tal as it never had before, the only barrier between him and the beating, and he realized that Rania was directing most of what she held to him, fortifying him against the torment. The tiny part of his mind still capable of rational thought thanked her as he tried in vain to hold back the screams.

His throat was raw and produced only hoarse croaks when at length the blows finally stopped falling. He feebly struggled to regain his feet, but couldn't support himself. Pain pressed in on him, making his breath short with its urgency, even through the buffering of the Sephira. Without it shielding him from the agony, he'd probably have lost consciousness by now. Perhaps mercifully so.

Mercy didn't seem to be in the stars for Tal, though. Once Joren had re-coiled the scourge, he stepped close and slowly ran a dark hand across the mass of open wounds on Tal's back. The frigid touch on top of the burning agony of the fresh injuries plunged Tal into a whole new world of torment. With each touch it seemed he could feel his life force ebbing away. He shuddered weakly as it went on, until even that was beyond him.

After he had dangled limply for a time, his chin was pulled roughly up again and his eyes thumbed open by the same icy hands. He managed only a whimper and a feeble twitch in response to the sensation that his eyes were about to freeze in their sockets.

"Still conscious, Tal?" Joren asked. "I admit, I'm a little bit impressed. And delighted that you got to experience all of that. I'll be back again soon for more, when it's less likely to kill you. Heal quickly." His laughter faded with his body as he melted into the shadows and was gone.

Tal simply hung by his arms, unable to muster the effort for aught else. He still held the Sephira, still held his link to Rania. She was weeping, he realized, feeling her anguish and frustration at having been unable to do anything more to assist him. There was something else, too. A hint of nervousness, growing stronger by the second. When he felt her pulled around on her chain to be fed and watered, he understood.

Steeling himself, Tal shunted as much of the Sephira as he could through the link to Rania. The pain that wracked his body seemed to grow all the much greater, and he groaned as his vision started to darken, but struggled his way back from the plunge into unconsciousness. Rania had helped him through his ordeal, now he had to return the favor.

He felt the first lash fall upon Rania's back. It was distant, separate from him, not like being struck himself, but knowing that the pain he felt was Rania's more than made up for any physical sensation lost in the translation. Tal squeezed his eyes shut against the tears that leaked out as he suffered through a second beating, this one crueler than the first.

So it went for what must have been days. Tal and Rania would be left in the dark, alone with their bond to each other. Whenever the light came, they were fed and watered perfunctorily and then beaten to the edge of consciousness, always by Joren and always with unholy delight. He stopped wearing *Edyamar* when he came to them after the first day, though. Perhaps he'd taken Tal's threat to use the weapon to kill himself seriously. The time between each visit was just enough for the Sephira to close the wounds of the Shevestra'ken with tender pink skin. When exhaustion took one of them, the other would maintain the bond while the first slept, allowing both to continue to regenerate at a slightly reduced rate. The few times the bond did fail, Tal had little difficulty picking it right back up again. All the time they were spending bonded seemed to be improving his sensitivity to Rania. Sadly, that was the only thing that improved. So long had Tal been chained to the ceiling, he didn't think his arms would work properly even if the chains were to be removed. Days of minimal food, water, and sleep coupled with regular beatings left his body so weak he usually couldn't stand on his own. He felt broken, his will battered down until only a shred remained that he dared not let go of.

When the light came again after Tal had endured his fifteenth scourging, he was already preparing himself, drawing back in his mind to that one corner where a scrap of sanity remained, his fortress against the abuse. When the soldier who opened the cell door came in carrying a rickety little wooden table, Tal blinked in surprise. The table was soon followed by two chairs, placed across from one another. A bowl of stew, the aroma from which made Tal's mouth water, was placed on the table along with a cup and battered teapot. The soldier exited the room after placing all th'e things alongside one wall, and as soon as he disappeared into the hallway, Kherzul entered. The scrape of metal announced the door being barred again as the King of Bhellus studied his captive.

"You look dreadful, Lord Solus," Kherzul rasped. "I told you this would go badly for you if you wouldn't listen to me. Now you begin to understand the truth of my words. Perhaps this show of goodwill will open your ears." He made an offhand gesture, and the chains about Tal's wrists writhed serpentinely, loosing him from their hold. No longer supported by them, Tal stumbled and fell on his face.

Unseen hands pulled Tal to his feet and helped hold him up as he hobbled over to the chair Kherzul gestured toward. The hands disappeared as Tal took the seat. He wobbled a bit, but didn't fall. Sitting was somewhat easier than standing.

"Please, eat," Kherzul said as he settled into the other chair. "I understand Joren hasn't been feeding you very well. He seems to dislike you rather intensely, and the Marquess by extension."

Tal's arms felt limp and rubbery, and having them no longer held above his head felt strangely unnatural, but he forced them to work. Pain lanced up his shoulders as he willed his arms and hands to move, but he wasn't about to let any amount of pain stand between him and real food after so long. Kherzul watched on silently as Tal licked the bowl clean and then downed two cups of tea in rapid succession.

"Now, perhaps you'll hear me out?" Kherzul asked when Tal put the cup down and didn't move to refill it.

"You can torture me as long as you like, Kherzul. I'll still never serve the likes of you." Tal's voice rasped almost as much as the spectre's did, and words felt odd on his tongue.

"Talaren, I'm not doing this to you. You're doing it to yourself. I'm giving you every chance I can to escape this unfortunate situation. You did try to kill me, you'll recall. I'm afraid I can't just let assassins go; you never know when they might try to kill you again. If you were to swear to obey me, though, I would take your word on the honor of the Shevestra'ken. I'd know I wouldn't have to worry about you then. You could walk free again." A shadowy arm gestured toward the door. "Say the words, and you can leave now."

Tal shook his head disgustedly. "If you know the first thing about Shevestra'ken honor, you know that I couldn't give that oath without betraying the one I gave to the Maiden."

"You couldn't be more wrong," Kherzul replied in what Tal guessed was meant to be a reasonable tone. "I'd require nothing of you that would violate your oaths. I'll need someone to keep the peace and maintain order in my kingdom, and I believe a Shevestra'ka would be ideal for such a task. Would it stain your honor to mete out justice? Would it not serve the people you swore to defend to stand by my side and help me unite them in a peaceful kingdom, with a mighty army and an immortal King to protect them?"

"An army of the dead and a King who rules through fear," Tal spat right back.

Kherzul leaned forward ominously. "Fear is a tool. You should know that. A useful tool, I'll grant you, but just a tool nonetheless. As for the dead, would you prefer I send the living to feed the ravens? Would that really be so much better? I employ the methods I must. This age is coming to an end, Lord Solus, can you not feel it? People whisper of it in the streets; the mighty see it from their thrones; your friends within the Jhessaillian Order know it is coming. The Guardian who came to me in my youth, who secretly began my training in the Sephiral Arts said as much. It's the very reason he chose me – no, they chose me! Because I have the will to do what is needed to prepare us for what is coming. Ancient threats begin to waken. Nations crumble, and order is lost. Everywhere, civilization is falling apart, and prophecy tells us that we will soon face the day of our greatest need. Now, of all times, the North must be strong! All the splintered nations must be forged anew! I can do that for them! Is that not worth whatever price must be paid?"

Tal shook his head stubbornly. "How you do something is as important as that you do it. If you become a monster to save the world, it doesn't make you any less a monster. You make a good monster, Kherzul, but a poor savior. You'd destroy the people to save them. How terribly heroic. I can't imagine that the Jhessaillian Prophecy would have any use for a creature such as you."

"Fool!" Kherzul roared, slashing his hand toward Tal as he stood angrily. An unseen force hurled Tal from his chair to hold him splayed out helplessly against the wall. Kherzul glided over to stare up at Tal with flaming eyes. "I could kill you with a thought right now," he said menacingly, "but I won't, not yet. You will have another chance to change your mind. But remember, my patience is not infinite and when it runs out, I'll find another way for you to serve."

The force holding Tal to the wall vanished as the door slammed shut behind Kherzul, and he collapsed in a heap on the floor. Though pain still wracked his body and he could barely stand on his own, he found himself shaking with silent laughter. The chains that had held him remained unbound.

31
Waiting in the Twilight

The Jhessaillian Chapterhouse in Val Zherrane was filling up. Every day saw the arrival of several more Guardians and Godtouched pulled from their usual duties across the continent. Already the Chapterhouse's hundred beds were full, and newcomers were having to take rooms at inns throughout the city. Only very rarely in the history of the Order had there been such a gathering for war. The power assembled under that one roof would have put to rout any normal army; it just might have a chance of holding back the onslaught that would come with spring.

Kyril made a point of meeting with every group as they came in to brief them and see if they carried any word for him from other lands. The contingent from Scithis in Amberyl, among the smallest to arrive but also among the first, brought heartening news: they had informed King Soren of the plight of his neighbor to the north, and the nation that had broken away from Valeran nineteen years past, at the height of the Bhellan Revolution, was sending troops to join the fight against Kherzul. Permission for those troops to cross the border had been easily obtained from the King's Council. After seeing Talaren's reports from Val Jerak, they were eager for any assistance that might be offered.

Though in the depths of winter the sun barely peeked over the horizon before setting again, the entire city buzzed chaotically through the long nights like a kicked anthill. Soldiers trained at every hour of the day wherever there was room to do so, new recruits being readied for the war and grizzled veterans re-sharpening their skills. Forges burned constantly throughout the city, pounding out armor and weapons for the burgeoning army. Wagons loaded down with foodstuffs rumbled into the city, paid for by the crown to feed all the extra mouths the military buildup was bringing into Val Zherrane. Yes, preparations for war had begun in earnest, and the host that was gathering would be worthy of song. Kyril still held out hope that none of it would be necessary, though.

It was a week short of two months since Kyril had last seen Tal, enough time that he and Rania should have arrived in Bhel Meravos by now. Kyril expected that any day could bring a raven with news of Kherzul's demise.

The news that occupied the Guardian now, though, was of a different nature and from farther away. One of the his fellows had arrived earlier in the day from Cardon bearing a sealed scrollcase for Kyril, and it was over the contents of that case that he now pored. There were several pages scribed in the runic of the ancient tongue, and a single page in a hand Kyril immediately recognized.

> Effarim'zor Damarrian,
> Your report, though tardy, was much appreciated. We are pleased that our preliminary projections for the Solus boy appear to have been correct. As for the matter of the Amoran heir, we will take your beliefs under advisement until conclusive proof becomes available. Based on the information you provided about this pair, one of your brothers in the Word of Jhessail has found a passage from a tome in the Great Collection that may be applicable. If so, it may well support your theory. A transcript of the relevant pages is included with this missive. Our disappointment must be noted, however, that both subjects have been allowed to place themselves at risk. Consider yourself reprimanded. You are ordered to use any and all means you deem necessary to effect their recovery, and thereafter to keep both from danger as best you are able.
> Jhessaillarim'zan Davor Venrath

Kyril went on to the pages appended to the letter. The books in the Great Collection were those that had been recovered by Jhessail from Felmorinen in the days following the Harrowing. They all dated back to before the Great Purge, an era of history that few remembered and none well. The knowledge contained in those books was the Jhessaillian Order's greatest treasure. The pages Kyril pored over now appeared to be excerpted from a scholarly work analyzing the interaction of Shevestra'ken with the Sephira. The text was complicated and technical, as works from the Great Collection tended to be, and Kyril had to read through it a second time to be sure he had understood it correctly.

Kyril stroked his beard thoughtfully as he finished his second read of the document. The pages described a rare phenomena amongst Shevestra'ken that the author referred to alternately as Binary Essences or Sephiral Conjunction. It would explain a number of things if it applied to Tal and Rania, and raise several interesting new questions besides. Unfortunately, Kyril couldn't tell if it *was* applicable. He tucked the information away in the back of his head for later reference. He glanced at the window of his study to check the time, and shook his head ruefully at the everpresent darkness outside. He still hadn't gotten used to northern winters yet. It was somehow offensive that it should be dark through most of the day.

A tentative knock at his door snapped Kyril's head around. "Enter."

A slender, swarthy Guardian with short dark hair entered and bowed to him. Eryk, Kyril thought his name was, a Guardian of the Hand called up from one of the southern nations. "Guardian Damarrian, King Garant sends for you. His courier said that important news has arrived from the east."

A smile spread across Kyril's face. "Excellent!" He declared, bounding out of his chair. "Thank you, Guardian Eryk, I shall go consult with the King at once."

"You're welcome, brother." Eryk bowed again and left.

Kyril found he was actually humming happily to himself as he put on a heavy cloak to brave the cold that lay between the Chapterhouse and the Palace.

The pleased smile on Kyril's face faded as soon as he was ushered into Garant's study. Across from the King sat Duke Solus, and both of their faces were like thunderclouds. A heavy air seemed to hang over the room.

"What's happened?" Kyril asked.

"A raven arrived from the east a short while ago," Garant replied somberly, "We don't know specifically where or whom it was from. The message tube was sealed but bore no sigil, and the writer gives no indication of his identity. This is the message it contained." Garant slid a thin sheet of paper across the desk, still creased and curled from its journey.

Kyril picked up the sheet and glanced quickly through the small, precisely printed letters.

> Friends in the Valerite Court,
> I recently made the acquaintance of a young man from your lands who came here on a matter of some urgent business. I believe he is known to you. I was able to assist him in reaching his destination, but I regret that once there, he fell afoul of a very powerful individual. The young man and his companion have, to the best of my knowledge, been imprisoned. I wish I could offer you gladder tidings, but sadly the best I can give you is this: In the days to come, know that there are those among your

enemies who are reluctant and would wish
peace between us.

By the time he finished the note, Kyril's heart was trying to beat through his chest. Tal *couldn't* have failed! But there it was, right in front of his eyes. The sour taste of bile came to his mouth. Could the Jhessaillian Prophecy have been wrong? Or had he simply failed in executing its edicts?

Kyril slowly laid the message back on the desk. "Imprisoned," he said, the word bitter on his tongue.

"At least imprisoned still means alive," Daron responded gravely. His face was creased with concern for his son.

"Alive, yes," Garant agreed. "But as troubling as this news is to us personally," he gave Daron a sympathetic look, "we must bear in mind that if we are to be of any use to Talaren now, we must look at what this means to us strategically. It appears that we can no longer hope for him to slay Kherzul before the spring. We're going to have to rely on a military solution now. Unless either of you have another idea?" His eyes shifted between the two men before him.

"I wonder," Kyril mused, fingering the note on the desk. "Maybe this tells us a bit more than it seems to."

"How so?" Asked the King.

"Whoever wrote it obviously took pains not to reveal who they might be and to be vague as to exactly what they were telling us," The Guardian noted. "That suggests someone with both position to lose and practice at the intrigues of court, which means that we're dealing with some form of nobility. The closing sentences of this missive, then, would seem to confirm that fear of Kherzul is the primary motivation of this war. Without him, the Bhellan will to fight will probably disappear. Kherzul is the key."

"We already knew that," Daron grumbled irritably.

"No, we suspected," Kyril corrected. "Nationalism can be a touchy thing when it gets stirred up. It can compel a nation to war even when all reason, righteousness, or hope has abandoned their cause. Now we know at least that some of the Bhellan nobility have kept their heads. We can use that."

"Just what are you driving at, Guardian Damarrian?" Garant asked.

"Tal had the right idea about this war," Kyril replied, "It will be won by defeating Kherzul, not by fighting his armies. Even with all the Guardians who've come to aid Valeran, the carnage from this war will likely cripple the North. We have to strike at Kherzul himself if we're to have any hope for a real victory."

"With Talaren captured and Trazeri's Sword in Kherzul's hands, that would mean we'd have to use Godtouched." The King's snowy eyebrows lowered meaningfully. "Do you think one of them can succeed where Talaren and Marquess Amoran failed?"

Kyril shook his head slowly. "One? No. Godtouched are meant to fight sorcerers, not armies. Kherzul's guards would slay our man before ever he got in sight of the King." He grinned suddenly. "But a hundred Godtouched, or maybe even two hundred, might present Kherzul a problem. Especially if they come for him while the bulk of his army is busy attacking the rest of us."

The King nodded thoughtfully. "How do you intend to accomplish this?"

Kyril shrugged. "Once we near the end of winter, it should be possible to get that many men through the Felmorr's high passes with the assistance of the Pathfinders. The Godtouched could travel in small groups to avoid attracting notice, and they should have a reasonable chance of avoiding the forces Kherzul will be sending to the Gap. We'll still have to defend Val Jerak, of course, but this way at least we'll know that even should we fail, we'll have bought time for the Godtouched to end this."

"Shall I command the defense of Val Jerak, then?" Duke Solus asked his King grimly.

Garant shook his head. "No, Daron. I'm not so frail that I can no longer hold a sword. I'll command. It's my duty as King." He smiled kindly at his old friend. "I would appreciate it if you would be my strategic advisor, though. You always did have better instincts for war than I." The King turned his eyes back to Kyril. "Send your Godtouched to Bhel Meravos, Guardian Damarrian. We'll buy them the time they'll need."

There was little else to be decided after that. They adjourned for the evening, and Kyril returned to the Jhessaillian chapterhouse, his thoughts troubled. Talaren and Rania captured. *Kallevamar* under Kherzul's control. The carnage that would come with facing Kherzul's armies. And still no word yet in reply to the more surreptitious inquiries he'd made back to Cardon. None pleasant thoughts, and nothing Kyril could do about any of them except wait and see how events played out. With almost two months yet to go until the Godtouched would even be able to attempt a crossing of the Felmorr, it was shaping up to be a dark winter indeed.

32
Slipping Into the Abyss

Tal's elation at his unbound hands was unfortunately short lived. He quickly found that weeks of being bound as they had been had left his arms even weaker and less willing to cooperate than the rest of his body. He was free to roam about his cell now on unsteady legs, but no matter how hard he threw himself at the door, even with the Sephira filling him, the cold iron was utterly unyielding.

Kherzul was with Rania now. Tal felt the chains loose themselves from her wrists, and the sharp spike of rage that came from her whenever she set eyes on the Bhellan King. Before long, he became aware of the pain being inflicted on the woman he loved. He grit his teeth in anger as he channeled Sephiral power to her, an act that had become nearly reflex now. Thankfully it was all over shortly, and Rania had also been left unbound. Apparently Kherzul hadn't made a mistake, after all.

Within a few minutes Tal had another visitor. The door grated open to admit the hatefully familiar form of Joren, carrying a length of chain with shackles on its ends.

Tal lunged for the door as it opened, but Joren anticipated him and smashed a gauntleted fist into Tal's jaw, knocking the Shevestra'ka to the ground with a sharp crack. Pain washed through Tal, and he knew his jaw had been broken. The door clanged shut as he crawled to his hands and knees, and then he was kicked viciously in the abdomen. While he still wheezed for breath, a heavy boot stepped on his back and pressed him down to the floor.

"Time for your new bonds, Tal," Joren announced with a hollow laugh.

Tal's hands were pulled roughly back and then the shackles snapped closed around his wrists, binding his arms behind his back. Seconds later, another set of shackles were clamped around his ankles. He felt Joren get off his back before a fist tangled itself in his hair and yanked him up to a kneeling position.

Joren walked around to stand before Tal, chuckling darkly the whole while. With the snap of breaking ribs, the spectre kicked Tal brutally back to the floor. Mercilessly the kicks kept coming, one after another after another, and Joren laughed all the harder with each one. Tal balled himself up as best he could against the blows that rained down on him. The punishment continued long enough that he began to think maybe this time it would kill him. It was a strangely comforting thought. At least death would end his pain. But death didn't come, and the kicking finally stopped.

Before Joren left, he held the door wide open for several seconds, taunting Tal with the unblocked portal. The Shevestra'ka struggled to rise, but so soon after the abuse he'd just taken, his muscles refused to respond. A final chilling chuckle emanated from the spectre, and then he slammed the door shut. Tal lay in a fog of agony, bracing himself for the sensations he knew were about to come to him as the process was repeated for Rania. He didn't have long to wait.

Rania huddled alone in the darkness, striving to ignore the pain that burned all across her body. It had been hours since Kherzul and then Joren had come to her cell, but it would be some time yet before the Sephira would mend her hurts and Tal's. Their captors had been even less gentle than usual.

With nothing else to occupy her, Rania concentrated on picturing Tal's face in the pitch black before her eyes: the strong line of his jaw, the way his sandy hair just brushed his shoulders, the deep gray-blue eyes she could lose herself in. Forsaking the torment she was in now, she traveled back through her memories to better times, remembering the contentment of being in Tal's arms, the bliss of her body pressed against his, the thrill of their lips meeting. They'd had far too little time together between realizing their feelings for one another and being taken by Kherzul.

In a strange way, Tal's hurts pained Rania more than her own. Knowing through the Sephira what was done to him, and knowing that she couldn't do anything to stop it, made her shake with rage at her own impotence. Compared to that, physical torment was merely an irritation. It kept her strong, though, fueled her will to resist Kherzul and not to give in to despair. Somehow, she would find a way to get out of here and to be with Tal again. That was all that mattered. So she waited, waited to see what the next torture would be, and while she waited, she lost herself in remembrance.

More time slipped by, and Rania managed to get a little bit of fitful sleep. Sleeping with wrists and ankles chained wasn't particularly comfortable, but it was still a far cry better than it had been whilst chained to the ceiling. She had no idea how long she had slept for, but shortly after she awoke, flickering torchlight filled the hall outside her cell again.

Two spectres entered the room this time, the first ones aside from Joren and Kherzul she'd seen since her capture. Rania was hauled to her feet, and then prodded toward the door. Compliantly, she shuffled out of the cell with the tiny steps that were all the chain connecting her ankles allowed her. With one spectre before her and the other behind, she was herded through several twists of the corridor and then down a set of stairs. Her Sephiral link to Tal grew more strained with every step until, as she carefully descended the stairs, it vanished. Rania paused, wanting to howl at the loss of her sense of Tal, and the spectre behind her gave her a shove forward that resulted in her tumbling down the last several steps. The spectre who had stood in front of her reached down and grabbed the chain between Rania's wrists and pulled her back upright, nearly dislocating her shoulders in the process. At the bottom of the stairs was a short hallway with a stout, iron-bound door at the far end. The lead spectre opened the door, while the one behind Rania pushed her ahead of him into the room beyond.

Rania found herself in a scene from a sadist's most twisted imaginings. Four torches burning at the corners of the room shed their light on a bloodstained stone block with restraints at its corners. Racks on the walls held all manner of torture implements, knives and hooks and pincers and clamps and other things Rania didn't even know the name for. A raised stone enclosure in the far corner seemed to be intended to hold hot coals, with brands neatly arrayed on an adjacent shelf. In the opposite corner stood a sarcophagus-like case worked at the top into the semblance of a face contorted with suffering.

A slight, balding man wearing a worn leather apron gave a thin-lipped smile as Rania was escorted into the room. "Welcome to my workshop," he said blandly. Beady, close set eyes looked her up and down. "What a lovely prisoner. I think I may enjoy this."

Rania attempted to struggle as the spectres pushed her down on the stone block and began fastening the restraints, but weakened as she was, she felt like a kitten struggling with a pair of wolves. She managed to wriggle a leg free when the shackles on her ankles were opened, and for her trouble earned a backhand across the face that left her ears ringing. Once she was firmly secured spread-eagle to the stone, the pair of spectres departed in silence. She heard them slide a heavy metal bar across the door behind them.

"You really shouldn't struggle, you know," the little man said absently as he surveyed a rack of knives. "If you behave yourself, you get to sleep in your cell. If not, you go in there." He gestured toward the sarcophagus contraption with a knife before testing the blade's edge. "The inside is covered in spikes, very sharp spikes. If you don't stand completely still in there, well, I'm sure you can imagine."

"You'd have to kill me before I'd ever cooperate with Kherzul," Rania snarled, "or one of his dogs." Her voice dripped with contempt.

"Ah, yes," again that tight little smile, devoid of any mirth whatsoever, crossed the man's face, "His Majesty said you have an unusually strong will." As he spoke, he casually grasped the bottom of Rania's filthy and torn tunic and slid the knife under it, slicing neatly up the side from waist to sleeve. "You and that young man you arrived with. That's why he gave you both to me. I'm the best here at what I do." He beamed with pride for a moment, and then calmly cut away the other side of Rania's tunic, tossing the rags of the garment off to the side when he finished. "You'd probably have been sent to me sooner, but we had to let the big boys soften you up a bit first. A pity, really. Their methods are so crude." The knife began cutting at Rania's breeches. "But they seem to have had their desired effect. I really am quite excited about this, you know. I've never had the opportunity to work with a Shevestra'ka, after all. I expect this will be quite the fascinating challenge. I hope you won't let me down."

Rania glared hate at the little man. "One day soon, I'll kill you," she growled.

"That's the spirit," he murmured. "Now, shall we begin?" He selected a new knife from the rack beside him with a short, narrow blade. He began humming as he gently placed the tip just below Rania's collarbone, drawing a single drop of blood.

Rania's restraints pulled taut as she tensed in anticipation of the cut. The little man smiled as he began drawing the blade downward, the first time the smile actually reached his eyes.

Tal lay limp on the floor of his cell. Standing on his own was well beyond him now, especially after having been forced to do so for several hours in that accursed spike-filled box his tormenter seemed so fond of. Tal had been put in it more times than he could remember now. It had turned into a sick sort of game. The short balding man plied his trade on Tal with his knives and clamps and hooks and knowledge of how to cause the most pain with the least real injury to his helpless subject. Each session was several hours of unadulterated agony and terror for Tal, the only thought in his head during those times being not to cry out. Sometimes he failed. When he succeeded, his reward was to be put in the spiked box. That, and the satisfaction of having denied the beady-eyed torturer the pleasure of his screams. It was the only way he had to strike out at Kherzul's foul little minion. A sick game, and one in which Tal was the loser either way.

He had found that his training could help him when he was put in the dark of the box, where any movement greater than a fraction of an inch meant being pierced by several sharpened barbs. The meditations with which he had begun his initiation into the ways of the Armslords and Shevestra'ken made it easier to stand completely unmoving for hours at a stretch, resisting the pull of gravity on his battered and undernourished body. It also helped hold the smothering fear at bay. Had it not been for being able to so blank his thoughts, Tal had no doubt his sanity would have shattered by now. It still felt fragile, as though one single sharp blow could break his mind into a thousand gibbering pieces. That was the fate that terrified him beyond all others, that he fought with everything he could muster. He was afraid he might be losing that struggle.

It seemed an eternity since he'd had any contact with Rania. The only way he still even knew she lived was that the torturer frequently taunted Tal by describing the torments he applied to the other Shevestra'ka. The hateful creature had discovered quickly the nature of Tal and Rania's feelings for one another, and had just as quickly moved to turn those feelings against them. For that, if nothing else, Tal had promised himself he'd see the man die an agonizing death. It was one of the few pleasant thoughts left to him.

Sleep. That was what he needed now, needed desperately after his most recent ordeal. He lay there on the floor, imagining the hateful pig eyes of the torturer going wide as Tal's hands tightened about his throat, hoping that sleep would come soon, the dark dreamless sleep that had become his greatest refuge. If it came soon, he might actually get some real rest before he was sent for again.

Such was not to be, it seemed. As his thoughts drifted, taking on the fuzzy incoherence of the far end of consciousness, the bar on the door to Tal's cell was drawn back and Kherzul drifted into the room, followed by two of his spectral minions.

Kherzul gestured imperiously at his prisoner as Tal tried to focus his eyes on the necromancer. "Bring him."

As the generals closed on Tal, he noticed with a start that they both wore their swords. None of his captors had come armed to the cell since the first day when Joren had taunted him with *Edyamar*. Just enough time for that realization, and then the spectres were hauling Tal up by his shoulders, dragging him between the two of them like a sack of potatoes. His flesh cringed away from the numbing spectral fingers, but compared to what he had to endure regularly now the pain seemed almost negligible.

"You should feel lucky, Talaren," Kherzul said in his hollow voice as he led the way down black corridors and up rough hewn stairs, "you get to witness history today. The conquering army of Bhellus is about to march. I'm sorry to drag you out like this; I understand you've just had a very trying night. But you're a powerful symbol after your ' Battle of the Falling Snows,' to my people as well as yours." Kherzul chuckled ominously. "Besides, under the circumstances, I think it safest to bring you out before you've a chance to recuperate from last night."

They emerged from the dungeons into the basements, and from there proceeded up to the ground floor of the Citadel. Tal watched listlessly as turnings in the hallways passed him by along with servants, their eyes downcast as their King swept past them. When they emerged from the front gates into the daylight, he had to squint his eyes almost all the way shut against the unaccustomed brightness. Even then, the light still seemed to stab at his eyes, but he wouldn't miss out on a glimpse of sunlight for any amount of pain. He filled his lungs with fresh air. It tasted strange, after so long sitting in the fetid stench of his cell.

The spectres took Tal up to the inner side of the wall by the southern gate. To either side of the gates, a set of stairs climbed up to the walkway atop the wall and the enclosure above the gate where Tal had failed to slay Kherzul. He could hear the cacophonous roar on the other side of the wall of what sounded like an enormous crowd.

Kherzul mounted the steps while his generals halted at their base with Tal between them. As Kherzul ascended, the roar beyond the wall went from confused to united in applause. After a few moments the crowd fell silent, and Kherzul's voice boomed over the square, clearly audible to Tal.

"Brave soldiers of Bhellus, today marks a grand day in the history of our great nation. Generations from now, this day will be remembered as the day that Bhellus began her reunification of the North. The day the tide finally began to turn against the chaos and decay that have eroded all the lands around us. The day we began to forge a great new nation under the benevolent protection of an immortal King. Today is the outset of the greatest undertaking of our time. The other nations will fight us, of course. So caught up are they in propping up their own failing hegemonies, they refuse to see that a strong and unified North is in their own best interests. They resist to their own detriment. We find ourselves, then, in the difficult situation of fighting against the very people we are actually fighting for. It is a hard thing to do, but it is natural for the strong and wise to thus lead the weak and foolish."

Kherzul paused, and cheers filled the gap in his speech. Once the cheers died down, the spectre King continued. "And we are strong, my loyal followers. You, our military, have long been recognized as being among the finest soldiers anywhere. Combined with the forces I have raised with the ancient wisdom I've learned, you will be unstoppable. With the dead fighting for us, we may keep our real casualties to a minimum, and you may be secure in the knowledge that the more we fight, the more powerful we shall become. We shall sweep like a wave over our enemies, gaining strength as we do until nothing may stand in our way."

"Some of you, I know, still have your doubts. The memory of the Felmorr Gap is too fresh still, of a seemingly unstoppable force being defeated by the trickery of the Snowfox, Talaren Solus. I am here today to show you how unfounded such doubts are. You already know how mightily the Snowfox resisted me. Now you shall see to what his resistance came."

Taking the cue, the spectres standing to either side of Tal dragged him up the stairs and under the enclosure. The square was filled to overflowing with armed and armored men in Bhellan red and gold, all jeering up at Talaren as he was thrown to his knees before Kherzul's crimson-draped form.

Unclothed, filthy, and covered head to toe with cuts and bruises, Tal fought past the pain and weariness that filled him to hold his back straight and his head high. "Your cause is doomed," he yelled as loudly as his parched and raw throat would let him.

One of the spectres behind Tal kicked him in the back, sending him sprawling on his face. Raucous laughter rolled up from the crowd.

Kherzul's voice cut off the mirth. "Our cause is righteous, our might peerless. None can stand in the face of our resolve. What we here begin cannot be stopped. Go forth, then, my glorious army, and reunite the North! Go, and claim your place in history!"

As the assembled soldiers erupted in cheers, Tal was seized by the shoulders again and hauled back behind the wall. Kherzul followed after several minutes of adulation from his men. He said not a word, only gestured curtly to his generals, who fell into step behind the King with their prisoner between them. The four wound their way back through the palace and down to the dungeons. Tal wished he had the strength to struggle, but realized that under the circumstances his chances of escape were non-existent. After they cast him down on the floor of his cell again, the spectral generals departed in silence. Kherzul remained behind.

"From your petty show of defiance I assume you haven't changed your mind yet."

"Nor will I ever," Tal replied from the floor. He didn't even bother to raise his head; Kherzul didn't deserve that much respect, and the effort probably would have been too great anyway.

"I do wish I could make you understand, Talaren. What I said to the men outside was absolute truth, about how the strong and wise must lead the foolish and weak. It is the nature of society. Without that leadership, humankind would still be wallowing in the mud. Your ability to interact with the Sephira shows your wisdom, and you've demonstrated your strength in both mind and body enough that I'm convinced of your value. A high place awaits you in my new kingdom, if only you will take it. I want to have you as an ally, not an enemy." The sound of Kherzul's hollow, grating voice trying to be reasonable was almost enough to make Tal laugh.

"You don't lead, Kherzul," he croaked, "you dominate, intimidate, and subjugate. In your search for ever greater strength, you've left wisdom behind. That you believe your cause just and right doesn't earn you my respect; it earns you my pity."

"Save your pity for yourself," Kherzul retorted irritably. "My time for these games grows short, Talaren, and my patience shorter yet. Would you like to know what I'll do when both run out, to you and the girl? I understand there are feelings between you and Marquess Amoran."

Tal managed to crane his neck around to glare at the indistinct shape of the King. "What's to know? You'll kill us and turn us into spectre slaves, like your so-called generals." His voice dripped with scorn.

A chilling chuckle rose from Kherzul. "Only one of you. That is the fate that awaits the Marquess should she fail to give me her allegiance."

"After all she's suffered by your hand, Kherzul, that will never happen."

"She hates me, true," Kherzul agreed, "but hate is something I understand. Hate can be used, channeled, redirected. Love is more troublesome. I believe Marquess Amoran's love for you is all that prevents me from breaking her will now. We shall see if I'm right after she witnesses what I intend for you. I have a special use for you, Talaren. You should be honored, though I doubt you'll see it that way."

"You see, that sword you so thoughtfully brought to me is far more than you imagined. Clearly you understood that it had a Sephiral presence that makes it possible for it to destroy those such as myself, but the power that weapon contains goes far beyond that. I found references to it in Anakara's notes. She spent a great deal of time studying it, and learned some very interesting things. Obviously, the sword is a relic from the times of the ancients. The Sephiral power it contains is far greater than is needed to simply injure spectres or other immaterial foes, yet that is the only unusual ability it seems to display. Anakara found that to be because the weapon is incomplete. Fortunately it has the ability to finish itself, if its bearer wills it to at the moment he takes a life with it. Once that happens, Anakara believed the sword would become a Sephiral amplifier, lending the strength of the spirits bound in it to that of its bearer. All that it needs to awaken that potential is one more soul bound into it. A single Sephiral essence absorbed into the blade, and it will grant me power unheard of in this age." Kherzul's voice adopted a sly tone. "Considering the strength of will you've demonstrated these past few months and your Sephiral abilities, I think you make an excellent candidate for that final spirit."

Tal snarled and yanked at the shackles on wrists and ankles as he tried to thrash closer to Kherzul. "Even then I'll never serve you, demon! I'll..."

"You'll do nothing." Kherzul's voice was final, the voice of judgment. "You'll be a living object, your will bound forever to that of whoever holds the blade that contains you. My will. That is the reward that awaits you for the inconvenience you've caused me. That is what will happen the next time you see me, if you continue to deny my offer of friendship. I hope it's everything you hoped for." The spectral King melded into the shadows of the cell, disappearing completely into the darkness. His laughter seemed to echo from the walls long after he was gone.

33
To Ride Into Shadow

Kyril snugged his riding gloves closer as he gazed upon the tightly packed snow in the Felmorr Gap. He shrugged his shoulders uncomfortably under the unfamiliar weight of his mail shirt. He *was* riding to battle, after all, and had deemed it wisest to don some armor for when matters inevitably got unfriendly.

As the weather began to warm and the snow to melt, the dead buried beneath it all had begun, as Tal had predicted, to dig themselves free from their icy tomb. Patrols had been set to climb around atop the perilous snow and destroy any charnel soldiers they found, but today the patrols had been reeled back in to get them out of the way.

In the strategy sessions at Val Jerak, Duke Solus had theorized that the Valerite forces would be in a much stronger position if they could reach the Bhellan end of the Gap before the enemy host had gathered. Given sufficient time, they could reinforce against the coming horde there, and hopefully attack the Bhellan units piecemeal as they arrived. Of course, that particular plan still presented the not inconsiderable difficulty of actually reaching the other side of the Felmorr when the Gap was still buried under tons upon tons of frozen debris. It had been Kyril who offered the solution to that problem.

Studying the wall of ice and snow before him, Kyril shook his head sadly to himself. He hadn't thought it would come to this. Everything had gone far from how he had expected when he departed Cardon, and what should have been a fairly straightforward mission had become horribly tangled and confused. The Guardian was still haunted by the information his contacts had dug up for him. Learning what he had, he now felt in some way responsible for the suffering that had come to the north. He had, after all, been a part of the Order's script here, if an unwitting one at first. *When this is done, when I tell him what I know, will Tal be able to forgive me? Will either of us even be there for him to be able to try?*

Kyril desperately hoped Tal and Rania still clung to life in Bhel Meravos; if they died, the personal consequences to the Guardian would pale beside those the entire world would face. Without the pair of Shevestra'ken, the coming of the Unifier would never happen. Compared to what was yet to come, Kherzul was but an annoyance. With the Unifier to lead them, mankind would at least have a chance. Without the prophesied savior, they were already doomed. Those two *had* to be alive. The Godtouched would find them when they arrived in Bhel Meravos, Kyril kept telling himself. They had begun their trek across the heights of the Felmorr Range a week gone, a full eight score of them. Establishing a Valerite presence on the eastern end of the Gap was as much about distracting the Bhellans from the Godtouched traveling to the capital as it was about gaining a strategic edge. In the final analysis, theirs was the fight that would end this war.

Kyril heard the horse ride up alongside him. "Are we ready?" Daron's voice asked him calmly.

The Jhessaillian nodded. "As ready as we'll ever be." He glanced at the three other Guardians mounted abreast of him and took a breath. "Guardians, stand ready," he said loudly. As he spoke, he reached out and took hold of the Sephira, as he knew the three with him also would be. They understood their task. Kyril waited for several breaths before speaking again. "Now."

Four identical jagged fire runes appeared in the air at the opening of the Gap, each easily as tall as the walls around Val Jerak and glowing with a gentle blue radiance. The runes seemed to merge into each other at the edges, and as more and more power was funneled into them by Kyril and his fellows, their color began to shift from the calming blue to an angry crimson. Brighter and brighter they burned, until suddenly they seemed to shatter and melt into a colossal wall of flame. In the blink of an eye, ice and snow flashed into water and then steam.

"Very good," Daron murmured, then wheeled his horse to face the host waiting behind himself and the four Guardians. "Advance!" Bellowed the Duke.

Kyril nudged his horse forward at a walk and his fellows did likewise, the wall of flames moving ahead as the Guardians maintaining it did. Behind them, ten thousand pairs of feet began to march at the same slow, steady pace. Those making this first march represented but a fraction of the might gathered at Val Jerak. The remainder would follow soon after, but for this initial foray Daron and Garant had deemed ten thousand sufficient for any unpleasant surprises that might await them on the other end of the Gap, especially considering that among that ten thousand were a hundred Guardians. The Jhessaillians were to work in shifts to create and maintain the walls of fire; shaping so much Sephiral power would be tiring, and a single team of Guardians would exhaust themselves long before the army was even a tenth of the way through the pass.

The same flames that steamed away the blockage in the Gap served a secondary purpose, one in many ways as important as clearing the way for the Valerite forces to position themselves. As the covering snow and ice were melted away, the supernatural flames hungrily consumed the bodies of the animated dead beneath, leaving behind only the occasional bits of charred bones and teeth and partially melted weaponry. The entombed legions, those who had not already freed themselves, would never join Kherzul's already bloated army. A small tactical victory, in the long view, but Valeran needed every victory she could win right at the moment. Denying the enemy thousands of troops, with a cost to Valeran's army of no lives whatsoever, was a bargain they were not likely to have the opportunity for again.

The army's pace was out of necessity kept to a snail's crawl. While the Sephiral flames blazed with a heat unknown to any natural fire, the massive volume of snow obstructing the way, piled high and deep and compacted to terrific density, gave way only so fast. The effort involved for the Guardians was immense; in little over an hour, Kyril was sweating profusely from a combination of the heat and strain. It was very shortly thereafter that the first of the other Guardians withdrew to rest, his place quickly filled by another riding up from behind.

A pace at a time the snow gave way, and slowly the entry to the Gap dwindled away behind Kyril. The second Guardian stepped back to be relieved, and then the third. Still Kyril fed his portion of the blaze, but then he was among the strongest in the entire Order. He owed his swift rise almost as much to that fact as he did to his talent for information gathering. At length, Kyril too reached the limits of his endurance and withdrew. He fell back and took up position alongside Daron Solus, riding at the head of the troops.

"You look exhausted," the Duke observed.

"Ever try carrying a mountain on your back across treacherous ground in the dark?" Kyril asked with a wry grin. "It's not too dissimilar to what I've been doing for the last few hours."

"I couldn't imagine," Daron said with a wondering shake of his head, "what it must feel like for you to channel the Sephira. Is it like that for Tal, as well, when he touches it?"

"I don't think so," Kyril mused. "I take hold of it and bend it to my will with the assistance of runic diagrams and focus implements when I need them. It's rather like trying to wrestle something with no form and no substance into the shell of an idea in my head. Talaren, as I understand it, doesn't shape or alter the Sephira so much as he attunes himself to it and becomes part of it. What I do saps my strength and tires me out. What Tal does gives him strength and vigor. I've seen him hold the Sephira from sunup to dark and into the next day. For a Guardian to do that would require strength beyond what any of us could even imagine. I doubt even Jhessail himself could have accomplished it, and he's generally recognized as having been the most powerful of us. The Shevestra'ken disciplines fall largely outside the Order's understanding of the Sephira. They are perhaps the last great wonder still alive from before the Purge."

Daron grunted in acknowledgement. "I hope those disciplines are helping Tal now."

"I'm sure they are, your Grace," Kyril said sympathetically. "I'm sure they are."

The journey to the east end of the Felmorr Gap, which normally took only a few hours to accomplish, took the army the entire day to finish. Their pace improved considerably once they reached the far end of the remains of the avalanche Kyril had triggered at the beginning of the winter and only had to melt through winter's accumulation of snow. The Bhellan end of the Gap was not undefended, of course, nor had the defenders failed to notice the ruddy glow of the wall of flames that preceded the Valerite vanguard. Perhaps two hundred men manned gates nearly identical to those on Valeran's end. Those were swept aside swiftly with the aid of several Guardians who had not been needed to assist with the clearing of the snow. As the army surged through gates cast open by invisible Sephiral battering rams, they found that the men on the wall had been but part of a force ten times as large encamped at the opening of the Gap. Though the Bhellans had a defensible position and showed considerable discipline in the fight, the greater numbers of the Valerite army and a punishing barrage of flames and lightning from the Guardians forced them into a hasty retreat after little more than a skirmish. Daron dispatched a sizable force of his light cavalry to harry the fleeing troops and in the same breath ordered his scouts out to make sure there were no other forces nearby. As the cavalry and scouts peeled off from the main body of the army, those left behind got to work.

Squads of soldiers fanned out and established a wide perimeter amongst the snow-covered hills. Tents were erected, firepits dug, lines of horses set up. Weapons were stacked neatly central to clusters of tents and men set out to gather wood from the scattered stands of trees that dotted the landscape, all with practiced military precision. The encampment seemed small in the midst of all the ground Daron had ordered his men to secure, but they were preparing the way for the greater part of the Valerite host which would begin arriving in the morning. Those Guardians not already exhausted from burning through the Gap had their own tasks, as well. Those skilled in Sephiral healing went to work among the men wounded in the brief fight with the Bhellans, mending instantly injuries that otherwise would have required weeks or months of rest and recuperation.

Kyril's talents and interests had never leaned much toward the healing arts. Having abstained from any Sephiral working since the morning, though, he felt rested enough to lend a hand again, so he found himself riding with Daron and several other Guardians as the Duke directed the other task the army had for its Jhessaillian allies.

"I want pits," Daron explained from horseback, gesturing to take in the ground just beyond the soldiers watching the perimeter. "All around the camp. As soon as we can, I'll have the men line them with stakes and hopefully we'll have time to erect a wall behind the pits, but I want to limit the avenues the Bhellans can come at us from as quickly as possible. Can you do that?"

Kyril nodded and flashed Tal's father a toothy smile. "We can do even better than that, Your Grace." He took hold of the Sephira and visualized a complex phrase of runes. All was still for a few seconds, and then the earth began slowly to stir. Soil mounded itself up, evacuating itself from the intended pit and piling up behind it. As the pit grew deeper, the growing mound of dirt began to compact itself, pressing in ever more tightly to form a hardpacked earthen wall slightly taller than a man. When the pit was finished, row upon row of sharply pointed stone barbs thrust their way out of the ground, slanting out away from the wall.

Daron rode up beside the pit and studied Kyril's handiwork in detail. He shook his head slowly and said in wonder, "You Guardians are worth more than your weight in gold to an army. Do you have any idea how incredibly useful what you just did is?"

Kyril nodded gravely. "That's precisely why we don't really call attention to it, and why those who are trained by the Order but don't join us as Guardians are forbidden from any sort of military service even though we never teach them the destructive arts."

"I hadn't heard of any such stricture," Daron noted with a raised eyebrow.

"I'd be surprised if you had," Kyril replied with a faint smile.

The Duke sighed in exasperation. "Is there anything your Order doesn't habitually try to keep secret?"

Kyril's smile withered a bit. *No, we try to keep all the damaging truths buried,* he wanted to say, *sometimes even from our own people.* Instead he tapped the side of his nose slyly and said, "We just appreciate how precious, powerful, and dangerous knowledge can be." To change the subject, he added, "I take it the wall is acceptable, then? Shall we continue to fortify in this manner?"

Daron nodded. "Yes, this is better than I could have expected." He eyed Kyril askance. "Assuming it won't tire you out too much, that is. I wouldn't want you to burn yourself out before the fighting even begins."

Kyril waved off the Duke's concern. "I'm mostly rested from the morning, and doing this is really quite easy compared to that wall of flames. The results may look impressive, but I'm really just changing what was already here, not calling into being something that wasn't. It makes a world of difference in terms of the effort involved."

Daron acquiesced, and Kyril and the other Guardians set to work clearing pits and raising walls. They worked in tandem, each raising their

296

section of the wall so it was flush with the last. The work proceeded quickly, but there was an enormous amount of ground to cover. About half the night was gone, and just under half the wall raised, when Kyril finally decided it was time to seek some rest. He imagined he could still handle the Sephira for some time yet, but he'd already had a long day and it was becoming difficult to keep his eyelids open. Before curling up in his bedroll, though, he did send several more Guardians to assist in finishing up the fortifications.

It was midmorning when Kyril awakened again to the shouts of men. At first, as he roused himself from bed, he thought the camp might be under attack, but he found when he left his tent that the commotion was due to the remainder of the Valerite host beginning to arrive. Like a titanic steel serpent they emerged from the Felmorr Gap, with King Garant riding at the head resplendent in plate and mail lacquered black and red. Cheers rose from the camp as the wizened monarch rode into their midst. Upon dismounting, Garant handed his horse off to a squire and ducked into the large tent of the command center. Kyril followed.

Inside, Duke Solus was poring over a map of the region with a handful of officers. As the King entered the tent, they all bowed.

"Rise, please," Garant murmured. "Your encampment and fortifications look excellent, Daron. My compliments to your men and the Jhessaillians for a superb job." He nodded to Kyril with his mention of the Order. "Have any of your scouts reported back yet?"

"A few, Majesty. Our short range patrols have reported a small force headed this way from the North. Their banners indicate that they originate from Bhel Femoryan, but what's especially interesting is that they also march under a flag of truce."

"A trap, perhaps?" Garant wondered aloud.

"Perhaps," Daron allowed. "I wouldn't put such trickery past Kherzul, but it doesn't feel right. They number barely more than a thousand, so there's little threat they present to a force of our size without significant additional strength. We've had no reports of any such reinforcements in the area yet. Also of note is that they're entirely composed of regular troops, no walking dead among them. Based on their last reported position, they should be here within a few hours. I advise caution, naturally, but if they seek to open a dialogue I think we should hear them out."

"Agreed," the King said. "We'll all have our fill of fighting soon enough. No reason to start early if we can avoid it."

The tent flap was pushed aside and Tazmin Joseth entered, clad in a shirt of heavy metal scales.

"Lord Tazmin," Daron greeted him, "I hadn't expected you to be here. I thought your father was leading Val Joseth's forces."

"He is," Tazmin said. "I'm here with Val Jerak's troops."

"You didn't have to come, lad," Garant said. "General Krovar could have led those men. He's a bit more experience with this sort of thing."

"I know," Tazmin murmured quietly. Then he looked up with fire in his eyes and steel in his voice. "But Tal risked everything to try ending this war without a thought for himself. What kind of friend would I be if I didn't follow his example as best I can? I came for him. It may not be much, but it's all I can do to help him."

"I understand, Tazmin," Daron said with a catch in his voice. "I'm glad my son has friends like you. It'll make me proud to have you stand with me."

Tazmin bowed to Val Solus's Duke. "Thank you, Uncle."

A short time later that day found Kyril sitting a saddle to one side of King Garant several hundred yards in front of the encampment's fortifications. On the other side of the King was Lord Tazmin, and arrayed around the three were a dozen mailed soldiers. Before them, well out of bowshot, stood the force that the scouts had reported.

The Bhellan ranks disgorged a party of equal size to the one that awaited them, which came forward at a walk with the white banner signaling truce flapping in the air above them. When they drew within twenty feet, the man at their head called out, "Lord Brant Femor requests parlay with King Garant Zherrane."

"The request is granted," responded Garant, "what would you have of me, Lord Femor?"

"I am one who would wish peace between us," announced the Lord, echoing the message that had arrived in Val Zherrane months ago. "I offer what forces I have to your cause."

"You would betray your King?" Garant asked with a raised eyebrow.

"I already have by assisting Talaren Solus," Brant replied. "My King has betrayed his lands and his people, and it is with them that my loyalty lies. Besides, I have a debt to repay."

"What debt is that?"

"That I still live means that Talaren hasn't divulged to Kherzul my role in helping him, despite the torments I'm sure he's been exposed to. Such devotion to even so poor an ally as myself demands to be observed."

Tazmin nodded proudly. "That's our Tal," he murmured.

Garant chuckled. "That young man truly is amazing. He seems unable to do anything without soon commanding the loyalty of those he comes in contact with. If you wish to join us, Lord Brant, you may do so. But if you're contemplating any sort of treachery..."

"I offer myself as hostage if you have such concerns," Brant interjected. "I just want to do what I see as right."

"That shouldn't be necessary," Garant countered. "I believe you speak honestly."

Brant turned to an officer beside him. "Major, bring the men into the encampment. Tell them to obey all Valerite officers and nobles as though they spoke with my voice." He heeled his steed forward to approach the King. "Your Majesty, the forces of Bhel Femoryan are yours to command. I offer you the hand of friendship." As Garant took the hand he held out, Brant leaned forward and said quietly, "I also have information for you."

Garant motioned for his party to withdraw back to the fortifications. "What can you tell us?" he asked as they began riding.

Brant sighed. "I wish any of the tidings I had for you were good, but I'm afraid they aren't. Before I left Bhel Femoryan, I received my marching orders from King Kherzul, and based on those I can give you an estimate of what we'll be facing here. I'm sure your scouts will confirm my approximation soon enough. Kherzul will be fielding roughly fifty to sixty thousand soldiers, but you no doubt realize that they're the smallest of your concerns. Considering the size of your encampment, I'm guessing that you could probably match such a force once all your men are in place. The problem is the dead. Kherzul's unholy generals have been crisscrossing Bhellus all winter gathering them up. One would be hard pressed to find an unmoving corpse in our lands these days. It's hard to get an accurate estimate of their numbers, but my sources in the capital insist that Kherzul has a few hundred thousand such troops. We can expect the bulk of those to be coming our way. My orders were to join up with the main body of the army, which should be arriving within the week."

"We knew we'd be dealing with overwhelming numbers here, but so many..." Garant shuddered.

"And I'm afraid there's more, on a personal note," Brant said with a sad shake of his head. "I've caught word that Lord Solus and his friend Rania Amoran are to be executed shortly. Probably about the same time we'll be joining battle. I've a handful of people within the palace and I've given them orders to do anything they can to help those two, but I honestly can't say how much they'll be able to accomplish. Access to the Shevestra'ken has been tightly restricted. Kherzul isn't taking many chances with them."

Kyril felt bile rising in his throat. Brant's operatives had better be able to do something. The Godtouched wouldn't arrive in Bhel Meravos in time, if the Lord's estimate was accurate. If Tal and Rania perished this war might yet be won, but the greater battle for the life of the world would be lost before it was joined.

34
The Sea of Despair

Kyril stood atop the earthen wall around the Valerite encampment, watching grimly as the darkness on the eastern horizon moved slowly and inexorably closer. He was but one of the Guardians who stood every twenty paces around the entire length of the wall, with archers bearing heavy quarrel-throwing crossbows between. After the demonstrated ineffectiveness of arrows on the dead at the Battle of the Falling Snows, it was hoped that the more powerful but slower-firing crossbows would prove to have a greater impact on the enemy advance.

Before the wall, rank upon rank of horsemen and infantry awaited the start of battle. Under other circumstances they would have been an intimidating force, nearly fifteen thousand strong and with many more waiting in reserve, but the battle fought today would be far from ordinary. Not since the ancient war that had led to the Great Purge had there been so large an engagement involving Sephira-wielding combatants.

Questions and doubts raced through the Guardian's mind while he waited. Did Tal still live? Rania? Had all hope disappeared beyond recall already? Would he even live long enough to find out?

Kyril's morose thoughts were interrupted by the archer beside him breathing in shock, "Gods! Is there no end to them?"

The Guardian cast a somber gaze across the approaching army. They dwarfed the size of the force that had attacked Val Jerak at winter's beginning, an undulating carpet of animate carcasses blanketing the landscape. And there was no hint yet of their back ranks coming into sight. Their ranks stretched for miles.

"We're their end, soldier," Kyril murmured, "or they ours. Let's see that it's the former and not the latter."

"Not much choice there," the archer grumbled. "I doubt there's anyplace to run from something like that."

"There's no need to run, we'll destroy them." Kyril wished he was as confident as he sounded.

"That's optimistic of you."

"Were you at the Battle of the Falling Snows?" Kyril asked.

The archer shook his head.

"I was. I saw the Snowfox win against odds nearly this bad. We can, too."

"I might feel better if he were here," the soldier replied. "I hear he's for the chop soon, though."

"I know Talaren Solus," Kyril said. "He won't die easily and he won't die alone." He hoped. "Do you know why?"

"No. Why's that?"

"Because he never gives up. He'll fight to his last breath, and even then I won't believe him dead until I see the body."

"You've a great deal of faith in him."

"I've a great deal of faith in the Jhessaillian Prophecy. The Snowfox isn't fated to die now, and we're not fated to lose here." Empty words to one who understood how prophecy truly worked, but they had their desired effect.

The archer drew his back up straight and set his jaw resolutely. "Well if that's the case, let's send these things back to the hell that spawned them."

Kyril nodded approvingly. "That's the attitude that'll get you through this alive. May your aim be true."

"Hard to miss when there's so many targets. Fry a few of the bastards for me."

"How about more than a few?"

"Fine by me," the archer laughed.

It was almost time. The dead were nearly close enough.

"Guardians, stand by!" Kyril yelled. He took hold of the Sephira along with his brethren.

The role that Duke Solus had assigned the Guardians in his strategy was to use the wanton destruction they unleashed to carve the enemy into manageable chunks for the Valerite forces to engage and obliterate. Kyril selected a point several ranks back in the enemy advance for his first strike. His brothers would then target their own attacks based on his.

Kyril visualized his rune forms, and a swirling ball of flame exploded amidst the shambling corpses. Of the various destructive forces, he had always been most comfortable with fire.

Before Kyril's fireball had finished expanding, chaos erupted amongst the dead hordes as the other Guardians released their powers. Snaking lines of fire seared necrotic flesh and bone to cinders, ball lightning hurtled through the ranks of corpses, wreaking havoc, and upthrust spikes of rock sprang from the earth to impale their victims and impede the Bhellan advance. Spinning maelstroms of ice hurled jagged lances that exploded on impact into glittering razor-sharp shards, and bodies detonated seemingly of their own accord as healers inverted their arts to destroy flesh rather than mend it.

A horn sounded below, and Valeran's soldiers surged forward with a roar to attack the unhindered Bhellan front ranks. They met with a colossal crash, the heavy cavalry bursting through the Bhellan lines and wheeling their mounts to attack from behind while the infantry engaged the front.

The dead marched on heedless of the destruction being wrought on them. They hurled themselves upon the spears of stone, piling up bodies which those behind climbed over. Even the elemental fury commanded by the Guardians succeeded only at slowing their single-minded push forward.

The second wave of dead reached the Valerite forces before they had quite finished off the first. As the fighting intensified, Kyril and the other Guardians redoubled their efforts to hold back the main advance. Steel clashed on steel, bone talons rended at flesh, Sephiral devastation filled the air, and the field rapidly became a wasteland of carrion. So it continued for hours, the seemingly infinite swarms of dead pushing relentlessly on, claiming ground a few yards at a time while Valeran and her allies struggled to stem the tide.

With the fourth wave it became necessary to commit a portion of the reserves to the field. Guardians around the continuous wall lowered several sections of it, filling in the pits before them with the displaced earth, to allow the reinforcements to ride out before once more raising the fortifications.

The constant shaping of the Sephira began to exhaust many of the Jhessaillians. They retired from the wall to rest and recover while fresh Guardians took their places. Kyril himself was beginning to feel the strain from creating conflagration after conflagration, but he stubbornly refused to step down from his position. He set his jaw and resolutely continued to weave destruction.

Eventually the fighting moved close enough to bring the crossbows into play. Flights of quarrels arched over allies to pepper the dead. Though still not as effective as sword or mace or axe, their impacts proved far better than arrows had been at knocking body parts from the animated dead. The archer by Kyril's side emptied quiver after quiver as the Bhellan formations drew closer, ever closer.

By the time night was beginning to fall, Kyril had come to a dismaying realization. *We're going to run out of space before we run out of strength.* The walls around the Valerite encampment were a daunting impediment, but Kyril had no doubts that they'd eventually be breached by the Bhellans' costly but effective tactic of simply piling up corpses until an obstacle could be climbed over. Once that happened, the inability to maneuver freely would severely handicap Valeran's men. Their defeat could not but follow soon after that happened.

Fortunately it appeared that Duke Solus had come to a similar conclusion, for when Kyril spared a glance back he saw that there were already men taking up position on the wall within the Gap to provide a fallback point. The situation was dire, but perhaps not yet beyond retrieval.

One other thing gnawed at Kyril, a detail that seemed at first heartening. None of the Valerite dead had yet begun to reanimate. But that begged the question: if not raising corpses, what was Kherzul doing? There had been no indication thus far of his Sephiral arts being employed, and that made the Guardian nervous. Surely the necromancer had a plan, but what could it be?

No time to speculate, though. The battle still raged at a fever pitch. Drenched in sweat from the exertion, Kyril summoned another column of flame.

For what must have been the twelfth time, Tazmin resettled the shirt of scale mail on his shoulders, full of nervous energy. It was almost time for him and his men to ride out into that ocean of death on the other side of the walls, along with his father and Lord Brant and the forces they commanded. The bulk of the Valerite army was beginning to withdraw into the Gap, and it fell to Tazmin and company to provide the extra force to hold the Bhellans long enough to cover the shift in positions.

"Relax, son," Baron Remarr said beside him. "Just hit anything that comes within reach of you till it stops moving and you'll be fine."

"I'm just worried about Tal," Tazmin lied.

"He'll be fine," Brant said from the Baron's other side. "My people will find a way to help him."

"I thought you said you weren't sure they could?"

"I'm not," the Bhellan Lord admitted, "but you have to keep believing. If you don't, it's the same as giving up on him."

Tazmin nodded. "You're right." He laughed hesitantly. "Tal promised me in the letter he left that we'd have a drink together once this was all over, and he never breaks his promises."

Brant smiled. "If you don't mind, I may want to join you two for that. I didn't have much time to get to know him, but Talaren seemed a good sort to be friends with."

"He's the best," Tazmin agreed, "and his sweetheart, Rania, isn't so bad either, once you get used to her temper."

"She came within inches of going to war with my entire household guard when she thought I'd captured her and Talaren for Kherzul," Brant commented. "From what I saw, she just might have won, too."

"That sounds like her, to be sure."

"I'm sure we'll all see them both again soon," Remarr murmured. "We just have to finish saving the North first."

"All in a day's work," Tazmin laughed. Looking at the faces of his companions, the grim set of their jaws, the creases about their eyes, he realized that they had all been trying to comfort one another though none felt as hopeful as their words might suggest. "I remember something Tal told me once," he said. "He was talking about the Shevestra'ken oaths and how there's one part of them he particularly liked. 'I am the candle that holds the night at bay.' He said it means that a single light, no matter how weak, is all it takes to keep back the darkness. So long as you hold that fire in you and never let it go out, you don't have to fear the night. With all the candles we've got here, Kherzul doesn't have a prayer."

The wall before them glowed briefly and melted back into the earth as a Guardian opened the way for them. It was time.

"Well then," Baron Remarr said, "let's go hold back some darkness. Since our Battleborn friends aren't here to, I'll say the words for them: may Shevestra favor your blades this night."

Tazmin looked to the sky as he nudged his horse forward after his father. With the day's light gone he could see striated clouds of sapphire blue Sephiral energy hovering over the field, wisps of which would detach themselves before coalescing into the fire or ice or lightning the Guardians directed against the enemy. It was one of the most beautiful sights Tazmin had ever beheld, and at the same time one of the most terrifying.

"I'm thinking of you, Tal," he murmured skyward. "I hope your light hasn't gone out."

They rode out through the opening and into the night, turning the formations of men following them eastward after clearing the barrier. Tazmin shuddered as he surveyed the battle he was about to join. If the hells of the underworld were real, surely he gazed upon them now. Armored men hacked and hewed at an ocean of semi-human creatures of nightmare amidst a constant flicker of fire and lightning that cast the brutal struggle into stark relief. Bodies lay everywhere, some trampled into unrecognizability, others piled up in mounds where it was impossible to discern which parts belonged to what corpse.

Tazmin became sharply aware of the cacophony that had seemed like background noise on the other side of the wall. The clash of steel mingled with the cries of the dying punctuated by the rumble of thunder, with the roar of flames and the soft hissing of ice maelstroms for a background. *The Song of the Damned,* he couldn't help but think. *Curse my ears for ever hearing such a thing!*

"The One have mercy," Tazmin breathed, "The Lords of Frost keep us whole and the Lost Ones stand watch over our souls. Shevestra grant us strength and courage." He'd never had much use for religion, but he thought he might have just found one. If he'd known of any other Gods to call to for aid, he would have.

"Amen," Remarr said. Then he raised his Sephirally-worked battle axe, an heirloom of House Joseth, over his head and bellowed, "For Valeran, the North, and the light, charge!"

They hurtled forward. For terrifying seconds Tazmin watched the gap between himself and the enemy closing, and then they were amongst the dead. The momentum of their charge carried them deep into the enemy ranks, mounts' hooves crushing bodies as they bulled their way into the midst of the walking dead.

Tazmin laid about himself with his sword, blood racing and pounding in his ears. Adrenaline coursed through his body, lending him strength and speed to batter down corpse after corpse as he fought like a man possessed. To his one side Lord Brant's blade flickered like a serpent's tongue, striking off upraised arms seeking to pull him down from the saddle. To the other Baron Remarr cackled like a madman, the wicked axe clutched in his hand splitting skulls with ease as he marauded gleefully about.

The three noblemen acted like a spearhead for the troops they led, opening the way to dig deeper and deeper into the enemy ranks. Time seemed to disappear for Tazmin. He drifted through an everpresent now, the only thoughts in his mind being the nearest enemy and the words that repeated in his head like a mantra. *Keep moving, keep cutting, kill anything that comes close to you.*

The initial burst of frenzied energy from their entering the fray eventually wore off, and still they fought on. There was no other choice. There were always three more enemies waiting after the next, and the slightest pause to rest could bring swift death.

A rusted blade managed to sneak in past Brant's guard to open a long gash down his leg. The Lord yelled angrily with the pain of his injury even as he smote down another foe to the other side. Before Brant could turn to face his attacker, Tazmin rode down the corpse and split it down the torso with a mighty overhead blow. The Bhellan Lord flashed him a tight smile of thanks from behind the bars of his helmet.

Remarr continued his mad rampage, cleaving through everything in his path. He was famed throughout Valeran for the might of his battle rage; It had served him well in the Bhellan Revolution, and tonight it did so once again.

From the midst of the Bhellan horde rode a night-black figure atop a rotting carcass of a steed, bearing down on the enraged Baron. Tazmin's breath caught in his throat at recognition of the countenance of a spectre, and one intent on his father.

Remarr turned to face the dark minion, and the instant it was within his reach he swung his battle axe at it with all his might. The blow was well-aimed, and the axe's blade tore through the spectre's helm to send the top half spinning off into the night. Baleful red eyes glared from the ruined helm, and Remarr's backswing was met by the spectre's sword, severing his arm just below the elbow. Baron Joseth's axe fell to the ground along with his forearm.

"Father!" Tazmin screamed. He knew he couldn't harm the spectre, but he refused to stand by and watch his father be slaughtered. He spurred his mount at Kherzul's general and leapt from the saddle while the spectre's arm was drawing back to deliver the killing blow.

Tazmin's lungs constricted as numbing cold rushed into him at his collision with the nightmarish foe. He knocked the creature from its saddle and the two tumbled to the ground together. Tazmin landed on top, and he lunged out to clamp both hands around the spectre's sword arm and hold it to the ground, crying out at the numbing iciness. He could swear that the blood was freezing solid in his veins.

The spectre's free hand snaked down to draw a dagger from its swordbelt and it slammed the blade into Tazmin's shoulder, kicking with the impact of the strike to send the nobleman sprawling on his back.

Tazmin scrabbled back as the spectre got to its feet, desperately seeking a way to defend himself. His left arm was useless from pain with the dagger still protruding from his shoulder, and he had dropped his sword in his leap from the saddle. His right hand found the broken-off end of a spear and grasped it, holding the pitiful weapon before him like a talisman.

An ominous laugh emanated from the spectre as it advanced menacingly on him. "Just another frail mortal," it taunted as it raised its weapon.

35
Blades of Fate

"This is the last time I'll see you," the torturer said to Tal as he cleaned the blade he'd just been plying his trade with on a dirty rag. "I suppose I should congratulate you for not being broken after the months you've been in my care, but the truth is that I'm quite disappointed to have you taken from me." He wiped his bloody hands absent-mindedly on the rag and tucked it back in his pocket. "At least I can console myself with the indulgence I'm to be granted. Tonight, after she's watched you die, the girl will be brought to me again if she doesn't swear loyalty to King Kherzul. His Majesty has removed all strictures from me for that session, including the one that says she has to survive. He wants her to suffer a long and lingering death, and I'm quite excited with such a request. I'm terribly looking forward to finding out just how much one of you can endure before it becomes too much for the body to withstand. It's a pity, really, that I can't have both of you, but that's just my selfishness speaking."

Through the haze of his agony, Tal glared daggers at the repulsive creature. "You'll never have her," he croaked.

The beady-eyed little man chuckled. "I'm afraid you don't have much say about that. None, in fact." He glanced over to the door as the bar was raised gratingly. "Looks like your escort is here to take you to the King. Farewell, Talaren Solus. You've been an uncooperative and obnoxious subject. I hope your passing is an especially painful one." He turned and began replacing his implements on their racks, humming to himself.

Tal kept staring hate at the torturer's back without sparing a look for the spectre that had come to take him to his execution. Maybe there was one last thing he could do for Rania before the end came. It was a small mercy, but it was the best Tal could manage. He carefully judged the distance to his sadistic tormentor. He would only have one chance, and the possibility of failure frightened him far more than any consequences he would face. After all, it might be for the best if he incited his captors to kill him before Kherzul was able to carry out his designs.

He felt the icy grip around his wrist as the first manacle was snapped on before the chain binding that same arm down was released to allow the spectre to chain his other wrist to the first.

"Hey, friend," Tal called to the torturer.

The torturer turned around with a questioning look, and his movement brought him a few inches closer. Close enough.

Tal pulled in more of the Sephira than he had ever before dared, letting his hatred for this wretched excuse of a human being buffer his sense of self against the scathing torrent. He used all that power to buttress weakened muscles and heaved himself from the spectre's grip, throwing his body across the torture table and swinging his manacled arm around in a broad arc with all his strength.

Shock flashed across the torturer's face for an instant, and then the open cuff on the loose end of the chain slammed into the side of his head with a wet crack. The man's legs went to rubber and he collapsed in a heap. Blood began slowly to pool on the floor beneath him.

The spectre hauled Tal back and brutally backhanded him across the face before again focusing its attention on his restraints.

Through the rough treatment, Tal managed a wracking laugh. "I told you you'd never have her." He realized there were tears in his eyes.

"Are you ready to see your hope's end?"

Rania looked up reproachfully as Joren entered her cell followed by another spectre. They carried no torches so the only light source was the glow of their eyes, but Joren was easy enough to identify by his habitually mocking tone.

"This is going to be a good night," Joren chortled. "We're going to go now and watch Talaren's death. You should thank Kherzul for allowing you two to see each other this one last time."

"I'd thank him more to let me see you die," Rania retorted.

"I'm afraid you arrived a bit late for that," Joren said airily, "but I'm sure it would have satisfied you. It was quite unpleasant. But, oh, what it gained me!" His voice took on a slyly insinuating tone. "And tonight I'll get to handle your disposal, since Tal went and killed our best torturer when he threw a tantrum a short while ago. It won't be as satisfying for me as killing Tal would be, but I suppose I'll just have to settle for the woman he loves."

"Are you really so bitter about how much better than you he is?" Rania asked angrily.

That struck a nerve. Joren kicked her savagely to the floor. "Shut up! If he's so much better, how come I won in the end?"

Rania spat blood on the floor. "This isn't over quite yet, Joren."

"No, it's not," the spectre agreed, "but it will be soon. Let's go."

Joren's companion hauled Rania up by the chain that bound her hands together before her and half led, half dragged her out of the cell with Joren following behind. They took her up through the Citadel by corridors strangely devoid of guards or serving staff until they reached a pair of tall double doors. Two guards in red and gold, the first living people Rania had seen in the entire trip up from the dungeons, stood to either side of the door.

"We're not to be disturbed for any reason until we're finished," Joren said to the guards.

308

"Yes, his Majesty already told us," one of them replied. The other opened one of the doors, and Rania was shoved through into Kherzul's throne room.

Tal was chained with arms spread against the wall, his head lolling forward against his chest. He was naked, filthy, and covered with barely healed cuts, burns, and abrasions. Greasy, tangled hair hung over his face. A few paces in front of him stood Kherzul, *Kallevamar* cradled carefully in his arms.

The spectre King turned his head her way as Rania staggered into the room. "Welcome, Marquess, to the celebration of my impending victory."

Rania ignored him, her eyes locked on Tal. She reached out to him with the Sephira, letting it flow through her to him. Almost immediately upon the Sephiral aura flickering alight around him, he groaned, head stirring.

"Tal!" Rania cried.

He raised his head, eyes blearily coming into focus as he took hold of the Sephira for himself. A faint smile crossed his face. "Rania, my love," he rasped. He looked past her, and strangely his smile broadened when his gaze touched Joren. "I'm afraid it looks like we're just about out of options."

"That's the wisest thing I've heard you say in months, Talaren," Kherzul chuckled. When Rania had been carried to about twenty paces from Tal, Kherzul raised a hand to his minions. "I think that's close enough. We wouldn't want to present the Marquess an opportunity to try anything foolish."

The spectres accompanying Rania held her in place by the shoulders. The cold of their touch spread down through her arms, but she paid it barely any mind. Tal was here, in the same room as her, and that was what mattered. And unless she mistook herself, she thought she felt a faint sense of hope coming from him through their bond.

"At last you've reached the end, my stubborn friends," Kherzul announced. "You might be interested to know that my forces joined battle against Valeran earlier today. Your friends have been putting up a valiant struggle, but just like you they're about to discover the futility of resisting me." He rumbled with a malicious laugh. "I hope you appreciate the irony here, Talaren. You were the deciding factor in my loss at Val Jerak, and now you're going to become the key to my victory in this battle. Once your soul awakens the Blade of the Accursed, your friends will be the first to taste the extent of my new power."

"Kherzul, hold," Tal said. His eyes were clear now and there was in his voice a note of command. "You win. I'll swear to obey you."

"Tal, no!" Rania yelled.

He turned his eyes to her. His gaze was piercing, demanding her attention. "Quiet, Rania. I'm doing this for you. For the both of us." He looked back at Kherzul. "I swear on the honor of the Shevestra'ken to serve and obey you in all things if you'll let Rania go. Order Joren to give her sword back right now and let her walk out of here, and you'll have yourself a Shevestra'ka for a liegeman." He met Rania's gaze again, and now his eyes were pleading.

Rania nodded once, slowly, that she understood. Glancing from the corner of her eye, she saw that Joren did indeed wear her blade. *Edyamar* was but a few feet away.

Kherzul chuckled. "It's too late for that, Talaren, and your conditions are unacceptable anyway. I'll thank you, though, for having finally let me hear you plead for your lives. I'd thought you were made of sterner stuff." He raised *Kallevamar*. "I've waited too long for this power, and I'll not be put off now." A Sephiral glow seemed to seep from *Kallevamar's* blade, a midnight blue so deep as to be nearly black.

Tal's aura flared like the sun as Kherzul approached him slowly and deliberately, and he channeled everything he held to Rania. The extra energy seemed to crackle through her, dimming the pain and weakness from her months of imprisonment and torture.

Rania lunged suddenly downward and to the side, tearing free from the spectres' grips as she reached across Joren's body with her bound hands. Sephiral celerity would give her a small amount of time, maybe half a second or so, before they could react to her. She hoped it would be enough.

Her hands found *Edyamar's* hilt and she pulled it from the sheath, twisting with the motion of the draw towards Kherzul, who was just beginning to turn to see what the commotion was.

Joren smashed Rania to the floor with a gauntleted fist between her shoulderblades, but *Edyamar* had already left her grip an instant prior.

The Blade of Unity spun sideways through the air, a shining brand of hope amidst the darkness that had swallowed Tal and Rania's world. Rania's aim had been imperfect in her haste, but it was close enough. The blade spun past Kherzul, the last couple inches of its tip dipping through his side and opening a small tear in his robe with its passage.

The necromancer began to laugh, but the laughter was cut off by a pained grunt. Kherzul looked at his side, where dark mist was steaming out from where the blade had scored him, then his gaze darted to the sword lying on the floor beside the wall.

"There were two blades, Kherzul," Tal said, eyes hard and voice even harder. "You've just been cut by *Edyamar*."

"What?!" Kherzul snarled. "No! I was to be immortal! I was to rule the world! I..." He tottered toward Tal with *Kallevamar* raised, but coordination was swiftly leaving him as the energies that composed his body bled off.

"You were a pawn of the Order, just as we have been," Tal said sadly. "And now your part in their game is finished. Time to leave the board. If it's any consolation, I don't intend to play by their rules anymore. I doubt Rania does, either."

Kallevamar fell from Kherzul's grip, its blade fading once more to quiescence. He looked up at Tal with rapidly dimming eyes. "What are you?" His voice was distant, as if it emanated from some immense deep gulf. He struggled to pull himself from the floor one last time and then his substance completely disintegrated, his robe and crown falling to the ground.

"I don't know," Tal murmured. "I'm Shevestra'ka, and that's enough for me."

"Talaren, you bastard!" Joren howled. With Kherzul's destruction, his own body was beginning to dissipate, boiling out from the cracks in his armor. On the other side of Rania's prone form, the other spectre was struggling to free its blade from the sheath, but didn't seem to have the strength to do so. Seconds later all that remained of the two were a pair of empty suits of armor.

"Hey," Tal called gently to Rania, "please tell me you're alright."

She raised her head, and tears glistened on her cheeks. "I hurt, Tal, but I'll live. We did it! My parents' ghosts can finally rest." The last was a wondering whisper.

"You did it," Tal corrected. "I was busy being chained here. It was your hand that struck down Kherzul."

Rania shook her head. "No, it was both of us. I'd not have known what to do if you hadn't managed to let me know that Joren had *Edyamar*. And I couldn't have done it without the strength you gave me. We both did it."

Tal smiled down at her, tears of joy making tracks in the grime on his face. "I'm glad I could help you, after all. I love you, Rania."

"I love you, too, Tal. I wish I was strong enough to get you down from there."

"Someone will come along eventually. I'm not sure what will happen then, but I guess it doesn't much matter. The North is safe again."

They wept together in relief, and waited.

Tazmin breathed heavily as he watched the spectre closing on him. He knew he was about to die, and there didn't seem to be a damn thing he could do about it. His eyes fixed defiantly on the creature that was about to end his life. *I may die,* he told himself, *but at least I'll face it like a warrior.* He gritted his teeth in anticipation of the final blow.

Not three paces away from Tazmin, the spectre stopped, a shudder running through its body. It wavered and staggered back a step.

Tazmin looked up at it in confusion. Dark mist was seeping from the spectre's armor, and the point of its blade dropped down as though the creature could no longer hold it up. The spectre fell to its knees, and then its ornate armor crashed empty to the ground.

Tazmin cast his gaze about disbelievingly. All around him, across the entire field as far as he could tell, the dead were toppling over, lifeless corpses once again. The nobleman's mind raced. Kyril had said that the Godtouched shouldn't be reaching Bhel Meravos yet for a week at the least. Though he admitted to himself that his thinking probably wasn't at its clearest, Tazmin could only grasp one possibility.

"He did it," he whispered. He laughed hesitantly, half-afraid that his verbalizing it would negate what his eyes told him. When the bodies failed to get back up, Tazmin's laughter became almost hysterical, the pain in his shoulder forgotten momentarily.

Horns were sounding across the field. For what, Tazmin wasn't sure, nor did he care. He was sure of one thing, and it was the only thing of any importance.

"Tal did it!" he yelled exultantly. "Kherzul is slain!"

36
An Empty Throne

Tal and Rania didn't have long to wait in the throne room after Kherzul's demise before being discovered. Within a few minutes there was a timid knock at the door and when it wasn't answered the door cracked open.

"Your Majesty," a messenger said tremulously as he poked his head in, "a thousand apologies for disturbing you, but your legions outside the city have..." He gasped as his eyes fell upon Kherzul's robe and crown, and he bolted back out of the room, the door slamming behind him.

Almost immediately there was a great clamor in the hall outside, and soon after the doors were thrown open to admit the guards who had stood in the hall outside.

"Gods above," one of them breathed in disbelief. He looked at his companion with wild eyes. "What do we do?"

The other shook his head. "I don't know. I say we wait for an officer to get here and give us orders. Let any consequences come down on his head, not ours."

"Right," the other one nodded. He looked at Tal. "You, prisoner, what happened here?"

"Just what it looks like," Tal replied. "We destroyed your abomination of a King."

"An admission of guilt, given freely from the perpetrator's mouth," declared a Captain as he strode into the room followed by a double column of twenty guardsmen. "Kill them."

"No, wait!" yelled another officer, this one with the insignia of a Lieutenant on his breast, as he ran breathless into the room. "Belay that order!" He darted forward to stand between the Shevestra'ken and the guardsmen, facing his comrades with arms held out to either side.

The Captain glared angrily at the lesser officer. "You're out of order, Lieutenant! Stand aside!"

"That may be so, sir, but please hear me out," replied the Lieutenant. "I'm trying to keep you from making a tragic mistake."

"Explain," the Captain ordered tersely.

The Lieutenant nodded gratefully. "Thank you, sir. King Kherzul is dead, the line of Meravos ended, and Kherzul's legions have returned to the grave with him. The war is over, or will be soon. These two may have slain our sovereign, but they're heroes in Valeran and of noble blood besides. If we kill them out of hand, the Valerites may well continue the war in retaliation. I don't know about you, but I'm not at all sure we can stand against the might they gathered to fight Kherzul. At the very least, they need a trial, and a crime of this magnitude requires the King to stand as judge, once the nobles determine who is to assume the throne now. Do you really want to issue an order that may bring ruin to Bhellus?"

"We both swear in the name of Shevestra that we'll submit to such a trial," Tal volunteered.

Rania had pulled herself up to a sitting position beside Tal against the wall, and she nodded. "Yes we do, on the honor of the Shevestra'ken. You surely know that such an oath, once given, cannot be broken."

The Captain frowned, and then sighed. "I don't like it, but you may be right, Lieutenant. Have quarters prepared for these two appropriate to their station. They are to be afforded every courtesy possible, except in that they are to be confined to their rooms and placed under guard. For their own protection, of course."

"One set of rooms," Tal said. "You can double the guard on it if you like, but we won't be separated again."

"First give me your oath that you won't conspire together to escape justice for your acts," the Captain demanded.

"You have it," Tal said.

"Agreed," echoed Rania.

"Very well." The Captain turned to address his men and gestured at Tal. "Get him down from there."

"I suppose it's too much to ask that our blades be returned to us?" Tal asked as a pair of guards began unfastening the chains on his arms.

"It is, for now," the Captain replied. "That will be determined at your trial. If it means that much to you, I can promise that your weapons will be held secure in storage. I'll allow you to inspect them periodically if you keep your word in good faith."

"That'll be acceptable. Thank you, Captain."

The officer nodded grudgingly.

A short while later, after robes had been brought for them to cover themselves, the Lieutenant who had saved them escorted Tal and Rania to the room that had been prepared for them.

On the way through the hallways of the Palace the Lieutenant said quietly, "Lord Solus, Marquess Amoran, I'm in the employ of Lord Brant Femor, and in his name I'd like to thank you for removing Kherzul. I had orders to aid you any way I could, and I apologize for not having been able to intervene until I did. If it will make it up to you, I can try to help you escape the Palace."

Tal shook his head. "That won't be necessary. We gave our word, and we intend to honor it. You helped when you could, and when we needed it, and for that you've our gratitude. There's no debt to be settled as far as I'm concerned."

314

"Well, if you change your mind or if there's anything else I can do for you, let me know. My name is Lorek."

"Thank you, Lieutenant Lorek," Rania smiled, "but right now I think all we want is a bath, a decent meal, and several days' rest in a real bed."

"Oh, yes," Tal agreed fervently.

Lorek laughed sheepishly. "After what you've been through, that's not surprising. I'll see if I can get a healer brought to you as well."

A healer was indeed sent to tend them, a very talented one with Order training by the name of Orlen. His gentle ministrations mended the hurts to Tal and Rania's bodies from their ordeal in short order, but there were other deeper and less apparent wounds about which he could do nothing.

Aside from the ravages of confinement and malnutrition that could only be mended by food, exercise, and time, Tal and Rania's experience had left both scarred emotionally. They frequently awoke screaming and thrashing in the middle of the night from nightmares of their imprisonment and torture. Occasionally while waking one or the other would be overwhelmed by what had happened to them, and during these times they turned to each other for support and reassurance. Though neither was comfortable talking about the specifics of their experiences, each knew that the other understood as nobody else could as they sought solace in one another's presence and embrace.

There was a single exception to their not talking about the details of their imprisonment. Tal told Rania about his last encounter with the torturer, whose name neither had ever been told nor wanted to know. He told her because he hoped that hearing the account of how the beady-eyed little sadist met his end would help her as much as the retelling of it did him.

"It's good to know I don't have to worry about that fiend roaming free in the world," Rania said when Tal reached the point in his tale with the torturer lying in a pool of his own blood with a shattered skull.

Within the week, several dozen Godtouched arrived in Bhel Meravos, and a few were allowed to visit the Shevestra'ken. By that point Tal and Rania were both beginning to look a bit less emaciated, and their storms of depression, hopelessness, and unreasoning terror were becoming more infrequent, if still not completely abating.

The Jhessaillians were naturally full of questions, most of which Tal refused to answer. He pleaded that the experience was too painful to revisit, which was partially true, but his primary motivation lay in that he could think of no way to explain Kherzul's destruction without bringing *Edyamar* into the story. Even were it not for his promise to keep it secret for Rania, he had too many doubts about the Order at the moment to share that piece of information with any of them.

After repeating the same questions over and over and getting the same refusals every time, the Godtouched acceded to Tal's desire not to discuss what had happened in the throne room. Rania, unsurprisingly, was no more cooperative.

In the face of such a frosty reception, the Godtouched were surprisingly helpful. They readily volunteered what news they had from Valeran prior to their departure, and Tal was informed that they had lodged a formal request on behalf of the Order for his and Rania's immediate release. Despite his reservations, Tal had to admit to himself that they appeared to be acting with the best of intentions. And he found it of particular interest that according to those he spoke with, a full one hundred and sixty Godtouched had been sent with orders to secure his and Rania's safety by any means. It appeared that he had a great deal to talk with Kyril about when he saw the Guardian again.

Almost two weeks later, another visitor came to them. Tal was sitting and reading a book while Rania meditated in the next room when the knock sounded at the door.

"Yes?" Tal asked curiously. He hadn't been expecting anyone for some hours yet, when servants brought up the evening meal.

The door opened, and standing in it was a grinning Lord Brant. Even more surprising than his presence was that he had Tal and Rania's sheathed swords with him.

"It's good to see you again, Talaren," Brant said as he stepped into the room and proffered *Kallevamar* to the Shevestra'ka.

Tal eyed the blade and looked up at Brant without taking it. "Is this another offer of assistance in escaping? If it is, I can't accept."

Brant laughed. "Yes, yes, word of honor and all that. Lorek told me all about it. No, Tal, it's not an escape attempt. The new Regent, in his inestimable wisdom, has granted you and Rania a full pardon, and even given you both a commendation for saving Bhellus from Kherzul's madness."

Rania, roused from her meditation, walked into the room. "And who is this new Regent? We haven't heard anything about anyone being chosen yet."

Brant smiled like the proverbial fox in the henyard. "Well, he wanted to tell you himself."

"You?" Tal asked with a raised eyebrow. He took *Kallevamar* from Brant's hands. "I think you've got a story for us as well, my friend."

Brant walked over to Rania and handed *Edyamar* off to her before responding. "It all began when in a fit of altruistic insanity, which I blame on you two, incidentally, I took all of my men who were willing to follow and

316

joined up with your nation's forces to fight Kherzul. I'm sure you're curious, so before you ask, your father and Lord Tazmin Joseth were both there, and both are currently alive and well."

"When the dead keeled over all at once in the middle of battle, it wasn't terribly difficult for anyone to guess what had happened, and my remaining countrymen on the field suddenly found themselves badly outmatched. They offered surrender almost immediately, and I volunteered to mediate negotiations for the terms. Kherzul had a handful of holdout loyalists, but for the most part the Bhellan nobility present were coming out of the woodwork to distance themselves from his acts. They're the ones I owe my unanticipated advancement to, because once we turned to the matter of selecting a new leader, they united in endorsing me for my 'moral and ethical leadership' in being the first and only Bhellan noble to openly defy Kherzul with military force. Personally, I find the whole situation rather absurd. An act which I had been certain would prove to be political suicide looks now like it may end up putting me on the throne. I need the confirmation of a full assembly of the noble Houses first, so in the meantime I'm only Regent."

"My congratulations," Tal murmured. "I think you'll make an excellent King."

"Yes, well, that remains to be seen," Brant replied modestly. "Right now, my biggest concern is that those loyalists of Kherzul's that I mentioned might try to prevent my coronation by eliminating me before the Houses can confirm me. Bhel Meravos probably isn't the safest place for me at the moment. Truth be told, I'd not have come back if it weren't for my having to set matters right between us. Fortunately, I've an affair of state that I should really attend, and now a pair of travelling companions who I wouldn't hesitate to trust with my life. After all, I'm sure you'll want to be present for the event as well. We'll depart in the morning."

"Affair of state?" Tal asked.

"Why, yes, you hadn't heard?" Brant asked in mock surprise. "The ceremony officially announcing King Garant's heir apparent. He intends to adopt Duke Solus, your father, as his son."

37

Blood of Heroes

Tal and Rania's journey back to Val Jerak in the company of Brant and a contingent of guardsmen from Bhel Femoryan passed uneventfully. Spring was truly beginning to take hold now. The air was pleasantly warm and filled with the songs of newly returned migratory birds, the land fresh with new growth and the budding of plants. The world seemed alive with signs of new beginnings.

Both of the Shevestra'ken still suffered from bouts of morose introverted reflection and nightmares in which they relived their torment. They continued to improve, and faster now that they were free, but the progress was still slow overall. Tal imagined it would be a long time yet, perhaps never, before they could put it entirely behind them. Luckily, Brant was wise enough not to bother them when the dark moods overtook them. The sympathy in his eyes at such times clearly announced that he wished he could help, but his silence revealed that he knew he could never wholly understand their pain. That tacit acknowledgement, in fact, was the most help he could offer in this case.

There were still signs of the battle that had taken place when they reached the Felmorr Gap, churned earth and scattered bits of armor or weapons that had been missed in the cleanup. And then there were the dozens of glassy patches of ground, charred at the edges, where the dead had been given to the flames. Jhessaillian-conjured flames, unless Tal missed his guess.

They paused on the battlefield at the request of Tal and Rania, who went together to kneel in silent reverence for several minutes where one of the pyres had stood.

"I'm sorry," Tal whispered before leaving. "We tried to stop this. I'm sorry we weren't fast enough to save you all." He hoped the dead would understand.

Their passage through the Gap didn't go unnoticed, for when they arrived at Val Jerak's eastern gate, Tazmin was waiting for them.

"Tal!" he yelled as he ran toward them waving. "Rania! Thank the Gods you're back! I'm so glad to see you two again!"

"Tazmin," Tal nodded with a smile. Noticing the axe riding on Tazmin's hip in place of a sword, he asked sadly, "Or should I call you Baron now?"

"No," Tazmin shook his head. "My father's alive. He nearly died of blood loss but the Jhessaillians managed to patch him up again, just minus a hand. He gave me the family axe since he can't wield it anymore, and in recognition for my saving his life." Tazmin blushed and looked downward. "Even though it was probably the stupidest thing I've done in my life, tackling a spectre. Bloody thing would have gutted me like a fish if you hadn't done for Kherzul when you did."

"Then you should be thanking Rania, not me," Tal said. "I helped a little, but she's the one who actually killed Kherzul."

Tazmin flashed his usual flippant grin and dropped an overly elaborate bow to Rania. "Marquess Rania Amoran, Lord Tazmin Joseth thanks you from the bottom of his heart for saving his sorry behind."

"You're welcome, Tazmin," Rania replied with a hint of a smile.

The young Lord sighed dramatically as he rose again. "You two are far too somber for the part of our vanquishing heroes. Luckily, I know just the cure for that. You'll join me for that drink you promised me tonight, and you can tell me all about your exploits. I'm sure it's quite a story."

"I'd love to have that drink with you, Tazmin," Tal said, "but no story this time. What we accomplished came at a price I'm not ready to talk about yet."

"I suppose it would have," Tazmin said, crestfallen. "I'm sorry to have brought it up, Tal."

"It's alright, my friend. We're happy to be back, we just need some time."

"Take all you need. I doubt anyone would begrudge you that, after all you've done." Tazmin's tone brightened. "Shall we go up to the Keep? Your father and the King are both anxious to see you again."

"And I them," Tal agreed.

King Garant met them on the steps of Jerak Keep with Duke Daron in tow. "Lord Talaren Solus and Marquess Rania Amoran," the King intoned formally, "Valeran owes you an enormous debt of gratitude."

Tal dropped to one knee, Rania doing likewise by his side. "Thank you, your Majesty, but we were simply fulfilling our oaths to Shevestra."

"I'm afraid you can't hide behind modesty this time, Tal," Garant said with a kindly smile. "What the two of you did went far beyond the call of duty, even for Shevestra'ken. Your names will be remembered in song for generations because of your selfless acts. My heart swells with pride to know two of Valeran's nobles are such superb Adepts of Shevestra."

"Begging your pardon, Majesty," Rania murmured, "but we lost claim to our titles when we swore our oaths."

"That's not entirely true," the King said as he descended the steps, motioning for them to rise. He stood between the Shevestra'ken and laid a hand on each's shoulder in a gesture of confidence. "I had some research done into the precedents regarding such situations. Though no noble of Valeran has ever before sworn the oaths of the Battleborn, we did find record of the tradition in the old Northern kingdoms. The Throne has decided to honor this tradition, and the Royal Council supports my decision."

"We recognize your titles within your respective Houses, along with all the rights and responsibilities accordant with those titles. You are excused from any duties which would violate your oaths as Shevestra'ken. In the absence of an heir of suitable age to assume those duties, you may appoint a Steward to oversee rulership of your lands. For any situation in which you feel your oaths may clash with your title, we will defer to your judgment."

"Thank you, Majesty," Tal said.

Garant turned his eyes to Brant. "I welcome you in friendship, Regent Femor. Rooms have been prepared for you and your party. I hope they're to your satisfaction. I'll have some of the household staff show you up."

"No need, Majesty," Tazmin volunteered, "I can show them the way."

"Thank you, Lord Joseth," Garant murmured before turning to Rania once more. "So, Marquess, we meet again. I thought the last time that I recognized in your face the child I once met. It pleases me to know she wasn't lost to us, after all." He offered her his arm. "Shall we talk? I'd like to get reacquainted with you after all these years, and I think we should allow Talaren and Daron some privacy for their reunion. Besides," he added with a wink as he led Rania off, "I have to introduce you to my Master Armorer to have you sized."

"Sized for what?" Rania asked curiously.

"For your new armor. I'm having a suit similar to Talaren's made for you. A gift for your service to Valeran, and one I'm sure you'll look quite impressive in at the Announcement of Succession."

Rania smiled over her shoulder at Tal before disappearing around the corner of the Keep with Garant, headed toward the armorer's forge nestled among the outbuildings.

Tal and Daron stepped forward while Tazmin led Brant and his men into the Keep. As the last of them disappeared into the tall doorway, father and son embraced each other in a fierce hug.

"Son," Daron said, "I'm overjoyed to see you safe. I was terribly worried about you."

"It's good to see you again, father," Tal replied. "Would you like to walk?"

Daron smiled. He'd always said walking helped with thinking, and they had often gone on walks for their weightier conversations. "Of course." They set out side-by-side in the opposite direction from Garant and Rania, out towards the practice yards. "How are you?" the Duke asked awkwardly. "I mean, after..."

"I understand now why you were bothered when I put up that tapestry of the Gilden Hills," Tal said with a sad smile, hearing the question under his father's question. "I've seen horrible things, experienced horrible things, had to myself take actions that caused me sorrow and shame. It still hurts, that loss of innocence, knowing first hand the depraved things people are capable of doing to each other. I'll need some time to reconcile myself with it, but I'll be alright." There was a different matter they had to talk about, even though Tal had been dreading this conversation since Val Jerak. He took a deep breath to steel himself. "I'm sorry, father, I hope I haven't disappointed you too much."

Daron gave his son a puzzled look. "Disappointed? Whatever by?"

"When it came time to choose, I went chasing after legends rather than honoring my obligations as your heir."

The Duke shook his head in disbelief. "Oh, Tal, Tal, Tal," he said. "If I know you, you've probably been worrying over that for months, haven't you?"

"Ever since I took the oaths," Tal admitted, surprised at his father's reaction.

"You really needn't have. Maybe you didn't choose the course I'd intended for you, but you found your own way in the world. You stood and fought when most any other would have fled, bringing great honor to yourself and our house while you were at it. And you won a war that by all rights should have been the deathknell for this poor, battered nation of ours. You didn't go chasing legends, Tal. You became one." Daron put a paternal arm around Tal's shoulders. "Have I ever told you what I think the greatest hope is that a father could have?"

Tal pondered a moment. "No, I don't think you have."

"It's for his son to become a greater man than he was himself. I'd say you're doing quite the job of that, and it fills me with pride. All of Valeran is proud of you, but none of them as much as I am."

The Announcement of Succession was held a week later atop the steps of Jerak Keep. Garant had declared the day a holiday, and a great cheering throng greeted Talaren and Rania as they strode out of the front gate in their formal Shevestra'ken armor flanking Duke Solus. Daron was garbed in an exquisite black and red robe trimmed in silver, carefully chosen to emphasize his recognition as the heir to House Zherrane while acknowledging that he was of House Solus.

King Garant followed them out, leading a group composed of the members of the Royal Council along with Regent Brant and General Elgar, who commanded the forces King Soren of Amberyl had sent to join the fight against Kherzul. Kyril also stood among that group as a representative of the

Jhessaillian Order. Tal had been putting off speaking with the Guardian, and he could see the frustration in Kyril's eyes when their gazes briefly met. He'd have to deal with that soon, but not quite yet. He had questions for the Jhessaillian, but he wasn't yet sure he could trust his own response to the answers.

Garant's group arrayed themselves around the three standing at the top of the steps, and the King stepped forward to speak.

"My loyal subjects, countrymen, and friends," Garant began, "today is a day of great joy for Valeran. The reason we celebrate is twofold. First, we honor the names of Lord Talaren Solus and Marquess Rania Amoran, Shevestra'ken both, for the succor they have brought to the North. Through their valiant deeds and peerless courage they have prevented us from being plunged back into the darkness from which Valeran was founded. They have stopped short a senseless war which would have devastated all our lands and blackened our hearts against one another. And they have shown us the way to Valeran's future."

"When first the North fell under the shadow of the walking dead, Valeran was founded by the man who eliminated that threat, my ancestor, Korven Zherrane. Now, as Korven's line draws to an end we are reminded that from the very beginning, Valeran's crown has been bound to that act of heroism. It is only appropriate that at a moment such as this we should renew our throne with the blood of heroes. That is the second cause we have to celebrate this day, for today Valeran has a new heir. House Solus has long provided exemplary service to the crown and to the people of Valeran, and has now given us in two generations two of our most celebrated heroes. Such great acts deserve the greatest of recognition, and for that reason I now recognize Daron Solus, Duke of House Solus, as my adoptive son and successor to my throne."

Cheers rolled from the crowd as Garant approached the kneeling Duke Solus, producing a narrow band of gold which he placed carefully upon Daron's brow. The King turned back toward the assemblage as he gave Daron his hand and motioned for him to rise.

"People of Valeran, I give you Prince Daron Solus!"

The roar of applause was deafening.

"Tal!" Kyril greeted his friend with some surprise when the Shevestra'ka walked unannounced into his study. "I'm glad you've finally come to see me. I was starting to worry that I'd given offense somehow. There's a few matters I rather need to discuss with you."

Tal grimaced as he drew his sword and placed it flat on the desk in front of Kyril. "Like what this is?" he asked in a subdued tone.

The Guardian looked at the blade and then back to Tal's face, brow furrowed in consternation. "I don't understand what you mean, Tal," he sighed. "That's the sword Trazeri asked you to carry and protect. One of the Blades of Unity. *Kallevamar*."

In an accusing tone Tal asked, "Then you didn't know that *Kallevamar* is incomplete? That it needs to absorb a soul to waken it? That it *can* absorb a soul into itself?"

"No, I didn't. Not any of that. How did you come by this information?"

"Kherzul," Tal growled. "He said he found notes Anakara took while studying it. He didn't know that it was a Blade of Unity, but he knew a lot more than I did about how it works and what it does."

"And you believed him?"

"Not everything he said, but I believe what he told me about the sword. I nearly ended up being the soul that completed it."

Kyril nodded. "That would have been about when Rania killed Kherzul, unless I miss my guess. I've been reading the reports our Godtouched made on the information they gathered about that event. They're inconclusive, you know. Based on what we know about where and how you were found, the placement of the remnants of the spectres who were with you, and where your blades were, we can't reconstruct a plausible scenario for how you did it." He gave Tal a thoughtful look. "Unless, that is, if both of your weapons could kill spectres. Tal, I can see that something has made you suspicious of the Order, quite probably for good reason. But I promise you as your friend that anything you tell me won't leave this room. I won't put any of it in my reports back to Cardon, but I have to know. Rania has *Edyamar*, doesn't she?"

"If I knew the answer to that, I couldn't tell you unless I was certain I could trust you," Tal said softly. "And while I do count you my friend, Kyril, I'm not sure at the moment how far I really can trust you. I need proof, and you can start to provide it by answering a question for me."

"What question?"

"During my imprisonment, Kherzul told me that he had been secretly trained in the Sephiral Arts by a Guardian. Was he telling the truth? And did the Order know about it all along?" Tal locked gazes with Kyril as he waited for the answer.

For long seconds the Guardian was silent before dropping his eyes and saying, "Yes, on both counts."

Tal lunged up out of his seat and across the desk, hand balling into a fist that he smashed into his friend's jaw.

Kyril found himself on the floor beside the chair he'd been sitting in, ears ringing. Tal was glaring down at him with cold eyes.

"I waited to come here until I could be sure I wouldn't kill you if that was your answer," Tal said, voice wavering between towering rage and depthless sorrow. "As it stands, I would still kill you if I weren't convinced that you genuinely believed you were serving some greater good. Just tell me what your Order hoped to accomplish by helping Kherzul."

Kyril put a hand to his lip that came away bloody as he took his seat once more. "You're not going to hit me again?"

"Believe me, I want to, but I think I can restrain myself," Tal replied.

"I hope you'll at least let me present my defense before you do," Kyril said with a wince. "I can understand that you feel betrayed. To be honest, I feel it myself. At first I only knew a part of what was going on here. It was after the Battle of the Falling Snows that I grew suspicious that there was more to the Order's involvement than I had been allowed to know. I had to call in quite a few favors to get to the bottom of the matter and confirm what you already seem to have figured out."

"It all goes back eighteen or so years, long before either you or I had become entangled with the Order." The Guardian frowned. "Well, technically, it goes much farther back than that, but that's when the events of concern to us now began to unfold. The Bhellan Revolution had recently ended and an order came down from the Word of Jhessail, who are charged with the keeping of all our secret knowledge, including the Prophecy itself. The reputation we Jhessaillians have for being secretive applies tenfold to the Word, and a hundredfold where the Prophecy is concerned. They almost never let the actual passages involved in prophetic events be known even to our own people, and even then they limit it to the operatives actually involved. This was one such case. 'Kindle a flame in the heart of ambition's scion,' the Prophecy told us, 'for the fire he ignites will illumine the path to salvation.'"

"It was decided that Prince Kherzul had to be the one the passage was referring to. His father's ambition was notorious following the war, and even as young as he was Kherzul was both clever and remarkably cruel. Within a year the Eye managed to place a number of informants and operatives close to the Prince to assist in guiding him. He was already a twisted, vile individual when we found him, but with our people there to nudge him in the right direction now and then and to help cover his tracks, he was allowed to grow into the monster you defeated. And yes, in the years following his attack on Felmorinen, we provided him instruction in the basics of the Sephiral Arts to help him decipher Anakara's notes. The man we sent was posing as a member of a rogue branch of the Order that never actually existed, and if it's any consolation to you, Kherzul eventually had him killed to keep his studies secret."

"Why?" Tal was virtually quivering with rage, his eyes flinty and accusing. "Why would you help him that way? Did your Order have no concept of the consequences?"

"'The fire he ignites will illumine the path to salvation,'" Kyril said again, sadly. "The consequences were the entire point, Tal. The Order wanted this war to happen. They wanted the hero who would emerge from it. They wanted you, needed you, so they created a threat for you to vanquish."

"I still don't understand, Kyril," Tal snapped irritably. "What purpose do I serve for the Order now that I've fought your damned war?"

"That remains to be seen," the Guardian replied, "though I think I could hazard a guess. Remember, I knew none of what I just told you when I came to the North. That I do know it now is a major breach of protocol, and telling you means I'd be subject to extraordinarily unpleasant disciplinary measures were any of my brothers to learn about this little chat. When I was briefed before being sent here, I received a cursory review of Kherzul's activities with all mention of Order involvement removed. The first part of my mission, as I told you and the Council when I arrived in Val Zherrane, was to meet one of our operatives in Bhel Meravos and evaluate the accuracy of our estimates. I believe now that my contact's being exposed and the subsequent attack that I barely escaped from were all orchestrated by the Order to prompt me to take the exact actions I did and trigger the war. But that was only the first and lesser part of my assignment."

Kyril looked soberly across his desk at the young Shevestra'ka. "The primary part of my mission was to find a certain Valerite nobleman in whom the Order had already invested a great deal of effort. We'd arranged during the Bhellan Revolution for his father to make the acquaintance of an Armslord by the name of Malry Zhierren. And later we provided some gentle encouragement through one of our operatives to have the father let his son train under that Armslord. You may not like it, Tal, but from the beginning you yourself have been at least partially a creation of the Jhessaillian Order. So I was sent with orders to befriend and serve you as confidant and advisor, and to render you all possible assistance when required. I know that telling you this might cause you to question the authenticity of what has gone before, but I hope you'll understand that I'm doing so as an act of trust. I do genuinely consider you a friend, Tal."

"Be that as it may," Tal growled, "you still haven't answered my most important question. What does the Order expect of me? Why go to such lengths to influence me? Just what is it that you're trying to accomplish with me?"

"I did mention that I think I may know the answer to that," Kyril said slowly, "but to confirm if I'm on the right track or not, I'll have to ask some questions you may not want to answer."

"I'll answer, within reason."

"I've noticed some odd things about you and Rania. The way you fought at the Battle of the Falling Snows as if a single mind controlled both of you. The uncanny sense you seem to have of each other's state of mind. The way you tend to look at a door seconds before Rania walks through it. Do you know what causes it? Do you two truly share an unseen sensory connection?"

Tal pondered a moment before answering. Kyril was right that he didn't like answering these questions, but the Guardian seemed already to have guessed and he might be able to tell Tal something of use. "Yes, there is a bond," he said cautiously. "We don't understand it, but it's been there from the moment Rania gave me the Warrior Soul. When we're close enough, when the Sephira flows through us, we can sense each other. Feelings, physical sensations, a few other things."

"And you can share the Sephira with one another through it, can't you?"

"Yes," Tal nodded, "though we only found that out on the way to Bhel Meravos."

"It is true," Kyril murmured in wonder. Excitedly, he leaned toward Tal. "The phenomena you're experiencing was known to the ancient Shevestra'ken and studied by them. They referred to it as Sephiral Conjunction. I made a few official inquiries with the Word of Jhessail when I first noticed it, and they managed to find a tome in the Great Collection containing a brief analysis of its causes. Their studies found it was caused when Binary Essences, two souls so closely aligned as to be nearly identical, both took on the unique Sephiral traits associated with becoming an Adept of Shevestra. The leading theory as to how Binary Essences happened was that in the mingling and reiteration of Sephiral energies that comes between death and rebirth, two souls could end up each with a significant portion of energies associated with one another in a previous lifetime."

Tal's brow furrowed. "So you're saying that Rania and I are two halves of the same soul?"

"That's a very romantic way to put it," Kyril chuckled, "if not particularly accurate. Better to think of it as two complete and separate souls,

326

but with numerous significant similarities. Binary Essences themselves supposedly aren't that uncommon. Those who possess them tend to have an immediate affinity and enhanced empathy for each other and to be drawn together once they come into contact. That you and Rania are also Shevestra'ken amplifies those traits by several magnitudes and generates a Sephiral resonance between you that allows the shared sensations you experience."

"I see," Tal murmured. "So what significance does that have to the questions I asked you?"

Kyril drew in a deep breath. "The mission I was sent here on is one of those I mentioned earlier with a very direct involvement in the Prophecy, and as such I was told the relevant passage. 'From fire and strife will emerge the two perfect blades. Belief and Understanding, hand in hand, of the bonds they form will the Unifier be born.' It's interesting to note that in the ancient tongue, 'understanding' translates as '*kallevamar*.' And 'belief' is..."

"*Edyamar*," Tal finished for him.

The Guardian nodded. "So you see, this entire time I've been expecting the Blades of Unity to surface. That's another reason why I believe that Rania possesses *Edyamar*. But in retrospect, I'm beginning to think that may be only part of the puzzle. I think that 'the two perfect blades' refers as much to the wielders as to the weapons themselves."

"Rania and I..." Tal mused wonderingly, eyes widening.

"If I'm right, I think you'll agree the interpretation of the passage is somewhat obvious," Kyril affirmed. "You and Rania will bring the Unifier into the world. And now you see why it's important for me to know if Rania carries the other Blade of Unity."

Tal stared over at Kyril for several breaths. At length, he said softly, "I swore not to answer any questions like that."

"You know an answer like that is little short of confirmation?"

"I won't break my promise," Tal muttered, "but you've earned a certain degree of trust. More than I'd expected. Just don't put any of this in your reports back to the Order. I need time to think." He stood to leave, picking up and sheathing *Kallevamar*.

"Tal?" Kyril asked. "If I've earned some trust, does that extend to telling me what you'll do next?"

Tal looked back from the doorway and shrugged. "I'm going to Felmorinen with Rania. She has to return the books and notes Kherzul stole, among other business. We'll stay there for a while. Felmorinen is remote, quiet, peaceful. A good place for us to heal the hurts inside." He paused a moment, considering. "I'll also be reading Anakara's writings while I'm there."

"Tal!" Kyril gasped.

"There's no threat, Kyril, no temptation," Tal said quietly. "I'm a Shevestra'ka, not a Guardian. I won't be able to use any of it the way Anakara or Kherzul did. But there's information in there about my sword, information I need to know. I need to know what it is that I'm carrying. I need to know what I'll be asked to give..." he paused awkwardly, "my son. My daughter. Do you know which it's supposed to be?"

Kyril shook his head. "The Prophecy doesn't specify, not that I'm aware of, anyway."

Tal shrugged. "Best to have some things be a surprise, I suppose. Where will you be?"

"Val Zherrane," Kyril replied. "The official story is that because of my interactions here during the war, I've been appointed special envoy to the Throne of Valeran. Of course, I'm really here to observe and maintain contact with you while avoiding drawing any suspicion as to my true purpose."

"You're doing a great job," Tal smirked before departing.

"Thanks," Kyril said to the empty room. "Good luck, my friend."

Epilogue
Peace

"Mother, Father, I did it," Rania whispered as she pressed her cheek to the cold stone of the alcove that held her parent's remains. "I avenged your murders. I got back everything Kherzul stole. I even helped save the North while I was at it."

"I had help, though. His name is Talaren. Tal. He's the one we were waiting for, the one who would wield *Kallevamar* by right. I wish I could introduce you to him. He means a lot to me. I love him."

Rania smiled through the tears in her eyes. "So much was taken from us. So many times we should have spent together. I've missed you both terribly. And after everything that's happened, all I want is to be able to tell you that your little girl is happy. I've learned not to let my pain hold me back or ruin me. I'll keep moving forward. I'll live my life. I'll make you both proud of me. I love you."

When she emerged from the mountainside tomb, Tal was waiting crouched against a stone outcropping. He looked up at her and smiled gently. "Is it done?"

Rania nodded as she wiped the tears from her cheeks. "I said what I needed to. I can go home now."

Tal stood and took her hand warmly. "I can't wait to see it with you."

The tombs were located in the base of one of the mountains ringing the valley in which Felmorinen stood, just beyond the edge of the Sephiral haze that moderated the climate around the city and ancient fortress. As Tal and Rania walked in toward the center, the temperature rose rapidly over the course of a hundred paces until they found themselves stripping off their heavy winter clothing to enjoy the warm spring afternoon. They stashed their coats, cloaks, and heavy woolen outerclothes in their packs and continued walking hand in hand toward the great stone spire of Felmorinen.

Farmers sowing fields looked up curiously to watch the couple pass. Most returned to their work smiling.

Tal and Rania were met at the wall surrounding the city by a group of Pathfinders including Toven, the Ranger Tal had met on their first excursion through the Felmorr Range.

Toven stepped forward with a hand raised in greeting as the Shevestra'ken drew near. "Hail, friends! We heard about what happened in Bhellus. We also heard that you were coming here. Does that mean..."

Rania nodded happily. "Your Marquess has returned to you. For a time, at least."

Toven smiled broadly. "This is grand news! We'll have to have a celebration, naturally. I can't promise anything as spectacular as you'll have already had, considering we're more like a large village here than a city, but..."

"But it'll be at my home. That makes it far more exciting than any gaudiness would," Rania cut him off. "If you don't mind, though, could you take a few days to organize it? Tal and I would like a bit of time to acclimate ourselves first."

"Of course, Marquess," Toven deferred. "Shall we escort you to the fortress?"

"No, thank you," Rania replied. "I'd like to show Tal there by myself."

"Very well, your Grace." Toven cast his eyes down shyly. "I hope you'll excuse our leaping to conclusions, but when we heard you were coming this way we had the Marquess's suite made ready."

"That was quite thoughtful of you, Toven. I see nothing to excuse."

Rania led Tal down the central street leading to the fortress and up through the echoing passages of Felmorinen to the spacious set of rooms near its top.

"I'm back," Rania murmured as she walked into the familiar quarters that had once belonged to her parents.

"Welcome home," Tal whispered, giving her a brief kiss.

"Now that we're here," Rania said, taking Tal by the hand. She led him to the bed and sat him down on its edge, settling down behind him to gently knead the muscles in his shoulders. "I've noticed that you've been unusually tense these last few days. Is it something about your talk with Kyril?"

Tal nodded. "He knows you've got *Edyamar*, or close enough as makes no difference. I asked him not to let the rest of the Order know."

"Can we trust him?" Rania asked.

"I'm not sure," Tal answered, "but I think so. He told me some other things that the Order wouldn't approve of me knowing. Of us knowing."

"Like what?"

"Like why the Order is interested in us. Rania, Kyril seems to believe that the Unifier will be our child."

Rania's hands stopped dead. Her body shook, and after several seconds she began to laugh. "Don't you think it just a bit soon for us to be thinking about children?"

"Kyril's the one thinking about it, not me," Tal replied, laughing with her.

"So next time he brings it up, tell him our love life is none of his concern. A Guardian like him should be able to find other things to occupy himself with."

330

They both fell over laughing on the bed.

"Rania," Tal asked seriously after their laughter had subsided, "do you believe in fate?"

"I believe our choices matter," she replied, "and that the future is built from those choices. Fate's just an excuse for not choosing, or choosing badly. Whatever future our choices bring us we'll face together."

"Together, yes," Tal murmured. He pulled her close to gaze deeply into her eyes. "I love you, Rania."

They made love that night in the pale glow of the Sephira that crept in from outside. After lying contented in Tal's arms for a long time afterward, Rania gently slipped away from him and went to the next room to stand before a tall open window, gazing down on a sight she hadn't seen in fifteen years. This time there were no flames, no screams. Felmorinen slept in peace.

Within a few moments, Tal crept up behind her and wrapped his arms gently around her waist. He leaned forward to smell her hair, and whispered in her ear, "Rania, I think we're going to be alright."

She sighed contentedly and snuggled closer into his embrace. "Yes, I believe we are."

Further adventures await in the forthcoming

A Prayer For War

Age of the Unifier: Volume Two

Visit www.ageoftheunifier.com for more information